THE
KLUANARIANS

BRENDA M. HOKENSON

authorHOUSE®

AuthorHouse™
1663 Liberty Drive
Bloomington, IN 47403
www.authorhouse.com
Phone: 833-262-8899

© 2022 Brenda M. Hokenson. All rights reserved.

No part of this book may be reproduced, stored in a retrieval system, or transmitted by any means without the written permission of the author.

Published by AuthorHouse 06/09/2022

ISBN: 978-1-6655-6204-1 (sc)
ISBN: 978-1-6655-6203-4 (hc)
ISBN: 978-1-6655-6202-7 (e)

Library of Congress Control Number: 2022911129

Print information available on the last page.

Any people depicted in stock imagery provided by Getty Images are models, and such images are being used for illustrative purposes only. Certain stock imagery © Getty Images.

This book is printed on acid-free paper.

Because of the dynamic nature of the Internet, any web addresses or links contained in this book may have changed since publication and may no longer be valid. The views expressed in this work are solely those of the author and do not necessarily reflect the views of the publisher, and the publisher hereby disclaims any responsibility for them.

DARKNESS RISING

ENCOUNTER WITH THE PAST AND PRESENT

Thanias entered the courtyard of the dark citadel of Nagazthastar. Uncertain of what would be laying in wait he was prepared for anything. He drew his short sword and motioned his companion to follow him. "We can make camp in that building; it looks most promising." Thanias said under his breath as he slowly pushed the door open.

The two cleared the small building that had been abandoned long ago and built a small fire in the hearth. The sky was growing dark as evening began to fade. Rain was expected, as the water swollen clouds stacked against the mountains.

"When is this Llylandra supposed to meet us?" Rynn asked as she placed the fresh caught quail over the fire.

"In the light of day, I would hope, but the Fraeloch are not so civilized. I will venture a guess and say that it may be somewhat hostile for an encounter, as her domain does not like our kind whatsoever. So, we must be prepared for anything."

"I shall take first watch. You need rest, since this quest is yours. I will be up in the loft where mine arrow will fly true."

"Thank you, Rynn. I am pleased that you accompanied me on this most important quest"

Rynn smiled and served the quail. Thanias prepared the bread and two draughts of ale for their meal.

"Alright, there is enough wood for the night. The rain is quite thick, Rynn. Take care in your sight, as we have not encountered these folk before and I am unsure of what they look like." Thanias prepared his bedroll and also set up Rynn's while she went to the loft.

"Aye, it will be most curious when this quest is at its height, I believe," Rynn spoke as she climbed a set of hidden stairs to the loft. She took in the air from outside as she opened the vent enough to peer out into the rain filled sky. She wandered about the small room, examining the objects left behind. A small leather-bound stack of parchment caught her eye. As she made her rounds, she read the details concerning the abandonment of the courtyard and the advancement of the Legion from Forest Mithdrool.

The Mithdroolean Legion approaches. Llylandra has abandoned us to our own devices. The women and children fled to Kaprius weeks ago. I am uncertain what Mithdrool will gain with his over running of our citadel, but it cannot be for the good. We Fraelochans are not exactly friends with those of Kaprius, but they have made the women and children welcome, for now. I hope soon, this siege will end and they will return.

If anyone finds these writings, please, keep them safe from those who would use it against the good. We are not, by nature, the warmest of the Orders, but, we too, are of this world and have much to share with those whom inquire.

I am Wryn. My twin sister, Rynn, was lost in a city we visited once with our family. We searched for weeks, only to the dismay of our parents, she was never found. I am a sorcerer and she, at such a young age, was taking up archery and swords. I hope to one day meet her again. Mother and father asked that when their time came, I place a spell upon them so that when Rynn returns they may see her as well.

If anyone finds this, please seek me in the sand cavern beneath Mithdrool Forest…

Rynn was startled as she turned, she caught Thanias out of the corner of her eye. "Is it your shift already?

"Yes, now get some rest. Tomorrow is almost upon us."

"Very well. I will see you later then. Good night, friend." Rynn placed the drawn arrow along with the parchment in her quiver and headed down the stairs. She laid her head on the pillow as she heard Thanias pacing in the loft. She heard him walk down the steps and across the floor near the door. She heard him take a seat and place his feet on the window ledge. "Is everything alright, Thanias?"

"Yes, quite. You seemed bewildered. Are you well?"

"Aye. Just a little confused, but I think I will be fine."

"Why, what has transpired in the last four hours?" He came over and sat beside her. "What has rattled your nerves so, friend?"

Rynn sat up and looked Thanias in the eyes. "I found a bit of parchment in the loft. It says I have a twin from here and that I was lost in a village. I wish to know more, but I don't know where to begin to find answers here. I don't even know if it is true. You have to help me with this, please, Thanias. I never knew my family."

"Curious. I think we can manage that. So we may want to search the town hall before Llylandra gets here. I am not sure how she would react to this news." Thanias put his arm around Rynn and comforted her as best he could. He eventually fell asleep next to Rynn.

First light arrived with a flash of lightning. Rynn jumped to her feet as Thanias rose quickly. Rynn pulled some cured meat from her satchel and handed it to Thanias. He handed her a skein of water and some bread. They ate at a small table in the room.

Hastily, they packed their bedrolls and prepared for the inevitable. "I think we should go over there," Thanias said pointing to the chapel. "That would have family records, if this place is anything like other cities."

The two made their way across the courtyard to the chapel. The door was ajar and Rynn followed Thanias as always. Finding no living beings, they searched for clues to Rynn's past. Thanias looked on the shelves of books and Rynn went to a spiral staircase. She felt beneath the first step and found what she had been looking for. She pressed a slightly raised stone that made up the foundation and a slight door opened between two panels of books. Thanias quirked an eyebrow and followed her inside.

"How did you know it was there?"

"I didn't, but something said look over here. Not sure where or what this something is. I am very afraid though." Rynn sighed and squeezed Thanias' hand.

He smiled, "We will see this through, no matter what. I promise."

There was a desk with many charts of many different things on it. As they approached the desk, the door closed behind them, and a small orb illuminated the room.

"I believe," Thanias paused briefly, "that this is your father's command. These belong to you, Rynn. His name looks to be Beryth according to the inscription, anyway." Thanias sat down in a chair and watched as Rynn looked at things. He never saw someone examine every detail as she did. He rose and walked up to the desk. Placing a hand on her shoulder, "Rynn, your family was destroyed by Mithdrool and his Legion. Actually, it looks more like your father's entire land was decimated by them. I am so sorry dear friend."

"It cannot be. Why? Why here, what advantage does this give this darn Mithdrool. Or does it actually give Llylandra an advantage somehow. We are Fraeloch, I am guessing more human-like than 'scary monsters.'"

"Well, we will find out, but I think this strong hold here is impenetrable to those of evil. I bet there is a second floor or something that will have answers."

The two searched records that were kept and Thanias stumbled upon another passage as he searched the collections. He gently pulled a shelf from the wall. It swung open and another orb lit another small chamber. The two entered it and the passageway sealed.

"Well, now, this is more like it." Thanias smiled. He found a written account of the siege of the citadel and the betrayal of Llylandra to her Fraelochs. He read as Rynn examined the entire room.

High Lord Beryth's Escape

Mithdrool conducted a raid on the most prized citadel of the Fraeloch, Nagazthastar. The warlock convinced Llylandra that it would benefit both sides, if she were to cede the land to him, or risk losing all of the lands surrounding the citadel. Mithdrool had no idea of the wealth and knowledge contained within the walls of the citadel. As his Legion approached from the North and East, the women and children left to the South into Kaprius, where Beryth had made arrangements, as he suspected some sort of treacherous deal. What was not known to Llylandra was that the knowledge and a great portion of the wealth were also sent to Kaprius for safekeeping.

Beryth himself went to Kaprius, where he took his daughter, Rynn, age 12, to the house of Impresaria. Impresaria raised Rynn as her own daughter with a Paladin, Lucien, at her side. Lucien is to wed Impresaria during winter aft the comet. This marriage will solidify the realm as three major Orders are united by this union.

When Beryth returned, he along with his wife, and son made provisions for a very long engagement with Mithdrool. Lady Phallas (named after a star cluster) set spiritual peace throughout the citadel. She generated a special shield wall that would protect these inner sanctums from the approaching onslaught and helped with safe passage to those who were not willing to travel earlier.

Wryn was advanced for his age. He was a sorcerer. With help of his mother, he created a sanctuary for the refugees, deep underground, out of the sight of Mithdrool and Llylandra. He also cast a spell upon his parents at their request. When the last inhabitant of the citadel passed through the portal to the sanctuary, Wryn sealed it from inside.

I am writing this for those who have come to our glorious citadel who are looking for the truth. You will find no ally with Llylandra or kinship with Mithdrool. For Mithdrool is a foul, loathsome warlock, corrupted by greed and by Llylandra. Do not seek peace from either of these.

-Menosh -

"Hmm." Thanias pondered on this account of a battle that never got fought.

Rynn approached Thanias. "Are you alright? I mean, well, something isn't right. I feel very ill." She collapsed across Thanias' knees.

Thanias took the bedroll from her pack and laid her upon it. He took a small cloth soaked in water and placed it on Rynn's forehead. "Please wake up. I can't do this alone." He sat in silence for an hour while he monitored Rynn's breathing and very gently adjusting her head.

"Where am I? How did we get here?" She opened her eyes slowly to see Thanias examining her face.

"Well, we are in your parents' sanctuary within Nagazthastar where a siege took place, when you lost your family and somehow ended up in Kaprius, with my oldest brother and Impresaria. It seems your family maybe alive, by the readings of this, but it is giving me doubts on my quest and if it will actually accomplish anything now. Are you feeling any better?"

"A bit. Do you have any water?" Rynn took the skein from Thanias and drank slowly. "Is there a way out of here?"

"I hope so. We are supposed to meet Llylandra soon. It is best we not share your family history with her."

"That is most wise, Thanias. Thank you." She took some artifacts that belonged to her family and stowed them in a special pocket inside her quiver while Thanias was opening the door.

"Alright, let's go. I think exploring was quite interesting today." He extended his arm to Rynn and steadied her as they walked through the chapel and into a couple other buildings within the citadel walls.

A figure appeared near the entrance of the citadel. "I see you found the way, Thanias. Did you bring what I asked?" The figure slowly entered into the light shining through a cloud break and extended her hand.

"It is here, in safe keeping at this moment."

"I see you found a second missing piece to the puzzle. How nice. What is it you want from me Thanias?"

Rynn was slowly regaining her strength. Thanias left her by the building and approached the Fraeloch cautiously. Rynn watched as Thanias interacted with the treacherous Llylandra. If only she could remember the escape route through the small building. Memories came flooding back. She could see the day she left clearly.

"Mother, why do I have to go to this Morket place? Can't I stay and help father. Wryn gets to help. Please."

"No my child, you need to go for our people." A shadow orb struck Lady Phallas as she loaded Rynn into the cart. Lady Phallas then charged the shade, Mithdrool, sword drawn. She knocked him to the ground in which his head slammed into the well at the center of the citadel. "Find your father, Rynn. Run!" Lady Phallas was surrounded by several Mithdroolean Legion foes...

"Wryn....Wryn. Where is father?" Rynn was breathless as she sprinted all the way to the chapel.

"Inside. Most of the people are safe now, in the chambers. We have to wait for mother..."

He was cut off as Rynn ran past him and entered the chamber. "Father, its mother. She....she is going to die."

Beryth raced outside. He watched as Lady Phallas used hymnal of truth and caused the surrounding Legion to vanquish. She ran toward her husband. "Now is the time!" She went to Wryn who closed the chamber.

Beryth opened a gate that went straight to Kaprius. He saw Lucien and Impresaria waiting. He motioned for Rynn to come forward with her people. She took her father's hand and passed through the arch way.

An hour passed as Beryth met with the Morket and Paladin. Rynn paced. She was scared and nervous. A servant brought her a snack and drink, but she refused. "Rynn, you must relax." Her father said as he approached. "Everything will be fine. Your mother and brother are safe, along with everyone else. When the time comes, you will find us again."

"Don't leave me, father. Please, don't go." Rynn sobbed as Beryth embraced her and vanished into a bright light.

Rynn cried to herself, and then realized Llylandra's plot. She remembered the small entrance and how it opens with a word. She saw the package near where she was sitting. It was now or never. Rynn reached for the package while Thanias and Llylandra were making plans. As her hand grasped the satchel, she turned and ran straight into the armory. "*Nieama kalicsh nuehi.*" There was a bright light. Rynn was gone.

"Tell me, Thanias. What is it you most desire?"

"Absolute power. The end of my brothers."

"We must do this secretly then. Where is the feldstar?"

"What, where?" Thanias was baffled as he turned to find the small package and Rynn both gone. "I swear to you."

Llylandra used her powers to summon an opaque arm which levitated Thanias by the throat. "I am not one to be trifled with by a mere Truncheon. But alas…" The hand released and Thanias fell to the ground. "You would not have known."

"So, this shall be carried out in secret. How shall I communicate with you?"

"This pouch has small crystals. Drop one on the ground, it opens up a channel in which I can communicate with you. I will also be able to transport you, if need arises."

"Very well. I shall return at once to my Burwash."

"I will send word to you through a network already established within your cities and alliances' cities. When the Orders meet for the first time in centuries, as the comet passes, I will be there, briefly. I will raise Mithdrool. Lady Phallas will fall for her treachery and darned Beryth. Of course, I don't mind extra casualties from the Truncheon, Star, Moon, and even a certain Enygminite.

Rynn, after speaking the incantation she remembered from childhood, found herself in a very familiar place, or so it seemed. The halls were

Brenda M. Hokenson

illuminated with a golden hue and a silvery light. The columns were sturdy and unshaken. She examined them as she walked toward the great hall. She noticed four thrones atop the stairs. Home, or as near as home can be in the sand cavern beneath the rotting Mithdrool Forest. "Wryn!"

VACATION

SUMMER IS HALF OVER. THE days are long and warm, with beautiful lands glistening in the morning sun. The evenings are cool, but not uncomfortable. The mountain village of Ruan is spectacular for those wishing escape from the cities. It has everything anyone could possibly want to do – without conventional means. It is a perfect place to reflect and practice the old ways. This is where Myron has chosen for the vacation.

The village being a "tourist" community offers only the best in fresh ingredients. Each dwelling for visitors has personal gardens, already ripening, for the guests to use in their own food preparation. A butcher set up shop a year ago and has offered services for the guests. The rooms are all set in antiquity. Very simple yet very detailed at the same time. The washroom is the only thing modern. Vehicles park nearby, with no more than a fifteen minute walk from the village. A beautiful lake was a ten-minute walk to the west. Rumors of druids always ran rampant in the village, as the druids were thought to have helped establish the village as a stronghold away from the mediocrity of city life.

Myron decided his family needed a nice break from the city he and his wife, Iris, made home. The city was alright, but many adjustments had to be made to better feel at peace. He often worried about his children and their future. A vacation was in order and Ruan was a perfect place to be normal.

Paul, the oldest, hated the idea. "Why can't we bring anything with us Dad?"

"Ruan is a small village which is based on simplicity and kindness son.

Real food- not store bought is going to change your mind. There is a lake for fishing and swimming. There are trails to be hiked to the summits of towering peaks, and quite a lot of local experiences. It is even rumored to have a chivalrous tournament each weekend."

"Oh, joy a tournament. I can't wait. Tell me why I have to go?"

"You are my son and I said so."

"Fine, just so Edwina doesn't go gaga over all the guys wearing tights."

"Ah, you are jealous then?" Myron winked and laughed at his son.

"No, but you know she will, and she will want a costume as will Tatiana."

"They have their costumes and so do you," added Iris. "It will be a breath of fresh air – quite literally and a good time to be a real family instead of everyone doing their own thing."

"Yes mom, I suppose that would be good, since next year is my last year of high school, then I am going to study at that aeronautical school I found online." Paul looked quite serious at his father. "Is that still a good choice dad"

"You bet son! You will do well in anything you so choose to study."

"Mom, can we go now???" Tatiana raced through the house to make sure everything was locked up.

"Hop in the car. Ah, I see Edwina is already set," replied Myron.

The drive was long to Ruan, but worthwhile. As they approached the kids looked in awe at the beautiful, jagged peaks with gentle rolling hills that adorned the valley. A stream flowed from a lake that looked endless. Birds, other than robins and blackbirds, flew overhead. A small village was in the distance.

"Dad, it is perfect! Can we move here?" Tatiana was admiring the land. "Look, a deer, I have never seen one 'til now."

"It is really nice, how long are we here?" Edwina was eager to visit and leave as soon as possible.

Iris became irritated. "What is the hurry, Edwina? Your father wanted this to be special. Don't ruin it for all of us. Besides it will do you some good to be with the family instead of with your friends. I think this is the longest you have been around us since you started junior high."

"And your point is? I like my friends and they get to do cool stuff and have all the new things. Why can't I, oh, I mean we?"

The Kluanarians

"We are saving up money to send you all to college. New things are not always good, especially when you don't remember your place, Edwina."

Myron pulled into the parking area. "Ok, it is time to unload."

A man with a cart pulled by a horse approached. "Would you like help to the village sir?" The man bowed.

"Please. It is so good to see you again, Tomas."

"I didn't think you would remember me, Sir."

"Who could forget you? That was a very wild time at the…" Myron was interrupted.

"Dad, what is that?" Paul pointed to the left of the village.

"Tournament set up. I told you they do a tournament each weekend."

They loaded the cart with their bags of clothing and began the descent in to Ruan. The path was worn smooth. Tatiana stopped every so often and smelled the flowers. She noticed rabbits and squirrels on the way. Not one of the kids noticed the mist they passed through to enter Ruan.

"Here we are Master Myron." Tomas helped unload the cart and went on his way. "I will see you at a later time."

"Let me find out if this still works. Myron walked up to the door of their residence and used a very old double sided skeleton key. "Looks like they cleaned it up nice, Iris." He checked out each room.

Iris entered the bungalow. "It is as I remember it. The garden is perfect as well."

"Wait, we have been here before? When…" Edwina lost her thought and just looked at her dad.

"We lived here when you were quite small, Paul was but 9 when we moved here. You were just a little girl with pony tails and an unending smile." Myron reminisced as he unpacked his clothing. "Each of you has a room, keep it neat, please."

"Yes dad." The kids went to their rooms and unpacked. They observed the beautiful décor and explored the abode. They went out back and saw a large thriving garden and a sitting area. It had a shade tree occupied by a family of squirrels and a few birds.

"This is really nice. Maybe we should give it a try." Paul glanced at Edwina.

"You are right Paul. I was rude and I need to make it right. Tatiana, where is Mom?"

Edwina went off in search of her parents as Paul and Tatiana relaxed in the sitting area...

"Do you want some help Mom?" Edwina found her parents in the kitchen.

"Yes, would you please try and be nice for once Ed?"

"About that, I came in to apologize. I know this will be a really wonderful vacation and I was wrong."

Myron hugged Edwina. "We know. We wanted you to know. Now how about going with me to the butcher?"

"Ok." Edwina whispered, "On our way back, we should get some flowers for Mom."

Myron nodded in agreement.

The butcher was not far. In fact, it was across the greenway. The path through town was cobblestone, which Edwina had just noted. She noticed the many shops lining the greenway and a palisade to the east of the lake.

"Do you have spareribs, sir?" Myron examined the various cuts in the display as he waited.

"Aye, how many would you like Myron?"

"Probably four pounds, as Paul is growing."

"Excellent, I have my famous seasoning if you would care to try it."

"Yes, please, let me get a couple pouches of it. Will you be by later?"

"Aye, me and the missus will stop by before eve's end."

"Great to see you, Henry. We will have tea and crumb cake."

"Very good, then."

Myron and Edwina left the butcher and went straight to the millist. "Edwina take this to the florist, she will know the arrangement. She is right there." Myron pointed at the small shop.

Edwina spoke to the florist and retrieved the bouquet. Myron came out with a sack of flour and spices. They walked back to their home and unpacked. Myron had Paul help with the fire pit. He was taught how to set up a grill over it. Edwina and Tatiana selected vegetables from the garden and helped Iris prepare dinner. Paul retrieved the spare ribs from the kitchen and placed them on the grill. Myron monitored it.

"You and Edwina should go explore. Or should we all venture to the tournament?"

The Kluanarians

"Tournament, Dad. Definitely tournament! I have seen a lot of people arriving today. Are they all lucky like us and have a spot already?"

"No. They will be in campgrounds and at Innshaven down the path a bit more. Someone will prepare food and such for them —and they have to pay a lot more than we do."

"Why?" Paul was intrigued by this.

"We helped build Ruan. When we moved from our homeland, we came here. It was chosen as it had all the ideals we respect. Those who did not help in the construction, well, are considered visitors. Since they are visiting, they are treated as tourists and get waited on, but pay a good fee. Since there are eight families here who built this, the families run it as a kingdom and monies after taxes go to repair and add things – that go with our ideals. I am the Sheriff here. Your mother provided information to us about when to sow seeds, when to store, when to winterize and all the other good things that can be determined by stars and sun." Myron smiled, reflecting on his village and his family's returning.

Dinner was served at the table. Everyone was talking over each other about what a wonderful experience it had been, just on the first day. Iris checked the crumb cake in the oven. "Is it done yet, Mom?" Tatiana was waiting patiently for it to finish.

"Almost dear, but we will have guest in a bit to share with us."

THE ADVENTURE BEGINS

A KNOCK ON THE HEAVY FRONT door was resonating through the home. Myron got up and walked to the door. He slowly opened it, reflecting on the last time he had guests in Ruan.

"Welcome Tomas, Henry and Luly." He bowed and showed them to the main room. Please make yourselves at home. It is wonderful to see you."

"How is your vacation so far, Myron?" Luly smiled.

"Excellent, the kids seem to be enjoying themselves. When is the tournament ceremony?"

"In an hour or so, by the sun. Are you attending?" Tomas was eager to find out.

"Yes young man. Are you competing?"

"Aye, sir. Father said it was time."

"Great. Would you escort Edwina then this evening?"

"It would be an honor sir."

"I don't want to be escorted." Edwina interjected.

"It is a requirement of the tournament that all young ladies be escorted by a young man." Myron smiled as this amused him. "You will learn to be a lady, or at least ladylike whilst you are here."

"Oh, ok then. What do I wear?"

Iris brought Edwina her new garments for the tournament. "Oh, a dress. I should have seen that coming." Edwina examined the dress and all of its exquisite detail. "I love it Mom! I am sorry for being..."

"No worries." Tomas replied as he studied her face.

Dessert was served and everyone readied for the walk to the tournament.

"Wow, these are almost too big Iris." Myron had to uncinch his belt a little.

"Well better than bursting buttons dear." Iris smiled and took his arm as they left with their friends and children.

Paul and Edwina told Tomas all about their city and Paul's car, and Tatiana drifted off in thought as she held Paul's hand. The adults walked ahead, turning many heads.

"Sir Myron, you have returned. We are so glad. Iris you have not aged a day." Many townsfolk commented along the way.

Tomas described everything in and around Ruan and where he fun places are and most adventuresome. "Druids are said to be in the hills. We don't try to find them though, they keep balance here."

Tatiana said, "Are they like the ones that change shape, do they? Do they have long capes and robes? Are they invisible?"

"Shoosh, Tat." Myron was quite frank. "We never discuss druids here. They are very important and it is disrespectful to talk of them in that manner."

"I just want to know – in case I meet one when I am looking at flowers and stuff." She kicked the dirt.

Trumpets sounded as they entered the tournament grounds. The heads of the eight founding families stood at the center of the ring.

"Welcome to Ruan. This is our eightieth season of tournaments. Please be respectful to all participants." Myron beamed as he was the one to start the tournament. "Enter, please all champions."

Tomas took Edwina to the center with many other young adults. Paul was escorted by Tatiana. There were twenty contestants all told. Iris took pictures of her children and of the entire cadre.

"This will be a momentous evening and I hope all of you will enjoy!" With that Myron and the founders exited as the tournament started with a cordial and everyone was in the ring. There was live music and food and fireworks – which was a first this year. Criers handed out the tournament schedule, which would start the next day.

Tatiana played with kids her age as the bigger kids and adults danced and spoke. Two of them she liked a lot. She raced everywhere with them. They took her to the lake and showed her the canoes and rafts.

"Tomorrow maybe, we can go rafting?" Tatiana was so happy to have made friends so quickly.

"Yes, that would be fine. We live next to you. I am Thallas and this is Gwendolyn."

"I am Tatiana. My brother is Paul and Edwina is my sister. This is a really neat place to be."

Myron found her after two hours. "Tat, it is time to go. My you two have grown I remember when I got to keep watch of you for two days while your mother and father had a series of meetings. You were so small."

"You remember us, Sir Myron? That was a long time ago." Thallas smiled.

"Not that long ago. It has only been six years. I am glad you have met Tatiana."

"See you tomorrow Tat," said Gwendolyn. "Good night."

The families returned home for the night. Clothing was hung up and everyone drifted to sleep. The kids had vivid dreams inspired by the day's events. Myron slept heavily as did Iris.

"No, it cannot be." Iris sat up as she spoke.

Myron lurched awake. "What can't be?"

"The kids are …"

"Asleep." Myron finished her sentence. "Now please go back to sleep, search for meaning in the morning dear."

The morning arrived too early for the kids liking. They met in Paul's room to have their secret meeting, as they did on every vacation. They made a list of stuff to do here, not related to the town; after all it was their vacation. They discussed the wild idea of their dad that the family helped build it and decided it was to make them feel special while here. They decide the tournament thing was ok, since it was only for two days. Paul pulled out a map that Tomas had given him that had all the neat places to go marked.

"We should start here, by the lake and enjoy the lake today," proclaimed Paul.

"Aren't you competing today?" Edwina inquired with a grin.

"Nope, I don't know how to fight, but I couldn't let Dad down and not take the field, after all he 'helped build the town.'"

"Umm, how do we slip away to explore?" Tatiana paused while she looked out the door, "they have super kid locating powers you know."

"Let's go eat and sneak out the window. Edwina, you are super quiet. Do you think you can grab a bag to stuff food in to? Tatiana, find the hiking pack – it has some skeins for water plus a small tent in it in case of rain."

The girls chimed in, "What about you?"

"Wait, I'll get the pack. Tat, you can fill the skeins in a minute. Or we should eat first."

"Hello, Edwina to Paul. Do you read me? There is no fast breakfast, remember, no cereal, no frig for milk, yada, yada, yada."

"Ok, there are biscuits on the counter, a loaf of bread, honey, and I snuck peanut butter, just in case. Plus I got some of those instant meals you can heat or eat cold for just such an occasion." Paul grabbed the hiking pack and loaded it with the instant meals and three blankets. Tatiana filled the skeins with water. She grabbed he smaller pack and put the skeins in it. Edwina ran to the kitchen a prepared a quick breakfast for them. They ate in a hurry and cleaned up. Myron was stirring. It was now, or wait.

"Out the window, now!" Paul held it open as the girls climbed out.

"Here is the map Paul?" Edwina said as she handed it over to him.

The kids slipped quietly out of town down the path. Edwina took pictures on the way. Tatiana took notes on various things she saw, so she could reflect in her detective book when she gets home for vacation.

"Edwina, what do you think of checking out the Palisade first? I really need something good to go in my detective book ya know." Tatiana stopped, waiting for a response.

"Sure, that is where we are headed." Now come on before Paul leaves us in the dust."

"I am so glad to be in my real clothes again, Ed! I was afraid I would get the dress dirty."

"Paul, wait up. You know Tat is little."

Paul stopped checked his route against the map. "It looks to be about a mile, will you make it or should we stop for a bit?"

"I need some water; we've been walkin an hour!" Tatiana removed a skein from her pack and shared it with the group. "Much better, plus if we run out, we can get fresh water from the stream."

"I don't have Iodine tablets to purify it." Paul replied as he searched the pockets of the pack."

"We can boil it or catch it in the pan, if we are out super late." Edwina was excited to be out in the wilds.

"No the water here is clean!" Tatiana added

"Ok then. It is settled. We will explore the Palisade and go from there. Tatiana, can you write down anything we might find and Edwina you take pictures."

Both girls nodded and the trio set off. Quaking aspens lined the stream, Tatiana busily wrote down each variety of plant and animal she saw on the way. Paul topped at the stream and found some broken limbs and branches.

"Here we are! Walkin sticks. Please no fighting with them." He hand the girls each a branch.

They continued on to the gate of the Palisade. There were guards present, and all eyes were on them.

The Palisade reminded Paul of an old fortress, made of stone. He noticed the patchwork on some of the protective walls. It was, however, unique. It was more triangular in design with a large courtyard. Toward the left rear were barracks, a well, a tower, and it appeared to be the armory and chow hall – as he called it. The walls as he walked through the area were 3 feet thick. There were bridges that crossed the corners, and special slits in the stones for archers. He noticed a strange portion at the very center which seemed to be for more archers, although its design was too bizarre for that.

"Tatiana, can you draw a picture of this?" Paul inquired.

"I got the pictures, here," Edwina answered. "Tat, just write a bit about what we see."

"Ok, I can do that."

They continued looking around as the guards studied them. Whisperings were afoot.

"Do you think Thanias will want to know of them?"

"Doubt it. He is too busy dealing with his all important quest."

Rumors raced through as the kids poked around without interfering with the activities of the Palisade.

An older gentleman noticed them from the Seat and began his journey down the staircase. He noticed a great resemblance of the children and his family. He wondered a bit as he approached, *could it be Iris' kids, my grandkids?* He decided to not say anything until he was certain.

Tatiana spotted the older man. "Why is he Edwina's size but beefy?"

I am not sure, Tat." Paul responded. "We can ask, I guess."

There was an arbor over the bench with wildflowers growing and two rabbits near the well caught the eye of Tatiana. As she started racing toward the bench, Edwina snapped a picture to preserve the peace before the havoc. The girls looked around and saw a garden of wildflowers with some song birds on an aspen attached to the bench and arbor.

Harold observed as he made his way across the courtyard. Paul caught his attention. He saw Paul drawing the Palisade freehand on some parchment with great care in the details. He stood over Paul's shoulder and just watched. He then moved on to see what the girls were doing. He heard the chef yell.

"Get out of my herbs. Those aren't wildflowers to pick! You eat them. Quit chasing after supper! War help us!"

Amused by someone thinking of War as an entity to save the cook and the cook not knowing the history, Harold said "I will handle this."

EDWINA OF THE MOONS

"WHAT BRINGS YOU HERE SO far from the village?" An older man grumbled as he approached. He wore chain mail and carried a staff and sword. "I am Harold, keeper of the Palisade. We reside here and on occasion venture to Ruan for supplies. Rarely do we have visitors."

"I am Paul, and this is Tatiana and Edwina. We are in Ruan on vacation with our parents, and as we do every year, we snuck out to explore for a bit. We saw the Palisade from Ruan and thought it would be a good place to start our exploring."

"Well, you are here now, come on in." Harold began explaining what a Palisade was and why it was located at that location. He showed them many artifacts and sites within rich in history. "If you wish to stay for the evening, you are most welcome young adventurers."

Edwina wandered off and observed a stone that was not quite due east. As she approached, she noticed symbols around the base. She felt a strange energy from the stone, as she knelt beside it examining the symbols. Something inside her told her to press the stone. She rose and followed her feeling. The stone sunk in slightly, revealing a small door.

"What have you found child?" Harold ran over with sword drawn.

"I am not certain. Do you feel it too?"

"No Edwina, but I do see the door. You were meant to open it, if you figured out all that. I will protect you."

Edwina nodded and opened a door. It was a very small ornate door, and behind it was a small chamber that was only big enough to hold a box. Edwina lifted the box from the chamber and removed the lid.

The Kluanarians

"You need a priestess probably, to understand what that says, lass." Harold ran his fingers over the object.

"It is a book, Sir Harold. I believe it belongs to the Moons. I heard about the people from a story Mom used to tell me at bedtime. May I have it Sir?"

"Yes. My men and I have no use for a book. But you, on the other hand, will benefit from this treasure. We have a watcher amongst us who might be able to help you. Bring Altus to me Walther."

"Aye, he is already enroute," proclaimed Walther.

"The book is found by its rightful owner," Altus rushed across the square and studied Edwina. "Where are your siblings?"

"Chatting with the guards, we are staying here this eve."

"Very well, I will help you learn some of this. Please also be aware, your grandmother will have her hand in this. She will come to you when it is time."

"What? Are you mad? I don't even know my grandmothers."

"You will in short time. But for now, let me see you left shoulder."

Edwina had a tank top on, so just turned and said, "See. It has been tingling and itching for a couple weeks. I tried calamine lotion, but it made it red."

"It is because a symbol has formed and is slightly raised. Do not worry, it isn't bad. Fairly small, I wouldn't go spreading it through your house just yet, at least not until its purpose is discovered."

"Ok, can it be hidden then?"

"No, not really. But I can see someone who can. Harold, can you hide this?" Altus showed the symbol to Harold.

"Yes, it will be easy, and no bloodshed or branding required. Walther, my kit."

The kit was delivered, and Harold dug through and found his paicely root and frog spit. He crushed the root and mixed it with the frog spit and a drop of water. He pulled his dagger from its sheath. "This will not hurt, I promise." He placed the dagger in the paste and carefully smeared it on the symbol. He recited an incantation in a language unknown to Edwina. "Good as gone and nothing can break the enchantment except for me."

"Thank you. And the itching stopped as well."

Altus took Edwina to a library full of many ancient works. "First, I need to school you on the language." He took time to ensure she understood the lettering and the basic words. After four hours she was allowed a break.

She was excited to see Paul learning how to hold a sword and Tatiana was learning about messenger birds.

"To the chamber everyone, our meal is prepared." Harold announced as he motioned to the children. "This great meal is in honor of our guests. The rest of today is a day of leisure. Dessert will be after the meal – should you have room."

All celebrated. The kids had never seen such a huge amount of food and drink served, or how fast it dwindled as the guards returned for more. They too found themselves gorging and drinking. Dessert, the kids looked bloated- but somehow had room for two helpings of dessert, as there were many desserts to choose from, they took a bit of each. When the meal was done the kids returned to their instructors.

"You have learned much Edwina. The rest of the day, I would like you to read these three books. One is a history of the Moons; one is a book a made that will help you relate Kluanarian to English. The third is a book on Kluanaria."

"Kluanaria?" Edwina quirked an eyebrow.

"Just read, it will make sense. And again, you must not tell anyone of this knowledge." Altus provided a waterproof bag that books could be carried in. "Tomorrow, I will select some for you to take with you. And I can switch them out with translocation as you complete each one and understand its contents. Do you have questions young lady?"

"The Moons is a symbol rarely given according to what I just read. What does it mean when a mere normal person gets it?"

"You have a great sleeping ability that is beginning to stir. You would not have been able to retrieve the Book of Moons without this gift. It will all make sense after you read these books. I will teach you some in the late hours, as that is when your powers are strongest."

"How do you know so much?"

"Lunacerian is the Head of our Order. He has sent me to keep watch over this stone until the gifted one was able to retrieve the book. It was a test, one of which you passed. He has selected you to be a part of the Order and I am here as a teacher to prepare you for your acceptance in the order. Lunacerian will request you when it is time. Until then, I am your teacher and protector."

"This is way too weird for me. I think there is a mistake."

"Nonsense, girl. Lunacerian does not make mistakes. Now take these books with you and relax. I will summon for you late this eve."

Altus showed Edwina to the door. She walked down the long corridor and found a familiar face. "Tomas, why are you here?"

"My tournament begins this evening. I was hoping to find you here. Why were you with the creepy man?"

"He was sharing his library with me. Kind of a neat place. What do you know about here?"

"Umm, not much. I bring supplies for the guards and sort of act like a - what you would call- a cab service so travel time is lessened."

"The guards taught me to fight, so I am excited most are going to watch me this evening. Will you go with?"

"Yes, but I don't have..," Edwina was interrupted.

"I have robes for your caliber for the tourney lass." Harold approached. "If you two will follow me."

"Your parents will not recognize you. I sent tell that you were found safe and enjoying the Palisade so they would not interrupt your learning." Harold showed Tomas and Edwina to a huge chamber. "There, you two can pick out a good robe for the Moons' representative to wear. Altus of course will be attending and seated beside you. Tomas is your Champion."

"Wow, all of that, for one simple vacation. I was just supposed to relax and do nothing and maybe explore – not all of this."

"I understand if you choose nigh." Tomas bowed.

"No, Tomas. I will be most pleased to have you as my Champion." She hugged Tomas. "I think this is meant to be. Please help me look through all of these fine robes."

They settled on one which was very fine. The material was a silvery sheen of silk with mithril woven throughout with the Moons symbol repeated from the neck down to waist. The sleeves had the same pattern around the cuffs. An open face hood was made in the same manner, with its base having the pattern and a large mithril symbol place at the very center in the front.

Harold then showed Tomas the Champion's gear - adorned mithril mail with the collar of the tunic having the same pattern. The helm was highly polished as was the mail. The sword hilt had the Moons symbol and an inscription emblazoned in to the blade. Edwina recited the inscription thrice. She looked at the shield and could feel a great connection. She knelt beside it and focused with her head pressed against it. Tomas walked over and also knelt.

"This is to be Tomas." Edwina kissed his forehead. You are my Champion. And I will be present for your battles. Please accept this," she removed a ribbon from her hair and fastened it to his wrist.

He smiled. "If only you were a couple years older."

"I would have you wait for me then." She said we must ready lest we be late."

"Aye, young lass. I will send for a maid to assist you." Harold motioned for a guard but halted as Edwina spoke.

"I can manage. Thank you." She ran to the robes and took them to a changing area at the far end of the room.

Harold assisted Tomas with his gear.

Tatiana and Paul were busy telling stories to the men of the Palisade to notice their sister leave with Harold, Altus and Tomas.

Quiet settled on the tournament site as the four entered the arena. Tomas and Edwina bowed to each other. "May I kiss your cheek Sir Tomas?" She did not wait for an answer, she did it anyway. "Where I normally live – it is considered good luck." She said as she walked with Harold and Altus to her seat. Her mother was two seats away with her father also in the Noble Box. All stood and bowed before Altus.

"You never come to tourneys Altus, what brings you from the Palisade?" Henry was prying, as he often did when the unexpected happens in Ruan.

"The gifted has been found, and Tomas is her representative." Altus mused.

"Is that? No it can't be. Can it?" Myron glanced at Edwina.

"Nonsense, Myron. Edwina is with Paul and Tatiana at the Palisade." Iris arose and bowed to Edwina. "Welcome to the tourney. Forgive my husband." She then noticed the faint smile semi concealed by the shade of the evening. She put the thought from her mind and sat down. "Myron, it is Edwina," Iris whispered.

"No, really. I told you she would be trouble." Myron said jokingly.

The Kluanarians

The tournament was quite spectacular. The onlookers were charged as Tomas was in the final round. Altus on numerous occasions restrained her from being boisterous during combat. "It is not lady –like to shout such things, Edwina. I would think you were a man by those words."

"I said nothing foul; I was just supporting my Champion. Not your Champion, MINE. In case you didn't notice, he wears MY mark."

"Woman-child you have much to learn about being civil, especially when representing an Order. Notice your mother. She is quite calm and cheers only after points for each round. Notice how she is sitting. You need to emulate that. Not this slouchy - excuse me – get your foot off of that seat. Help me Lunacerian, please!!"

"Well I am a kid, a stinky little brat, if you must know. I am on vacation and I keep getting in deeper and deeper to some weird cult thing from what I am told. I hope the cops show up and save me."

"I am no cop, lady," Tomas bowed before her. "But I will escort you back to the Palisade, or are you returning to the bungalow with your parents?"

"I believe she should be at the bungalow tonight, so that she might sleep well and soak in this long day," Altus replied in an exasperated tone. "Please escort her to her residence here."

Myron approached, "This is a shock, Ed. I never knew this would become of you. Not in my wildest nightmares." He paused and reflected. "Tomas will you escort her home and be there this night as Champion?"

"Aye, my Lord. What else would you have me do this late eve?"

"Please just make yourself at home. I assume Altus already had servants of the Order there preparing your sleeping area."

"Yes, Myron, I did. I hope that I was not too intrusive. Did the messenger pigeon arrive timely?"

"Aye and we were in disbelief, until now. Thank you for your wisdom and guidance. Why couldn't you leave this alone until tomorrow, is my only question."

Ignoring the question Altus continued, "Please make sure she gets plenty of rest. Reading is tomorrow, she need not be at the Palisade for that. And Edwina, as you walk home, see if you notice anything different about things."

"Yes Altus. Thank you for attending the tournament with me. I am very glad that Tomas won." She bowed and took Tomas' arm. They walked slowly into the darkness toward the bungalow.

"Beautiful night isn't it, Tomas?"

"Yes Lady. It most certainly is, and so you know, I shall also wait for you as you had stated earlier."

They entered the bungalow and noticed all was modified, reflecting to Orders' presence in the home. There was now an upstairs with two rooms both adorned in Moon. Two rooms on the main floor were adorned with Star. Tomas noted this and pointed it out to Edwina.

"We should be quite respectful here as I believe this has great importance," suggested Tomas.

"Where is your place here, Tomas? Umm, it is beside you. See there are two beds; one is yours one is mine. I am your protector, so that is my place. Do you prefer window side or wall side?"

"Either, I just know I am very tired. The other room is a changing room for one of us, I suppose, so I will change there and you change here."

"Very well, Lady. Please knock before you come back in here though."

"I will, I will." Edwina smiled and closed the door as she walked across to the changing room.

Edwina knocked, Tomas opened the door. "Ok, now should I tuck you in, as I do not know exactly what a Protector does at night."

"No, I am good. Good night Tomas."

"Good night Edwina."

Both crawled into their respective beds and were instantly out.

Myron and Iris arrived shortly after and tucked both of them in.

"What the heck? Why can't that man stay out of affairs that are not his to meddle in!" Iris was ranting as she walked through the bungalow and saw how distorted it was from the Moon and the Star enchantments. It didn't seem at rest. "You know there is great distrust between our Orders, Myron. I will not allow her to become a Moon. I will fight this. My father will hear me. Come back here, I am not done talking to you!"

Myron had gone up to his room and was out. A surprise visitor knocked on the door.

"Thanias, what a surprise!" Iris was happy to see him. "Myron won't do anything, but you will."

"What happened?"

"That darn Altus happened. He is twisting Edwina!"

"Why is that? Did she go to the Palisade?"

"Yes, and her curiosity has got her in to some trouble. You know how well Moons and Stars get along."

"Ah, this is really about my mother then." Thanias said whimsically. "You did bring that encounter on yourself, when you ran."

"This…This has nothing to do with…her"

Thanias quirked an eyebrow. "It does, as you can't even speak in a complete sentence. Now I will see about fixing this mess tomorrow. Where is Myron?"

"Asleep, as usual."

"I must be going. Do not tell him I was here."

"Why, are you on some sort of 'secret' quest?" Iris said mockingly.

"Actually I just returned from that and have lost my companion, Rynn. I was hoping on my journey from Nagazthastar by stopping here and asking you for aide…"

"I will look for her, Thanias."

"Thank you." He bowed to Iris. "I will see you tomorrow."

At dawn, there was a whispering as Tomas went down the hall toward Myron's sleeping chamber.

"Sir Myron? Are you awake?"

"What is it, son?" Myron stretched and quietly got dressed.

"It is me, Tomas. I cannot be her protector. There is no way that this will work out to my liking."

"What is your liking?"

"Well, a good night's sleep. But I don't see that happening."

Myron laughed. "Truthfully, Tomas, I was not expecting her to be an Order. Not in my wildest dreams. I am Iris' protector, I will watch over Edwina until the facts are clear. You don't worry about that part. You are much too young for such a duty right now. I will get word to my brother, Thanias, and he will help me fix this. Out of curiosity, why didn't you sleep?"

"Well, she rambled on and on for an hour, so I tried cotton in my ears. That kind of helped, that and I ignored her, so then she was "hurt". She finally said her irksome words and fell asleep. I fell asleep after an hour of enjoying silence. Then the loud snoring began. It was like a den full of thirty bears for most of the night."

Myron almost fell over laughing. "Oh dear, that would be horrible. I am terribly sorry the Moons are such a pain to deal with. I mean the teacher should have realized you are both way too young to be worried about such things. I will handle Altus in a bit. Sir Harold will be more understanding, as we spoke in great length after your win, which by the way was the best combat I have seen in many years."

"Thank you. Please do not be angry with me for being so blunt, but I do not like putting sugar coating on things."

"I understand, Tomas. Join me for breakfast."

The two drank tea and discussed combat for some time. Iris soon awoke and started preparing the meal. "How did you sleep, dear?" Iris asked as she peeled potatoes.

A loud roar came from the two men. Both laughed for a bit and settled down. "Iris, the Champion is relinquishing his duties to me, until they are a more realistic age and we might need to send him to an ear specialist. I thought it was my imagination, but it was confirmed this morning. Our Edwina snores extremely loud."

"Well, that being said, is there anything else that disturbs the young man?"

"No, ma'am. Just not ready to be put in harm's way for something I know nothing about. The fighting would be great, but if it is fighting snoring, I will never win. Please excuse my abruptness."

"How rude. But I accept your apology, as I too believe that Altus needs his head examined. Myron."

"I am going to speak with him after breakfast. Hopefully Thanias shows up, he knew we would be here."

THE PALISADES

Paul and Tatiana became tired of waiting on Edwina to show. They supped with the guards and learned many valorous songs, that Tat jotted down- as future reference – just in case a mystery requiring a tune developed. Paul observed the customs and precision throughout the day. He too took notes, as he felt it important. He, after Tatiana was asleep, went to the observation area where some older telescopes were placed in a slight room. He scanned the skies and noted various patterns in the heavens. He mused often that one day he will be a great aerospace engineer and be able to travel to those far-away places and discover new lands with many more cultures, preferably a place less violent.

Tatiana grew bored and found Paul atop the tower with the telescope. He pointed out stars and galaxies to her and she took notes. "Does that book ever run out of pages, Tat?"

"Yes, I brought ten with me in the pack, just in case. Wonder where Ed is at, she should be enjoying the view."

Paul thought for a bit, "Maybe she got scared and ran back. Maybe a troll chased her," he started laughing at the thought.

"Well, anyway, I am tired and we need sleep. Walther, could you show us to our room, please?" Tatiana bowed as Walther came up the tower.

"This way young-uns. It is right here." He led them in to an extravagant room with a monstrous bed that Tat thought could hold twenty people. They surveyed the room and Tat, as always recorded interesting details. Walther even sat down beside Tatiana and told her a bedtime story before he left.

Brenda M. Hokenson

Walther's Bedtime Story

"Ok, young lass and Paul here it goes."

There was once a village in the shadow of a vast plateau that was in the East. A stable boy tended the horses every day. He took special care of the foals and colts as they were born and grew. One day something on the edge of the plateau caught his eye. He saw four riders mounted on horses. He found it strange, as no one was ever on the edge plateau. The boy ran to the Elders and asked they raise the alarm.

"Why would we do that, Malos?"

"They are evil!"

"You don't know this. Let them come, we will welcome any visitor."

"You don't understand, they are on the plateau." Malos pointed toward the East.

The four started down the side of the plateau. Their mounts seemed to not have to touch the ground as they approached the base of the plateau.

"If you won't, I will." Malos screamed as he raced to the church and climbed into the bell tower where the alarm was stored. A loud rumbling horn echoed through the valley. He was successful!

The villagers gathered in the square and waited for an Elder to speak.

"Go back to you business, all of you!" The Elder said mocking Malos. "There is no danger."

"No danger! What do you call those four approaching from the East?"

"Visitors." The Elder laughed.

"No, the boy is right." The priest spoke up. "We must go to the sanctuary. We do not want the destruction they will bring."

The Elders laughed, but the villagers followed the priest.

A slight passageway opened as the priest moved the cloth on the offering table and pressed a slight button. The women and children were first to enter the large room. An eight-year-old approached Malos and they started talking.

"At last, it is time." Malos said to the boy. "How have you been William?"

"Yes, and I am not certain why this is happening now. And I have been fine. The home I am in is really nice. The lady is quite sincere in caring for me, even though I am not hers."

The priest overhearing the conversation approached. "She is happy to keep you, William. We are not sure where your family went, but you have brought her much joy."

"Malos, we need to check the village." William said as he remembered first meeting his new "mother".

"You both are too young." The priest interjected.

The boys ignored him and they went to the church entry way. They saw only one of the four riders approaching. William led the way back through the entry way. "We must seal it now!"

The two sealed the entry way temporarily while the priest stood in awe. "Stop, stop I say. We will be trapped."

"Better trapped than dead!" Malos said as he looked at the villagers.

A man approached. "You two have caused enough commotion today. He took off his belt and was ready to beat their backside as they heard horse steps above. "What's that?"

"Trouble, worse than your wildest nightmares. It is a horseman."

"We have done nothing." The man said.

"Exactly!" Malos said as he looked at the Elders. "You all have done nothing for so long and grew complacent to everything, that a darkness grows here. Now the horsemen are free again."

"You know too much." One of the Elders said. "We have always looked after the village."

"No, you haven't. There are ailing folk whom you refuse to aide. There are families in need of food and shelter, that you ignore daily. There, is me, a stable boy, who has no home, no family, no anything. I am ignored no longer, nor are these suffering people. The horsemen are here to teach you, Elders!"

The horse stopped and the rider dismounted. He searched for the way in to the chamber.

"We must open the inner sanctum!" Malos whispered.

Toward the back of the room there was a goblet with a liquid in it. Malos searched for a way to remove the liquid. "We cannot tip it!"

William found some small pebbles and began placing them in the goblet. The man with the belt started helping as well. After a bit, the liquid ran over the top of the goblet and as the last pebbles were added, a rumble filled the room. A bright light came from behind a large rock. Malos and the man moved the rock. The villagers panicked yet silent, as they heard the horseman roaring unfriendly words, went into the second room.

Brenda M. Hokenson

"Ok, I must seal you all in now." Malos said as he ran back through the opening.

The man said, "It is better you than me. I brought my medicinal to treat everyone." He helped Malos push the rock into place.

"Seal it, William!" A command came through the crack as Malos quickly pulled the rocks from the goblet and tossed them everywhere.

"You will not win, Malos!" A booming voice roared as the horseman crushed the hidden door with his fist and foot. He made his way down the stairs.

"I must go to his aide!" William shouted. He ran toward the rock.

"No, you can't. I will not lose you to this horseman!" William's mother, Malificence, screamed, grabbing him by the shoulders.

"Let me go woman." William said.

"How dare you speak to me in that tone!" Malificence slapped him on the cheek.

"You leave me no choice then." He stomped on her toe and ran through the rock.

"Who do we have here, Malos? You have a new friend, I see."

"Yes, and you will return to the realm of unliving at once." William said. "Now, War. Where is your trinket?"

"Not this time. I am here to help you."

"Why would you help us?"

"I carry the red dagger. I am here because a little girl interests the unholy one and Death is to find her and take her to him."

"So why are all four of you free?" Malos said as the three paced, unsure of who would strike first.

In the chamber women and children cried and the men paced and gathered arms.

"First of all, the unholy one isn't who you think, this time. We are uncertain of how this dwarf freed us."

"What dwarf?"

"The one who summoned us from our realm."

"Well, let's not waste any more time. We will start be freeing this town."

"Plague is outside." War added. "He has taken the extremely ill and possibly the cause of this hamlet's downfall. I will lead the way. You will have to trust me."

32

The Kluanarians

"We cannot trust you, but for this instant in time." William nodded as the trio left the outer chamber.

All was quiet in the town square. War pointed to a home a block away. "He is there."

The two boys went to the rear of the home and War to the door.

"Are you home, Plague?" War shouted.

"Yesss. I am home. I have missed torturing the living. Missed the screams of pain and agony. Missed the tears of family mourning." He went to the porch. "Did you find the villagers?"

"I think..." War was interrupted by two boys.

"Your time is over." Malos said as he ripped the trinket from Plague. "Quick the unending pockets!" Malos placed the trinket into the unending pockets that William held open.

"How can this beeeeeeeee." Plague yelled as he dispersed into nothing.

"Three more to go!" William shouted.

"First, let the villagers out." War said amusingly. "They need to know they are safe by my hand."

Malos and William looked at each other and shrugged. The three returned to the sealed room and let the villagers loose. The priest saw War standing before him and fainted.

"You there." War said to the Elders. "You five have brought this to your village. I hereby appoint Zanor as the High Lord of Ruan. His children and friends will rebuild this place! You five will go with me." War waved his arm as if grasping each one and they shrunk into the palm of his hand. "You will be my next general's, if you survive." The five were absorbed into the red dagger.

"Zanor, bring order back to this village."

"We must go now; the others are rampant upon the land." said as they prepared to leave.

"You aren't going anywhere young man." Malificence said.

"I am no child of 8." As William spoke, he transmuted to a man of about thirty in human years.

"How... how is this..." Malificence was cut off.

"Ahh, at last." Malos also shifted and appeared in his forties.

"Not too bad for being 900 Malos." William chimed in.

"Well, you're one to speak, elf of 1200. At least I didn't got to the extreme and be a helpless baby."

"She needed me. She was on the brink."

"I was. And I am grateful. I always thought it odd that I could hear you speaking late in the night from your cradle."

"We must be off now. Thank you for understanding." William bowed to the lady who tended him since he was small (in human guise).

"She cannot stay here." War commanded. *"She is not safe here."*

"Well, then, what do you recommend?"

"She goes with us, of course." Malos added. *"First, we need horses. As he spoke two horses approached.*

"Where is my mount?" Malificence inquired.

"There." Malos pointed at a pegasus. *"He will keep you safe."*

The group left, leaving Zanor to rebuild Ruan.

"What exactly are you looking for?" Malifice asked as she hovered on the Pegasus.

"Well, Pestilence first. He is easy, just follow the carrion birds." William answered. *"After that, not sure."*

"I do." War added as he wringed his hands with the thoughts of destruction flashing in his mind. *'A small girl, probably 6-8 years old with red hair. She is in a small village."*

"How do you have such details? How can a small child have anything to do with the horsemen?" Malos asked as he came to an abrupt halt. *"She can summon the Warlock?"*

"I hope not, for all our sake." William said as he dismounted near Malos. *"That is where our next mark is. See the great flock?"*

Malificence wondered aloud. *"What warlock?"*

"Oh, just a very, very evil one. Mithdrool is his name and once summoned, it is painfully hard to put him to rest." War paused as he looked at the village. *"HE is undead and has risen many times. The people of that village are called Fraeloch. They aren't much different from humans, except for their minds – much quicker and they respect nature. Many druids are Fraeloch."*

"Now is our chance!" William motioned for the group. He entered a house where the horseman was and managed to get behind him with a drawn sword.

"Too late William!" Pestilence spun about with his bird balanced on his shoulder. He plucked William off of his feet by his neck. *"You're next."*

Malos used the distraction to his advantage and ripped the trinket off of the belt. He opened the endless pocket and dropped the trinket inside.

"How could you, brother? Waaaaarrrrr! Coward." Pestilence was contained.

Malificence breathed a sigh of relief. Something caught her eye as she was looking around."Over there, look. It's a child running into the forest."

"Yes. That is Mithdrool Forest. I am thinking we need to give chase and find Bob."

"Bob?"

"Death, Bob, same thing. His real name used to be Bob, when he was alive as a Titan. Not many Titans left. They have intermingled with humans and Fraeloch. But that is for another day. Any way, he prefers to be called Bob." War responded, reflecting on his life as a elven soldier.

William removed a golden ring from his pocket and placed it on the ground. A great dragon emerged from it.

"Why?" War inquired. "She is but a small child with no clue of what is going on."

"To contain the magic this child possesses." Malos replied. "The dragon belongs to Menosh. He has ultimate say, even though he lets the races fumble about. Mithdrool must not rise. The girl must be stopped. Fred, you know what to do."

The dragon nodded and took flight. The group followed as the dragon observed the child's path. He set down near the base of a large hill that had a cave part way up and waited for the riders to catch up. "Go forth riders. She is looking for someone, near that stream."

The riders followed the small path and found the girl. William and Malos built a small fire and prepared a meal for all. Malificence fetched water and set up a tent and placed the bedrolls inside. War gathered wood for the fire.

"Why are you gathering wood?" Malificence asked as she helped stack the pieces. "You are undead."

"You are not though, lady Malificence. I will not see you be chilled as it gets quite cold here at night."

Malificence blushed. "Thank you. Do you not go by you living name anymore?"

"No, I hated it."

"It can be no worse than Malificence."

"It is Harold. I belong to the dwarves. My father is a High King or was a

Brenda M. Hokenson

High King. I can't remember much, but Menosh asked that I fill this role. So I am more undying than walking dead."

"Thank you, Harold. Will you help me find the child?"

"Yes, she will need to eat as well."

The two spotted her near a stream where she was huddled in a blanket.

"Child, why do you run from us?" Malificence asked as she approached the girl.

"I wasn't running from you. I was running from that man who had the birds following him. He kept saying I was chosen and that he would take me to Bob. Who is Bob?"

"Don't worry about Bob." War said as he gently picked the child up. "We have food and shelter to share with you. Where is your family?" The trio set off toward the campsite.

"That man with the birds, he took them away." The girl cried. "He said I can't have them back until I see Bob."

"Well, then, we will see Bob together. I will get your family back." War promised as he placed her on a log near the fire.

The group ate their fill and went to sleep. Heavy rain fell all night long. The girl peered out a flap and noticed it no longer striking the campsite, but all around it.

"That's what dragons are for." William responded as he caught the girl's eye. "Please sleep. Tomorrow will be long, and you will need your strength for that hill." He picked her up and told her a short tale that put her to sleep. "Thank you for the sleeping breath, Fred." William said as he placed the girl back on the rather fluffy bedroll. "Sheep's wool, really. How many did you eat to get that bedroll that fluffy?"

"Oh, only a heard of twenty-five."

"Ah, only twenty-five."

"Hey, I refrained from eating the expectant ewes, babies and those in their 'prime'."

"I know, all of the rolls are really fluffy, thank you."

"Menosh has work for you."

"Really!" Harold exclaimed.

"Yes, you are to wed this Malificence and the line of Morket will be restored."

"Ah, and why do we want the Morket Order back?"

"They are the only ones who can defeat Mithdrool."

"I thought that is why Zanor is in Ruan?"

"Well, no, he has to rebuild it. You will be in charge of the Palisade. The Orders will need protected in not too far off a time. Plus you are a Morket."

"I am not…"

"You are and you will or two worlds will fail as darkness returns."

"Very well. For the sake of two worlds. I guess." War yawned. "See, now I am exhausted. Sleep well, Fred." War went to his place after adding wood to the fire and was soon asleep.

The dragon kept watch as he slumbered using his special vision. He had also cast deep sleep over the group as the quest was most important and he had to do some defending and wanted no interruptions.

The group awoke by mid-day. A small feast was set before them by the dragon. After the meal, the task was at hand, the climb to the cave.

"Why do I have to be on the dragon?" The girl inquired.

"He will protect you from Bob." War responded. After this is done, and if we can't find your family…" he paused as he placed the girl on the dragon's neck, "you are most welcome to reside with me and Malificence."

"Really?" Malificence's eyes opened wide.

"Yes, and we shall be wed and reside in my Kaprius." He smiled at the two.

The group set off up the slope of the hill. The dragon said, "Luly must be used. We must convince Bob that she is here to help him."

Malos nodded. Luly dismounted the dragon and ran up the hill and in to the cave.

"Are you Bob?" Luly asked as she entered the cave.

"I am. Do you know why you are here?"

"The mean guy took my family. He said I had to find you to get them back."

"Ah, I see." Bob paced. "Turns out, I don't need you after all." Death approached her as she slowly backed toward the entrance.

"Please, Bob. No. I haven't done anything to you."

Death quickly turned his head toward a sound at the rear of the cave. As he changed course, Luly ran out the entrance. He turned back and ran after her. "You cannot escape Death!"

"And you won't be killing another being this day." War pulled the trinket from Death's grip and the endless pocket was presented another gift.

"You are too late you fools. The warlock is risen!" Death vanished.

"I am terribly sorry, Luly." Malificence embraced her as the child wept. "Please come with us and be part of our family." Luly nodded.

"What about Mithdrool?" William asked of Malos.

"Menosh has said it is to be, for now. He is too weak and there are none who will assist him. Beryth and Lady Phallas are in Nagazthastar and will protect all secrets."

A week later in the city of Kaprius, Harold wed Malificence. Together, they raised Luly who became a Eupepsian, learning beside Truance. They also had two daughters, Impresaria and Iris.

To this day, no one has heard from Mithdrool. He is out there, somewhere, waiting for the right time to wage war on the twin planets.

Tatiana was out cold, with visions of the Palisades and fighting dragons and other wicked creatures running wildly through her mind. Paul remembered the names used. They seemed familiar for some reason. He wondered if it was oral history and not a story. He too fell asleep.

In the morning, they ate with their new made friends and as they were walking across the courtyard, glanced upon a familiar face.

"Dad, dad!" Tatiana burst into a sprint and leapt into his arms. "We can't find Ed anywhere, and what happened to the little girl?"

"She is at home. She went with Tomas and Harold to the tournament. What little girl?

"The one in Walther's bedtime story. Her name was Luly. We have been learning about messenger birds and Paul has been learning about swords too. I got to send a message to you. Did you get it?"

"First question's answer is what bedtime story? Second part, yes, I did, and your writing is improved, Tatiana." Myron saw Harold approaching. "Good morn to you Harold. Is Altus in, or is he hanging out in Ruan?"

"I believe we should both speak to him. It will be interesting to see what happens next."

"Let us go then." Myron gestured for Harold to lead.

The long corridor seemed to take forever to navigate. At the end of it was a short set of spiral steps to Altus' sitting room.

"Altus, are you here, Sir?" Harold inquired in a low vice so as to not startle anyone.

"I am. What is it that is pressing this day? Ah, I see. You are both here and have a similar concern."

"Altus, what madness led you to the decision that since my daughter, Edwina, is of the Moons Order, and that she immediately needs a protector? I am her father and will do quite well in her defense. You ask way too much of such a young lad as Tomas. Harold and I have discussed this. I will be responsible for her safety until she is fully trained and ready to move forth as Lunacerian requires. Until such time, Tomas will remain with Henry and Luly, his parents and receive training from Harold and Walther."

"I understand your dilemma gentleman. However," Altus was cut short.

Harold spoke up, "Listen here you pansy. I am telling you; Tomas is not prepared for being a Protector. I have sent word to both Lunacerian and Thanias. I am tired of your crap, old man and it will be settled once and for all."

Paul and Tatiana were in the courtyard when Thanias arrived. They watched everyone migrate to him and bow.

"Is that you Paul?" Thanias acknowledged the guards and walked to Paul and Tatiana.

"Yes, sir. I remember you from when I was little. You are someone important," replied Paul.

"I am. I am your uncle and it seems your father needs my assistance. Do you know where he is?"

"In the library place, with an older gentleman and Harold."

"Oh yeah, and why is Harold as big as Edwina and beefy?" Tatiana's question was left alone as a very tall thin man entered. "Who is he?" Tatiana grabbed Thanias sword hilt so he would stop and look.

"Oh, him, that is Lunacerian, he is a pain in the heiney on most days. What is your name so I can introduce you?"

"I am Tatiana, Paul's little sister." She smiled and took his hand.

"Lunacerian, welcome to the Palisade." Thanias walked forward and greeted Lunacerian. "This is Tatiana and Paul, my niece and nephew."

Lunacerian greeted the kids. "It is my pleasure to meet you both. Now you should both go with, umm, Walther for a tour."

"We did that yesterday. As I understand, Thanias has reign at the Palisade." Paul replied.

"Hey, I can ask him about Luly!" Tatiana beamed with new excitement.

Thanias grinned, "Technically, Harold is the overseer. I am in charge of the Truncheon and rotating them. Harold uses what he is given in defense of Ruan and the Palisade. My Truncheon and Harold's soldiers have been watching over this rock forever and it seems they can go back to normal now that it's just a rock again."

"It is not just a rock it is a protected…"

"Rock," Thanias interjected. "Now let us see about the dilemma caused by your darn rock, since it pertains to my kin. It has better be a good reason to stir the ire of a Star."

All four walked down the hallway. Myron, Harold and Altus greeted the new arrivals to the library.

Thanias said, "Let's cut to the chase. From the message we received, Edwina is part of Lunacerian's Order. Tomas is not yet a protector, but Altus decided he will be the protector, and cause some anxiety amongst the kids and force my brother's home to be renovated to include the Moons ideals and tradition. Is this correct and what Lunacerian received?"

"Yes Thanias." Harold responded, looking toward Tomas he contiued. "Tomas is but a boy who delivers supplies to us and provides us quick returns to Ruan. We have been training him in his spare time, but he is not required to do anything."

Myron interjected. "My daughter has no inkling as to the gravity you have placed on her or what is expected of her. She and Tomas were placed in an unnecessary predicament by Altus. I am quite capable of protecting her and my wife, who is quite perturbed by this incident and wants it resolved now."

Paul took Tatiana by the arm, "Let's find Walther now!"

"Let's sit down and come to a peaceable solution that does not jeopardize the Order or the kids." Lunacerian gestured toward the chairs and seated himself. "First of all, Edwina is of my Order. Altus stepped over the line by putting so much on her and by renovating the bungalow. It is being restored as we speak. Edwina will not be ready for some time. I am asking that the library remain here so the books may change out as she reads and fully understands the material. I do not ask her to have everything memorized. She must be comfortable with it and capable of controlling herself. Altus, you are here by resolved to return to Kluanaria and resume your old post as scribe." Lunacerian paused briefly as Altus left and then began again. "Please forgive his expeditious behavior. I am sure he was running on adrenaline when all of this came to be. Tomas, I apologize for the position you were placed in."

"It is ok, Lunacerian. I kind of enjoyed having everyone look at me as someone important. I even enjoyed having to stay at Myron's house, up to a point." Tomas started laughing again.

The laughter was contagious. All were laughing, but no one except Myron and Tomas knew the reason.

"Your willingness to protect an innocent through this and to be the Moons' Champion has shown me that you are our next Protector. You will be more than likely paired to Edwina, but not for some time." Thanias was quite pleased with his announcement and added, "Harold, please train him. I have already spent time with Henry and Luly. They are quite pleased of this decision and have asked that he be allowed to visit home."

Harold bowed. "Yes Sir. There is a great area in the commons of Ruan where I can train him. He only needs to come here to learn smith work and that is not for some time."

"Very well. Are all parties satisfied with the resolution?" Lunacerian asked nicely.

All nodded in agreement. "Then to town with everyone, we shall celebrate the children and the guards and the future." Harold ordered the bell to toll for the dismissal of the guards.

Lunacerian walked with Edwina and explained everything to her as best he could. Iris watched from across the commons as the meeting took place. She after all had a deep distrust of the Moons Order and wanted nothing to do with the meeting.

A bit later, Edwina was excused by and she ran home to relax. Her mother fixed her some shortcake and tea to help calm her down.

Myron and Thanias walked together. Harold joined them, along with most of the soldiers and Truncheon. Walther rode a horse with Tatiana and gave Paul and Tomas mounts to keep up.

"So, how do you know there was great ire stirred in my residence, Thanias?"

"I stopped by last eve, but you were just asleep, according to Iris. She said many words and one was to fix the problem."

"Well, it isn't fixed now, is it?" Myron said gruffly. "Why can't you stay away from her and us?"

"Well, now, that isn't very friendly, especially since I have not seen you in at least 5 years. You really should look after your wife better."

"Why, what's wrong with Iris?"

"Well, for one, she does not know her place. Second, she thinks this is my fault somehow."

"She knows her place, and it is your fault."

"No, it isn't. I only thought a long, long time ago that she and I would be great together and that we could do awesome things as a team."

"No, no. She thought and still thinks that you are up to no good."

"Well, she is wrong, as usual. But I did ask her for help. Rynn is missing and I don't know where to find her. Rynn is the closest I probably will have to a special someone."

Myron choked back laughter and reflected for a bit. "So the elf is your companion for life?"

"I had hoped that maybe..."

"Thanias, come on now. I am your little brother. Why her?"

"She is not judgmental, temperamental, or any other 'ental.' She is however missing."

"Ok, you win. It would take an elf to make you see who you truly are and the fact that she is a tested archer."

"How did you know that?"

"Just like you Thanias, I have my ways."

The men entered Myron's bungalow. Iris was seated with tea already poured for the two in the living room.

"I saw you coming." Iris spoke as she got up and hugged both of them. "Tell me, is Edwina free of the Moons?"

"No dear." Myron responded.

"Why? What was sooo difficult to tell that 'rock monitor' to stay out of family business?"

Thanias rose. "Iris, by Kluanarian law, Edwina opened the darn rock's compartment and was fully understanding what was in front of her. There is no way on this great planet that she can be taken from the Order before she is trained and can make that decision on her own."

"Well, it should have been allowed to wait until she is of age." Iris said as she paced. "Did you see what those darn rock lovers did to this place? Did you? It was a disaster. Moon and Star do not go in the same residence. It just does not work."

"Well, now I see the whole picture, Iris. This is about Kira, me and Myron's mother. Get over it, you were dumb and beyond wrong!" Thanias added as he too began pacing.

THE LAND OF TREAH

THE REMAINDER OF THE DAY passed. Paul got permission to finish his exploration with Tatiana and Edwina. They were given horses to ride, which was a huge challenge as they had never been around horses. Tomas volunteered to go with them. A few mount and dismount lessons were given and a few commands were learned to make the horse move.

The group set off for the next destination on the map. Tatiana rode with Paul and took notes every so often. "I hope we see druids. Wouldn't it be neat to see druids? I wonder if they will like me."

"Tat, don't talk about them. They would have powerful magic, and it might not be good."

"Ok, Paul. Look, over there, the waterfall." Tatiana almost fell off the horse pointing.

"Let's have a look then." Tomas replied. He made a clicking noise that the horse responded to.

They rode up to the edge of the water basin and dismounted. The horses were tied to a huge branch on the ground. Edwina decided it would be a great place to set up camp.

"Paul, let's set up here. There is fresh water, and it is flat. Or should we be in the trees more?"

"Umm, closer to the trees, it will protect against the wind and we won't be right in the open."

"Ok." Edwina untied the horses and tied them under the trees.

Paul got the tent out of the pack. He and Tomas set it up. Tatiana started finding twigs and branches for a fire. Edwina took out a small spade and made a pit for a small fire. She pulled out a cooking pot and started heating water. Dinner was served. Paul had decided on the just add hot water for it was cooler than expected in the summer.

After dinner, they dispersed in the tree line and explored. Tatiana was busy drawing different flowers she saw and updated her list of animals. Exploring lasted until sunset. Edwina had smuggled marshmallows from home and pulled them out. She shared with everyone until the bag was empty. Tomas shared stories of the mountains and of mysterious things that happen near the mountains. The fire went out and the kids climbed in their blankets. Paul brought spares, which was a good thing, as the temperature was much cooler than he thought it would be.

The next day a quick breakfast was prepared, and Tomas showed them to some more out of the way places. Edwina took many pictures. Tatiana couldn't help but look back to the wood line. She just knew she would find a druid, and that was her goal.

"Please, can't we go look in the tunnel in the woods? I know they are there. They have to be, right. How much more close to nature can they get if they live under the ground?"

Paul was short with his sister. "Drop it, Tat! I have had enough of the druids. They don't want to be found. When they want you to see them, they will let you."

"Well, maybe one day they won't have a choice!"

"Please can we not argue, especially in front of our new partner?" Edwina chimed in.

"It is ok, we are here now." Tomas dismounted and led the way up a winding trail. "This is one of the highest points we go to, as the mountains are sheer, and the weather is unstable. Have a look around."

Edwina set up a tripod for her camera and took a delayed group photo. After much exploring, the kids hiked back down to the horses and made camp.

"The old guys in town call this area all the way down to the valley we camped at yesterday in Treah. I am not sure where the name came from." Tomas said as he was helping with the tent.

"It is a druid word, huh?" Tat mused.

"Enough already!" Paul was fed up with Tatiana.

"Well, I am just thinking out loud, nothing wrong with that is there?"

"Only if your name is Tatiana," Paul tossed in.

Tomas moved between them and spoke with Tatiana. "You are quite curious, Tat. But I am afraid we would have to ask your parents or someone else who built Ruan. I know someone in the village will know where the name came from."

"Ok, Tomas, I will wait and ask when we get back. I am sorry."

"It is ok, now just enjoy nature, you know that is what the druids do. Enjoy nature and protect it."

Tatiana smiled and gave Tomas a hug. She then started recording everything she saw and drew pictures. She settled down by the fire and watched it dance around the wood. She was interrupted by the howling wind.

As the wind picked up a bit so the fire was doused and buried. The tent was in the tree line and seemed to be holding well against the wind. Rain began falling. It started as mist and then turned down pour. The girls took shelter in the tents. Paul checked the horses with Tomas. The boys built a makeshift shelter for the horses. It was built into some brush with a few trees immediately around them. A tarp and rope and some sturdy branches created the roof and upper back wall. Tomas laid out some grain for them and the water was plentiful. The boys ran back to the tent and changed in their half.

"If I was a druid, I would make the water not fall on us or the horses." Tatiana thought out loud.

"That would be one good thing that I won't argue with you over, Tat," Paul added.

They all laughed and settled in for the night. Not an hour had passed when the four could here rain pouring but not landing on the campsite.

Paul opened the door and peered out. He was amazed to see what Tatiana had mused seemed to be happening. He returned to bed and said, "Well, Tat, you got your wish. No rain on the tent or the horses; very interesting."

"Really, maybe I should go out and thank the druid?"

"No way! It is far too dangerous and besides, maybe they like you and you can meet them. But don't provoke the... please." Paul yawned and went to sleep.

Everyone slept well through the night. This morning would be the journey back to Ruan, which would take all day into the eve.

Tomas prepared a fire and cooked some hasty rolls as he called biscuits. He also fried the bacon which his mother sent along. He prepared a pot of tea as Edwina was the second out. She prepared a place for everyone to eat. Tatiana slept in, as she stayed up most of the night wondering why the rain did that. Paul woke and had fetched some wood for the fire. It was quite cold for having only rain. He placed two logs on the fire after Tomas had cleared the cooking area.

No words were spoken throughout the morning. Tatiana finally woke up at mid-day and had warmed breakfast. Paul packed the horses and Tomas took down the makeshift horse stable. Edwina washed the remaining dishes and soon all were off. Everyone had a blanket wrapped about them as they descended the steep wall of Treah.

Off in the distance, Tatiana caught a glimpse of someone. "Look over there," she whispered to Edwina. "It is a druid. He is wearing leather or some brown clothes."

"Oh, I see. And no, we are not going to change our path to go over there. He seems to be focusing."

"No, he is walking toward us."

The horses abruptly stopped. A slender man and a semi-invisible creature approached. They walked to the horses and the man placed his hand on each horse's muzzle. Paul was scared. He wasn't sure what to do. The man looked at Tatiana and motioned her down.

Tatiana climbed off the horse and walked forward. She bowed. "I am Tatiana."

"I know all of your names. The horses told us." The slender man placed his hand on her forehead. "I am glad to meet you. I also am happy the rain stayed off of your campsite and that the bear did not attack."

"You prevented it all?"

"Not all, this being had a good part in it as well. Now I must ask you return to Ruan, as it is not safe here. A great slide is being prevented so long as you are here, but we cannot hold it for long."

"Thank you, Mr." Paul replied and bowed.

The creature aided Tatiana back onto the horse and commanded the horses to continue with a motion of his arm. He silently spoke to Tatiana as if to reassure her. The horses seemed to be travelling swifter than normal, but no one was in discomfort.

After four hours the group was at the entrance to Ruan. Paul removed a spyglass and looked back. He saw the landslide and shared the view with the others. All were humbled by their abrupt halt and then seeing the aftermath of the slide.

Tomas went to his home and told of the grand adventure to his parents and then after a bite of dinner, fell fast asleep.

Tatiana busily wrote down what happened in her book and raced in to her dad's arms. She shared all the details of the whole trip and of the encounter with the man and creature. He calmed her down enough that she fell asleep in his arms. Myron packed her to her bed and covered her. "She has had quite an adventure Iris. She should sleep."

"I agree, but that story is very disturbing. I will keep some food for her in the warmer, should she get up." Iris went off to the kitchen and finished preparing the meal.

"How long was the ride from Treah to here?" Myron inquired.

"Umm about four hours." Paul looked at his watch.

"Impossible. What time did you leave this morning?"

"It was about 1230pm or so by my watch."

"But how then?" Myron was completely taken aback by this. "How?"

"The creature waved its arm and the horses seemed to almost fly here. There weren't as many bumps on the way as going out."

"Hmmm. Tat maybe right. We should respect nature and not disturb it as much as possible. I will have a chat with my friends and see if they have seen these people before. Anyway, we have about two weeks left here before we decide if we want to go back or remain here."

"Dinner is ready." Iris said in a quiet voice so as to not disturb Tatiana's sleep.

After dinner Edwina and Paul retired to their rooms and were out like lights.

DECISIONS, DECISIONS

THE CHILDREN SLEPT UNTIL MID-DAY. Iris prepared a brunch, as she had a feeling it would be a very late start. Myron was busy getting supplies. The table was unusually quiet.

"Well, don't all speak at once?" Iris teased as she enjoyed the nice, argument free start.

"Mom, we are all drained. Did you check your picture of the landslide?" Paul replied.

All of a sudden, all three kids were in great debate over what was seen. "Ok, I stirred the hornets' nest, so calm down and one at a time, please."

Edwina went first with her explanation, followed by Paul and Tatiana.

"Well, at last you all agree on the same things. So the beings are real and we should respect their privacy." Iris responded. "Now, we all must decide as a family if we wish to remain her or return to the city soon, so take your time and weigh everything out and we will have a meeting later next week." With that Iris left them to their thoughts.

The kids went their own directions the rest of the day and Tatiana settled with playing in the commons with her friends Thallas and Gwendolyn. She promised not to speak of the encounter to anyone, as the "tourists" would damage a lot of land to try to find the two who stopped the horses in Treah. Tatiana had short daydreams about the week's events throughout the day. Gwendolyn and Thallas begged her to tell them what happened. She said no, it wouldn't be right.

"Are you magic, Tatiana?" Thallas inquired uncomfortably.

"No. I don't think so anyway. Why?"

"Because when you go into your daydream lots of butterflies show up." Gwendolyn replied.

"Umm, no. I think the butterflies are here for the flowers we are sitting by." Tatiana responded. "Besides, wouldn't I know if I was magic?"

The two shrugged their shoulders. "We need to get home. It is almost time to eat." Thallas said as he stood up.

"See you tomorrow?" Gwendolyn chimed in.

"Ok. I will come over to your place." Tatiana waved at them as her friends walked off toward their home.

"Mom. Mom....... Mom?" Tatiana raced through the home looking for Iris.

"What dear?"

"Thallas and Gwendolyn think I know magic."

"Why is that?"

"They said that whenever I am thinking of something more butterflies show up."

"That doesn't mean you know magic, don't worry about it. You all are quite young to be concerned over such silly things. Besides, there are always more butterflies in the afternoon – it is warmer then." Iris hugged Tatiana and sent her on her way.

Myron was asleep in the hammock he set up when Tatiana woke him. "Dad."

"Yes, huh hmm. Ok, I am awake now. What is it?" He picked Tatiana up and set her on the hammock next to him.

"My friends think I know magic because butterflies are around when I am thinking or daydreaming outside when we are playing. Mom says that I am not magic."

"Well, I don't think you are magic, Tat. What do you think?"

"No, I just keep hearing that creature talking to me and the man."

"What do they tell you?"

"In time I will know my purpose and to be a kid."

"Well then that is good advice. So don't dwell on your meeting of them and just know you met them. Pondering can cause you to start believing things like magic. None of you are magic."

"Ok, Dad. But how do I not think about them."

The Kluanarians

"By thinking about your friends and playing with your friends. And not dwelling on a past that will not happen again."

"I will try Daddy. Now go back to sleep."

"I can't now; I have to help with dinner. Don't tell your Mom I was napping."

"Why?"

"She thinks I was getting wood for the stove, but I already did that and I was enjoying some 'Me' time."

"Ok."

The two walked inside and helped make dinner. Tatiana set the table and Myron grilled the meat. Edwina and Paul returned from their outings and made a salad and more tea. Dinner was served and everyone spoke of the wonderful vacation they were on.

"When do we have to decide, Dad?" Paul asked after the ramblings slowed down.

"The sooner the better, but I want you to make sure you think of everything while you each decide."

"Yes." Iris agreed. "Why don't you make a sheet that shows the good and bad of both places? Then on the weekend we can discuss it."

"Ok, that will work well." Edwina tossed in. "Now can I be excused."

"Yes." Myron motioned for her to go.

"Where is she off to Myron?" Iris fretted.

"She is just hanging out with her new friends and Paul has a long day tomorrow, so off to bed son."

"Yes, Dad." Paul disappeared to his room and went straight to bed."

"Tatiana…" Myron was interrupted by a loud noise. "Oh what now?" Myron left the table to investigate.

"Myron. Please tell your little one to not worry of magic. It is straining us slightly. She is not ready, nor are you."

"Ah, so you are the mystery man she has been rambling of then. So what do the Intervals want with Tatiana?"

"The purpose will be revealed, but you must return to your city after your vacation. It is most imperative."

"Iris won't like this will she?"

"No. Most likely not. But she has no choice."

Myron folded his arms and paced. "Why, again, should I do this?"

51

"The balance needs to be there right now, very terrible things are upon us and we, the Intervals, are knowing of Edwina's indoctrination that is forthwith in the Moons' Order. You must keep her powers in check or it will be the beginning of the end."

"Ah, I see. And which evil has returned? Do I need to inform my wife – as she is quite capable of defending against this evil?"

"Not yet, we will come to you when it is time." With that the mysterious man left.

"Who were you talking to, dear?" Iris chimed as she dried her hands.

"Not important. Just a friend stopping by."

"Sounded important." Iris hugged Myron. "Well since it isn't important, then it must be hunting or something."

"Yeah. Hunting. Don't worry, just relax and enjoy the evening with me." He motioned for Tatiana to join them.

"Whatcha doing, Dad?"

"Well, getting ready to go for a stroll through town. Join us."

"Ok. Can we get ice cream?"

"Sure sweetie."

The three left for the small ice cream parlor at the far end of the commons. Tatiana pointed out her favorite places to play and when they arrived at the parlor, she pointed out the best flavors of ice cream. They picked their ice cream and slowly ate it.

"So, why did you let me have ice cream so late?" Tatiana was curious after all. "Not that it was bad, but you never let me have ice cream late."

"Just because, Tatiana. Just because." Myron replied. "I am thinking we need to go to our home for a while. I should be hearing back soon on that project I bid on."

Iris stopped walking, "Why the change of mind about here?"

"No real reason, just want to close up any loose ends is all. We can't have something bite us later."

"I suppose. How long until we come back Dad?"

"Oh, hard to say. I need to make sure all of my stuff is taken care of and put the house on the market." Myron rubbed his forehead. "You two are relentless. Now, let's get a move on before it is too dark."

The three walked briskly home. Tatiana cleaned up and got ready for bed. Iris and Myron tucked her in. Myron locked the doors and put out the candles.

"I have to be up early for Paul's big day, Iris. Sorry I am not up to talking for a while."

"It is fine. Get some sleep. You and he will have a grand time." With that Iris was out like a light as was Myron.

THE VISITORS

THE NIGHT PASSED. TATIANA HAD wild dreams that woke her several times, but she refused to be a baby and went back to sleep. She slept through most of the morning when Iris checked on her. When she saw the hard sleep of Tatiana, she tucked her in and covered the window with a blanket and closed the door.

Edwina raced out to be with her friends and the two men of the house were long gone.

Iris enjoyed the peace. That is until an unexpected visitor arrived. "Kira!?" Iris found herself looking at her mother-in-law. "Why are you here?"

"Visiting the kids, before they are whisked back to that overpopulated place you chose for a home. Besides, I wanted to see how Ruan was, since my older son helped us rebuild it. Tell me where is Myron?"

"He and Paul went on a 'Man Journey' fishing and hiking and hunting. They will be back in a couple days."

"Good then. I want to take Edwina with me for a bit this summer, if it is ok."

"Why, whatever for?"

"So she can be around the family and learn some manners. She is quite a rude person with an attitude to go along with that mouth of hers."

"She is becoming a lady just fine. She requires a little nudge now and then. Besides, Myron wants us to return to…." Iris was cut off.

"Well, we will just see about that! Where is she at now?"

"With her friends, being social."

Tatiana came into the room. "Who is this, Mom?"

"I am your grandmother, Tatiana. I saw you when you were just a wee little thing. My you have grown so quickly." Kira picked up Tatiana and placed her on her lap. "I hear you like horses and stuff?"

"Yes ma'am. They are my favorite animals and one day, I hope to get to have one for my very own."

"You have one at my place, when you are ready to visit, he is yours."

"Really?"

"Yes, my child. I named him Horace. I hope that is ok?"

"That is fine Grandma. Horace is a good name for a boy horse. Dad took Paul on a trip. They just left this morning. I heard them leave before the sun was up."

"You are very observant. Do you like Ruan so far?"

"Yes, and I already have two friends, but they think I know magic."

"That's enough Tat." Iris interjected.

"No, it is ok. Why do they think that?" Kira's curiosity peaked.

"I think a lot when I play and sometimes my mind wanders. They said more butterflies show up when I do that."

"Oh. I see. Well now, don't worry about it. I think butterflies do their own thing and that maybe the butterflies like people who can be still for more than a few seconds at a time."

"That makes sense, maybe they like me because I am not disturbing the plants they like by racing around."

"I think you are right," Kira replied as she hugged her granddaughter.

"When is Edwina returning?"

"I don't know, probably a few hours or so." Iris replied, exhausted from trying to outthink Kira.

"You go take a nap dear. I can watch Tatiana."

Iris took a nap as Kira taught Tatiana a few games she played when she was little.

"Wait Grandma, I need my notebook."

"Whatever for?"

"I like to write things down. Sometimes if I think it is good enough, I try to solve it, if it has a mystery anyway."

"Oh, ok. Then you can take notes and teach your friends."

They continued on well into early evening."

Brenda M. Hokenson

Edwina arrived. "Where's Mom?"

"Grandma made her take a nap. She is gonna stay with us a couple nights."

"Oh, ok. Hi Grandma."

"Well hello Edwina. I am your father's mother. My name is Kira. I would like you to come stay part of the summer with your grandfather and I."

"Ummm…. Well…. I don't get to decide things for myself. I am not responsible according to Mom."

"We'll see about that."

Edwina smiled and started dinner.

"Nonsense. You two go get cleaned up for dinner and I will fix supper."

"What's supper?" Tatiana asked as she and her sister walked off.

Edwina whispered, "It is the old word for dinner. Dinner used to be lunch and supper was the evening meal." They went to their rooms. "Wear a dress, Tat. Grandma is very old fashioned from what I can tell."

Tatiana put on a simple dress and walked down the hall to her parents' room. "She whispered, "Mom, are you ok."

Iris stirred. "Yes, how long was I asleep?"

"A long time. Grandma Kira is fixing something called supper."

"Oh, that is dinner." Iris stood up and straightened herself before taking Tat's hand and walking down the hall.

"Did you sleep well, Iris?" Kira asked as everyone seated themselves.

"Yes and thank you."

Everyone ate and went to the living room for a more comfortable visit.

"Grandma, Edwina and I fixed up a room for you." Tatiana said as she nudged Kira down a hall to show off the room.

"Thank you, dears. That is very sweet of you."

Tatiana took notes as the grown-ups chatted. She drew a picture of what she thought Grandma's home looked like. She included Horace in a stable and gave it to Kira.

"It is getting late. Off to bed everyone." Kira shooed everyone to their rooms and cleaned up the kitchen. After the kitchen, she too retired and was sound asleep.

Tatiana and Edwina did not go to sleep. Instead, the two questioned their mom.

The Kluanarians

"So, Grandma Kira is from Kentucky, according to my notes." Tatiana said as she flipped through her notebook.

"Kentucky?" Iris mused. "Where do you get Kentucky from?"

"She has a huge fancy house with horses, and one is mine." Tatiana replied. "Where else could have that many horses and a big house? After all they run a lot of horse races there. Maybe I can racehorses there too."

"She is not from Kentucky!" Edwina gasped at the thought.

"Well, where do you think she is from, huh?"

"Somewhere more open than Kentucky. I was thinking Montana, where the mountains are tall and the sky is big."

"Ok, off to bed. You are tired and need the sleep." Iris escorted both to their rooms and tucked them in.

Iris then turned in herself. She thought of her son and husband and of their visitor and of the wonderful conversation the girls were having before bed.

Myron and Paul returned earlier than planned. They snuck through the sitting room window and got ready for bed. Iris was startled by their early homecoming so late in the night.

"Why have you returned so soon?" Iris hugged Myron. "Your mother is here and wants Edwina for the rest of the summer."

"Oh, wow. Umm, did you say no? Paul is … umm very tired and needs his bed. He kind of had a fall. But I patched him up."

"Not yet, I haven't told her anything yet. Should I look at his injury?"

"We need to leave here in the next couple days. And I said I already fixed it"

"Why? What is going on? First Edwina, then the mystery people that stopped the kids on their adventure, then your mysterious friend, and now your mom." Iris paced. "What the hell is happening?"

"The Intervals request we return home as soon as we can as something is taking shape that affects both places."

"Why didn't they tell me?"

"Because last time they tried to tell you something of importance that concerned your Order, you ran. Now go to sleep."

Myron fell asleep after calming Iris back down. In the morning, everyone woke to the smell of breakfast. Myron went to the kitchen.

"Good morning son. How was your excursion?" Kira hugged Myron and then continued breakfast preparations.

"It was cut short. I have patched up Paul and gave him some strong pain killer so he doesn't notice the injury."

"Shall I tend to him for you or do you want your wife to?"

"Go ahead Mom. Iris would be hysterical."

Kira and Myron walked to Paul's room. He was in and out of sleep.

"What happened to this poor child?" Kira examined the extent of the wound.

"He fell. Our bridge across Latana Spring broke under him. I guess about twenty or thirty feet. Snapped his leg. I splinted it, gave him major pain killers, and waited a bit for him to sleep. Then as I was waiting and cleaning him up, the Intervals aided me in healing him a bit more and returning us here a bit quicker."

"Oh, that is good they helped you. They did a remarkable job. Should heal just fine how they set it. Did they give you healing herbs and salve?"

"Yes." Myron handed a shoulder pouch full of herbs and a thick creamy substance.

"This is the best medicine for him. But I think our healing house would be better."

"Let's talk to Iris first, ok Mom?"

"Ok. After breakfast then." Kira said as she elevated Paul's leg and covered him better. She added a couple blankets under the leg for stability. She then returned to the kitchen and set the table.

Myron opened the door. "Welcome Malos. Thank you for your aid earlier."

"You're welcome, friend."

"Please join us for breakfast." Myron showed Malos to a seat.

Tatiana and Edwina came into the kitchen with their mother. Malos stood up and bowed to the three and waited for them to sit down.

"Good morning, Malos." Iris stood again and poured tea. "Please sit down, Kira."

"Ok, you are in charge now."

"Where is Paul? Tatiana, go get Paul up."

"No, don't get him up. He is sleeping quite heavily." Myron said as he held Tatiana to her chair.

The Kluanarians

"Why is he so exhausted?" Iris added.

Malos stood up. "If I may, your son has a terrible break in his leg from a fall from Latana Spring Bridge which shattered. He fell a distance and Myron did all he could to repair the boy. My group and I happened by at that time and helped Myron lift him from the spring. We realigned your son's leg, and he should heal nicely. However, I recommend a healing house."

"What? Why? How could you let this happen, Myron?" Iris was hysterical. "How can a bridge just shatter? What is next?"

Myron made his wife sit down. He got her a warm, damp cloth to wipe her tear-stained face. Edwina and Tatiana sat silently as did Kira.

"How about some breakfast?" Kira started serving everyone. "Come on now, everyone eat. Paul is well cared for."

Everyone ate. The table was very silent. After the meal Malos went with Myron to check on Paul.

"He needs more blood." Myron said as he noticed how weak his son's pulse was.

"I agree. But my people do not have those means. Does the physician across the commons?"

"No. We need to get him to a hospital or healing house."

Iris entered the room and sat beside her son for some time. "Please, Myron. Take him to where he will recover better."

"Where are the girls?"

"Cleaning up the kitchen."

"Ok."

Kira showed up in the bedroom with the rest of the adults and Paul. "What shall we do?"

"Open a portal Iris, Malos and I will escort mother and Paul to the healing house. There he will have the best care."

"Alsonokama tele kama noheeklanam cata." As Iris spoke, a brilliant light shown in the center of the room.

"I will be back tomorrow, ok Iris?" Myron hugged her.

"Yes, please just get him to the house." She wiped away some tears. "Thank you again Malos."

Malos bowed. The two men made a cot to transport Paul. Paul stirred for a bit and told his mom not to worry. Kira led the way through the portal. The portal closed and Iris set off on her normal routine.

"Where's everyone at?" Tatiana yelled as she raced from room to room. "I wanted to visit Paul. Mom…Mom?"

"He is at a healing house. He is quite safe and will mend better there."

"Is he in Kentucky or Montana?" Tatiana blurted out.

"No, he is not in either of those states. But he is well cared for. We need to pack. Your father will be here tomorrow so we can drive home for a bit and get everything ready."

"Yes Mom." The girls replied in unison.

The girls packed up Paul's room first. He didn't have a whole lot to pack. Then they packed their things, except for enough to use the following day. They straightened the kitchen and stacked the wood on the patio in the covered area. Iris finished up packing her and Myron's things and tidied the sitting room and guest room.

When everything was done, the girls went to hang out with their friends for the rest of the day while Iris visited her friends. In the evening Iris took the girls to eat at the café next to the florist. Tomas and his family joined them. Iris invited Tomas to their home for a few weeks. His parents thought it would be a great experience for him.

Everyone returned to their homes to prepare for the next adventure. The girls went right to sleep. Iris stayed up a while and read. She then took out a small smooth stone, a worry rock.

"Tecumsal loderian vies" Iris waved her hand over her worry rock and was able to view her son and husband. She saw Paul was well looked after. *"Vies anol pertifin."* After she ended the vision, she went to sleep.

THE HEALING HOUSE

Upon arrival at the Healing House, Malos and Myron immediately situated Paul on a bed that had an elevating device for his leg. He was sound asleep. A tall, thin lady approached with blankets and vials.

"Nice to see you again, Myron. You have been gone many years now."

"Yes, I have, and it is nice to see you too, Truance. My son is in need of your aide. He has lost much blood."

"I will help. Dania, bring a bag."

"Yes, Lady." Dania retrieved a bag of blood from the storage unit. "Here it is."

Truance prepped Paul's arm for the blood. When it arrived, she verified it against the records and attached the bag to its tube. She sat quietly, observing Paul and finally methodically checking for other injuries.

"How high was the fall, Myron?"

"I guess twenty or thirty feet. He fell when the bridge collapsed, and he landed in semi-shallow water where he busted his leg on some boulders."

"He has two cracked ribs and dislocated shoulder."

Malos added, "The shoulder could be from us getting him out of the water."

"No one is to blame. I just have to fix it all. Your brother seeks you, Myron."

"Very well, I will go there at once as Paul is in safe hands."

Kira was outside, waiting. "How is he, dear?"

"Well, not good, Mom. He has the busted leg plus two cracked ribs and a dislocated shoulder. Where is Thanias?"

"Come along then, I will take you to him." Kira took her son's arm and showed him to Thanias.

"At last, Myron. You have returned." Thanias removed himself from a seat that sat in the center back of a great hall. "Welcome home, brother!" Thanias clasped Myron's wrist as that was the appropriate greeting.

"Thank you. How are things going here? I see you are now leading the Truncheon now."

"Yes. It was a long journey to this seat, but I earned it."

"That is good. I would hate to find from anyone that there is a different opinion."

"No, no different opinions. But there is a peace finally."

"That is wonderful. Truance is mending Paul."

"What happened to Paul?"

"A fall. The bridge spanning Latana Spring gave way and the poor lad landed in the shallows on some boulders. Malos and his companions aided me in Paul's retrieval."

"I shall visit him when he is a bit better then. How long will you be staying?"

"Only tonight. I have come to ask if Paul may reside with you when he is able to leave the Healing House, so he may recover in a calmer environment."

"Hmm…" Thanias pondered for a bit. "Yes. My nephew is welcome to stay until he is fully recovered and longer if he so chooses."

"Very well then. Thank you." Myron bowed, as was custom when leaving the High Seat.

"What about you, Myron? Please stay with me, you will be comfortable there."

"I will stay with Paul."

"Of course. I shall than as well. I need to check on things there anyway." Thanias saw his mother at the far end of the hall. "Come along Myron, I think Mother would like us to go with her."

"Ok." The men approached Kira, and each took an arm. They escorted her to her home where lunch was waiting.

Myron found his father tending the horses. "It is time to eat."

"My boy! I am so glad to see you here. How is the family? Did everyone come with you?"

"No just Paul. He is in the Healing House and will be there for a bit. Thanias will take him after Truance releases him and help him in his recovery."

"That is good of him. He doesn't have a family."

"Oh. I didn't know."

The two walked in to the dining area and sat down with Thanias and Kira.

"Zanor, you look parched?" Kira said to her husband.

"Yes, dear. But first I must ask everyone to stand and join hands."

As hands were joined the four spoke a prayer. "*Luftallawaheil candsume talekimacci.*"

They then returned to their seats and began to dine. News was shared between Myron and his family. All the strange occurrences were brought to the surface as well.

Kira said after listening to the words, "This can only mean one thing."

Zanor interjected, "Yes, the Shadowblyts have found an heir to their throne."

"There is much malice in their souls. It will be difficult to overcome this time around." Thanias spoke. "I have placed observers throughout our land and have been receiving reports."

Malos knocked on the door and entered. "I must return. The Intervals are working at both locations to secure lands and have found a possible leader."

"Good, make him ready, as the Orders will meet in my Hall in two nights.

"She is quite young and doesn't know her potential." Malos added.

"You can't be serious? She is just a child!" Myron stood up.

Thanias calmed the group. "Who is this new leader?"

"Tatiana. And she has no idea. But the Intervals are going to leave her some clues to guide her, as she seems very interested in solving puzzles."

"I will have no part of this. To ask this of my daughter is…"

"Not for us to decide, it was decided by the guardians, and the guardians dictate," added Thanias.

"Very well, then. I need to go to my son now." Myron abruptly left the house and went to his son.

He sat in deep thought, holding his son's hand. He pondered the reasoning behind the use of such young children for such high positions within a system the kids have no idea of.

Thanias arrived late in the afternoon. "Are you ok, Myron?"

"Well, what do you think? You think you have all the answers, since your seat in the Hall has gone to your head. Why don't you tell me? Where the hell is Lucien?"

Paul stirred. "Dad? Where am I?"

Myron raced back to his son. "You are in a healing house. Do you remember when you were little?"

"Yes, you mean at our real home?"

"Yes, son. Don't move too much you are sort of broken."

"I thought so. Did Mom come too?"

"No, she is packing the bungalow and tomorrow I will go back."

"What about me?"

"You will be safe here and will heal much better."

"No, I want to be with you guys."

"Your uncle is going to watch over you while you heal."

"No. If I remember, you can 't force me to stay here."

"I know, but I would like you too, so I can get the stuff out of the house and here without having to watch over you and coordinate the move and watch your mom and sisters all in hysterics."

"How long will you be?"

"A week or less. If it is more than a week, you will be brought there and recover there."

"Ok. Please don't go tomorrow. Grandpa!" Paul caught a glimpse of Zanor in the doorway.

Zanor walked over to the bed. "Tomorrow, I will go get your family and we will deal with the other house later. You need your family while you recover. No interfering Myron or Thanias." Zanor glared at both men. "Paul has gone through enough without the crap. Truance?"

Truance entered the room, "Yes Lord?"

"See to it that my sons are removed from the Healing House until I say they may enter again. Make Paul as comfortable as possible. Have you heard from Lucien?"

"Yes sir." Truance escorted Myron and Thanias out and had explained to the guards that neither are to enter. "I believe he is near Kaprius. I will send word to him that he is needed." She bowed and walked away.

Zanor sat beside his grandson and made him smile. He told stories and explained a bit of the mess going on, but not about his sisters. Kira arrived with his favorite snacks.

"Paul, Kira and I are going to open a portal now and get your mom and sisters, and Tomas."

"Tomas? Why Tomas?"

"His parents want him to be with your family for a bit. He is aware of this place and his parents agreed. Then once you are healed, you will go to your home and get ready for moving here. See your uncle thinks he knows how it will go, but he forgot. I see all and am pretty sure this way will work better."

"Ok, just come back safely with everyone."

"Truance, could you set up the guest rooms here for tonight?" Kira asked nicely.

"Yes. We will start at once. Don't worry, it will be perfect. Now get going"

With that a portal opened and Paul's grandparents stepped through. He thought he was imagining things when not more than fifteen minutes later the portal reappeared with his family and Tomas. Tomas exclaimed. "Wow that was fast!"

Truance gently placed Paul back on his bed. "Please don't move so much."

"Ok."

Iris raced over to him and hugged him. "May I sleep next to him, please?"

"Of course. I will have a bed set up next to him. Now, if you will all follow me. Your dinner is ready."

The girls and Tomas were in awe of the size of the room they stood in and more in awe as they walked down a long hall to the eating area. Kira and Zanor joined them at the meal.

"Where is Dad?" Tatiana inquired as she looked around.

"He is banned from here, so is your uncle."

"Why?"

"They were loud in my Healing House," Truance interjected. "Your

Brenda M. Hokenson

grandfather commands respect for all who are healing and by being loud and a bit obnoxious, they disrespected the House and may return only when your grandfather permits it."

Edwina decided to speak finally. "So, this is not Kentucky or Montana. Where are we? And how is Paul doing? We would like to spend time with him if that is ok?"

"You are right; it isn't either of those places. You are in the city of Burwash. Your grandfather is High King, although he doesn't always act like one. Your brother is healing well and stable and yes you may visit him, but only after you eat your meal." Truance smiled and walked away.

THE BANISHED BROTHERS

Shortly after Zanor banished them, Myron and Thanias walked silently off toward a small inn where they ate a small meal and drank ale.

"My daughter will have no part of the Intervals." Myron declared after a few pints.

"She has no choice, but I don't see her interacting with them for many years." Thanias reassured Myron.

"No matter, Malos spoke of some sort of unrest in the distance. Are you aware of this oh high pain in my backside?"

"Well, yes, that is why Paul shall stay with me. To prepare."

"Like hell." Myron stood and leaned across the table. "My boy is broken currently and is no way near ready to be trained by you or any of your minions."

"Minions! I have no minions." Thanias rose from his seat and forced Myron to sit down. "Look here coward. I was here when the land needed me. You ran off with that star gazer. I can't see you protecting anything but yourself."

"That star gazer is my wife, and she left because she had to. You gave her no choice, you wanted to use her to your advantage in something, that I haven't placed the last couple pieces of the puzzle to, but I am darn close. So I would be very careful so long as we are here, Thanias." With that Myron rose again and left the building.

The entire room was silent. Zanor entered and the inn became active again. He looked puzzled as he sat beside Thanias.

"What is going on here that Myron leaves without you?"

"Father, we had a minor misunderstanding. That is all."

"Good then, I expect to see the both of you at my home for dinner this eve. Don't be late. Now, I have to catch up to Myron and let him know of dinner." Zanor left.

Myron milled about town, pondering the recovery of his son and wishing Thanias would have kept himself out of sight. He found some beautiful flowers for his Iris and a doll for Tatiana. He came across a history compendium for Paul to read when he was able to stay awake long enough. He also picked up a special trinket for Edwina, which he decidedly hid in the bottom of a box for a Moons necklace. Tomas, what to get for Tomas? Myron mused for a bit and decided Tomas shall pick it out, it would save much time and it would be what Tomas wants that way. He was quite proud of his find and was deciding how to sneak into the healing house when he saw his father walking toward him.

"Father, I must ask of you, please let me go to my family. Thanias is stirring things and it has caused me to reconsider some things that you and I must discuss. But first, I would like to return to my Paul. It is my fault he is in such terrible shape."

"No son, it is not your fault. I believe things are in play now that have deeper purpose. Let's go inside and deliver your gifts." Zanor walked with Myron into the healing house and to the family. "Drop off your gifts and we will discuss things in about ten minutes. Malos will get you." With that Zanor departed down the hall to an antechamber where he relaxed with Kira. "Your son has reconsidered and will be here soon."

"Why the change of heart?"

"He didn't say but maybe he has come to his senses."

Myron spent considerable time with his family before approaching his parents. He walked with haste yet calmness. He knew what was asked of him and he knows now that balance must be maintained. Myron bowed before his parents. "Father, Mother. I have decided that I am needed here to help maintain balance and I take full responsibility of my duties of overseeing the Truncheon."

"Why the change of attitude, son?" Kira asked with a smile.

"I have seen many things, and if what is occurring as Malos has indicated, I am needed here."

"What of the Star?"

"Iris understands and is willing to come back. But she does not wish the children to learn of their abilities until they are of age."

"Understood. We will have a ceremony then tomorrow in your honor. Tell me, which portion of the Truncheon do you plan on governing? The defenses or the training."

"Where do you think I will best suit your needs, Father?"

"I am thinking you shall determine that after a month of each. Then decide where you feel more comfortable."

Truance escorted Thanias in. "He has been waiting patiently at the entrance to the healing house. Let him be heard."

"Speak, son." Zanor rose, staff in hand.

"Father. Forgive my rude, thoughtless behavior. I was reacting instead of understanding Myron's situation."

Zanor glanced at Myron and back to Thanias. "Very well. What's done is done. Tomorrow there will be a ceremony as Myron has returned to serve as your equal in the Truncheon. You will best remember that."

Thanias looked in awe at his brother. "Very well then." Thanias bowed to his parents and showed Myron the way out. "Come, we must find your garb. You can't look like you are muddle-fuddled here, wearing those strange leggings and tunic."

Before they could exit the Hall of the Ruler, a beam of silver/blue light flashed through the room. An older lady stepped through the intense beam. "Why has no one said anything about my grandchildren?" The woman approached the thrown and did not bow, as was considered custom.

Thanias and Myron walked toward her swords drawn. An incredible blue aura surrounded her. The shielded their eyes and waited.

"Your weapons bother me not." The aura slowly faded, and the figure was revealed.

Zanor rose from his seat with Kira and approached her. "Welcome Malificence."

"Why does Iris not answer my inquiries? Does she send tell to Harold?"

Myron bowed before her. "She is not communicating with you for some unknown reason, Lady Malificence. I cannot answer for her."

"Will she be arriving here?"

"Aye." Kira responded. "Perhaps we both shall have a nice conversation with her."

"Perhaps, at least you got to see the grandchildren. I think Harold has as well."

"Only from their adventure to the Palisade. Do you not stay there?"

"I do, but the Morket needed me, as I found from the great dragon years ago, that when I married Harold, my Order was restored. By chance, can you explain this?"

Zanor spoke up. "It is because he too is Morket and only Morket can marry Morket to save their line. I assume then that one of our grandchildren will have developed powers greater than any of the remaining Orders, time will dictate this. The Shadowblyts are ready to send their new member here for proper training and I was hoping you would be present for this."

Thanias found the interaction curious and observed.

"Has Harold arrived?"

"No, something terrible is occurring in Ruan. The Interval Order and his soldiers are attempting to root out the problem." Thanias added. "The Truncheon posted there are currently rebuilding the Latana Spring bridge. It was completely demolished."

Myron caught a glimpse as Thanias spoke. "How do you know it was completely demolished?"

"I have my ways. Haven't you heard of keeping in contact with your men? Oh, wait. I forgot. Your 'wife' made you move to a freakishly out of control place to hide."

"Thanias!" Zanor pointed to his son. "Be silent and sit down."

"I have a valid point, father." Myron interjected.

"In time it will be known. More than likely the message was sent through the scrying well."

"Please, Malificence, if you would, join me in visiting the grandchildren" Kira said as she extended her hand to Malificence.

The two ladies departed the Hall. "Kira, do you know much of our grandkids' abilities?"

"Aye. I am thinking, and from what little I have been able to observe, Edwina will be a Moon. Not for sure yet as her powers are similar to yours and mine. Paul, well, let me see. I think he already is headed toward being like his dad, but his will is very strong so it could be something greater. Little Tatiana, she is an Interval through and through. I have seen her do things and heard of some others by her writings."

"Hmm. Our work is cut out then. We must get them and prepare them. Mithdrool caused the mishap in Ruan. I think there is a traitor among us but am not sure who just yet. I have sent word to the Shadowblyts and Izmaa Orders to send their best to train those living in Kaprius and Treah. I am uncertain if the latter will respond positively. It is said that they have been working with Llylandra and her 'chosen' Fraeloch."

"This is news I have not heard. Tell me all you know, as we go to the healing house."

Tatiana and Edwina saw the two ladies enter the Eupepsian domain.

"Grandma Kira. I got to help with Paul today."Tatiana mused as she hugged her grandmother.

"Tatiana and Edwina, I would like to introduce someone equally as important as I am, your grandmother, Malificence."

"I heard about you and about Zanor and Harold." Tatiana smiled as she also hugged Malificence.

"How is this possible, young lady?"

"Walther at the Palisade to me and Paul a bedtime story. But I thought it was more like a true story, so I jotted names down."

"You are very bright, if I do say so myself. And you, Edwina, are quite the looker. Your Kira has said you are to be a Moon."

"Yes, ma'am, I don't understand though."

There was a challenge written on a stone many many years ago. It was to have had a special enchantment upon it that only the next heir to the Order of Moons, after Lunacerian of course, would be able to retrieve the items stored within the stone."

"How nice. No wonder Thanias calls it a darn rock. His men and Harold's have had to watch it forever from what I understand."

"Yes, Edwina. Your destiny is to the Moons Order. It will be very complex, but you grandmother will help you along the way."

"Not if Mom has anything to say about it."

"We'll see. Is she here?"

"Yes ma'am." Edwina pointed her out.

The two grandmothers hugged Edwina and Tatiana. They walked to Paul's chamber where he lay asleep. Both provided a special blessing to him for his recovery. When they finished that, they went to the ceremonial atrium where Iris was studying the water fountain.

"At last, daughter." Malificence said as she sat to the left of Iris. "Is all well with you?"

Kira sat to Iris' right. "Paul is healing well, according to Tatiana."

"Yes he is, Kira. I am well mother." Iris spoke to both as she stared at the water.

"We need to understand something right now." Kira spoke first. "We need to know why you left."

"Yes, why did you leave and why have you not spoken to your father and I?"

"You are all busy with 'Order's Duty' and have not the time to be bothered by such matters."

"That is load of babble if I ever I had heard it." Malificence responded. "Why did you leave? I won't ask again."

"I had to. Thanias."

"What about Thanias?" Kira quirked an eyebrow.

"Thanias, before I wed Myron, had tried to court me. He said that together we would build a great life. He said that we would rule all of Kluanaria and potentially the twin planet. I left as I feared what Thanias might become. I did love him once, but I had reservations that made it impossible to be near him. I told Myron of this and sought his counsel. He, for months and years before our marriage, I was kept hidden in Treah. Thanias was furious, so after Myron and I wed, we left. It was right."

"IT was not right! It was cowardice and caused great strife here. The Star Order disbanded because of you and your unwillingness to stand your ground to a mere Truncheon." Malificence added.

"You left Thanias for Myron?" Kira mused. "How odd is that? I would think a Star would want more power than…"

"Not power, violence." Malificence corrected. "I think Thanias is our spy."

"Hmm. Possibly." Kira pondered the thought and dismissed it. "Why have you returned now?"

"My son is gravely injured."

"Oh, and the healers of the place you ran away to are unable to mend bones?" Malificence and Kira said together.

"No. It is not just that. I am responsible for the disbanding of my Order. I am here to rectify that and pull it together."

"You can't. It's too late, dear." Kira said with a solemn look.

"It is now time for your children, our grandchildren, to learn who they are without being so hostile to the ideals of Orders Selection. They have no choice, just as you didn't," Malificence spoke quietly as she saw Edwin and Tatiana approach.

Tatiana exclaimed, "It's time, it's time. Truance is ready!"

PAUL AWAKENS

AFTER A FEW WEEKS IN the healing house, Paul was allowed to wake up. Truance had been giving him special herbs to keep him asleep while his tremendous injuries could heal. She was present as he woke and had brought food of all kinds to him.

"This will not be as bland as before, Paul. Please take your time eating and when you wish to get up, ask. We will need to assist you for a bit. Your ribs are healing beautifully, and the leg will need much more time before you can walk on it."

Paul listened as Truance was speaking. He wasn't quite sure where he was even. He recognized his family as they returned to see him. "Where are we?"

Iris sat beside him. "At a healing house. Truance and the others have all been monitoring your recovery very closely for some time. Your father has also decided that it will be best to tie up loose ends back home and then return here."

"Are we in…?" Paul winced in pain. "Kluanaria?" He grimaced again. Truance noticed from across the room and brought zephyr root for the pain. He swallowed it quickly as it was very bitter.

"Yes." Iris replied. "Do you want us to get you anything?"

"Nah, I just hurt badly and, how did my ribs and leg get broken?"

"Umm, well, you see…." Iris wasn't sure if she should tell him.

"You fell. The bridge at Latana Spring collapsed and you fell onto some rocks in shallow water." Myron said as he approached.

"An Interval was there. He said to sleep."

The Kluanarians

"Yes. Malos was there and he and his band helped me get you out of the spring and to Ruan, then we arrived here after much debate."

"I see. I think I need to res…" Paul was asleep before he finished his sentence.

"Well, I think he shall rest more tonight and tomorrow we will bring a special chair that is slightly reclined. He needs sunshine. It helps heal the body and the spirit." Truance interjected as she resituated him in his bed. "Tomorrow is your ceremony? Paul will go to this event in his chair if that is acceptable?"

"Yes, by all means." Myron said. "Thank you again, Truance." Myron escorted Iris out.

Meanwhile Tatiana, Edwina and Tomas had been exploring and making plans for adventures as soon as Paul was well enough to go. They spent a long time detailing paths and listing out equipment and food.

Tatiana raced in to Paul's room and actually caught him while he was awake. "We have been drawing out some plans for adventures here. How do you feel?"

"Hey Tat! I am so glad to see you. Can you help me sit up – just a bit?" Paul wriggled up and Tatiana slid a pillow behind him. "Yeah, that is perfect, thanks. Now can you hand me that water and a piece of that nasty root." He ate the root and drank the water. "Now, let me see. How long have we been here?"

"Umm, a long time to me. But probably a couple weeks. I got to ride a horse and Edwina is reading. Tomas has been fishing with Grandpa and Dad doesn't like Thanias. Mom is worried, but she always is."

"Ok. Do you know how long I have to stay here?"

"No, but I will ask Truance. Here she comes now."

Truance entered the room. "Well hello Tatiana. I see you make a great healer. Will you get that chair over there? We will get your brother into it so he can go outside for a bit today."

"Ok, I got it." Tatiana raced over to the chair and pushed it back to Truance. It seemed to float as she moved it. "That's cool. I gave him a piece of that root stuff, he asked for it. How long does he have to stay here?"

"Well done. I might see if I can keep you around. He needs to stay until the cast comes off, then we will help him learn to walk again. After that he can go. " Truance and a stout man lifted Paul carefully into the chair. The chair automatically adjusted for Paul's injuries and build. "Ok, Tatiana, you may lead the way. The chair will follow you."

Tatiana walked backwards so she could watch the chair follow her. "Paul, it IS following me!!" She took Paul out to the patio area for now as she wasn't sure how far away she could go with the chair.

Thanias was on the patio. "How are you doing Paul?"

"Ok. I guess. I hurt a lot. Tatiana was helping me earlier."

"That is good to hear. There is a ceremony today for your father. Will you attend?" Thanias asked the kids.

"Yes, I suppose. Does this chair thing have a range before it stops or returns to here?" Paul replied as he adjusted.

"I don't think so, but Truance will escort you to be safe. I need to be going now. I have some things to take care of and then I will return." With that Thanias left.

"I see Mom and Dad. I will go get them, or they might think you ran away." Iris and Myron had seen the kids on the patio and were headed that way when a wind swept by them and circled, then stopped as fast at is had begun. Puzzled, both glanced down and saw Tatiana.

"Hrmmm. Tatiana, how did you do that?" Myron asked with a smile.

"Do what, Daddy? I just ran over here to get you. I didn't want you to think Paul ran away."

"Never mind, Tat. Let's go see your brother."

The six spent hours talking and telling stories. Thanias returned with Truance.

Truance smiled, "Your son is healing quite well. I have not seen a more complex break, but it is much improved."

"Thank you, Truance." Iris bowed and smiled.

"Do I need to go to the ceremony Mom?" Edwina huffed and stared out into space.

"Yes, you will go and you will be proper. And yes, you have to wear your Order's garb." Myron answered. "Your mother is considering some things and doesn't need the grief today, Edwina. Tomas, would you like to attend with my family, as I consider you a part of our family?"

"I would really like to, sir." Tomas answered excitedly.

"Thanias, would you assist the kids in finding their appropriate attire for tonight? I would like to sit with Paul for a while. And please take Iris to the house, she needs some sleep."

"Yes, hrmmm, Myron. Will Tatiana be in her garb as well?"

"No."

"Why not Daddy? Do I belong to an Order? Do I have magic?"

Thanias seizing opportunity said "Let's go children." Iris took his arm and the group left.

First, Thanias escorted Iris to the home of Zanor and Kira, where they were greeted and dismissed as Iris was greeted by Kira. Then he escorted the kids to the Hall of the Ruler.

THE HALL OF THE RULER

Tatiana glanced around. "Wow, this is huge! I will get lost here."

"Nonsense, now stay with me while we traverse the halls. This room here is the Order of the Moons chamber. Edwina, you will find a servant of the House there to help you. But stay with me for now. Over here, to the right is the chamber for the Star. That is your mother's Order. The chamber diagonal to it is for the Intervals, whom have not been seen in many hundreds of years." He glanced at Tatiana. "Continuing on, there are several more Orders who use the next chambers, for instance the Truncheon here, I think Tomas would be comfortable using this chamber, and then we have the Seekers, who are sort of explorers. We also have some more chambers over here. They are extremely rare, and very, very dangerous. They include Izmaa, Aantiri, and the Chrinthold." Thanias paused and glanced down the hall to the empty chambers and pondered. "Ok, that is the tour. Let's go to the eating hall here, for our meal and then we will get you all ready for the ceremony." Thanias led them to dinner and contemplated Tatiana's knowledge.

Tatiana had wandered off, observing everything and still taking down notes in her binder. She thought each room should be investigated. She started taking notes in her small detective journal, which she had almost completely forgotten about. She decided the main section, where the "High Seat" was, was the second most important. Second because those who occupy the chambers will shape the decisions of the "Seat". She took a special interest in the Interval Chamber. She noted everything down to the smallest detail of everything, and wrote down incantations that seemed to come to her as she studied their symbols.

She was picked up by Paul and seated at the table. Paul glanced at her. "Why, Tat, do you wait until mealtime to jot stuff down?"

"Because that's how I roll. Maybe you should get a hobby instead of working at the library. Nothing ever happens at libraries."

Thanias interrupted. "Ahemm. Everyone please be seated. Do you all know what is about to transpire later?"

"Well, Dad is getting something done to him at a ceremony." Tatiana chirped in between huge bites of fruit.

"Yes. He is going to actually get his crown tonight. It will be like mine, and is very important to your Grandfather and Grandmother."

"Wow, do we get one too?" Tatiana mused looking into her uncle's deep gave.

"No, it is not time for you all to be crowned. You see the crown represents the Order in which a person belongs and the ceremony can be long or short depending on the presenting Order and how ritualistic it is. Like Moon and Stars take quite a while. Truncheons take about half that time and Intervals have never been viewed in my lifetime. They prefer to remain to themselves." Thanias paused briefly to eat and to let them take in what he had said.

"Thanias, sir." Tomas spoke. "Where do I fit in, please?"

"Well, young lad. It seems that you were chosen to be a defender of a Moon. You would fall in with the defenders of Orders as a Chrinthold. Chrinthold are revered by all Orders and have a special seating to the right side of their ward, for lack of a better word. The Truncheon and Chrinthold have always been close comrades and have sometimes shared Chambers during ceremonies and other events. I hope that answers your question."

"Yes, sir. Will I have to have a different trainer other than Harold? Harold is great and all, but I think he worries too much. Something is bothering him; I mean really bothering him."

"Can girls be in the Chrinthold?" Edwina asked, tapping her foot.

Thanias carefully answered the question. "I have never heard of a girl in the Chrinthold, but I think it is possible. There are no rules saying no girls allowed. In fact, the Truncheon have had a few women in the ranks who were quite adept and sometimes more skilled than the men."

"Will Altus be available for me to visit?"

"I don't know, Edwina. He may be. Ah, there he is now. Finish eating and I will permit you to speak to him briefly."

"Yes, Uncle."

Altus approached the group and seated himself in the Moons position at the table. "Tis alright if I join you, Thanias?"

"By all means, yes. I just finished up a tour of the Chambers with our guests and we decided it was time to eat before we ready ourselves for the ceremony."

"Edwina, I will send assistants for you to help with dressing. I assume you would like to meet with me about the Moons, how shall I say... business?"

"Yes, please, Altus." Edwina flashed a smile for the first time in a week.

"Am I an Interval?" Tatiana interjected. "I mean, is that where I am supposed to be? Am I a druid?"

Altus laughed. "Child, you are very young and should not dwell on things that have not come to pass. I would suggest you spend your time playing games with kids than worrying about your place. Even if you are an Interval, there is none left to train you. And no, druids are not intervals. There is one I know of who is in hiding."

"You don't know that old man. You don't know anything. I am glad Edwina found her place with another stuck up, bitter old person. She will fit right in." With that, Tatiana stomped off, scowling and grumbling.

She saw a flicker in the Interval Chamber. As she approached, she could hear a voice calling to her and soothing her inner rage. "You must not lash out. You must embrace all thoughts. You are an Interval. Please walk to the rear of the chamber."

As Tatiana did as the voice instructed, two familiar beings became visible to her. "You are the ones from Treah?"

"Yes child. And it is good that you know, as some very terrible times are approaching, and we need to not be discovered. We are extremely rare individuals, coming from almost any kind of life. As I am an Enygminite, I have seen many, many great and horrible things in my time. I must know that you are trustworthy enough to share my deep knowledge, as you will be our representative and have to be very secretive in our workings. Malos is your guardian. You met us at Treah, and I have a feeling we will meet again in the not-too-distant future."

Malos approached. He greeted Tatiana in proper Interval manner. "This is your first lesson, Tatiana. This is what you must learn, how to greet parties. It is extremely important that you are comfortable with this, as you are our ambassador. Ladies greet in such a manner as this." Malos grasped Tatiana's left hand with both of his crossed his left foot in front of right foot and bowed slightly from the waste. "Okay, now your turn."

Tatiana greeted Malos and Menosh as was taught. "Was that ok?"

"Yes, Lady of the Intervals. Now, you must know a few things, before the ceremony." Malos paused as he gazed upon the little girl. "We can speak all languages and can communicate with everything."

"What does Menosh do?"

"I... I oversee this planet. I know of some terrible things that will transpire sometime soon, either around the time of this ceremony, but that can still be shaped."

"How. Do you just stir some magical water and fix it?"

"No, but I must depart, as it is very dangerous for me here. Malos will be an excellent trainer for you."

"Will I see you again?"

"Yes, as I must teach you my knowledge, but only after Malos has taught you the Interval knowledge. You are also my representative, so keep that in mind and know that you shall be safe and have an answer for all the questions that will arise at this ceremony."

"Thank you Menosh." Tatiana said as he faded just as he appeared.

"Let's get you your garb. I believe Thanias is testing you. He might not be one to trust, ok."

"Yes, Malos. I won't hang around him."

"Here we are." Malos removed some very small dresses from the wardrobe and allowed Tatiana to select hers for the event. "A sprite, ah there she is. Anyway, the sprite will be your assistant. She is a servant, but all of our servants are free to leave and return as the want to. They all have very nice living arrangements and eat the same thing as we do. The nymph is like a wind. He will communicate with you when Menosh has important things for you to know. He also keeps an eye on things happening around you and remembers everything. He will be present at the ceremony. The sprite is named Alasha and the nymph is Kren. Both will be with you until your passing."

Kren appeared before Tatiana as almost a bit of sparkling dust hanging in the air. Alasha appeared as a small lady with thin dragonfly like wings.

"Now your head gear." Malos found a small crown of silver and gold thinly woven in one band with four points representing seasons. Malos spoke in Interval and the crown seemed to be alive with seasons dancing in a circle from point to point from spring to winter and repeating.

Alasha held a mirror for Tatiana to look in. "Wow that is neat! How?" Tatiana was amazed.

"Now I will let Alasha assist you and then we will go to the main room for the ceremony."

"Yes, sir." Tatiana smiled ear to ear. Before she changed though, she looked in every nook and cranny the Chamber had. "Do I sleep here too? What did Altus mean, that there is a druid in hiding?"

"You can sleep at your parent's home. That is expected, since you are so young and your parents would be very sad. Now please change. In hiding? When did he say this?"

"Before I ran in here."

Malos and Kren left the room looking for Altus while Alasha assisted Tatiana.

In the same time frame as Tatiana was learning her truth, Edwina and Tomas sat silently and ate. Altus and Thanias conversed. Malos entered the hallway and walked toward Altus. He closed his eyes and Altus excused himself from Thanias.

"What troubles you Malos?" Altus said as he greeted Malos.

"The young one said you told her a druid was in hiding. Did you mean Rynn?"

"No. She is not the druid, unfortunately." A scroll was handed to Altus. "I am thinking that this is related to the comet. Its brilliance peaks today and its trajectory shows potential impact that would give rise to the Shadowblyts again, or worse."

"Is this word from the house of Beryth?"

"Yes, it is. They are positioned to help us. They ask that Rynylla send word when it is time."

The Kluanarians

"Ok, I am done now, Uncle." Edwina spoke hastily, as she walked into the hallway. Altus slowly closed his thumb to his fingers which silenced her.

"Forgive me Malos, I must correct her, we will talk later?"

"Yes, of course."

"Now Edwina. Please do not speak out of turn. It is not how Moons behave. When I finish this sentence, then you may speak." Altus looked at her almost disappointed. "What will Lunacerian say?"

"As I was saying. I am now finished with my meal." Edwina said as she felt her lips.

"Very well, now I need to take you to the Moons chamber and prepare you for tonight."

Seeing opportunity, Thanias sat in a chair near Malos. "Is all well, Malos?"

"No, Thanias, something is about to transpire, and we will need to be vigilant through this ceremony."

Edwina nodded and followed Altus down the hallway.

"Well, Tomas, that leaves us." Thanias smiled. "I will show you to our chambers again and you can ready for the ceremony. I believe Altus should have left some Moons garb there, but we can make it more realistic. I think they go overboard in style."

"Ok. Do I have to be Edwina's watcher or whatever?"

"No, son, not at all. You see as a Chrinthold, you are one of the most respected of the Orders and have a say in what you do. No one can tie you to an Order other than your own. You may start with the Moons, get bored and then say go assist a Star or Izmaa or Seeker, or whomever you wish to be associated with. In fact, I think I better check and see if there is Chrinthold garb, if so, who cares what the Moons want you to wear."

"Thanks, Thanias. That makes me feel better." Thanias left Tomas to his own while he searched for the Chrinthold belongings. "Thanias. I think I found the stuff." A wardrobe appeared. In fact a whole section for the Chrinthold appeared, as well as a Master.

Thanias returned upon hearing his name. "Ah, I see that I would have looked in vain for this."

"Yes, Thanias. Indeed, you would have. I am Rynylla. I am the Priestess of the Chrinthold. I am here for Tomas." Rynylla gazed upon Tomas. "You are Tomas. Much has been said of you amongst our Order. Many have waited for this day. Welcome."

"So, why are you here?" Thanias questioned. "I was not aware that the Chrinthold meddled in Kluanarian affairs unless something bad was about to happen."

"You know why I am here, Thanias." Rynylla smiled. "Please Tomas; feel free to use anything in here. You are also welcome to sleep here if you wish, as it is a protected place for us." She paused briefly. "I have prepared a small memory book for you to help in your learning of our Order, Tomas. Read it at your leisure and I will answer all questions. Now, Thanias, please escort me around, for I have not been here for some time."

Thanias offered his arm to Rynylla. "Not much has changed priest. There is still much to do."

"What are you talking about? There is balance that has been sustained for many years."

"Not much longer, I fear. I have a concern, as these young people are being placed far too early in their lives."

"It is the way, and it probably means some shift in the balance but nothing to overly anxious about."

"Look here Rynylla; I have not seen you since we were in school together. I don't know whom gave you title, but I train and deploy the Truncheon every single day, to keep the darkness in check. The Izmaa challenge us, testing us. All at the whim of the Shadowblyts who are biding their time."

"Thanias, stop for a minute." She hugged him and whispered in his ear. "I know what is happening. That is why I am here, and I will be here for some time. Now let's go sit in the gardens while the children are prepared for the ceremony of Myron."

"Very well, then. It has been a long time since I sat in the gardens. It has been a very long time since I have seen you." Thanias smiled at Rynylla. "Why did you leave?"

"I had to go. It was my duty to go. Your path took you to the Truncheon, and I dislike war."

"War is a part of us, if the ancestors would have refused to take up arms against the Shadowblyts at Edziza, we would be no more. The Edziza Battle preserved our way of life."

"Yes, Thanias, I suppose so. But war is such a burden on all creatures. Anyway, I am here to aid in the instruction of Tomas. I will be here for some time I guess and will need a place to stay other than the Hall of Rulers."

"I have room at my home. You are most welcome there. I don't know if it will meet your standards though."

"Thank you. It will be fine, just so there is no food gone bad," Rynylla smiled at Thanias. "But you still have to be a gentleman and let me alone. I don't have time for drama. My focus is the development of Tomas into a true Chrinthold."

"Whatever, you can stay where you want, I only offered, as I am very hospitable."

"No, you have an enormous ego, just like when we were younger, and you didn't learn then. Nothing has changed. Anyway, we need to head and retrieve the new Orders members and place them accordingly."

"As you wish." Thanias abruptly walked off and wandered down the hall with the separate chambers. He greeted the trainers and new members. "Please accompany your trainer, guide, or priest to your area in the Hall. They will show you how to act." Thanias stared directly at Edwina. "Please do not interrupt the ceremony, or I will make your stay most unforgettable."

Tatiana noticed others entering rooms with people. "I didn't know there were elves here." She whispered to Malos.

"There are. Perhaps you should introduce yourself. I will give you some free time as the ceremony will be quite long."

Tatiana bounded off and ran straight for the elf. Panting she slowed her gait and greeted them. "Hello. My name is Tatiana. What is yours."

"Oh, hi. I am Irra. I have never seen one of you before."

"Really. I never saw an elf either." She smiled and hugged her new friend. "Let's see who else we can find." She took her notepad from her pocket and began writing.

"So what part of this thing do you belong in?" Irra asked.

"Oh, I think Malos said Interval, though I am not sure what that is."

"I have done a study on Intervals, you see, I too take notes and try to figure things out." Irra pulled out her notebook as well.

The two headed toward a long narrow passage where they encountered Onachala. The three were close in age and got along marvelously. Malos found them racing in the halls and decided this would be a good test for all of the members.

"Ok, children and young adults. Follow me to the end of the hall." Once there he placed his hand on the center of the wall and closed his eyes. The wall slowly vanished. A great room full of keys was in front of them. "If anything should ever happen which places your life at risk, you are able to escape to here with the use of a key. This key will be specific to your Order. I would like you all to work together to locate these keys. After this is done, we will exit and I will give you an incantation that will make the key return you to this room. Are there any questions?"

"Yes, please. What is an incantation?" Tatiana asked.

"A special sentence or word that causes something to happen."

"Ok, can we start now?"

"Yes, Tatiana, you may begin. Paul, I will escort you to the Eupepsians, you look in pain."

The three younger kids looked together, and three of the four older kids looked together.

"Please, Malos." As they left, he watched Tatiana interact with her new friends. "She is going to change how you perceive certain Orders."

"Yes, Paul, she will. That is what Menosh has intended."

"Thanias keeps secrets from you."

"He does?"

"Yes. All the time I have been here, before Mom and Dad got settled, he was in my room pacing. I was not always asleep and noticed some things."

"This is very important. Do you know what kind of things?"

"He drops a tablet of some kind on to a table and talks to someone name Llylandra. Something about Mithdrool. Owww, I hurt really bad!"

"We are almost there." Malos escorted him in to the Eupepsian area. "Help him, I must find Harold." Ten minutes later he returned with Harold and found Paul half awake. "Are you able to speak to us Paul?"

"Yes. Harold, your name is familiar. Are you related to the Harold in Walther's story?"

"Unfortunately, yes. I am Harold."

"Wow, you must be..."

"Old, yes, but I am truly War."

"Ok, I will go with Harold. Has Thanias hit you radar?"

"Radar?"

"Has he seemed odd toward you and the soldiers, to include Truncheon?"

"No."

"He should. Some lady named Llylandra is working with him to raise Mithdrool. I am thinking that this is bad. But then he is also in favor with some beings that look like Menosh, except for they aren't partially invisible and have fangs."

"Where are they from?"

"Phallas Minor. They are looking to destroy the House of Beryth."

"How do you know this?" Harold inquired half amused.

"There is a traitor amongst the ranks of all the Orders. He is just a guard, so he blends in well with everyone. They are searching for a druid. This druid is supposed to be the one who can end the skirmishes that will take place soon. Is there a druid in Beryth's home?"

"When did you hear all of this? No, there is no druid there. I suspect William can answer that better than I." Harold huffed.

"While he was in my room and once in a while a guard, the same one, repeatedly would stop with a briefing."

"Hmmm." Harold paced.

"Can you win favor of your uncle before he does something dumb?"

"Not sure, but I think it is too late."

"Why is that, boy?"

Malos interrupted, "The comet is today."

"Ah, that is the problem. Can Zanor contain him?"

"No, but Rynylla can. We need to find this druid." Malos left.

"Do you know the druid, Grandpa?"

"How did you know?"

"Just a hunch, and Mom talks to you. Why doesn't she talk to Grandma?"

"Because your mom left at a very bad time. Grandma Malificence is a Star, like your mom. When your mom came of age and was trained, she stepped down. Then Edziza happened and during this bloody siege, your mom ran away with Myron to Earth." Harold paused as Malos entered again. "And Malificence removed all powers from your mother except portals and viewing. The Order was all but destroyed."

A roar went through the Eupepsian chambers. A rather large figure emerged from the doorway.

"Welcome, old friend." Harold greeted William.

"Thank you. Malos sent word not moments ago. Luly is in danger."

"Is she the druid?"

"No. And who might you be, young man."

"My name is Paul, sir."

"I should say, you are an exact image of Zanor, when he was your age. Tell me what Order you belong to?"

"I don't think I belong to any. I had a Truncheon mark, then it vanished and so I am no one important. Who are you?"

"I am William. A Titan, Luly, I found out is also a Titan. I have raised her as my own daughter. She has strong powers, and it is not safe for her to attend this ceremony."

"So, then, if she is not the druid what puts her in danger?"

"Thanias does, Malos. He has a scroll from Nagazthastar and it mentions her. Rynylla has placed her in safekeeping."

A sudden outburst of giggles filled the long halls. Three small children raced into the room.

"Malos, we found them," chimed the three girls.

Malos smiled and introduced the new Order members to William. He then had them form and arch in front of him. "Repeat this word. *Laelochlancarti.*"

"*Laelochlancarti.*" The three children spoke and as they finished the word, vanished.

Edwina screamed, which was heard all the way back in the Eupepsian chambers. "It worked," Malos said as the three older kids ran into the room. "Now, you three are next." The process was repeated for the teens. "Ok, now back to the matter at hand." Malos added as the teens vanished. "William, do you know who the druid is?"

"No, Malos. It is not within my sight. Luly and her children are druids, but not the one that is supposed to be able to sway the upcoming events. She is most willing to train this person, however."

THE CEREMONY

Dinner had passed; Myron dressed in a mithril mail adorned with gold and a hunter green cape. He was given the golden waist and helm by his father. It was specially made for this ceremony. Iris dressed in a light golden silk gown with pearls placed amongst the braiding down the front, collar, and sleeve ends. She met Myron in their house and together walked over to his parents' residence. Kira, dressed in a charcoal shaded silk with silvery inlays, greeted them on the walkway. Zanor joined them. He wore the traditional High King attire, but also added the Aantiri symbolism in his cape.

Zanor pleased with their assembly, smiled, and spoke. "Thank you, Myron. I was concerned about many, many things. This will help me to be at ease and bring balance to my mind."

"I understand, father. I would prefer you to show me the trainees and the deployed Truncheon, as opposed to Thanias. He seems to think he will have say over everything, and I know that is not what is meant by my return."

"Very well. It will also give me opportunity to view our lands and interact with our people."

"Are the dark coming to this ceremony?" Iris inquired nervously.

"It is possible, but I doubt it. Although, we have been surprised by them before," Kira responded.

"Well, it is on armistice grounds, so there is no need for concern." Zanor added as they entered the hall.

Iris was stunned at the sight of her two younger children and Tomas.

She was seated in disbelief. She noticed all Orders were represented, to include the Izmaa and Shadowblyts. She was unable to speak to Myron as he was seated next to the High King, and she was in her Order's area.

A few minutes later all stood as a special guest entered the Hall along with Truance followed by Paul who was being escorted by two apprentice Eupesians. They bowed and placed Paul in the house of Aantiri for now, out of honor of the King. The special guest announced himself.

"Welcome all, to this momentous occasion. I am Gareth, of the Seekers. I am proud to announce the ceremony is to begin. Also, a welcome for one who has not set foot in the Hall before, Malificence of the Morket Order. There will be time for the Orders to interact with one another after this ceremony."

Malificence stood and bowed. Since she was honored in the opening, she was permitted to wander amongst the Orders and assess the strife if any.

With that, the leaders of Orders and new members rose and formed a procession to the center of the room forming a half circle facing the throne. Each Order eyed the others to see if there were any other "surprises" to occur.

Zanor approached the center court with Myron. Thanias stepped forward with a drawn two-handed sword, embellished with Truncheon symbols at the hilt and at the tip. Zanor motioned for the Eupesians to escort Paul to the center as well.

"Welcome all to this very special ceremony. It is very special to me as I am not only crowning my son, Myron, as Prince of Burwash and as Commander of Truncheon aside his brother, Thanias, but also witnessing the Induction of all of the new members into their Orders."

Zanor spoke as he walked to Myron, accompanied by Gareth who passed the Seal of the Truncheon to the King. The King stepped forward and placed the Seal into the premade inlay on the helm. Next, Zanor had Thanias step forward with him. They approached Paul and presented the Truncheon Sword as the Eupepsians assisted Paul in standing to receive it.

Following this, all members cleared except the High King and Gareth. First the Moons, represented by Lunacerian approached with Altus escorting Edwina to the center of the court. She was given a scepter by Lunacerian and recognized by Zanor.

They were followed by the Chrinthold. Priestess Rynylla who escorted Tomas to the center of the court where he was presented with a sword and shield by Gareth and also recognized by the King.

Next the Izmaa entered the center court. "Greetings, High King of Burwash. I am Guilles (pronounced Ghee). I bestow to you, our newest member, Irra." With that, an orb was presented to Irra and she was recognized by Zanor.

Something unexpected happened. Iris stood. Kira noticed this and looked in the direction of Iris's gaze.

"The sky lightens. What is the meaning of this?" Guilles wondered aloud.

Thanias and Myron stepped to the Hall entrance to observe the occurrence. Thanias announced, "Please be seated. It is the passing of a comet; all is right now."

The commotion ceased. Zanor re-recognized the Izmaa and continued in the ceremony. Shadowblyts followed. "I am Rithmas, Herald for the Shadowblyts. Our High Priest is ill and I am here to present to the Orders Lady Onachala. He bowed as he placed a tome in her hands. Zanor bowed in recognition of Onachala.

Finally, Malos stepped forward. "My King, I present to you Tatiana of the Intervals." Malos bowed and gave her a staff. Zanor smiled and also acknowledged the Intervals' newest member.

After all the Orders presented new members, the King returned to his throne. Gareth again spoke. "Keeping balance and continuing cross cooperation amongst all Orders for the benefit of all inhabitants of the Realm of Kluanaria." He asked for quick end to the siege which had begun not two days prior to the ceremony in the land of Kaprius.

Zanor interrupted. "With that note, I would like to see responsible parties whom are currently engaged in this combat following this ceremony. I have taken your abilities from you until this issue is discussed."

Gareth continued on with a formal status of each region, state, and land of Kluanaria. "Please keep in mind, our next ceremony will be elsewhere, and this status represents everything to present of each and every inhabited portion of Kluanaria and you as Orders and also the commons, must see to it that this is serious and not to be dismissed."

"You are aware of the significance of the comet, Lord Zanor?" Rithmas added.

"It is a mere comet, Rithmas, be at ease." Zanor paused. "Gareth check our scrolls, as you may have knowledge. And yes, in the winter, Lucien will wed Impresaria, as foretold."

The townsfolk dispersed, talking on about the new members and how young they are. Heads of Orders remained in the Center.

Zanor excused himself briefly with Gareth. "Find out something. You are a Seeker."

"Yes, I am, but you, Zanor are Aantiri and have much quicker methods of finding things out. So what do you say, we both look together."

"Very well, but first I need to see about this siege. Lucien has not returned yet."

Both men re-entered the Hall and the table was prepared. Seats were adjusted and all awaited the question.

"Tell me, Thanias, where is Lucien?"

"He... He is at Kaprius as we speak. He is engaged with the dark."

"Tell me Lunacerian, what is the meaning of the comet on this specific day?"

Lunacerian stood on the table at the center. He closed his eyes and spoke, "*Lumenseth Coimead.*" Darkness appeared under his feet with stars, moons, planets. It was a view of the heavens. All Orders could see the path of the comet. "The comet will return in six years. It originated near Phallas Minor and on its way back it will cross us in the opposite season as now. Something terrible has stirred with its passing. Its second passing will be another wave." With that, he removed himself from the table and was seated.

"Very well. Next matter." Zanor paused briefly. "Does Phallas Minor have beings?"

"Yes, Lord." Gareth responded. "They are not to be trifled with. I fear this comet can be seen by them and they can use it to plot things. They are power hungry and do not leave survivors from what I witnessed when visiting Mercurian on the other side of our planet."

"How long have they been there?"

"Probably a good year. They made Mercurian their stronghold. Its inhabitants are either dead or enslaved."

"Thanias, why have you done nothing about this?"

"The..." Thanias was interrupted.

"I'll tell you why, father." Lucien entered the room. "He has been stirring things. Things not meant to be stirred, to make him look better in your eyes. I stayed behind in Kaprius to seek peace and determine the cause of the skirmish."

Impresaria bowed to the High King of Burwash. "I finally get to meet you, Zanor. "Your son, Lucien has been quite instrumental in quelling the battle. I belong to a lesser order. Perhaps you have heard of Morket?"

"Yes, we thought all of the Order were gone."

"No, dear king. I am ruler of the Morket, and I am not one to be trifled with either. You know my mother Malificence, father Harold and ofcourse my sister, Iris. Your son has been plotting and seeking things not to be sought by mere Truncheons." She paused as all looked around. "If you want a fight, you will have one hell of a fight, and you will lose. Ah, and I see mother is here as well. I have much to discuss with you after this meeting, please."

Zanor looked at Thanias. "What have you done? Have you lost your mind?"

"No father, I have not lost my mind." Thanias grinned slyly, he walked toward the new members and looked at each one. "I have discovered a new power. And I will wield it against all who oppose me." At that moment he extended his arm toward the ceiling and a dark mist wrapped around him. He vanished.

Everyone stood. Lunacerian went into a trance. "I see him. He has retreated to Treah. The dark has embraced him, my lord."

"Impresaria, this is not your doing, nor mine. I sincerely regret the loss of life of your people. I apologize for the actions of my treacherous son. Please forgive us.

"Your son has unlocked an ancient darkness that cannot be quelled in normal battle. I fear for you and all of Kluanaria. Once the Fraeloch under Llylandra have this knowledge, they will join him, as he is the only one who controls this darkness. We Orders must unite to keep them separate. He has chosen to assist Llylandra with razing Mithdrool and his Legion. He also has allies with the invaders in Mercurian.

Kira stood. "I concur. We need to band together now and work

Brenda M. Hokenson

together." She paused briefly. "We will need Seekers and Aantiri to determine the source of this darkness and we will need the new members trained but kept secretly from here. My grandchildren and those wishing to go, will return to Earth and interact normally within the earthen societies. It will be far safer there and they can be trained discreetly. They can enter through Ruan, if Thanias has not destroyed it and the gateway."

Iris glanced at Myron in despair. "The Orders decided to go with this idea as it would be safest for the young ones."

Zanor spoke after great thought. "It is decided then. Please bring the children and their parents and siblings here at once. Orders, you need to explain the situation to them, make it quite clear that the entire family will go so as to not separate them for this long duration. Everyone will be in the same city suburb very well protected. If you wish to stay behind that is fine."

The kids' vacation ended. Kira cast a spell upon her grandchildren to remove their memories of Kluanaria until their time to return, or powers discovered. As the family stepped through a portal created by Iris, the memories faded.

NEW BEGINNINGS

Fall was well under way. Two additional families settled into their new homes and blended nicely into society of Earth. The kids interacted with each other as normal kids do and the adults also fit perfectly. Each was given a house with one bedroom per person and a nice yard with room for a decent sized garden.

The town itself was not great for any age kid – say unless they are college age. The activities were limited to a couple of playgrounds far away from their 'suburb" which took forever to walk to. Zanor saw this and had a special playground with activities that would simulate their training needs without threat of discovery.

Tatiana spent her days with friends from school and steeped in the task of learning to be a detective. She, having just turned ten, desired more than anything to escape her fearful personality. She was tired of being scared. Edwina mused at the thought of Tatiana even attempting to sever fear of basically everything. After all, Tat was still unable to tell fact from fiction. Edwina mocked her daily and became quite a prankster.

Fully convinced of her ability to shun her old habits of squealing and hiding during shows and movies with supernatural beings, Tatiana took it upon herself to watch scary things. She even borrowed Edwina's books, which were mostly of supernatural beings. The two held discussions concerning the possibilities of supernatural beings.

Paul had learned of the girls' beliefs and discussions and wanted to prove once and for all that once a coward, always a coward. He silently plotted daily of how to provide the best scare. He convinced both that they needed to watch more scary movies and he would bring better scary books home from library with him, where he worked after school. He bought devices for pranking, gadgets and gizmos. Paul would put on a great façade of the "we're not alone" and Tat, being more gullible than Edwina, would run in fear.

Edwina had found a gently used bookstore. She found an old manuscript that intrigued her. She bought it for a mere nickel, even though it seemed centuries old. She took the book straight away to her room and yelled for Tatiana. She showed her the book and asked it not be disturbed until she reads it a bit. Days passed and Tatiana's curiosity was overwhelming. She took the book while Edwina was gone and browsed through the pages. Toward the center of the book was a descriptive methodology on how to detect entities and interpret them. Tat, being a 'detective' took some notes and returned it before her sister returned.

Upon Edwina's return Tatiana raced to her and started rambling about the book. Outraged, Edwina ranted and raved for some time, and then an epiphany. She grabbed Tatiana by the arm and handed her a notebook and pencil. They began plotting out how to use the detection process without setting off the 'mom and dad alarms.

"Let's get Paul to help us. He is good with this stuff." Tatiana suggested.

"Ok, now we gotta wait til he gets here."

As Paul walked in the door, a sudden rush of sisters in his face hit him. Their words were inaudible as they spoke over one another saying help us, help us; look at this book. "Enough already! Where are Mom and Dad?"

"Grilling out back," came the unified answer. "What about our project?"

"Give me a minute, and then I will look at your book." With that Paul sprinted out the back door, with girls not far behind. They were very curious, as Paul usually did his own thing.

The kids have been waiting for the next camping trip. Maybe it was going to be an idea for the camping trip.

"Is this about the camping trip?" Tatiana chimed in before any words were said.

"Well it needs discussed," Myron added. "Son, can we do the camp trip discussion then your issue?" He whispered to Paul, "So the girls leave us alone."

The Kluanarians

"Umm, yeah sure, that's fine. My two cents are first I am bringing my surf board, since it is the coast, finally. And second, I want to drive too."

"Done, and done." Myron nodded in agreement.

Iris spoke, "All of this is going to depend on some things. First, Tatiana, you can't be loud and squelchy from now until the trip, during the trip and after the trip. That means that your "Supernatural Investigations" during the trip can happen, but while you are researching with Edwina and watching scary shows, you have to quell your loud interruptions before during and after shows and no fighting. Second, you have to be good and not throw rocks at the old house behind us. If you can do that, and then we are good, if not – well, the trip is off."

"Yes Mom," Tatiana looked down and swept her foot across the floor in front of her. "I promise to be good."

"Do I have to go?" Edwina looked at her parents.

"Yes," Myron responded. "We are going to the beach at Clamshoe. Plenty of sunshine, surf, clam digging before winter sets in."

"Yeah, for lame-o's." Edwina glared.

"For that, you get to help decide the menu and pack the car." Myron pointed at the chair to his left.

Edwina sat down and with notebook in hand; she began to jot down idea. "How long of vacation?"

"Three or four days." Iris added, "And no junk food allowed."

"Ok, done." Edwina handed the list to her dad.

Myron and Iris examined the list. "Ok, it is good. We'll go to the store and get this, you guys start packing your things." Myron motioned to Paul, "Come on, you're driving, and we are taking your wheels."

"Dad."

Myron laughed, "Well, the burbie has the tent, cook ware, dishware, sleeping bags and our clothes and your clothes. We need the food and your sisters' clothing."

"Alright, but don't wave at everyone, ok?"

"Yes, son." Myron chuckled. "Iris, you coming along?"

"No, I will make sure the girls get packed and recheck stuff."

"Ok, see you in a bit then." The men drove off.

"Now, Myron, what is on your mind? You were in a hurry to talk to us, but I didn't want to add fuel for Tatiana or Edwina."

"Something strange is happening to me. I woke up this morning with a small mark, kind of like the one Thanias has on his shoulder. It looks like the Truncheon symbol – a small hammer."

As they pulled to a stop in the store parking lot, Myron pulled up Paul's sleeve. "I agree. I also know that your Grandmother Kira suppressed all memories until you are deemed ready."

"I already knew about Kluanaria, she didn't hide my memories, I asked her not to. But weirder is that I was sleep walking or something. I woke up downstairs. My room is way at the end of the hall across from Tatiana."

"Well, your mom will want to see it, so we will have to listen to her carry on for a bit. So I will take the girls out to do a final checklist and you talk to your mom. Then we will load in the car, because she doesn't want the girls knowing anything."

"Anyway, Dad thanks. Now let's get those supplies – the surf is calling!"

After half an hour, the guys loaded up more than enough supplies for camping and drove home. Myron had the girls help him pack the supplies into coolers and boxes while Paul spoke to his mom.

"Ok, Mom, don't go ballistic please."

"What did you do? Do you have a ticket?"

"No, I want you to see this thing on my shoulder."

Iris immediately grabbed his wrist and pulled the sleeve up. "How long have you had this?"

"About two days. Dad said not to worry, so I'm not."

"Ok, how much do you know about it?"

"Nothing really." Paul played dumb so his mom wouldn't panic.

"Darn, MYRON…. Myron!" Iris yelled. Everyone ran into the room. "How long have you known about this, this…."

"Mark," replied Myron. "He has had it two days."

"I need to think about this."

"Ok, then think in the car on the way to some awesome camping." Myron pulled his wife to the burbie. "We will sort this out after vacation."

Iris sat in complete silence the entire length of the trip. She missed the lunch stop, the hurry up and stretch stop and even them pulling into their campsite.

THE OCEAN GETAWAY

TATIANA HELPED HER DAD AND brother set up the tent. Edwina arranged the table for a neat cooking and cleaning station. She also flung the bags to Paul and Tatiana grabbed the clothing. A second tent went up, where they could take turns changing. Edwina set up a mesh screen over the table and a second one over the folding chairs. Then she went back to the burbie and pulled her mom out of the car.

"Ok, ma, we're going swimming now!" Edwina grabbed her mom by the hand again and drug her to the water's edge. "C'mon, quit thinking and relax." She gave one last thought and decided to do something about this thought her mom was focused on.

"What the hell! Why did you do that? I am in my clothes. Godammit Ed. Wake up!"

Edwina laughed. "Well, you're not moping now and already wet…"

"Myron, your daughter is crazy."

"Not really, I told her it might work if she could get you to the water." He laughed heartily and winked at Edwina. "So, just relax and enjoy."

Tatiana walked along the beach and watch small crabs skitter across the wet sand. She looked at the sand dollars and starfish. A few glimmering rocks caught her eye, and she collected them. The light green one was clear and as she cast her gaze into it, she thought she could see someone looking back at her. She decided to see if the orange one did the same. As Tatiana gazed into the rock, it seemed to show her a battle. Disturbed by both she placed them in a small leather pouch about her waist and continued on. She jotted down what she had seen in her detective notebook.

Brenda M. Hokenson

Paul was on his surfboard swimming for the perfect wave. He got tired and relaxed as the board slowly drifted to the shoreline. "Hey, Tat! What are you writing?"

"Oh, nothing. Just some notes about this rock's unique properties. Will you look into this rock?" She pulled the green rock out of the pouch and handed it to Paul.

"Ok, what am I looking for?"

"I want you to tell me what you see when you look into it."

"Well, umm, honestly Tat, I don't see anything. It is clear but the light shines through it."

Look in this direction." Tatiana turned her brother by pulling his elbow.

"Ok, ok. I still don't see anything. Did you see something?"

"No." Tatiana kicked some sand and put the rock back in the pouch.

"Let me see your journal, Tat." Paul took the small notebook and read her last entries. "Hmm. You didn't see anything eh? Well, let's see if there is another rock out there that I can see in." He took Tatiana's hand and together the trolled along the water for another rock.

"Wait, you didn't try the orange one." She handed the rock to him.

"Ok, as I gaze through this small rock, I see…. I see… Sorry, Tat, I got nothing. Maybe you have some magic power, huh? But let's look for one more rock to satisfy my curiosity."

They spent another hour looking and found nothing. A nice wave was forming.

"Watch this, Tat." Paul took his board and sprinted out as far as he could and dove with his board into the churning water. He swam as if he was in a relay. Tatiana turned away briefly as a crab ran across her foot. She looked down and picked up a pale-yellow rock.

"Ok, Tat, here I come!" Paul was on a great wave. Tatiana snapped a picture as he was at the top of it and some more as he rode down the face of it. He came to a stop right in front of her. "Well, what did you think?"

"Nice. Oh, yeah, I found another rock, right where we were looking."

"Did you look in it yet?"

"No, I am afraid to."

"Well, go ahead, and if you see something scary, we can always leave the rock here."

"Ok, I will." Tatiana took a deep breath and look through the rock.

"What do you see? I know you see something."

"It is a town, some old people with us there, oh and a farm looking place with a castle!"

"Well, that isn't too scary."

"No, I guess not." She yawned. "We should head back. There is probably dinner for us."

The kids walked up the beach and decided to splash Edwina and their mom in the water, since they were already having fun in the water. Everyone splashed around until Myron interrupted.

"Foods on!" Paul had already plated the food and poured drinks. "Enjoy all. I have taken some awesome pics and tomorrow we can go hiking a bit too."

After the meal, Paul and Edwina cleared the table and cleaned the dishes. Tatiana sat in a chair staring out at the ocean.

"Something bugging my little detective," Myron said as he walked up to the chairs.

"Yes, and no, dad." Tatiana shifted as she was uncomfortable.

"Are you cold?"

"No, just something weird with some rocks I found. It doesn't make sense to me."

"What does a ten-year-old like you need to be so concerned over a rock?" Myron whispered to his youngest.

Tatiana whispered back. "Please, please don't tell Mom. Because I know something is up with Paul that upset her. This would make it worse."

Still whispering, Myron said, "Ok, you know you are sounding to wise for your age, so there is something going on with you too."

"I found these rocks and only I can see things when I look through them. I had Paul try and he didn't see anything." Tatiana handed the small stones to her dad.

"Hmmm, when there is light in the morning, we will look through them together. Right now, it is too dark and I would like to hold on to them, so they won't bug you while you sleep."

"Yes daddy." Tatiana got up and sat on her dad's knee for a while and sipped some hot chocolate her mom brought in.

Brenda M. Hokenson

Iris spoke after returning with her own drink. "You two are secretive today."

"No, Mom. Just relaxing and collecting things and taking notes."

"Oh, I see. Can I read your notes?"

"No, I have a mystery to solve in them first, and then you can."

"Ok. It is almost bedtime. But I see you already put your PJs on."

"Uh huh. Well, that's it for me I need to get some sleep." Tatiana ran to her comfy sleeping area and was out like a light.

Edwina and Paul toasted marshmallows for a while and turned in. Myron dowsed the fire and buried it to be safe.

Iris caught Myron by the arm. "What is going on with Tat?"

"Nothing."

"Liar. I can read you; you know."

"So, read all you want, she is only collecting rocks and shells. She hasn't brought anything major to me."

"Well, would you tell me if she did?"

"Well, you can read people so you should know."

Myron got free of Iris' grip and climbed into his bag and was out. Iris paced for a bit, and then went to sleep.

The entire family slept well past dawn. Tatiana was the first up and out the door. She took notes on the forest, where they camped and also on the beach. She decided that she would compare visions through the rocks at the two locations. Silently, Tatiana entered the tent and tried to retrieve the three rocks. Her dad grabbed her hand and slowly got up. He held his finger over his lips so Tat would not make a sound. They both exited the tent.

"Ok, come on, we need to get far away from tent, as your mom is suspicious."

Tatiana nodded and followed Myron along the tree line so as to not disturb the sand.

"Ok, this should be good here." Myron sat down on a rather large rock.

"Ok, here is my notebook. Now read it then I want to see if you see what I did when you look in them."

Myron read the journal and then he said, "Ok, I will start with the orange one." As Myron gazed into the stone something moved in the trees. "Well, let me see what that is first. Ah, only a rabbit." He looked in the rock again. "Sorry that one shows me nothing, and I am pretty sure I will have the same result with the others." He examined the small rocks to see I they were marked and found nothing.

"Well, am I crazy?"

"No, you are not, but you must not worry about it. You are seeing a real place, a real battle and a real being. This means you were meant to find the stones and in time you will get more knowledge that will make sense."

"Ok, Dad. I wonder if you would carve a small box for them."

"Sure thing, in fact let's find a piece of wood."

Together they gathered firewood and Tatiana found the perfect piece to carve the box from. They went back to camp and built a fire and started to prepare breakfast. After everything was almost ready, Tatiana was given the 'all clear' to wake everyone up.

Food was devoured quickly and while Iris and Tatiana cleaned up, Myron whittled on the piece of wood collected from the short hike. After everything was put up, the family packed light lunches and water for their hike up to the top of the bluff. The day long trip was uneventful.

Tatiana had taken notes on the plants, animals, rock formations and the small meandering brook. It fell from a gentle slope to the beach below where grass had grown along it with some trees and shrubs. She reflected for a minute.

"What's on your mind, dear?" Iris asked as she set the blanket down for their picnic.

"The view down there, it reminds me of our last vacation in the mountains. That's all. I remember the waterfall that Paul wouldn't let me go to get a better look."

"Ah, I see. Is that all you remember?"

"No. I had some friends there to play with, but they live in our neighborhood and I still play with them. I have a bunch of pictures I drew and am ready to put them on big paper so I might paint them. Then there was a tournament that you guys had to go to and we all looked so silly in dresses and funny pants. The food was awesome."

"Ok, ok. I will stop digging. Come eat lunch." The two sat down to eat as the rest caught up.

All had a nap under the canopy of intermingled conifers and deciduous trees. A brisk wind stirred Edwina. "Hey, we need to get down the bluff!"

"Huh, what?" Myron stirred. "A storm! Let's get back down quickly, but safely."

The picnic area was hastily packed, and all ran down the gentle slope. A light rain began to fall. Swirling low clouds encircled the top of the bluff. At the campsite, it had not begun to rain yet. Everything was packed into the "changing tent and it was given more stabilizing lines and a tarp. The family also secured a tarp over their tent and added more stabilizing lines.

"At least we are in the woods enough that the winds aren't as bad." Paul said as he sat down on his bag.

"That is true. And at least we didn't get to pack soaked items in the other tents." Edwina added with a grin.

A bit later, the winds picked up more and the rain poured down seemingly in buckets. The limbs swayed and the ocean crashed upon the shore. Tatiana fell asleep waiting for the rain to let up. Edwina followed Tat's lead and was out. Paul stirred, jotting notes down in a journal.

"What's this?" Myron said as he watched Paul write.

"Well, nothing else to do. So, I am following Tatiana's example and write down stuff, so I can remember it and figure out the meaning later." After an hour, Paul was tired and dropped the journal and pen as he tilted to the side onto his pillow.

Myron and Iris also took a nap, recounting events of their late autumn trip as they drifted off. Myron woke brief and turned on the emergency radio that had weather information for their location.

"Weather for Clamshoe and vicinity. A cyclone has moved into Clamshoe Bay and is expected to intensify overnight. If you are camping, please take shelter in a solid structure immediately. Coastal zones are expecting 20-30 foot waves. Heavy rain continuing through the night and next 3 days. – Repeat—Clamshoe Bay cyclone has moved into the vicinity. Expect torrential rain and wave cresting at 20-30 feet. This will continue through the next 3 days. Please take shelter immediately."

Myron turned the radio off and while his family slept, he asked for aid from his dad. Zanor obliged and helped dry the gear through a spell cast and the changing tent with everything self-packed how it was when they arrived.

"Ok, son. I have a small bubble over your area right now – though Tat would do better at this. It looks like a rainbow, so say to them, and "Come see the rainbow and we can load really fast! Did Tat find something of interest that may cause this?"

"I don't know – 3 rocks and she can see someone in one of them, a place in another and a battle in the third. I told her not to be concerned and that in time it will all make sense. She doesn't remember being in Kluanaria."

"Well, that is good then, it explains this very bad storm. It will cease soon, at least, I think, Malos will be informed." With that Zanor hugged his son and created a portal.

"Thanks Dad." Myron said as his father walked through the portal.

"Ok, guys. Wake up fast! We only have a small break in the weather to get this tent packed up!"

Quickly, the bags were rolled, the pillows placed, and the tent taken down. Everyone admired the rainbow that was above them and then as it dissipated, the torrential rain began again. The family quickly jumped into the burbie and Myron drove out of the low land camp area.

"Well, we can stay at the cabins over the next ridge. It will be less of a storm there. What do you guys think?" Myron asked as he considered options.

Unanimously all agreed to the cabins. It was a short 2-hour drive, normally, but in the downpour took 4. The family got out of the burbie and unpacked it quickly as the vehicle was parked tailgate to entrance. There, they watched it pour.

Tatiana felt strange. She ran to the window only to see a wisp of a figure looking in at her. The figure kept repeating the same exact motions. Tatiana decided that maybe if she copied it, it would talk to her. As the wisp brought his arms from his side to straight above his head, Tat repeated. Then the arms slowly went out in a V like shape, followed by dropping the elbows inward toward their bodies, finally with arms returned to their sides.

"What the hell?" Myron jumped up and ran to the window. How the hell?"

"What is this hell business?" Iris said as she ran to the window.

"Duh, the rain is stopped. Not a cloud in the sky. Earth to parents..." Edwina piped in sarcastically.

Paul had been watching Tatiana the whole time. "How did you do that?"

"Don't know, I saw something doing it outside so I thought I would copy it and maybe it would talk to me."

"That is very dangerous, Tat! Is the thing still there?"

"Nope, but he said I would see him soon enough and to not worry about my three rocks."

"Well then, that is good. But don't be messing with that stuff now."

"What stuff?"

"The wave the arms in the air to change weather thing you did." Paul threw her over his shoulder and went to the window where his parents were still staring in amazement.

"Anyway…" Iris paused a moment, "I say stay here just in case and we have more trails and can go to the beach quick enough from here."

"That's fine, dear. I don't really want to pack again." Myron sat in front of the fire and fell asleep.

"May we explore in here, mom? It is kind of large and there is lots to see." Tatiana asked as she hugged her mom.

"Of course, but don't break anything."

The three kids took off up the stairs. Each went a different direction. All had a notebook and pen, just in case.

Edwina ended up in a room with a nice library setting in front of the bed area. She decided it would be perfect for her. She browsed through some books and found some old papers on the small side table. One had her name on it.

"Edwina, if you are reading this, do not be alarmed. I am your grandmother (Myron's mom) and would like to help you to become stronger in your studies. I have devised a way to teach you, but it must not be discovered."

As Edwina read the note, she became more curious. She decided to write back and see what happens.

Paul found a cozy room for himself, putting things away and after that, lounging.

"Paul, where are you?" Tatiana yelled down the long hallway.

"Well, I was going to rest for a bit."

"Oh no. Not now. I found something. Something that I can't lift, but it has our family name on it."

Curiosity peaked and Paul went with Tatiana down the hall to a great library. It was full of many ancient books, old armor, weapons, and a gazing ball and in the center a large desk. On the desk sat a leather-bound book with an inscription.

Paul carefully opened the cover. He immediately recognized the names of family members at Kluanaria and his parents. "Well let's see here. This book belongs to the family Tat. It looks to be a book of guidance. These here look to be symbols of different things the "Old" family used to do.

"Ooooo. Well, I see it as some sort of old history book."

"Nah, this sort of tells what each family member did. It shows a battle and some stuff about the line of the High Lord that hasn't been fulfilled. I wonder if it has by now. I suppose.

"Hey, Paul. Do you think these lines are for mom and dad? It talks about people kinda like them and they have three kids like mom and dad."

"Hmm. 'let it be known in our hour of darkness, the middle son, ceased to be. His father disowned him as he chose the path of corruption and villainy. The Eldest, a great Paladin for the Truncheon, will make his way to far-off lands in order to bring ease to his younger brother and the other Orders' families that had been sent away for safety as the new members were kept secret.' Wow. That's not mom and dad but it's in our book.

"Here it lists the symbols and what Order it represents."

Myron, thinking it too quiet, decided to go up the stairs. He saw the gathering in the library and joined Paul and Tatiana.

"Anything interesting kids?"

"Yes." Paul stated as he closed the book. "This is our family history, right? I mean, well it is history?"

"Yes and yes, son." Myron opened the book and read the first few pages. "Hmm. I had no idea."

"Daddy, who is the great Paladin? Is that you?" Tatiana stared at her father with a curious look on her face.

"Ummm, well. No. This isn't our family. It is very curious though."

DECISIONS TO BE MADE

Tatiana had crossed her arms and spoke quite sternly. "Well, I think it is. Because I have strange dreams of places I seem to know that aren't in Colorado with us. In fact, I know it is, because something says deep inside me, Daddy."

"Fine, I will read this book later to see what I can determine from it."

That evening, after supper, a bright light appeared in the main room where everyone was gathered. A portal had opened and five people emerged.

"Greetings, Father!" Myron said as he moved toward his company.

Tatiana jumped to her feet. "I know them all! I know them all! I saw them in a rock!"

Lucien was struck by her statement. "You are truly a gifted child if you can see in to a rock. Please come with me." He motioned for Malos to go as well. He chose a study for a conference room. "So let me see these rocks of yours, Tatiana."

"Not until I know who you are and what you want with them. You see, I have a crazy uncle who disappeared, and I think he is evil, but no one listens."

"I am also your Uncle. I am the oldest. Your dad is the youngest. I too can see in rocks."

"Malos is this true?"

"Yes, Tatiana and Menosh have said it will be ok to share what you know with Lucien."

Tatiana brushed her foot across the floor and held her hand out, "These are the rocks. I guess you can have them."

The Kluanarians

"Oh, no. I don't need to have them; I want you to look into them while I am looking in mine. I want to compare what you see with what I see."

"Well, umm…Let's get comfy first. I like to sit upstairs with my animals and relax – that is where I feel safest." Tatiana pointed at the room she was using for her bedroom. She extended her hand to Lucien and Malos. Both followed her and sat amongst the stuffed animals on the floor.

After ten minutes, Tatiana took a deep breath and focused on the green rock from her pouch. "I see someone. I think it is Menosh." The image faded and a different person was in it. "That's him! That is my uncle! He vanished in some sort of black cloud or something when we were at a thingy for Dad. He is with someone. She seems quite …." Tatiana was silent.

"Ok, I see this too. See my rocks are the same as yours." Lucien held out his rocks for her to examine.

"Yes, but that lady – she is killing things." Tatiana was quite upset.

"Ok, let's try the pale yellow one now." Lucien picked her up and sat her on the bed.

"Hmmm. I see a castle, some horses, and a couple old people. Just like before."

"Yes. Yes, I see that too. So, tell me what is in the orange one, Tatiana?"

"A great battle. It looks like that lady is gonna take over a little place in the mountains."

"Are you sure, Tatiana?" Malos looked disturbed. He began pacing.

"Don't worry Malos, we can see this, they can't. That will be addressed."

A flash occurred in the room.

"Tatiana, I presume." A lady wearing silvery robes and caring a rather large staff stepped from the light.

"You are Impresaria?"

"Yes, I am. It is time you learn what you are seeing. You have been given several gifts, to what purpose I know and you will learn. Menosh will instruct you on the Interval ways. Your sprite will be with you from now on, as she is powerful on her own and you will need her soon. The rocks are clues. The clues guide us when we are lost. Right now you are not lost, but you have the ability to see things in them that is the future, current times and people's actions. I believe you can see your uncle because he allowed you to explore who you were while at the High Lord's keep. I believe he bonded with you as you asked many questions and he still cares, but wants to rule without limits. Malos is here to help you start to interpret reading the weather. It carries vital information, which is about the only thing I cannot have."

Lucien approached. "Don't scare her, she is young." He took Impresaria's hand and knelt.

"I understand." Impresaria picked up Tatiana, now don't worry, for all who know or know of you will protect you."

Malos stood in the doorway watching Iris pace. He shook his head and turned inward again as the Morket continued.

"Why did my uncle kneel before you?"

"Your family rules the people of the land; I rule the Orders and have dominion over all major decisions."

"What she means," Malos added, "is that she is basically the highest of all beings, and her equal is your mentor, Menosh. They work together to maintain this very special balance of our world and in a way of your planet that your parents went into hiding on."

"So, Impresaria, you are like a Super Queen?"

Lucien interrupted. "Let's say she is in charge and when she is with us, it means there is something important that must be done."

"Ok. So then what do these things mean in these rocks?"

"The rocks provided insight. Most of it is future and some it may be memories. The battle has yet to pass; the lady killing things is current. The people, in the other rock seem to be present mixed with some memories that aren't very old." Impresaria paused briefly and looked at the girl. "Now don't be frightened.

A great ball of blue energy filled the room and dispersed as quickly as it appeared,

"Ah, I see my young protégé has already had the pleasure of meeting you, my lady." Menosh appeared as the energy dissipated. "Tatiana. Dear child. I told you to not worry about these things. Now it has been determined that you have a gift of sight, as Lucien, so that part must be protected at all costs. Thanias will try and gain this knowledge if he knows about it."

Tatiana raced forward as Menosh was speaking and hugged him. "He kinda let me wander through the Great Hall and didn't bother to remove me from the "E" room. He sort of had this funny grin on his face like he knew I should be there."

"The "E" room can only be accessed by Intervals. He knows this and that is why you must not go seeking things that you are not ready for, child. Impresaria will have a Morket escort that will follow you everywhere and my escort will continue to follow you."

"Malos is my "E" escort?"

Malos approached. "Technically yes, but I am too obvious so your sprite will be doing this, and the nymph will represent Morket." He turned to Lucien and the others, "I have an idea, but it will need the vote of Council to accomplish this task."

"Iris, Myron, and Zanor, please enter the room." Impresaria spoke to them telepathically.

Malos began. "It has been many years since such a request has been made. Perhaps since the Battle of Edziza, but I believe now is the time to unite the Orders, well those who are soured by the actions of Thanias and some of the Fraeloch. It is time the new members learn from each others' mentors and grow together in knowledge to face this very terrible threat."

Menosh and Impresaria spoke off to the side and finally agreed.

"We will ask the Orders to arrive here by nightfall so we may start this process at once. Do we recall much of the Fraeloch, Impresaria?" Menosh inquired.

"They follow an ancient way, perhaps as old as time, Menosh. I do not know who is in power and driving them, other than Thanias."

"Excuse me." Tatiana raced into them. "The lady, in my rock is in charge of them."

"Show me this vision, please." Menosh and Impresaria said at the same time.

Tatiana removed the rock from Lucien's had and smiled. "Here we go!"

The image sharpened and all in the room could now see the image. Many subjects lay upon the ground with Thanias and a mysterious person inflicting death and destruction across the torn land. Great demons, vile scourges, and undeath appeared to be winning.

"Focus on the lady, Tatiana." Lucien requested as he too focused. "I know her. She, I thought, was a shaepling, but it appears I was deceived. Her name, when I met her in passing at least, was Llylandra. There is a distant realm, North and East of Burwash called Nagazthastar. It is said to be a haunted, tormented land and the people are few and far between." Lucien paced as he continued while Orders were arriving. "Shaeplings are a forest imp or at least I had thought, but I believe this woman can transmute into just about whatever she wants."

"Shaeplings are restricted in their movements across the land due to a treaty that Menosh and I signed on behalf of Shadowblyts, Izmaa, and Seekers. They entered adjacent lands willingly to cause ruin to the cultures and try to prevent knowledge from growing. It is possible that this shaepling is truly a Fraeloch and has unimaginable power to wield."

"What twisted Thanias' mind, my Lord Zanor?" Guilles inquired as he sat down at the large table in the room.

"I am uncertain at this time, but I do know all Orders will be here shortly for a decision, that will direct all of our futures."

For the next hour all the divisions of reality, at least the reality of Kluanaria, arrived. The High Lord presided as always and the elders, Menosh and Impresaria, explained in detail of the many things transpiring across their world.

Rynylla was first to speak. "We all must unite, as we have in the past, to squelch this major influx of violence. The Chrinthold are prepared. I say our new members should be located together, somewhere safe and unseen from those that wish to stop us."

"Agreed!" Rithmas and Guilles chimed in. Rithmas continued. "It is in our best interest to pick a place that Thanias and this Llylandra have not seen or cannot see with the gift. We are able to mask this until the fledging members are trained and have learned under the direct guidance of Menosh and Impresaria."

"Malos will remain present with the Newlings. He is very capable on teaching all of their basics. I will expect Orders to send their most skilled to prepare them. I will decide the pace of the rotations, as Malos sees fit. Zanor, I believe that your son and daughter-in-law have such a location already?" Impresaria spoke as she examined the crowded home's current occupants.

"Aye. Myron and Iris have a nice quiet place in mind. A village, not too big, but it has its quirks."

"Alright. Enough. My children will not take part in this!" Iris was quite enraged. "Be in the village, but mind you, I am not supportive of disrupting all of our children's lives because you all have grown too lazy over time."

"You are one to speak, woman. You left your place in Trembir to hide. Hide from the bitter truth. The Stars Order is failing because you chose not to ascend." Lunacerian spoke for the first time. "I should have your powers revoked by the Aantiri, but he is your father-in-law."

Kira stepped forward. "It is for the good of Kluanaria that we do this Iris. Everyone who agrees, please signal me." She tallied the illuminations as folk agreed. "Very well, it is decided. All will participate. The children, under 'protection' will not recall this meeting or anything prior until they are each of age or responsible enough, as Malos will dictate. As they age, they will start to remember. I am placing this protection on each new member of each Order and there is no way to break it once it is in place, except by me. Once the family passes into this realm, called Earth, they will be expected to be normal. Training will be conducted at Malos' discretion. So when each of you is ready, with your new member and his/her family, you will escort them through the portal opened by the Moons and Aantiri. The star has chosen to ignore us right now, so it is up to Myron to lead you there."

"The portal, please, Kira and Zanor." Myron said politely. The families were already present at the vacation home so timing was perfect. "I have given you each a key to a home, if you chose not to accept it last go-round... We are on the outskirts of town, sort of the last street on the edge, which is good. We can maintain close contact. All of your belongings have been placed in the homes as you receive this key. But you already know that, as it is common here. Earth is different. They don't understand balance and how everything needs to be synchronous. We will meet after everyone is settled and discuss matters as they arise. Now, please step through and welcome to Earth!" He smiled as his friends walked through the portal, no longer feeling so alone."

"Are you certain the spell will last, Kira?" Guilles inquired.

"Aye, as sure as I am that Truncheons smell." She winked at her son. "I am teasing you know. It is from all that laundry from when you were young and training."

"I know mother. Please, keep father healthy. I worry. I realize Lucien is near, but he needs monitored." With that Myron stepped through the portal. "Is this everyone, this time?"

Impresaria responded, "There is one missing still, but that will be later. All are with you on this final journey to the twin planet." As she finished her sentence, she saw Myron nod as the portal closed.

Myron held a quick meeting. "Sorry for the hasty departure from Clamshoe Bay. It is part of the Earthen world, but we needed to move quickly before Thanias or worse locate us. Here are the keys as promised. Ah, I see we have some additional members that are present. Welcome all. We will have a great celebration later this week. Here, they call it a block party. Anyway, let me show you to your homes."

Tatiana had run ahead with the children and the teens lingered, sizing each other up. The adults followed Myron and Iris. A familiar sight appeared as they approached the last bungalow. Menosh along with Malos.

"Myron, Mithdrool is awakened. Rynn was captured to do this. Rynylla and I will not be able to guise the older children much longer. I believe Thanias to be involved. They were good friends. High Lord Beryth seeks our council." Menosh said as he greeted the families.

"We must leave at once." Myron spoke as he held his wife's elbow.

"Malos, remain behind, with me, to prepare the older children." Iris said as she straightened her posture.

"The Star of Trembir has returned." Myron smiled and embraced Iris. "Portal please, dear."

BERYTH'S COUNSEL

As the portal closed behind them, Menosh and Myron found themselves in a cavern. A small stream flowed near the well-worn path. Light was brilliant, and no clouds. Wryn approached the two, staff in hand.

"I see you found your way, gentlemen." Wryn said as he bowed to Menosh. "My father awaits."

Do you know the reason for this meeting, other than Rynn being missing?" Myron inquired.

"It is worse than that. The Phallas Minor creatures are what we assumed were Shaeplings all this time. Llylandra is not one of them but is trying to sway the Shadowblyts to join her. There, however, is a slight issue with that."

"Oh, really?" Menosh looked quizzically.

"Yes, it seems that the heir to the throne is missing, along with the Izmaa Order's Newling."

"What a pity. I guess Llylandra will have to surrender peacefully." Myron huffed.

"No, the storm at Clamshoe Bay was a sign. Mithdrool is awakened. Weak, but awakened. The darkness is slowly spreading. Though we here in the cavern are uncertain of how the darkness failed in Clamshoe."

"Ah, that." Myron rubbed his chin. "Tatiana happened to Clamshoe. But I thought she is Interval not Druid."

Menosh spoke as they approached Beryth. "Lord Beryth, greetings. We have news for you and I hear you have some for us?"

"Yes, dear friend. It has been many long years since you were amongst us."

"Tatiana is an Interval. I want to make myself quite clear. Intervals are druids. There is no getting around this. Malificence has said that Luly and her children can train her. I think Luly would be a good place to start. I would also like to see Rithmas and Guilles agree to have their Newlings be trained alongside her. Those three hold the key and I have a feeling that Edwina will fail."

Rithmas and Guilles arrived shortly after tea. They were brought up to speed concerning Llylandra and Thanias.

"There is much in motion, Myron. Where is the High King?" Rithmas asked pointedly.

"He is trying to reach Lucien and Impresaria. I am hoping they will join us here."

"Can we stand as one, for once?" Guilles pondered aloud.

"Yes, we can." Impresaria's voice carried softly through the air. "Harold and Malificence will join us later. I am not well and am asking too much of all of you. I do not have the power to defeat them."

Lucien took her hand and helped her into a chair. "Myron, she is with child. Where is Paul?"

"What do you need with Paul?"

"Impresaria is going to mold him. His 'mark' fades and changes. His Order is not known. That is a tremendous advantage to us since, well since Malificence is a Morket."

Confusion filled the room. Menosh enlightened all. "I will tell you about Edziza now. Please pay attention."

The Battle of Edziza took place in Mercurian. Edziza is a mountain to Mercurian's west. During this conflict, Shadowblyts were amazingly powerful. Somehow, a mysterious energy was tapped by them. Their forces received aide from shades, Mithdroolean forces that had fought at Nagazthastar not more than a year prior, and Shaeplings.

Rynylla was the strongest in all of the Orders. Being Chrinthold, she was able to contain the darkness, however she unable to stop the siege. Our Morket, Impresaria, was able to remove powers from the Shaeplings. Harold, being who he is, had to stay out of the conflict as he would have had to be on both sides. William sought aide from his Titans, who were divided about whom to support. Lady Phallas and Beryth banished shades as best they could. This is the time that Iris truly ran away. I believe she saw or heard Thanias plotting a most horrific future for the lands. He chased her for months. Finally, the Star was able to escape in plain sight, with Myron.

The fight was even, both losing thousands. A Druid, the name escapes me now, but none the less, a Druid, er Interval, found the feldstar. This rock was the source of the power wielded by the Shadowblyts. It came from Phallas Minor with the Shaeplings. It was crushed in a special ceremony that only a Druid, er Interval, can perform. As the battle raged for four years, this druid developed a ritual to destroy the feldstar. Once destroyed, the Shadowblyts were humbled, humiliated and mocked.

Resentment remains amongst Shadowblyts, shades, and Mithdroolean forces. Now Thanias throws his name into their hat, along with this Llylandra and her necromancers and the Shaeplings. I feel the Shadowblyts will join us in halting this war that will destroy the twin planets.

As I am certain you all are aware, the comet has passed. Impresaria and Lucien will wed before winter. Mithdrool has returned, at the expense of our Rynn. Darkness has risen and we need the Order's Newlings to transcend and fulfill the most important work of maintaining balance. Tatiana must become an Interval.

As the days of autumn dwindled, the fledgling members of the Orders played in the vast meadow that surrounded the village Myron set up upon their arrival with the families. Parents were taking on challenging roles in the workforce and also in keeping alive tradition.

The village was an actual addition to the town of Weelin. Weelin consisted of about 800 residents. The town was set up in a wheel design. At the center was the city hall, two banks, a small market selling only what the villagers produced, and a small bookstore next door to the local library across the fountain in the town's center from the pub. All the houses were small, no larger than two stories with large lawns with room enough for games of fantasy.

MITHDROOL MANOR

"WELCOME BACK, THANIAS." LLYLANDRA SAID as she walked around the circular pool of silver water. "I see you have done well in forcing the Orders to point out their new members. That was very clever." She smirked as they walked toward a dining hall in Mithdrool Manor.

Thanias looked about, studying the lavish style the deceased warlock had used in his domicile. "Llylandra, what is our plan? Do we need to find the feldstar? Is Rynn dead as well?"

"Why does she concern you? She is a nobody, as far as your destiny is concerned. We must return to the citadel I abandoned, intentionally for it to be overran by the Mithdroolean Legion. The Fraelochs that were there were too weak to be a part of my grand scheme." Llylandra paused briefly as food was placed in front of her and those at her table. "You see, Fraelochs are not an Order, per se, but a race, just as humans, elves, dwarves, and titans are. There are some that found light in everything as they interacted with other races. The remainder stayed secluded and untrusting. Those ones, I bent to the dark, as the Orders see it. I wanted Mithdrool to capture the citadel. He has ways of unlocking what is hidden. No doubt you found some of what is hidden."

"I did, well Rynn sort of did. She said it called to her but she could only see some of what was there, as the room was enchanted and could sense the presence of darkness."

"We must return there. There should be another way to attain what we need. Tomorrow, at first light, we will journey to the citadel, with some help."

118

The Kluanarians

"You were able to raise Mithdrool?"

"Yes. He was more or less in a deep sleep for the priest damaged him severely during the siege. There is a medicine house that will have what I require to heal him fully. Everyone at this table will be at the silver pool at first light. Am I clear?"

"Yes, ma'am. Will Thanias know what to look for?" A titan asked as he ate his meal.

"Yes. I will be with him and a Mithdroolean mage will help, right Jaetoth?"

Jaetoth stood, "Yes, Llylandra. We will restore Mithdrool. I should have everything necessary to open that which is closed to darkness. Wryn will pay!" He smiled and raised his goblet to the head of the table. "For Mithdrool and our victory!"

All toasted and after diner retired to their quarters.

Thanias paced about a study and found Llylandra watching from the door. "I am thinking we need to strike Impresaria soon. She has held the peace of this land for too long. It is in need of new masters."

"Surely you realize that the Fraelochs who 'got away' are in constant communication with her? Your friend, Rynn, lived under theit guardianship, if you recall. She is now with her family and in the company of lesser Fraelochs."

"She can be swayed?"

"No, idiot! You led her to the citadel, not intentionally, albeit, but it awakened her. She will never trust you again."

"She has no special gifts. She is just an archer and good fighter."

"She is the druid everyone has been looking for. She can stop the whole thing, before it starts. This family of yours may have Orders not seen in millennia, but the druid is in ultimate power and doesn't realize it. Now go to bed, tomorrow will be enlightening." Llylandra left Thanias to his thoughts and retired for the night.

Morning arrived sooner than Thanias had hoped. He ate in the kitchen and walked slowly to the silver pool. Jaetoth walked with him. They studied each other for a bit as they walked.

"So, what do you think about this citadel, Thanias?"

"It should be rather easy. I know where these buttons are in the chapel, so maybe you can operate them?"

"I will try. It has been a while since I was in the chapel. Mithdrool's dark spells could not penetrate it. That is when Lady Phallas damaged him. She should have died, but somehow, she was able to live and take out 6 of our best Legion and escape. I hope she is there; I will kill her."

"I don't think they will return, Jaetoth."

"Rynn must have found something that caused her to leave like she did."

"No, she gave me a parchment she found." Thanias handed it to Jaetoth.

"She only gave you part of it. Wryn writes forever. It was horrible to be in class with him. She gave you enough to keep you looking."

"Darn. But all is not lost, for while she was studying some scrolls, I took this." Thanias handed over a short tome that had to be translated.

"This is mage work, most definitely. Wryn was stupid. This is how to get the tome. So we now have free access to everything, maybe even their sanctuary. I will examine this, if that is ok."

"Very well. We have some hours before we depart."

REALITY RETURNS

Tatiana raced up the stairs to her sister's room. She wanted answers. Edwina wasn't home from school yet. So Tatiana made herself at home in the papa san chair with her latest discovery, a very old book. Her imagination raced as she browsed the old book. She was unsure of the words as they seemed to be poetry or something. It didn't read like a normal book she thought. Tatiana flipped through pages and found a few illustrations that were neat in her eyes. Some symbols were scattered throughout with no explanations. She wanted to know what they were; she wanted to solve the mystery of the book.

An hour had passed; Edwina stomped up the stairs, flung her bag on the floor and threw herself on her bed. She looked at the papa san. "Now what is it, Tat? Did you find a flower outside I need to name? Is it fairies in the attic?"

"It is an old-time book. And I don't pick flowers or imagine fairies. Can you read it to me?"

"Let's have a look, before I start my science project." Edwina carefully examined the cover and searched for a table of contents or some reference as to what it contained. "Hmmm, this is a mystery! There isn't even an author listed, sort of weird. Where did you find it?"

"Umm, in the chest buried clear in the bottom, neath a loose board?"

"The chest, mom and dad said, is to be left alone? Your chest with your baby things and such in it?"

"They aren't baby things. It is some of toys they thought I should keep. And so you know I asked if I could empty it out and use it as my headquarters for my detective agency. Mom said I could." Tatiana was very matter of fact, as she generally was. She after all was a detective.

Edwina replied, "Did you ask Mom what it is? She should know."

Tatiana looked at the ground, "No, Mom was outside in the dumb garden, besides she would be mad."

"So where did you find the book then Tat, so we can figure out how to ask about the book without being yelled at?"

"The old house behind us that Dad says has a secret."

"Why were you there? The house is falling in. Honestly Tat, you are reckless sometimes"

"I wanted to solve the mystery." She breathed in very deep and continued. "I thought if I could solve its secret then I could be a real detective, not just one who solves mysteries in my house."

"Tatiana, it is a dangerous place to be and this book is very cool, looks like some enchantments or spells. See this- it looks like a seal of some kind. Maybe it belonged to a king or something. Is Paul home yet?"

"No he has to work till 5pm today, he told me that this morning. WE are gonna go see if there is a trap door in the old house when he gets home! Do you want to go?"

"Umm, no and since when does Paul tell you his doings?"

"All the time, I am his best sister."

"Girls come downstairs for dinner, and there better not be a huge mess Tatiana!" Iris hurriedly set the table and watched as her daughters washed up. "Are you two plotting again? I can tell ya know."

"No, we were reading a book together," the girls chimed together. "Is Paul home yet?" The girls were anxious to see him.

Confused by the excitement in the girls' voices, Iris replied, "In thirty minutes or so, why?"

"He has to help me with a mystery," Tatiana was quite serious in her tone.

"Ok, but remember to pick up after yourself, please."

"Yes ma'am. Is dad home yet?"

Iris quirked her eyebrow in puzzlement, "Yes, he is finishing the grilling."

Paul walked in the door with his dad. He followed the platter to the dinner table and sat silently in thought.

The Kluanarians

"Well Paul, how was the day for you," his dad said in his deep voice. Did anything exciting happen at the library?"

"Nope, just the same ole, same ole. Mrs. Lutinskin saw Tat at the old house behind us this afternoon. She stopped me when I was walking in. I hope she is wrong," Paul shot a glance at Tatiana.

"Oh really, that is interesting." Myron glanced at Tatiana, "Is this true?"

"Yes dad, I was there. But I didn't bust the window, Tommy did. I went inside it." Tatiana squirmed.

Iris became enraged, "Young lady, what do you think you were doing? That is a very unsafe place, even for a detective. How many times have you been there? What do you do there?"

"Enough, dear! I am sure there is a good reason our detective was there." Myron walked behind his wife and rubbed her back. "It will be ok, I promise," Myron whispered.

"Umm, can we eat now, I am starving!" Paul patiently waited for an answer.

"Go ahead dig in everyone." Iris walked to the kitchen and stared out the window. I hope for her sake she didn't go digging there, she thought.

"Hey, come eat," Myron said as he gently steered his wife back to the table and seated her. He smiled and sat down.

After dinner the most unusual occurred. "Paul, you need to come with me now!" Tatiana pulled on her older brother's arm. Up the stairs they climbed and ducked into a nook at the end of the hall.

"What is it Tat? Are you in trouble? Did you break something of Mom's?" He stood blocking the nook with a stern look upon his face.

"I found something, it's in Edwina's room so you can go with me to get it or wait here."

"I'll wait, Edwina is doing her homework and I don't want to argue why I am trespassing right now."

Tatiana raced into Edwina's room and grabbed her book. Edwina was busy writing but noticed. "Don't tell Mom or Dad."

"Ok." Tatiana ran back to Paul with the book.

"See it is very plain looking, almost like the cover of a real old, old book. But it isn't a Bible or textbook. And it has some picture things and a seal." Paul answered after looking at the book.

"A seal." Paul found the seal. "Wow, this is interesting. I thought everything I was learning was made up."

"What are you learning Paul? Is it scary?"

"Never mind about me, but you were meant to find this, don't ask me how I know, I just do. Has anything weird happened to you lately?"

"Nope, just mom telling me to quit leaving the water on outside when I wasn't even out there. I was playing with Tommy and Jake and Sally. We were gonna wish for a lot of water so we could float our raft we built on the stream. That night I had a dream about floating the raft and there was lots of water, and we used the raft to save people. Then Mom woke me up and asked why I flooded the yard with the hose."

"Wow, Tat!! I think you better try not to think about anything that can change things til I figure this out."

"Ok, Paul. Hey what is that on your shoulder?" Do Mom and Dad know you got it?"

"Got what." Paul looked at his shoulder. Yes, they do."

"Let me see." After examining the shoulder, Myron walked over to a book shelf and pulled a book from it. He flipped through the pages and found what he needed. "According to this you have a Mark of the Truncheon. Hmm. But we already know you have a mark."

"Tatiana asked me to look at a book for her, and then she saw this on my shoulder."

Iris ran in to the room. "What is all the commotion, is the world ending or something broke?"

"It is worse dear." Myron showed the seal to his wife. Our son was chosen, as well as Tat." Myron stood in wonderment for a bit. "But then we already knew of Paul."

"That explains the water issue yesterday when I scolded Tat. Does she know?"

Paul replied, "No, I don't think so but what do I not know??" He examined the page his father had been looking at.

"Well, we will not tell her, she is too young and not near ready for what is asked of her. We need to focus on Paul for now." Iris hugged her son and said, "All will make sense soon, I hope. We can't teach you."

"What are you talking about Mom? It is a funky bruise or something right? I am just a kid. And right now, I am gonna go take my wheels

The Kluanarians

through the car wash before it gets dark." Paul left more confused than ever.

"Your brother can help him Myron?" Iris paced back and forth.

"We refused our Orders' insistence in staying, we chose to come here. Now we must deal with this. I don't even know if I can contact him. The Orb of Distance was to be locked away, remember?"

"Yes, but we have no choice. We can port, but I fear they may not let us leave and I don't want the kids left alone. Come on Myron, we have to do something!"

"What we can do is treat our kids as normal kids and I know you can "hide" things, can you hide this Mark? So at least it will be invisible to all but you and me. I promise to figure this out."

"No, Myron. I walked away from my Order as they were out of line in the conduct of our resolutions within the Council of Trembir. I called them out for their dissent and asked the High Master to begin an inquiry as to the true purpose of their deceit. I would not go along with it. They became greedy and wanted total dominion over all of Kluanaria. To use my powers would subject me to my return to them and I am not ready to see how horrible the place is."

"It is the only way, Iris. Maybe the Council won't notice."

"Wait, Myron. You can do this. In your book of bindings, it has how to conceal things, I read over your shoulder on occasion when you were visiting Trembir. I remember well."

"Yes, you do dear, and you know what, I think I will pull that relic out and create the concealment." Myron busied himself in gathering his supplies that had been concealed for many many years.

"We need to start working with them as best we can, so they aren't terrified. Maybe tomorrow we can sit down and talk to Paul first."

"About what, Ma? I am back now." Paul was more confused now.

"Umm, come in here and sit down. Your father and I are going to talk with you for a bit. How is school going, and the library job? How is Jane doing?"

"Enough Iris. Ok, son, you have the Mark of the Truncheon. The Truncheon is an ancient order on Kluanaria. Your mother is a Star in the Council of Trembir and I am of the Truncheon. Yes, I know truncheon is related to fighting, and I am a warrior. Your mother, heh, umm, is well… one of them know it all types we warriors call…."

"Eh hem. Myron. We are like a mage but have an all seeing gift and usually are considered "Peace bringers" as our abilities are strong and none usually challenge us. Anyway, your dad, as a warrior learned art of concealment of things, so he is going to conceal your Mark until we figure out what is happening."

Paul shrieked, "So we aren't even from here? We have just sort of taken up a plot on the ground to blend in and not be noticed. Hello, in case you forgot we do participate in athletics, so the concealment won't hold. Why didn't you say something, why are we being left in the dark? What about Edwina? You know she practices some weird juju magic with her friends. It is rather odd. How come you are not looking at that?"

"I understand." Myron prepared a concoction that would deem the Mark invisible. He then smeared it on Paul's shoulder. A short incantation was said that Paul did not understand, and the Mark was gone! "There and no, it won't wash off. I have to remove the spell to remove invisibility. So just be normal and I will find a way to contact my brother, who is a Paladin. Get some sleep, tomorrow we will be busy."

"Good night son, please don't speak of this to your sisters until we figure out Edwina."

Iris tossed and turned; Myron held her still against the bed and comforted her as best he could. "Iris, don't worry. It is because we are needed. We are on this planet because you chose to abandon your order. I am your protector and will not let anything happen to you or our children. I will seek out my brother tomorrow, Paul will go with me."

"Yes dear, I am just terrified for them. I should never have left; I should not have come here to this planet which endangers them." Iris drifted to sleep.

THE MOON

A LOUD SHRIEKING SEEMED TO RACE up the stairs toward Edwina's room. It was accompanied by a shadow. Edwina awoke. She realized the attack. She grabbed a staff she had carved from an oak branch and had enchanted. She recited several phrases in Kluanarian. A great beam of light shot from the staff and struck the shadow. Myron raced up the stairs with sword in hand.

"What the hell! Edwina, get behind me and fetch your mother."

"No father, I can kill it." As her father fended the being off, Edwina focused inward and closed her eyes. She recited another incantation and raised her hand toward the shadow. The shadow hissed and struck at her, but as the creature's claws reached her, it imploded, and the battle was over.

"Where did you learn that? Where did you learn that language?" Myron dragged her downstairs. "Iris!"

"I have a book dad. I found it in a drawer at Grandma's house."

"When, we never went there. She lives very far away." Iris said.

"You mean not on this planet don't you Mom?"

"Yes. She lives on Kluanaria, and she gave you this book I assume?"

"Yes Mom. She said it was important that I have it. I don't know how I got there to see her though. She said something bad was developing and a great evil was awakening. I saw her I thought – in my dream, but when I woke up the book was with me and she said to tell you to open a portal for all of us."

"Edwina, do you have a mark, a symbol, or something you can't explain?" Iris frantically searched her daughter's head, neck and shoulder.

"There it is! Myron, bring the book." With some digging its meaning was discovered. "Oh no, not you too!"

Myron checked the book and looked at Edwina's forehead. There was a small symbol that glowed faintly when Edwina was fighting the creature, Myron verified the match in the book. "It is for the Moons. You will be in danger until we get you home, to Kluanaria."

Iris in disbelief, "It can't be. Do you know what that means?"

"Yes dear, now everyone go to bed and we will deal with this in the morning." Myron hugged Edwina and said what a great warrior she would make. Iris thought no, a caster. "Good night."

Iris curled up next to Myron, "Why now, why us?"

"We left; it was meant to be. Now please sleep, tomorrow you need to open that portal or it will get bad here." He braced Iris against him and brushed her hair until she drifted to sleep.

Myron was always up at 4am. He never varied from his routine. He got up after a couple hours sleep to find an individual seated in the kitchen.

"Myron, it is good to see you."

"Likewise, Truance, likewise. Tell me, why you couldn't wait a couple hours, I do so enjoy a couple hours peace before everyone else gets up."

Truance adjusted herself in the plush chair. "The girl needs help, the boy needs your brother, and your youngest is ready, believe it or not Myron. I am here to serve as an escort to Kluanaria; your brother will be here in an hour. Is the boy ready?"

"As ready as he will be. Would you like some tea?"

"Please and thank you Myron."

Myron and Truance sat peaceably drinking tea as the sun rose over the garden that Iris worked so hard in. They walked through the garden and discussed the future of the children. Iris awoke and glanced out the window. She immediately recognized Truance and hurriedly dressed and ran out the door.

"Why have you come? Are you taking my children? How was your trip? Would you like…"

Iris was cut off by Myron. "Truance is fine, her trip was short, she has tea, and she is escorting all of us to Kluanaria. Lucien will be here in an hour or so.

"Oh, ok. Should I wake the children?" Iris was puzzled.

"No Iris. Let them sleep. Lucien would want them to be well rested for this endeavor. In fact, I think we will be here for a bit to prepare them and reacquaint you two with customs. And so, you know Iris, the Council of Trembir was dissolved. The Order of Stars meet as a collective monthly to discuss whatever you discuss. They wanted to make it clear to you, that you are welcome – which is what the council has decided to call the High Order –out of respect for the Elders who formed the council to deal with the evil. I was also told that Tatiana belongs to the Order of Intervals. She is highly sought after right now as is your Moon child and Protector. I sense great things will be occurring in their lives and they are to become the new Doyen of their Orders."

Iris and Myron sat in disbelief. They spoke quietly with Truance so as to not awaken the kids.

"How is Lucien, Truance?" Iris was poking to see if there was still resentment.

"He is well. He has trained and replaced many commanders who were – as he would say- gutless swines who manipulated their regions. He is looking forward to seeing Myron. You know he is to marry Impresaria in a couple moons?"

Silence fell again as the tea was refilled and Iris prepared a breakfast befitting royalty. Myron set the table for seven as he knew Lucien would arrive shortly.

Myron watched as a stately man walked to the door and entered. "Welcome, Lucien! I am glad to see you. My son is in need of you and your Order. The girls have no memory of Kluanaria so it might be difficult."

"Thank you, brother. Tell me again, why this miserable planet? I assume Paul is well. Did he discover his Mark?

"Yes, and he is very confused." Iris stated as she plated food for the four present.

"You chose to run away Iris- you created the confusion." Lucien glared at her.

"I was not going to be with an Order that was self-destructing. There was no other choice."

Lucien said, "There is always a choice, Thanias offered you everything. You would have been his wife and would probably be our enemy as it turns out now. But at least you were somewhat intelligent and went with Myron."

Brenda M. Hokenson

Tatiana came down the stairs. "Good morning, Tat. Did you sleep well?"

"Yes mom." Tatiana hugged her mom and dad and looked at the two strangers. "Who are they?"

"I am Lucien, your uncle. This is Truance, a friend of our family. You must be the detective your dad was talking about earlier. He said you have solved many things."

"I have and I am trying to solve a riddle maybe you can help with Lucien," she gently pulled her uncle along behind her to her room where she had the book. "Paul said not to tell mom and dad, so I will show you what I have."

"This is a book of the Order of Intervals. This planet calls it Seasons. I believe you are to learn from this book. Let us take it with us and I will defend you should your mom and dad get mad."

"Ok, thanks Lucien." She went to her brother's room and woke him and did the same to Edwina. "This is Uncle Lucien. He is Dad's brother. Breakfast is ready and there is a very pretty lady there named, umm"

"Truance," interjected Lucien.

"Yeah, Truance... I wonder if she likes flowers." Tatiana was mumbling as the four walked down stairs and ate breakfast.

Lucien spoke as everyone was seated, "Would you like to learn about a place you have seen before?"

"What does that mean?" The children affixed their eyes to Lucien as he spoke.

"Kluanaria is a planet, kind of like this one, but is better. There are no wars there. There are very few people who are ill, and everyone has a real nice home. Everyone has a garden, like the one your mom works so hard in." He sighed and watched the kids' eyes light up. "There are two moons and many beautiful places to see. It is all protected by my Order, which is partly why I am here. You see kids, your mom needed to escape as her Order was in great turmoil. Your other uncle offered her safety, but she chose to move here with your dad. He is her protector and husband."

Lucien paused for moment to reflect and let the kids absorb all of what he has said. "I am the ruler of the Coterie of Truncheon. Truance is a friend of our family and rules over the Order of Eupepsia. She is the chief healer for all."

Tatiana was laughing hysterically. Just the notion of being from another place and then to also have parents who are some sort of leaders and an Uncle who is in charge of protecting all the people on that planet.

All eyes were fixed on her. Lucien continued, "She has a lot to take in and it is quite a lot for such a young person, especially when the Order of the Intervals needs her."

"You can't be serious, never has anyone been chosen for the Intervals, or by the Intervals, at least not in our lifetime. There has to be a mistake." Iris was in despair. "Myron, please."

Myron listened and observed as all was transpiring in front of his own eyes. He watched as his wife of 17 years broke down, he watched as his brother spoke to the children of the grand land he and his wife left in search of peace. "Iris, it will be ok. There are many, many years before the Order can use any of the kids. We will be together in our real home. Do you remember our real home? The small lake with waterfall, the wild horses…."

"Horses" inquired Tatiana and Edwina.

"Yes, horses. They roam freely and every so often you can ride one." Iris smiled as she spoke.

Truance glanced at Lucien. Truance spoke. "Yes, all will be fine at your home, your real home. Training will be provided when the children are deemed ready by the Elders of the Orders. In the meantime, we will require boarding until we feel the time is right to return."

"Agreed," Myron stated. "Make ready the guest rooms Edwina and Paul."

Edwina and Paul worked together to get the rooms ready. "What do you think about that line of crap from our "Uncle", mused Edwina?

"Well, it explains a lot, like why I remember a huge home and a huge yard and a lake from when I was eight. We moved shortly after a great storm. You were five then. And Tat, well, she was one, I think. Mom thought we would be safe here. We had to learn all about this place along with our parents. So, it has been terribly hard here and it would be…"

"Enough, Paul. I see Lucien has gotten to you. I think it is a bunch of hooey and I won't go! I will run away before that happens. I can protect myself. I did last night when that shadow thing came inside."

Paul was surprised by the statement she had made. "What are you blabbing about Edwina?"

"This loud, shrieking came from the hall last night. I opened my door and saw this shadow thing coming down the hall. It attacked me. I had crafted, from Grandma's advice, a staff and it was given a special crystal that was enchanted and placed in a bracer by Grandma. She said it would protect me and that I need a few recitations to learn and master before the third phase of five. Anyway, this thing attacked me and I used what Grandma taught me and demonstrated. It worked, I shattered it!"

"Right Ed, you have no proof."

"Dad was there doing his weird sword fighting stuff while I focused on what was taught to me."

"And I should believe this…"

"Just ask him."

"I will."

After the guest rooms were finished, the two went to the patio where the adults were talking.

"Last night Edwina saved us. A shade attacked us. I have not seen one since the Battle of Edziza. I never saw such a young person take out a shade!" Myron was both proud and discomforted by this memory.

"This is momentous. How does the girl know this advanced craft?" Truance was puzzled. "How should I say this? Either she is extremely gifted, or someone has been training her for some time."

"Impossible…" Iris interjected. "She has never gone anywhere except with us on vacation to the mountains."

Angered by the interruption Truance continued. "I am telling you from my perspective; the form is too advanced for anyone of such an age."

"Enough already, besides, we can ask Edwina right now, since she has just overheard our little discussion." Lucien motioned for the kids to enter. "Young lady it seems as you have a very special gift. Do you mind me asking how you came to master it so young?"

"Not at all!" Smiling, Edwina responded, "Grandmother would visit me, I thought in dreams. Until I found the book she gave me was physically with me when I woke up. I was at this incredible mansion like house and there was a large room and your parents, Lucien. I guess Dad's parents too. Umm she said I was very special, and something would harm me and

The Kluanarians

that she would not be able to protect me much more, so she taught me a couple things and Grandpa fashioned a staff from an oak branch I had picked out of a bunch of different types. Grandma had this bracer that a dude named Finly crafted and had this crystal socketed in the bracer. An incantation was said and the crystal seemed to grow bright and then dull. When I woke up I was at home and found all this stuff."

"Our mother did this?" Myron was furious. "Why can't she let things be, I be darned if she interferes with my children anymore."

"If your mother felt it necessary, then it was of grave importance," Truance said. "She never wastes time on unimportant things."

"And you know this how, Truance?"

"Ok, ok. So what is the big deal? Grandma saved me and all of you by teaching me this!" With that, Edwina left abruptly. "I am not going anywhere with you all. You tried to hide the true us, from us! That is what is not fair."

Lucien rubbed is chin. Iris was in shock. Truance pondered. Myron paced.

"I am still here, what about me?" Paul caused them all to stop.

"We will begin your training in the morn Paul, if it is alright with your father?"

Myron nodded in agreement.

"Then it is settled. Today will you show me about this place? I would like to explore the cultural aspects for a bit." Lucien leaned forward in anticipation of a no answer.

"Yes, Lucien, I will be honored to do so. I am just glad that I am not a psycho dude," Paul exclaimed. "How about we explore after lunch and this evening, and for a bit in the morning and then we can train after lunch?"

"Very well Paul." I will get transportation.

"No, I can drive us. I think you will like the wheels I have! I will get you after lunch. I have to find Ed before she does something dumb."

"Of course, and thank you Paul." Lucien sat down again.

"So, Tatiana, do you have questions or" Truance stopped speaking suddenly.

"Truance, Truance?" Tat yelled. "Do you see it too?"

"Yes, but I have not seen one since the Edziza battle. They are mysterious beings."

Lucien stood up and asked the creature to approach.

"I do not answer to anyone except the child."

Standing halfway between Lucien and the creature, Tat blinked. "My name is Tatiana, please, what is yours?"

"My name is Menosh; I am your mentor of the ways of Intervals. I am an Enygminite. We are few and aging. You are to be my predecessor when you are of age and prepared. I mean no harm and have protected you since birth."

"Welcome Menosh, please join us." Tatiana got a chair from the garden shed for Menosh.

"Do I need to leave with you, Menosh?"

"No, it is not time for you. But Edwina needs to be mentored soon. Her power is very strong, that is why your grandma gave her knowledge and tools."

"Is Grandma her teacher?"

"No young lass. Her mentor is Lunacerian. He trained your grandmother a very long time ago. Lunacerian does not like to waste time, so I am requesting that we expedite relocation of your family," Menosh slowly panned around and picked out Myron in the group and nodded, "whilst there is time to settle and make proper arrangements."

Tatiana left the adults to go spend time with her detective work. She started jotting notes down about the three guests in her notebook and asked Paul and Edwina questions. She was forming a theory. She drew out the symbols her siblings had.

SECOND SIEGE

IMPRESARIA PACED, IMPATIENTLY AS SHE watched as Lucien along with Menosh and Malos entered the portal. "This is late summer. The children need trained. Malos, please see to it that the Orders have sent instructors to Earth. I know for certain the guise is wearing on Myron's oldest child. They will know soon. The Moon is also beyond ready, your mother has seen to that, Lucien."

"Yes, Impresaria. We will meet at the predetermined location within 3 weeks as Orders to decide the outcome." Lucien bowed. "Please seek Beryth. It is time to protect what he has so well hidden."

"I will. Be safe. Thanias will more than likely have Mithdroolean shades seek to destroy what we are developing."

As the portal closed behind Lucien, Impesaria went to her scrying chamber and contacted Wryn. Wryn raced down the hall and found his father enjoying tea. "Impresaria needs you, father. It is most urgent."

"Very well. Find your sister and mother, I have a bad feeling about this conversation."

Wryn nodded and went to the gardens. He found both meditating with others. Rynn sensed him and nudged Lady Phallas. They rose and went to the scrying chamber where Beryth was waiting.

Wryn said "It will be easier to go there." He opened a portal and the four went through.

"Welcome all." Impresaria greeted them warmly. "Rynn, I have not seen you in several weeks. I am glad you found your family again. I do have some disturbing news."

"What has transpired, Impresaria?" Lady Phallas inquired.

Rynn spoke. "Remember my finding you? That is due to Thanias. He took me to the edge of Mithdrool Forest where a citadel stands vacant with much history. He went to meet Llylandra, the deceitful. I didn't know."

"You found my note?"

"Yes, Wryn and some other things. I fell into some kind of deep sleep, and I think Thanias had this and a book. The book was in his belt." Rynn handed the package to Beryth. "This is significant from what I heard. Llylandra called it 'feldstar'."

"Yes Rynn. And now it is home, with Impresaria. You are safe as well."

"What was on the book?" Lady Phallas inquired.

"Leather covers with a band holding it closed. It had silver and gold leaves on the band. No writing."

"Good. That one has what they think will open our gates to them."

"It was done by a mage. Any mage can unlock it!" Lady Phallas interjected.

"They don't have a mage! Llylandra hates mages." Wryn responded.

"It is not safe to be so arrogant."

"Enough, both of you!" Beryth raised his voice. "What's done is done. We must defend the citadel at all costs. It should take two days to relocate the knowledge, unless the Morket will help us?"

"Very well, we will assist. I am guessing Wryn will open a portal. We need to do this now!" Impresaria summoned twenty Morket to join them on this most important journey. "I believe they are trying to awaken Mithdrool."

The portal opened. The group was in the square when Lady Phallas defeated Mithdrool. It was a solemn scene as the siege reflected in everyone's mind. Rynylla appeared. "The dark will be here soon. We must be swift."

Wryn used one spell and all knowledge stored all over the citadel was revealed. With the help of the Morket and Rynylla, all was transported safely within three hours by portal. Impresaria created a vault for all these valued possessions in Kaprius. When all was moved, Wryn resealed the now empty hidden rooms.

"Rynylla, shall we wait and at least put up a bit of a fight?" Rynn asked in hopes of using her arrows.

"I think that is wise. We need to appear as though we haven't done anything."

Beryth went to work placing people in their locations to look as though things were being guarded. Each person was given a capsule to drop as their mock battle progressed. The capsule was automatic transport to Kaprius.

"I wish to speak with Thanias." Rynn said to her brother.

"Here is your chance." Wryn pointed at Thanias.

Rynn approached from Thanias' left. She watched until the Mithdrool followers passed. "Thanias!"

Thanias heard a whisper in his mind. He turned slowly and saw his last companion. "You are safe?" He reached out to her.

"What have you done? I don't understand. Please tell me what you have done."

"I have spoke with Llylandra. I am going to achieve my goals. Where did you go to?"

"I...I was not well. You left me by a small thing that reminded me of the past. The past I saw again as the siege went. And I remembered these words. I spoke the words and I vanished. I was somewhere, but nowhere for a long time."

"Where is the feldstar?"

"What feldstar? I have never heard or seen one. Is it magic? I have no use for this thing you are looking for Thanias. Please, come with me."

"No, Rynn. I can't. My destiny is tied to the success of this battle. Choose your side. We must raise Mithdrool and rebalance the world."

"That is not your destiny. Your destiny is to rule Burwash when your father passes. Not your brothers."

"You don't get it, do you? I want more than Burwash. I want all of Kluanaria. Llylandra can have what she wants, but I want to be in control of those who are allied with my father as well. Now get out of my way!"

Rynn tearfully stepped aside and nodded. "Then you leave me no choice, since you have broken my heart and my trust, I will bind you forever to this very citadel."

"You. You are a mere warrior who can shoot arrows and wield a short sword. You are no threat."

Rynn stood facing him with her left harm outstretched in Thanias direction. "Kanulach omminala lochcosi tyr lamanish ala zenno portiero…" she collapsed on the ground as Llylandra struck her with a weakening spell. "How could you, Thanias?" She whispered as she went unconscious.

Lady Phallas went to her aide. Wryn created a diversion. He conjured a large dragon from the storm clouds. It fended off several of the advancing Legion and then he caught a glimpse of Jaetoth. He knew this would be a most intriguing battle.

Llylandra commanded the Legion in a more ferocious manner than Mithdrool had ever done. "Leave no one alive, except the druid." She pointed at Rynn. "She is needed to raise Mithdrool!"

Thanias looked at Rynn. His heart hurt terribly after hearing this. He could hear Rynn speaking in his mind. "How dare you call yourself Truncheon, or friend! I regret knowing you, you monster. When I awaken, you best believe the Fraeloch from hell will be the first to perish. Too bad she didn't believe in all of us. And don't worry friend… You will follow soon after her." Thanias had tears in his eyes. "What have I done?" The siege came back into focus. He led Jaetoth to the chapel. He used the tome and unlocked rooms to plunder. The Legion was with him. The Morket and the group of three left using the capsules. Llylandra had taken Rynn before Lady Phallas could reach her.

"Leave her be, Llylandra," Rynylla called out.

"Or what? A noncombatant is going to stop the might of my Fraelochs and the Legion? I seriously doubt it. Now step aside." She waved her stave across her body, and it threw Rynylla several feet back. She had Rynn in an orbital that drifted behind her so as to keep from damaging the prize.

A bright light came from around Rynylla. "I belong to the Chrinthold! I have ultimate power over you and need no what did you say… help." The light burst forth knocking Llylandra to the ground and freed Rynn from the orbital. Lady Phallas grabbed her daughter and generated a protection orb about them. She healed her daughter, although the spell was quite weak because of the focus on the orb, Rynn regained consciousness.

Thanias saw this and a look of relief came to his face. However, a Legion grabbed Rynn while Lady Phallas was distracted and made it to Mithdrool Forest. Thanias followed.

Llylandra saw this act from the corner of her eye. She stood hunched over but had enough strength to raise her arms above her head and disperse

The Kluanarians

into nothing. She emerged in the chapel where Jaetoth was. "What have you found?"

"Nothing, yet. Some useless recipes, a doll, broken chair, and my favorite, firewood."

"Well, we will search all the buildings, it must be here!"

"Listen Llylandra, whatever was here is gone. Maybe there were only those few remnants here when Thanias brought the druid."

"That is possible. We will look any way! Leave nothing undisturbed." She sat in the High Seat as she waited for good news.

"My Lady," a commander approached her, "We have the druid."

"Excellent. We have all we should need to bring Mithdrool back."

"Llylandra, there is a medicine house. Please bring your knowledge there, as we are uncertain of the essence you need."

Llylandra rose and exited the chapel. Crossing the citadel she observed the busy Legion. The medicine house was small and fairly unruffled. She found a smile vile and opened it. "This is it. Let's go." She waived her hand and the entire force she brought with her vanished.

AFTERMATH

The returning Morket and Fraeloch emerged from the scrying chamber. There were some bumps and bruises, but no serious damage.

"What do we do about Rynn?" Wryn asked as he sat on a long bench in the hall. "They will use her to raise Mithdrool."

"I won't sit idly by and do nothing." Lady Phallas said. "I will stop them at all costs!"

"You can't, it is not your destiny." Impresaria motioned for the priest to sit. "The druid is the only one who can stop this."

"She is the druid." Wryn added as he began pacing. "Send word to Zanor. He is Aantiri, he will know."

"He has enough on his plate. Thanias is seeking the children of the Orders right now. He doesn't have time for this." Beryth said, taking pause to reflect on the two sieges of the citadel.

"I will stop Llylandra right now!" Wryn opened a portal, but it failed.

"I have temporarily suspended your abilities. It is important you stay here." Rynylla spoke as she entered the room. "Stay put or you will be suspended so to speak. I have sent word to Lucien and Zanor. They understand what is at stake here."

"My sister!"

"Is not the druid, Wryn. The druid still sleeps. However, they may use her to heal Mithdrool in the old manner."

DARKNESS RISEN

Llylandra found Thanias in the guest room doorway. He was observing their prisoner through the doorway. "Why do we need her? She is just an archer."

"She is the druid. We need her for the healing ceremony for Mithdrool. I have acquired the tincture from the medicine house at the citadel. If she won't willingly help us, then we will use the tincture and she will become his prize."

"Then let it be done. The warlocks are in the center hall as requested, along with Mithdrool. I shall wait for you there."

"No Thanias, you must convince the druid to heal him."

"No, she will, or I will kill her."

"You won't, you have feelings for her. But either way you will force her to participate in some manner." Llylandra left for the center hall.

"Wake up Rynn. Time has come for you to accept your fate." Thanias said as he shook her shoulder.

"Very well," she said as she slowly sat up. "Did we defeat Llylandra?"

"No, you are our guest, and you need to help us heal someone." With that Thanias led her to the center hall.

Mithdrool was seated in his throne. "Is this the druid who will heal me?" He laughed as he studied Rynn. "She is no druid!"

The warlocks cast a spell over Mithdrool and Rynn. Part of her life force left her and entered Mithdrool. It returned to her body as the incantation ended. Llylandra brought the tincture forward and placed it in Mithdrool's hand. As he consumed the vial, his powers restored. I guess I didn't need a druid, archer."

The skies all over Kluanaria grew dark. Lightning was intense and the coloring was not natural. The Orders' Powers waned briefly as they felt Mithdrool's return. Kira looked at Zanor and nodded. Signals were sent through the scrying devices that the greatest evil has returned.

The great Legion was restored and began its march across the lands as Mithdrool gave reign over the lands to Thanias as they conquer them. Llylandra and Mithdrool began plotting the course of destiny for all the people of Kluanaria.

"At last, Transcendence! I am ultimate ruler of this land!" Thanias took his army back to the now empty citadel and took place on the throne.

THE NEWLINGS

WEELIN

THE EARTH TOWN OF WEELIN sits in a meadow just near the footsteps of the Rockies in the northeast corner of Washington. It provides sanctuary for the Kluanarians who have blended in with the Earth residents well. The town has about 800 people. It is in a semi-isolated area about 100 miles from the nearest big city. This village, not an immediate tourist stop, but occasionally an influx of people for the hiking trails that are more challenging stop in for gear and supplies.

The town was set up in a wheel pattern with the center having many of the businesses located there. At the very center a 4-acre park which has many different things to do from a fishing pond to swimming pool, skating park, and the usual swings. The mayor managed to acquire a very old carousel which had been refurbished. North from the center, the first wedge held the city hall, police station, fire station, small jail, and a small court room above the city hall. The next wedge, clockwise from the civic wedge, houses an art gallery/museum, the library, and a bookstore. The third wedge contains a movie theater, theater for the arts, and studios which teach gymnastics, martial arts, and dance. The fourth wedge, called the health court as it has a 10-bed mini hospital which is home to doctors of all types and ambulatory services, veterinary clinic, dentist, optometrist, and counseling services. The fifth one is the "spiritual" wedge. In the very center, was the original chapel that was built by the pioneers in 1835. Some of the outbuildings are still intact and preserved. Three congregations share the wedge. The sixth wedge was for hospitality and supplies. There are two hotels, two strip malls, local eateries, and of course grocery and hardware stores. The seventh wedge contains the school district and the three schools (K-5, 6-9, 10-12), plus a vocational/technological school. The eighth wedge toward the center was for parking. After the main wedges end, housing begins.

The Kluanarians were in the northeastern section wedge of the wedges, almost out of the city limits. Myron had amassed a bit of money from working which he used to purchase the entire section and developed it into a style fitting to the culture of Kluanaria. He provided homes for each family that had come with them for safety. He built a "learning zone" for the children which had a riding stable, learning center for tutoring in Earthen or Kluanarian requirements, playground, plus a "no shoes" area. Zanor built a special house that everyone assumed was abandoned, intentionally, for the children to explore and learn from.

The parents worked in Weelin, for the most part, and would continue to integrate the Earth ways with their ways and keep the children focused on their ways. Some of the older kids took on after school and summer jobs because they liked the nifty gadgets sold in town. None had been around self-propelled transportation before and everyone was learning. They were also not used to having to purchase all of their supplies. It was a totally new concept.

As summer turned to fall the children of the Orders grew more accustomed to the Earth ways. It was quite different. School was "mandatory" as it was the "law". As with most kids, the ominous groaning and dragging feet to the bus became the norm. When school was out the majority would go home and race around. This was the norm, at least on Kluanaria. The children who came to Weelin with their families were very special. All got along marvelously and would re-enact battles from both Earth and Kluanaria.

Tatiana and her friends loved the "no-shoes" zone. It somehow invigorated them, and their senses were sharper as well as their thoughts. They also loved the "forbidden" house. They spent many hours exploring it and once in a while would throw rocks at the windows and watch the glass reform. She had been lectured previously for entering it with Tommy months earlier. She still snuck in. All the kids did. They found cool items that only some of them could use.

"Alright, everyone." Edwina spoke as the group met in the basement of the "forbidden" house. "I think today we will explore inch by inch to see what we can find. Tat, hand out the notebooks and mechanical pencils." Tatiana nodded and began her delivery. "I don't think this place is haunted or we would have seen or heard something by now. If you find something write it down. I got something called a camera that takes pictures, so we don't have to draw it now!" With that being said and the last notebook and pencil handed out, everyone scattered.

Tatiana and Tommy raced to the attic where they remember seeing stuff that looked important. They had Paul pull the latch in the ceiling, again, for them as they were too short. Slowly they climbed the stair which were built into the ceiling door and stepped inside. Tommy went to the left and Tatiana to the right. It was empty.

"My sister got a book at the bookstore downtown last spring. It has weird symbols in it. Some of them match what is in here." Tatiana said as she examined the frame around the window. "Looky here!" Tatiana found a circlet that had snow, rain, brightness, and leaves that turned color each of which was suspended above the circlet and rotated gradually around the circlet. The current season seemed to be suspended above the moving symbols. "What do you think?" She turned to find Tommy had gone. She left the attic and found Paul at the bottom of the stairs.

"Ok, are you done up there?"

"Yes. Look what I found! See…"

Paul nodded and the two walked back to the basement where the others were waiting.

"I can't believe you left me." Tatiana said as she walked past Tommy. "And to think, I found you first."

"You didn't find me. I was never lost to be found. I got here when you did."

"No you didn't. I always lived here."

"Tatiana, enough!" Edwina took her by the hand. "You have to be nice. He doesn't know we always lived here." She dragged her out of the abandoned house and walked her home. "Wait til Dad finds out!"

Paul smiled at Tommy. "Don't worry about that. She thinks she is a princess all the time."

Tommy nodded and smiled. "I found something…something in that

Brenda M. Hokenson

small room by the drop down for the attic." He removed a brilliant object that seemed to emanate random energy fields that each had different hues.

"That is weird. I never saw anything like that." Paul said as he looked at the other kids. "Did everyone find something?"

All of the young ones squealed yes and held out their quarry.

"Ok, then. I think we should go back to the learning zone." He let everyone go first and made sure the windows and doors were closed. A movement caught his attention. "Who's down there?" Paul abruptly spoke as the kids ran screaming out of the building.

The figure did not answer.

"I said answer me." Paul demanded as he grasped it with a dagger in hand at its neck.

"You are most unwise, Newling." The figure transformed into a very tall man.

"Whoa, how? What?" Paul stumbled back, landing on his rear with the dagger just out of his reach.

"It has been a while since I saw you last." William said. "Where is everyone gathering?"

"The 'learning zone', back toward the house a bit. You need to talk to them. They all have found something here, except me. So I am more like the babysitter, I guess."

"Young man. You are very important. Fred and I are watching over you. Soon, I will be taking you with me so you may be trained."

"What for? Why can't I be trained here?"

"This is very serious. You are going to be shaping events soon enough. Your gift is far stronger than any of the Orders' Newlings here. Let's say your skill, as I noticed you are able to control all of your powers, will be life altering for all Kluanaria and possibly here. However, I am thinking Tatiana and Onachala and Irra will be more useful here."

The two walked out of the house together to the learning zone where all were patiently waiting and testing out their newly found objects.

"Good morning, Newlings!" William said as his very long shadow cast over them as he approached.

"Good morning." Tommy said as he stood up. "I… I am Tommy. I found this thing and I don't know what it is for. Can you show me, please?"

"Yes, I will. First let me introduce myself. My name is William. I have an assistant," he paused as he looked to the skies and pointed, "ah, there he is. This is Fred."

As he spoke a great green dragon landed gracefully behind him. The children were frozen in terror.

"I will be helping you figure out what your objects are used for and Fred, is very special. He is going to have a snack with each of you and he will help you advance your knowledge before we leave."

Zanor arrived as he noticed the flying dragon. "No grand entrances, huh. The normal people on this darn rock have never seen a live dragon for an extremely long time. So try and be cautious." He smiled and walked to the center of the learning zone. "You are early William. Let them be for a bit while we discuss everything."

Fred picked Zanor up with his long, talon claws. The kids watched as Zanor was lifted up directly in front of the dragon's snout. They could see a glow of fire as the creature opened his mouth to speak. His deep, grumbling voice echoed in their meadow. "This happens now, Aantiri. I hold all the pieces, and if we want to have advantage, it is now!"

"Ok, Fred. What advantage does this give us? None of them have any idea of what is about to take place."

"I will show them." He set Zanor down amongst the kids. "Be seated all of you." He moved forward some, the ground quaking under his weight. As he seated himself, "Watch the smoke. It will tell you a story of what happened and a story about each of you." The children heard a great rumble from deep within the dragon's belly. Too afraid to move they stared at the smoke the dragon created.

Fred narrated as scenes went by. "I know some of you had been privy to the story told by Walther. I am going to show you what truly happened." As Walther's story was repeated by the dragon, Tatiana grew more excited and antsy. At the end of this vision, "That was then; this was a few months ago to my recollection." Fred was able to recreate the image of the Orders' leaders traveling to the sanctuary and returning what was missing for many ages. "Today, Newlings, I am here to help you understand your gift and your place. One day, you will be called forth to protect all, just like the current leaders of your Orders are doing now. Who will be first to visit me?"

Paul stood up and walked forward. The dragon had him step into the palm of his claws and raised him to eye level.

"Paul, you will be joining William and me this day. It is not safe for you here."

"I don't understand. I have no mark that stays; I have no item that I found."

"You are very, very important. Zanor approach."

Zanor went forward and knelt. "Yes, I am here."

Fred plucked him into the air landing him next to Paul. "Show Paul your mark."

"I have no mark."

Paul was astounded. "But you are High Lord of Burwash. Surely you are Truncheon."

"No lad, I am Aantiri. We sort of rule all for Menosh, William, and the dragon. My Order has ultimate say, counsel from other Orders is considered and matters are presented to the trio, but I have ultimate responsibility to handle all things on Kluanaria. Why does this concern you dragon?"

"He is your protégé, Zanor. He must leave with us for his safety."

"Aye. Does Myron or Iris know?"

"No, Grandfather. They think I am normal."

"Does Harold or Malificence know?"

"Not yet. Before he goes, Menosh has asked them to meet us here."

"You know Mom doesn't like things like this, right?"

"She will be fine. Her parents will be here and well, your dad's parents are already here. It will be fine."

The two were lowered and Zanor escorted Paul away to share some things.

"Next child."

The dragon received Tommy with his special crystalline object that had many colors radiating out.

"Quite impressive, Tommy. You have a truly pure soul and will be learning from Wryn. He is a very special sorcerer who has some really, how do you say, cool powers. You will be learning some history too. This crystal will go in a special stave carved from a limb of the Dracaena (dragon tree)." Fred let the small lad out of his palm and continued on.

"Irra, is it?" The dragon paused to smile slightly. "Don't be afraid, lass."

Irra stepped into the dragon's palm and spoke. "Dragon, please light a fire in our camp pit."

The dragon nodded. "Now what, child?"

She stepped out of his palm and made her hands rotate as if they were circling around a ball, but each going in opposite directions. Irra then closed her eyes and took in a large amount of air. As she exhaled, the fire went out and a cloud of smoke went up along with a cloud of swirling dust and a third column of fine sediments. She turned and looked at the dragon, which, at that moment in time lost his flame and breath.

The kids stood in amazement as they watched a mighty dragon succumb to a small person like themselves. And they were more amazed when they saw the camp pit dust and smoke separate at the same time.

William ran forward. "What have you done, Irra? How did you do that?"

"Well, first of all, William. I am an Izmaa. We are able to quickly figure out weaknesses and use them to our advantage. Don't worry, your pet is returning to normal now." She snapped her fingers and the seemingly long pause ended.

The dragon smiled. "Well done, Izmaa. I should have thought that through beforehand." Fred patted her on the shoulder. "Guilles will continue your training, but I would like to see if you can learn some Chrinthold tactics. It will give you a major advantage."

"Who is next?" The dragon waited impatiently as another Newling made his way forward.

"I am Tomas. I was told that I am Truncheon. Then someone else told me I am Chrinthold."

"You sort of are both. The first thing Chrinthold learn is combat. This is why the person told you that you are Truncheon. When your trainer decides you are ready, you go with Rynylla and she will provide the delicate lessons that all Chrinthold learn."

Lucien appeared as the dragon spoke. "Fred, Tomas will go with me. I have spoken to Rynylla and will train him as a Truncheon and such."

"Very well, Paladin. Tomas, please go with Lucien. He will be your mentor. Next Newling."

Tatiana, seeing her brother whisked off with Zanor and Irra and her stifling the dragon approached at a brisk pace.

"Yes, Tatiana?" The dragon mused.

"Come down here closer, please."

The dragon lowered his head and waited.

"What is the meaning of taking my brother away?"

"He needs to be protected."

"I doubt it. He is the bravest, strongest guy I know. Anyway, watch this." Tatiana used what she learned while camping and it began pour rain. Lightning flashed, the wind howled. The she became very stoic in expression and extended her arms to the sky. Rain changed to snow. Shortly after the snowfall, she relaxed her thoughts and butterflies appeared as the snow melted in the summer air.

"Very good, little one. Malos will have fun with your training."

As Tatiana walked away a tear appeared in the air around the "no shoes" zone. Edwina caught glimpse of someone walking through the tear and used her powers to knock the kids toward the dragon. As she did so, Llylandra grabbed an arm and Thanias the other and just as they appeared, the three disappeared.

"Nooooooo!" Tatiana screamed. She ran to where the tear was and attempted to separate the air.

Onachala ran to her side. "Step back!" She focused her thought on the shape of the tear and with her left he she traced the tear in the air and it reopened. "Let's go!" She motioned for those who were helping to go through.

"Halt this instant!" Malificence ran forward. "We will go!" She yelled as Kira joined her along with Lady Phallas. The three women jumped through the tear and as Onachala held the tear open, Lucien and Myron leapt through.

Iris was sprinting as she had seen everything from the kitchen window and was further away. "Darn you, Thanias. I curse you 'til the day you meet the creators." She reached Tatiana and hugged her. "I will bring her back."

Fred saw this. "No, Iris. You are needed here for the sake of the Newlings. You and 'Zanor and the other Orders' mentors are needed here. All will work out."

Onachala released the tear and Iris made a run for it. The dragon plucked

The Kluanarians

her from the ground. "Did you not learn after all these years?" He placed her in the middle of the zone and spoke again. "Newlings, I will work with you some more tomorrow. I know some of you are anxious to know what your powers are for, so tomorrow after you morning meal, we will continue."

As the kids headed for their homes, he could hear all of the talk of the cool things that they witnessed and of how awesome it was to see a great chase underway.

Iris went to the scrying basin which was built over a high energy vortex for optimum power. She concentrated on both Wryn and Harold.

"You won't hear from Harold," a voice from behind her cautioned.

"Why?" Iris spoke as she turned around. "Never mind then, father." She hugged Harold and went back to the basin.

Wryn's face appeared in the water. Iris explained the situation and Wryn departed from the basin's reflecting pool and briefed Beryth and Impresaria.

"Tell me what happened, Iris."

Tatiana burst in and saw Harold. "Papa, it was awful. The air opened and a man and a lady took Edwina! The dragon took mom up in the air and told her to stay here."

"Where is Paul?" Harold asked.

"He went with Papa Zanor, but then Papa Zanor went through a tear that my friend made to save Edwina."

"Ok, so where is your brother now?"

"I don't know. I can only tell you what I know."

He smiled. Walther entered the room. "The men await your command."

"They can bivouac here, are the paladins on their way?"

"Yes. Impresaria sent Ingvar as their lead."

"Very well. I think this might be ugly, have we heard from Beryth or Rynylla yet?

"No, sir. But I am hoping soon."

Iris glanced at the scrying basin and noticed it was glowing. "Wryn is reporting that Mithdrool is forming his legions again. He is thinking that the enemy believes Edwina is the key to controlling Kluanaria and Earth. He has also noted a rift between the parallel worlds is forming and soon entry can be made to here much more easily. They have sent Rynn and some of the Silver Mages to capture Jaetoth, since he created the rift."

She paused as a Fred appeared in the room in his mortal form. "I have asked my kin and Malos to temper the rift until the Silvers gain control."

Wryn nodded and shared the news with those in the scrying chamber with him. He held up a seeing stone. And then faded out.

"Ok, they will use the seeing stones like those that Tatiana has to observe the actions by those who went through the tear and those who are on stand-by," Fred said. "Tatiana, please help me find Paul."

The two left the house and went in the direction Zanor and Paul had previously journeyed. Tatiana grabbed Fred's hand, "This way, hurry!"

As they ran Fred asked, "Why are we running?"

"I have a feeling that he can save us all."

Fred stopped immediately. "How does your feeling have such knowledge?"

"You need to watch more TV. I don't know. I just have this funny feeling."

"Very well. Let us start here." Fred pointed at the home of Zanor and Kira.

"Fred. Why do they want my sister?"

"They think that since she belongs to the Moons Order and has received significant training via your Grandmother Kira that she already has superior ability that they can use to control dark creatures."

"What are dark creatures?"

The conversation was disrupted as Paul exited the house. "What is going on? Grandpa just left me here and said that I would be safe, and no one must know."

Fred looked at Tatiana. "Girl, I am going to snap my fingers and you will be frozen in time briefly." As he finished his sentence, he snapped his fingers. He saw Tatiana's question freeze on her lips. "Ok, Paul, now you can talk."

"Do you know what he meant?"

"Yes lad. Has Zanor talked to you about your gift yet?"

"He was explaining how he figured out his strengths with this gift and how he stumbled on it a long time ago. He also said that the big book that Tatiana found during our last camping trip would be of great use."

Fred snapped his finger again, only to hear the infamous question from Tatiana. "Why?"

A BRIEF JAUNT

WILLIAM CAUGHT UP TO THEM. "Iris is in the house going ballistic. We need to get her to calm down."

Fred nodded. "First we four have a short journey to make."

"Where to? Do I get to go? Should I tell Mom?

Fred transformed in to his normal form and wrapped his tail around the others. "Grab a tail scale and don't let go."

In the blink of an eye, the group was transported to the home above Clamshoe Bay. Paul sprinted into the room where the book was still open to the last page he had read to Myron. He gently closed the book and closed the hasp along the edge. He raced back down the stairs and met back with the group.

Fred once again asked them to grasp his scales and they vanished. The destination was unknown to the kids. The land was semi-desolate. A large valley lay below them. They saw many rare herbs and flowers. Small stone paths lead both down into the valley and up to the summit of the hill.

"Fred. May I harvest some of these herbs for my practice?" Paul inquired as he looked about.

"Yes. That is partly why we are here. William, the bag please."

William nodded. "Son, you will find that this bag will hold as much as you would like to stuff into it. In fact you can put in different herbs, and this enchantment that I am casting will separate them for you and as you need, it will produce the herb required." He placed the bag on a slight grey petrified stump and recited the enchantment. "Here you are lad. Take as much of the herbs as possible."

"Fred what is that up there, circling?"

"Oh that. That is Ermenya. She is a crystal dragon and is very powerful. You will have your chance to meet her in a while, Tatiana."

"Is Ermenya bound to the girl?" William asked.

"To her brother, but Ermenya will like her and probably help her learn as well."

"So it is true then what Malos and Menosh were saying that the two would be linked in some way." William pondered.

Fred nodded. "It was foreseen and will come to pass. I am hopeful that the Moon will be rescued."

After two hours Paul had picked a multitude of every possible variety of herbs that was located at this unknown place. The group walked up the hill together. As they climbed, Paul recognized some of scenery. "Is this Edziza?"

"Yes. Most of the scars are covered as the battle was long ago. Looking out to your left you can see the large depiction on the valley wall. To your right is one of the memorials, and at the top of this hill an altar." William explained. "We brought the Orders here, after the Clamshoe incident to remind them of the balance needed. Mithdrool is very dangerous and now he has the help of Llylandra who is quite deadly on her own. Your uncle has aligned himself in such a way that he will most likely lose his soul and/ or perish on the battlefield."

"That is why it is most important for us to go to the altar, Paul." Fred added as the group reached the summit.

William took the book from Paul. "This ritual you must perform when you are prepared to choose your path. The Aantiri are very special, very powerful. Your gift is masked as all Aantiris are. If the worlds knew of this power, you would become a target."

Paul nodded. "May I have time to study this? I would like to read my history and absorb some of this."

"Very well; Tatiana, come with me." William motioned to her as he walked over to a well. "We are here to give your brother some space. He has some very important reading to do."

"Will he get hurt? I mean will becoming this Aantiri thing, will it hurt him?"

"No. I promise. Once he is comfortable with what he has read, he will perform a short ritual and it will bring that rather large crystal dragon down. When she lands, her breath which is icefire will encompass Paul. He will be given all knowledge of the Aantiri. You see, his kind is very special as no one can teach them because of the knowledge each possess. It is shared and it is also rare to have more than one alive at the same time."

"Does that mean Grandpa Zanor will die?"

"It could possibly mean that. He, after all, went through the portal to get your sister."

Tatiana nodded. She looked toward her brother and watched him set the book down and walk to the altar.

Paul retrieved a few special herbs from the grasses around the altar along with a staff carved from a wyrmwood tree. "Draconia vi sumi la serva en ti en iterni." Ermenya landed, and her icefire engulfed Paul. Once it cleared, Ermenya shrunk to a small crystalline statue. "Tatiana, you will carry her."

Tatiana ran up and took the small dragon from Paul. She smiled and put it in her leather pouch with the seeing stones. "Are you ok, Paul? Did it hurt?"

"I am fine Tat. The icefire wasn't hot or cold. But it taught me a lot about a lot and I understand now." He hugged his little sister. "William what now?"

"Now, we return to Weelin and wait for news."

Fred once again had them grasp scales for the return trip.

As the tear created by Onachala closed, the group looked to Lady Phallas for guidance. Kira and Malificence new the road would be dangerous. Lucien and Myron along with Tomas drew swords. The way was a broken narrow path winding through dense fauna. Bristlethorn overgrew parts of the broken path. Horrific screeches were heard in the sky above. The landscape appeared almost colorless grays and browns. The green grass had a purple hue from the red star. In the distance strange creatures circled in the air. A crumbling ruin lay in the West. The East had a barren plain.

Kira removed a scrying dish from a pouch on her side. She filled it with a dust that turned liquid on contact. "Lunacerian guide me." An image formed as she opened her eyes. She could see Edwina in a prison, but well cared for. She saw Llylandra, so she ended the vision before she was seen. "The ruins, Lady Phallas. In the tunnel, below the mire where the shades reside. But they aren't the worst. The worst is the...."

Onachala froze in her tracks. She grabbed Malificence by the sleeve and pointed. Under her breath she said, "Everyone behind me!" After everyone was behind her she said, "Invisiblis en tote cruciento." Onachala motioned the group to follow her. They passed the creature. After about a mile, she found a well shielded place for them to rest for bit. The spell wore off and had taken its toll on her.

Malificence offered her some squash cakes and bittersweet water. "This will help you recover, Onachala." She prepared a blanket and conjured pillows to lean against. Clouds rolled in, so Malificence added a roof and walls that blended to the surroundings exactly. "Everyone please rest. I will protect us. Kira, you will have the night?"

"Aye. Lucien, you will brief Tomas on what to expect, please."

Lucien nodded and casting a knowing glance over the now sleeping Onachala began to explain the bad and the worse of the quest. Lady Phallas listened for rumors, as she has traversed this place more than he.

"Enough already!" Myron spoke after two hours. "We need to get food and firewood."

Kira snapped her fingers, and everything needed was provided. "Now, don't be griping, son." She smiled and checked on Onachala. "How are you dear?"

Onachala was stirring. "Drained, but better. I am not ready for this."

"No child, you are not. Rithmas will be here soon. Once he is here, you will walk through the portal he comes from. Then you must find Zanor. Take him this note."

"I will. Is Guilles going to help?"

"Yes. He will be here as well. Irra will be waiting for you at the portal location. You two have an important task ahead. After the note is given to Zanor, find Iris."

After three hours, nightfall set in. A portal appeared in the enclosure and two figures emerged. Rithmas and Guilles stepped out. Onachala hugged Rithmas.

"You have done well Newling. You are advancing faster than I had thought you would. Please, go now. Do as Kira asked; find Zanor and Iris."

She nodded and walked into the portal.

Irra was at the other side holding it open with blood berries. "See, there is more than one way to get into Vale Kilowas. Are you strong enough to walk?"

"Not so fast." A familiar voice spoke. Zanor appeared from behind them. "I was told you will have a message for me."

Onachala nodded and handed the parchment to him.

"Ok, now to get you two to a safer place than this dead thicket." Zanor grasped their shoulders and they vanished, reappearing in Iris' home.

Iris had prepared a place for the girls to recover from their exhaustive use of power to help save their friend. "Please rest. We will talk after you both have recovered more. I will be contacting Wryn with an update."

She escorted the girls to a room where Truance met with them and provided a mind soothing beverage which helped them relax.

Iris went back to the family room where Zanor was seated. "What is happening? Why was I not permitted to go after Thanias? What does Edwina know or have?"

"Calm down. This is exactly why you did not go. You can't control your emotions and would hinder the quest. The group does not have time to comfort anyone. I am assuming that the kids stood there and stared at you. Thanias is out of control and his brothers will deal with him. Edwina neither knows anything nor has anything that will benefit his cause. He is hoping to lure out a supposed druid who in all reality was in his midst the whole time and benefits him less than Edwina."

"Yes, the kids stared at me."

"So, what did you do?"

"I dismissed them to their homes and set up the scrying chamber to communicate with Wryn. Then I came here and started preparing."

"For what?"

"You need to watch more TV. You sound like a cop or high inquisitor."

"I am the inquisitor. You are not permitted to partake on a quest to free Edwina. All the players that are needed are present."

"I am her mother. Surely that gives me enough status to go."

"You need to wake up and quit acting like a child. Your mother and mother-in-law will handle it. Not to mention Lady Phallas and my two sons with Tomas."

"You are too proud and stubborn to even see reason." Iris took two steps back and tossed a brilliant vial to the ground. As the vial shattered, she spoke. "Illumeni ya Kilowas." She disappeared into the flash of light released from the vial.

Zanor stood in awe. He went to Truance with the events that had just unfolded. "I must meet with all the Newlings. If the Shadowblyt and Izmaa are able, they may join us in the morning. Right now, I will prepare the rest for our quest."

"Sire, what shall I relay to Malos? He will be joining me here before nightfall."

"Nothing. I have sent Tatiana's sprite with a message to Menosh. Malos should know by the time he gets here."

Truance nodded and returned to observing the girls.

In Vale Kilowas, the night had set in. The temperature dropped down and a light mist fell upon the shelter prepared by Malificence. The group rested peacefully for a few hours. Shades and trincotts hovered not far from the camp. Tomas stirred as a brilliant light shown in the atmosphere. The trincotts screeched off in fear and the shades vanished.

"Who's there?" Tomas whispered as he drew his sword.

"Shhh. It is me, Iris."

"What?" Kira jumped to her feet and grabbed Iris by the arm and pulled her in. "Why are you here Iris?"

"Because Edwina is my daughter."

"You are going to hinder us. Leave now."

"No."

Myron woke and saw his wife and mother in heated discussion. He shook his head and grabbed Iris to his side. "You should not be here. You need to be with Paul and Tatiana. They are our children too."

"Your mind is affected by your mother's presence."

Malificence awakened. "Contanimiente le satellite, quas."

A brilliant light appeared in the tent. As Iris turned as her mother finished the spell and as she turned, the light encapsulated her in a small crystal.

"What!" Myron yelled. "Are you raving mad? That is my wife and your daughter!"

"She is fine and will not hamper our quest. When we are done, I will release her."

Kira smiled. "We must get a move on. The darkness of this dismal place is thickening, the later in the night we go. Sleep, I will wake you when it is time."

"Agreed." Malificence responded. She placed her hand on Myron's forehead and he drifted to sleep.

A light rain fell on the campsite. Tomas stirred and built a fire outside the tent. Kira conjured a sustainment table for everyone. Myron and Guilles were busy planning the next steps while Rithmas and Malificence rolled the blankets and shrunk them to a more portable size. Lady Phallas took down the structure after everyone had finished eating under its protection.

Guilles led the way further into the mire with Lucien at his side. "So, Paladin, what do you think our chances are of remaining unseen by the trincotts?"

"Yes, Kira and Lady Phallas have us hidden now. We are almost to the ruins. Thank you for sharing your knowledge with us."

Guilles nodded and continued. The group stopped before they reached the openness of the ruins and supped. Tomas, being nervous, and youngest, sat quietly in thought. He had many versions of what was about to happen. He tried to block out the thoughts by getting up and pacing.

Lucien rose and went to Tomas. "Come lad, relax. This group is very good at what they do. No harm will come to you. I am still not certain why they brought you. That will reveal itself soon enough. Malificence, do you have chamomile? It may calm him some."

Malificence went to them. "I have something better. Please sit Tomas." She focused her energy. "Tomas, I am teleporting you to Menosh and Zanor. You are not ready for what is ahead."

Tomas nodded. "Please be careful."

"Illumeni ta Weelin par Tomas." Malificence dropped a small vial in front of Tomas. As the brilliant light flashed and dissipated, Tomas found himself in Zanor's home.

Familiar faces eagerly greeted him. Paul and Tatiana ran up to him and began asking questions, in turn, they described their adventure with William and Fred.

THE BOWELS OF VALE KILOWAS

Edwina was not restrained by her captors. She took the time, while they were plotting to explore some of the intriguing structure. There were ancient tapestries hanging in the great hall. Chandeliers with candles hung from the rafters. She closely examined some of the tapestries. She had her camera in her pocket, so she began recording them. She discovered a library with many books. There were several books from ancient orders that no longer existed. She took it upon herself to shrink them and stow them in her camera. She migrated back toward Thanias and observed the chaos.

"Tell me, Edwina, what do you think of Vale Kilowas?"

"Lovely, simply lovely. So, why am I here?"

"You are here, because I have to show them that I am strong."

"You don't have anything to prove to my dad and Lucien, let alone your dad. How long had you deceived them? What do you get out of this? As I see it, you have lost everything near and dear to you. Dad was absolutely crushed."

"I gain everything. You see, there is more to this than just family. I have already gained control of the Mithdroolean Legion. Llylandra has given me control of her vast armies. I will have the druid, and you are my lure."

"You already know the druid. She was with you as a friend forever. Too bad you are too arrogant to see things as they are." Edwina paused and walked around the table Thanias was leaning on. She put her hands on his shoulders, "Too bad Uncle. I did not want this to come to this point, but I have no choice. Containimiente la truncheon, quas!"

Brenda M. Hokenson

"Nooooo!" Thanias was encapsulated.

"Lunillumeni ya Kira." A few seconds later, Edwina was standing beside the rescue group. "Don't bother going there on my account," she said as everyone noticed her. "Where is Tomas? Thanias said Tomas was going to be here. He has plans for him."

"That is why I sent him to Zanor." Malificence said as she hugged her. "Rithmas, can you rift here?"

"Yes. Everyone through, quickly."

Zanor joined the group, now standing in his great room. "That was much easier than I expected."

"She got out on her own. I am not sure why Thanias didn't pursue." Lucien responded.

All eyes were on Edwina. "Well, he can't pursue. I have him locked up," she smiled.

"But, how? You have not got that far in your training yet."

"All of that reading Altus had me do over the summer. I learned a lot and have had time to practice. Oh, which reminds me, Malos, do you have use for these?" Edwina removed her camera and popped the miniaturized books from the battery slot."

"Wherever did you find them?"

"In a vast library, unused, with way more knowledge than our current library downtown. Oh, and I took pictures of some tapestries that were on the walls." She rushed over to the laptop she had at Zanor's home and uploaded the images. "Some of these look like battle scenes from a long time ago."

Malos studied the photos. "It was Edziza. Though I am not certain who lived in Kilowas after the battle to depict it in such detail."

Tatiana's pouch with Ermenya inside fell to the floor. A dainty figure emerged. "I did the tapestries. I had also relocated very important texts to that library as well." Ermenya bowed to Zanor. Malos, and William. "But there is more to the story than the tapestries. While the land healed, with my help, I would take solace there and reflect. I found Vale Kilowas to be very peaceable and a long-forgotten realm had reestablished there for centuries. Darkness came and this lost realm vanished. This realm is a major key. Are the Paladins here?"

"Yes Lady Ermenya. Ingvar awaits command. Where is Thanias?" Malos responded.

"Liberato la truncheon pir restani tus." Thanias emerged from the crystal with bindings on his hands. "Here he is, back by popular demand." Edwina mused and walked off.

"Hmmmm." Malificence paused. "Liberarto la satellite." An extremely radiant pulse of light burst through the charm Iris was held in.

Iris spoke as she regained her stature. "Well now, what do we have here? What brings the crystal to life at this hour? There is no impending doom. My daughter is safe."

"Silence Star! Know your place." William scolded as he pressed down on her shoulder forcing her to her knees."You almost cost us an advantage. If you continue this path, you will be removed."

Malificence stepped toward Ermenya. "Do you know where the lost realm went? I am thinking in your collection, there must be some information to track it down."

"We would have to take over Vale Kilowas. I am not sure we are prepared for such an undertaking, given the Star is lost in her own world and is unable to focus on duty."

Iris forced William back as she stood again. "You are fools to think that realm can help stop this. We need to stop Mithdrool."

"You won't let go of your children. They are necessary!" William said as he exited the home.

Fred was outside. "What is going on? You never walk away from a battle, no matter how petty."

"That woman will cost us and our allies."

"Oh, her. Malificence will put her in her place."

"No, she let her back out of the charm. We will not get anything done as she will second guess everything, like Edziza, when we lost twenty five percent of our forces in one battle, because we opted to follow her plan instead sticking with the battle plan."

"Maybe Malificence should be questioned as well."

A small, brilliant beam shot between them. From it, a familiar creature emerged. "I will deal with both of them." The three walked back into the home. "Get those children trained. It is very apparent that it has to be the elders and the Newlings to save these realms. Iris, you are hereby forbidden from communicating with your children, until a time as such presents itself." Menosh spoke as he conjured a table and chairs for all. "Harold, I need you to work with Impresaria and Beryth and develop a battle strategy. Kira, I need you to work with Guilles, Rynylla, Rithmas and Gareth. You need to locate the missing realm. Once it is located, Lady Phallas will give you further instructions. I have purposely left out Myron, Lucien, Zanor, Malos, and Lunacerian. Your focus is training the children. Develop a training plan and let Truance and Malos help." Menosh paused as he acknowledged Tatiana enter the room. "Child, you need to rest. Everything is just fine."

"Menosh. Thank you for sparing her." She smiled and hugged the Enygminite.

Malos escorted Tatiana to the other children. "Newlings, I am sorry for this abrupt thrust into training. There is a major battle getting underway. Tomorrow will be the start of your training. I have prepared a feast of sorts in your honor. After your meal, I suggest sleep. Training will be very intense and exhausting."

After the evening meal, some of the parents loaded the Newlings up in an old hay truck and headed into Weelin. Kira sat in back with the kids. She answered questions and told stories. "This trip is special for you kids. Don't let training scare you. It is more fun than anything. Tonight, will be movies and ice cream and the carnival that just came in."

The truck parked nearest to the center of town, with help of a little teleport that landed them perfectly in the parking space. A family in the row over did a double take. The father walked over as the group was heading into town and poked the truck, just to see if it was really there. "I don't know what we saw honey. The rig is solid."

"Well, if it is solid how did it just show up? Something hooky is going on and I am sure it is those devil worshippers."

"We don't have devil worshipers. We have about seven congregations, and none are like that."

"Don't be dumb, of course they want you to think they are 'believers' but when you aren't paying attention, stuff like this truck happens. Come on kids, don't make a scene."

Meanwhile, Tomas and Edwina led the group down the sidewalk. Paul was in the center of the group pointing out cool places to visit. Tatiana broke into a sprint along with Irra, Tommy, and Onachala. The ice cream cart was at the end of the sidewalk. Lucien left abruptly, as the kids were entering the carnival.

Menosh took Iris, Guilles and Gareth through the Veil between the two realms. "You will notice the Veil Guardians have been summoned." The guardians acknowledged Menosh as the group passed through. "The Newlings shall be safe in the realm of Earth. Kluanaria however is in grave peril and that alone threatens Earth's safety. We must hurry to the Sand Cavern, Lady Phallas has news, and I am positive that it is not good. I realize this is horrifying Iris, but you must trust what we are doing."

"I will not have any part in this supposed war Menosh. Where is Myron?"

Your breath needs to be used to help us, not argue. Now be silent while we traverse the through the greystone. Guilles, if you don't mind."

Guilles nodded and inserted a small granule of silver into the center of the rune inscribed stone, which is similar to the one at the Palisade. "I am a bit rusty with keys of such nature." As Guilles pressed the sliver deep into the small crevice, the rock opened. A bright lunar glow surrounded the stone, and the group passed through. Wryn awaited them at the entry in the caverns. "Welcome. Long has it been since we hosted other Orders. This is a perilous time and Mother, Lady Phallas, has information to assist.

MIITHDROOL AND LLYLANDRA

"I SEE THE HIGH SEAT OF the Nagazthastar was not good enough for Thanias." Mithdrool spoke in his low grumbling voice that sent chills through the halls of his keep. "Tell me, Llylandra, what happened that caused you to seek out Vale Kilowas? Was I not good enough to provide you my warlocks and deadmages? I also have Mercurian at hand. The giants will be of great value to our efforts."

Do we still hold Nagazthastar and was there anything useful there?"

"Yes, my lord. I do escape because I always have a way out. Thanias has the information gleaned from Nagazthastar and I am going to set him free."

"What information and why did you disturb Vale Kilowas?"

"Let me finish answering all of your questions. Nagazthastar still had some Fraelochs at the keep, remnants of Beryth's once elite guard. There was a slight rebellion and a young archer, Beryth's daughter, was with Thanias showing him everything and trying to rescue artifacts from the first clash with you and your armies. I am aware of a scroll that he managed to keep from the girl. During the small siege, her mother clobbered us with some major injuries to herself, and she escaped.

Mithdrool tipped his head back and laughed. It echoed down the long, empty corridors. "Very well, I will get him out since he is necessary. Tell me now, how he was captured."

"Lord, forgive me. We took Vale Kilowas with ease…"

"It was not necessary, and you have disturbed a greater presence than Menosh, that blasted Enygminite. Thanias is held in a gem, and you are here, kneeling because a Moon and a darn Paladin stopped you."

"We entered Vale Kilowas, assuming it to be inhabited at the castle. It was empty, just books on various subjects and tapestries. Trincotts roam the entire vale. This made the perfect location to cut through the Veil and take what we could from the fleeing Orders. Thanias managed to take hold of Edwina, Myron and Iris' daughter. She was worthless to our cause."

"You let a Moon go? You are aware of how terribly difficult to destroy them."

"Come with me. We will make short work of freeing Thanias. I will speak on our journey."

Llylandra nodded in agreement. She said not a word as Mithdrool spoke of ancient history, long forgotten.

"Llylandra, I have been in stasis off and on for millennia. The Fraeloch have a relic, a living relic that can easily destroy everything or restore everything to perfect peace."

Before Mount Edziza battle, there was the Truncheon Wars. Menosh had let the land be governed by the people in a society friendly to all. The Orders were in harmony and races were at peace. Harold, or War as the realm of Earth calls him, was running amuck and beginning to stir rebellion. He and his brothers of battle, the realm of Earth calls them collectively the Four Horsemen, started at one end of Kluanaria and created a large swath of destruction. A great battle ensued as War understood the determination of the last village he tried to destroy, and the lengths that the ancient orders went to protect those innocent people, even though it was not their place. Word has it that the girl saved by War and trained as a Eupepsian, or healer in Earth words, got tired of being selfless to all and to have no time to herself. She is rumored to have disappeared sometime after Harold and Malificence' last child, Impresaria, took over Kaprius, the homeland of the Morket, which restored Harold as a mortal, yet keeping with his undying duties as War. The girl's name was Luly."

Llylandra looked puzzled for a moment as Mithdrool continued.

"Are you Fraeloch, Llylandra? Or something else?"

"Why do you say that?

"Because Nagazthastar is the homeland of Mercurians and Fraelochs, once overseen by High Lord Beryth and it has been decimated at least three times. The true knowledge of this race is locked in scrolls and oral history. They spoke more than they wrote, at least that is how it was. They each behold a certain magical aura that has to be learned over a lifetime or from a certain artifact."

"What artifact?"

"Somehow and some way, we will find the Morket/Fraeloch as she learned both cultures and all rituals. As you know Morket can be dark and secretive, if they want. Whereas Fraeloch are more reactive toward conflict and prefer peace. This girl will be broken so to speak. She can unleash Death upon the realm of Earth and here. For she has the knowledge of where to find the pouch of endless pockets in which resides the key. Truthfully, Llylandra, I have not seen any word of you in any writings until now. I believe you changed you name."

"Oh, Luly, I am definitely not Luly. She resides in Ruan, with Henry, the butcher. Their son, Tomas, is Edwina's friend."

"Very well, then we will free Thanias. I believe we can get the pouch from William or that darned dragon he is with. It will take planning."

As the two reached the altar a floor above the dungeons, Mithdrool paused. He took a deep breath and fumbled about in his spells.

"What do you need my lord?"

"Do you have anything of Thanias' belongings? Where exactly is Thanias? And this Edwina?"

Llylandra handed a masterfully engraved dagger to the warlock. "The girl has a powerful gift. I believe she is stronger than the Moons realize. Her Grandmother…"

"Kira?"

"Yes Lord. Kira. She has trained her for some time but she also has a strong knowledge of Fraelochan rituals that are beyond our convention. Thanias is held in prism around her neck."

"Maybe he should remain there. What do you know of the Moons' Order?"

"They are I believe the most powerful Order we must vanquish. We need to gain the aid of Altus. He remains neutral as he desires power and knowledge. Perhaps we can persuade him to look the other way while we go to the library."

Take Jaetoth with you as Myron and Zanor will have increased the guard at the Veil and at their villages. Before you go, take a seat over there." Mithdrool pointed to a seat near a small table and shelf. She saw Jaetoth enter with several other warlocks and deadmages. "We will retrieve Thanias and then, Jaetoth, seek out Altus with Llylandra."

Jaetoth bowed and took his place with the warlocks.

Mithdrool studied the dagger for some time. "Interesting. This blade singlehandedly decimated fourteen of my strongest Legionaries. It shall work marvelously." Mithdrool paused to unclutter his focus. "Uni uncarsare di Truncheon a Thanias. Uni uncarse di loc ensiedre ensad di capratorium a Edwina!"

At that moment, on Earth, pain shot through Edwina, and she collapsed to the ground. Tomas ran to catch her but was too far away. He saw a dark mist rise from her amulet which was the prison of Thanias. As Tomas supported her head, he watched the amulet shatter. He heaved a great sigh of despair. Kira rushed to the teenagers followed by Malos and Myron who had joined the group.

"Mithdrool has freed him, Myron. If we cannot free your brother from the wicked, he is lost to us." Kira spoke softly. "Your father must learn of this. Seek him out now!"

Myron nodded and took Tomas on the rather swift walk to the truck. The passersby were watching indiscriminately as Myron placed a blue stone on the ground. "Ok, at the count of three, we jump on it and we will be in Zanor's presence."

The family that parked near them was headed to their vehicle when the two jumped on to the stone and vanished along with it. Shrieking ensued in the parking lot, followed by 911 calls and then the police.

"I told you. Didn't I tell you, the ones on the edge of town are devil worshippers? Please officer, believe me, they just went straight to hell by jumping on a blue rock. And earlier they landed this truck here, perfectly in the middle of these two cars."

The police officer could find no evidence of wrongdoing and checked the license plate. "Ma'am, I need you to blow into this device."

"What for?"

"I believe you have spent too much time at the beer garden."

"I don't drink beer."

"Well, just to be absolutely certain, please breathe into this device."

The woman cooperated and it was good.

"Mr...."

"Oh, Adams, Ronald Adams."

"Ok, Mr. Adams. I think your wife has been in the sun too long. Would you please escort her home so she can rest? Also give her plenty of water. Lack of water will cause delusions."

"Well, officer, considering 8 other witnesses are here, probably with video of some kind, I would interview everyone first before declaring my wife sauced and delusional."

Thanias appeared before Mithdrool and Llylandra, very weak. "Welcome back." Mithdrool said as he continued to question Llylandra.

"Llylandra added some information. "Edwina has a very powerful gift. She is stronger than what the Moons know, because of her lineage of Morket and Fraeloch on her mother's side. Kira has also been teaching her an old art in which I am unfamiliar. Perhaps it is from a text used by Aantiri who have all vanished so long ago."

"Do you not know Llylandra, that there is still one Aantiri alive today."

Thanias huffed from the cot he was stretched out on was carried by Legionnaires as the group walked back to the main floor. "My father, Zanor."

"Yes. Now you must rest. Llylandra and Jaetoth will be going to the Palisade."

"Are they, truly? If so, destroy the darn rock that sits in the courtyard. I hate that thing. Although it did yield to Edwina."

"Edwina will not be alive much longer."

"It yielded her a book." Thanias spoke as he drifted to sleep. "This book is Morket and Fraeloch. It has some Inscription on it in Chrinthold. I wish they would use the same written language, since they all speak the same language."

Llylandra looked on as Mithdrool paced. "It is done so because no one Order can read it. It takes all the Orders to translate their scribbles." She began pacing.

"Llylandra, it is time." Jaetoth took her by the arm. "We shall be fine. Most likely they will be looking for an attack from Mithdrool Forest and will have fortified Treah and Ruan. We shall enter the Palisade through the greystone inside."

"You can do this, Jaetoth?"

"Yes, if Thanias truly has the scroll, a sliverette of silver would be tucked under the small wooden knob. It should match this greystone to allow us to pass into the Palisade greystone."

Mithdrool smiled. "Very well, I shall arrange a strike against Kaprius by the Legion and some of your newly formed deathwards within the hour."

Jaetoth inserted the silver in to the greystone. The large overly inscribed rock split open and the two were sent through the Veil and to the Palisades rather quickly."

Walther and a couple of Newling Paladins noticed the rock shake slightly and split open. Pure energy shot from the rock, so bright was the light, they closed their eyes. Llylandra and Jaetoth emerged further from the stone where they weren't noticed for a bit.

"The Palisade is mostly deserted. There is the old man, Altus. He will be easy."

"The old man knows nothing Jaetoth. He desires power and power is something we can offer him. He just has to get us into the tower."

"No, there is one much older than Altus. I speak of Harold. He never leaves this place."

"So, just another slight challenge, but I have something for him."

Jaetoth chuckled. "What is that Llylandra?

"You will see in due time."

"Do you truly know who Harold is?"

"Yes, but right now, War is vanquished with peace and tranquility."

"The ancients always side with the good."

"Yes, and I have that worked out too."

"We must go back to the stone and turn the sliverette slightly. It will take us right to the tower library." As they approached the stone, none focused on them. The silver was turned and the two were at the tower entrance. "Strange, Harold is not here for you to dispose of Llylandra." Jaetoth chuckled.

Walther and Altus approached with several Truncheons following behind in procession. Altus spoke carefully as he judged the two in his mind. "I have never seen the greystone used as a portal in my long, long life. What brings you here, to my Palisade?"

"We thirst for knowledge Altus."

"How do you know me?"

"Since before your time," Jaetoth said as he studied the old man in Moon garb. "We seek knowledge and history of the Fraeloch."

"Why do you want their knowledge? Did you not attend a school or something that provides free history lessons?"

"I was not so fortunate, Altus. The Fraeloch intrigue me." Jaetoth saw a group approaching from the greystone.

Llylandra caught glimpse of a Veil Guardian emerging from the tear. Her heart raced as if it was trying to escape a prison. She grabbed Jaetoth by the arm and nodded. "Do you have a place to rest? We are just travelers and have seen many towers. We were hoping to learn about Fraelochs at one of them. We have been on foot for days and used our sliverette as a last resort."

"Aye." An unfamiliar voice answered. "Please follow me. Thank you, Altus. That will be all."

Llylandra and Thanias were taken aback. "How are you Thanias?" Llylandra mused.

"Fine. Now in this room there are two beds, and plenty of water, tea, malt liquor, and food, whatever you fancy to fill your bellies. Please rest." The man left them to their own devices and went to the tower.

"Are you certain that is Thanias, Llylandra?"

"Yes, I recognized him. I worked with him up until he was captured."

Altus returned to the room and the two stopped speaking. "Here is what I have on the Fraeloch, although, you should already know everything about them Llylandra. You, after all, are one."

"How did you know?"

"The Veil Guardians found you out as soon as you used the sliverette meant for Edwina. Now what else would you like to know?"

"What does Edwina know, Altus?"

"She is constantly learning and much focused. I never had such a good pupil to watch over for the Moons. She resents her parents for fleeing to the Earth realm. She is self-taught except for Moon teachings."

"Will you share your knowledge with us?" Jaetoth inquired.

"No, I may be just the scribe for the Moons and librarian for Edwina, but I am not one to join disrupters of balance."

"Oh, I think you will help us, willingly, or otherwise." Llylandra smiled.

"Llylandra, that won't be necessary." Jaetoth spoke as raised his arm and extended it in a pushing motion toward Altus. Altus was flung into the air with a great force. He landed at the back of the room as a crumpled heap of bones. "There, he will rise in our favor when it is time; now, to the tower."

The two exited the building and crossed the courtyard where they saw Thanias giving instruction to Newling paladins.

"Those are Newlings! What is that idiot doing? How does he know paladin teachings?" Llylandra whispered.

"Because that is not the idiot you are referring to. Let me introduce you." Walther said as he approached the two. The three then went to the instructor. All training halted as the man turned toward them.

"You willingly invade our land and dare stand upon the most sacred of sites to my paladins? I know who you are and I will permit no further advance on my premises." He kept their attentions. "I have long waited to see your demise Jaetoth. Llylandra, you have forgotten where you are from, your race, and the generous nature you had so many years ago. What happened? Oh, yes, Talaharian. I almost forgot. Where is your boyfriend now deadmage?" As he spoke a Veil Guardian appeared. "The wretch you call Thanias is imprisoned as you shall soon be."

"No, we freed him and Edwina's life hangs in the balance."

"I am Lucien, and I will be your worst dreams realized." The sword he drew shown blindingly as it was the most sacred of all paladin blades, Trillean. "Magic will do you no good in this courtyard. Ryatt please bring the conjurer prison," Lucien said to a small framed archer on the wall.

The archer nodded and approached with a small silver box with a dragon on the lid. The Veil Guardian stepped in front of Jaetoth and received the box from Ryatt. He turned and faced the warlock.

Having seen this box in use before, Jaetoth spoke. "Do not open that box, keeper of Trillean. I will reduce the archer to dust as I have Altus." He grabbed Ryatt's shoulder and forced her to the ground.

A moon glow started shining down on the courtyard. As the box was carefully opened a silvery light emerged from the moon glow and intensified as the lid was completely opened. The engraved dragon on the lid lifted off and hovered about Jaetoth. Lunacerian stepped from the intense light. This caught Jaetoth off guard and Ryatt broke free and shoved him toward the

Veil Guardian. The dragon flew rapidly around the deadmage until both vanished and the box slammed closed, taking the moon glow with it. The dragon reappeared on the lid with its claws across the seal.

"Now for you Llylandra." Lucien said as he raised his sword to her.

"Too late, Paladin." She vanished into thin air.

The group stood mesmerized for a moment. "She is in the tower!" Walther shouted as he saw her emerge from a grey cloud. He motioned to the Newling paladins and ran toward the tower entrance. Lunacerian snapped his fingers and both he and Lucian reappeared in front of Llylandra. The Newlings and Walther entered the second level and sealed themselves in the library.

"How dare you set foot in my tower, unwelcome half-mage!" Lunacerian cast a spell that knocked Llylandra off her feet.

She stood and returned the favor. Lunacerian was not rising very quickly. Lucien cast a protective spell as he has fought deadmages before. He slowly moved toward her. "What do you want from here?"

"Wouldn't you like to know; I see you are unconcerned for the girl, Edwina, I believe."

"She has many with her who can save her. My responsibility at the moment is taking your life."

"Strong words, I thought paladins were against death?"

"Not in this case, in fact it would be the best thing that ever happened for our Order." Lucian paced as he watched Llylandra, who was powerless. *"Imprisi li necri magi. Imprisi la Tillean!"* Llylandra was sucked into the gem on the sword, Trillean. "Now, I can take you to Impresaria. She has a better cage for you." Lucien walked over to Lunacerian and assisted him in standing. "Careful, there. We have her locked in the gem."

"Good, no about my partially disintegrated rib."

Lucien healed Lunacerian and both unsealed the library. "It is time for a break." Both leaders proclaimed as they sat down with the group. Walther documented all the details.

"Can we repair Altus?" Lunacerian mused as he drank conjured tea.

"I think that Altus knows more than we think." Lucien said as Altus slowly walked into the room. *"Mendi a Altus! Mendi aspriti tachini!"* Lucien spoke as Altus approached the table. The group watched as the spells healed the keeper of the library.

TATIANA EMPOWERED

Edwina did not know what hit her. One minute she was walking down the sidewalk with Tomas and the other Newlings, the next, she was on the ground, writhing in pain and with a shattered prison beside her. "He took the sliverette!" She went unconscious.

Edwina stirred a bit in the house of her family after a few hours. Tatiana hovered over her. "Are you ok? Who did this? Daddy won't tell me anything."

"Not now, Tat. I have a burning feeling in my mind. Where is Paul?"

Oh, so you will tell Paul but not me."

"No, silly. I want to know if he is ok."

"He is fine. The dragon he got is here, in this pouch. So he can't be too far, can he?"

Tatiana ran out of the room and got a pitcher of water for her sister. She ran out again and brought some biscuits she made. Irra and Onachala entered as well. They watched Tatiana care for her sister. They noticed how thorough she was, even the placing of the damp cloth on the forehead was exacting. After an hour of watching Edwina rest, the two left to speak to Rithmas about a protective spell for Edwina.

"Ed, can you hear me?" Tatiana whispered.

"Yes, Tat. You need to rest."

"I am gonna fix you. And then fix the monster that did this to you!"

"Tat, no. I will be ok, and I am not sure who did this."

"I have my seeing stones, so shhhhhh for a minute." Tatiana used one seeing stone at a time. She watched Edwina collapse through the orange stone. So, she then focused that knowledge through her blue stone. She pulled out her notebook and jotted down specific details about what she saw. The green stone showed her Edwina's mind and what was damaged and how. "Ed, I can fix this."

"Why?"

"That super bad guy did this. But he only used an incantation that broke Thanias out and some of it scrambled your brain."

"Leave my brain alone Tat."

Tatiana stepped forward and placed her hands on her sister's head and looked her straight in the eye. "Hold still, it will only take a second." Edwina was too weak to stop her sister. *"Lumini a Edwina, reparis la Edwina, immendis la cerebre."* A cold sensation flowed through the room. All of the elements were flashing through Edwina's eyes. She could feel the burning sensation in her head slowly dissipating. She could clearly see her assailant and Thanias. She breathed a heavy sigh and fell asleep. Tatiana, after the spell was complete collapsed to the ground. She woke in her bed with Malos and Truance watching her.

"Little one, you have much passion in your work. Please rest." Truance spoke as she gently tucked Tatiana in again.

"My sister is she ok."

Malos smiled. "Yes child. She is recovering much better thanks to you. Do you need some food or drink?"

"I saw something worse than this coming. There is a forgotten land, on the northeast tip of the land that Kaprius is on. Mer..." Tatiana yawned. "..curian. They are going to go for Kaprius and they know that Llylandra is imprisoned there. Can I have some warm milk, please?"

Malos went for the milk and a small tray of cheese, crackers, fruit and carrots. He paused briefly where Kira was seated and told her of Edwina recovering and Tatiana's vision. Kira entertained the news for a moment and looked at Myron.

Tomas entered the room where Tatiana was resting. "Tat, are you awake?"

"Uh huh. Is my sister okay?"

"Yes, she is sleeping. How did you do that anyway?"

"Do what?" Tatiana yawned.

The Kluanarians

"Your grandmother and dad are trying to figure at where you learned that spell. They looked in all the spell books of all of the known Orders."

"Hmm. I just knew it. Maybe the crystal dragon told me in my sleep."

"What crystal dragon?"

"It's in my pocket. She belongs to Paul. He had to earn it during a special ceremony for his Order and had to live through her fire that was ice cold and searing hot."

"Where is Paul, Tat?"

"Grandpa Z took him for training somewhere in Kluanaria, I guess. He said Paul is very special. That is why I helped Ed, to prove that I am special too. Everyone just talks about her and him and what they can do, and I am just little."

"You are special Tat. The grown-ups couldn't even help her. But you, you saved her."

"Thanks Tomas. Would you give her a hug for me? I need to go back to sleep."

"Ok Tat. Do you need anything?"

"Just my orange frog, over there on the chair."

Tomas retrieved the frog and tucked Tatiana in with it. "Get some rest." He left the room and headed toward Edwina.

Edwina was stirring after four hours of rest. She noticed Tomas leaning on the door frame. "How is Tat?"

"Well, she is very tired and has got your family confused." Tomas smiled. "She asked me to give you something for her." Tomas walked over and gave Edwina a hug. "They can't let the spell thing go."

"Well, maybe it is her part of her 'Interval' culture. Maybe ideas just pass into their minds and things happen as a result. I have seen her make it rain a couple times and he r anger once brought this massive storm to Clamshoe Bay, where we were camping."

"That is one theory. Tatiana still thinks the crystal dragon told her."

"There is no such thing."

"Well, evidently your brother had to live through its fiery breath to get it."

"Paul is too chicken to do anything other than work in a library."

"Chicken?"

"Oh, sorry Tomas. It is a different word for afraid or cowardly. Where did he go to anyway?"

Zanor took him somewhere and Rynylla will be here for me shortly. She said she has a master trainer waiting for me."

"That sounds bad. Do you know what the Chrinthold do as an Order?"

"Not much other than slight ego, exquisite armor and weapons."

"Hand me that small bag." Tomas passed the bag to her, and she pulled a book, *A History of the Orders*, out of it. "Well, hmmm. Chrinthold are a lot like Paladins, but they can cast spells of any Order they want and are looked to during conflict to restore the peace. Eupepsians or healers are also in the neutral zone but can only heal. So, to me it looks like the Eupepsians will teach you some healing stuff to balance the brutal stuff you are going to have to learn. Your body, mind, and spirit will be greatly affected, and you will need to prepare yourself with lots of rest. Did they figure out what Paul was?"

"Not sure, Ed. But they sure whisked him away quickly."

"Maybe he doesn't belong to any Order. Perhaps he is truly normal, and they have to protect him from Thanias."

"No, I am pretty sure Fred said that he is very important and needs to get to his Order." Tomas paced deep in thought.

Zanor appeared in bright flash as Tomas walked into him. "Pardon me, Tomas." He went to Edwina's bedside and sat on a chair. "What happened, Edwina? What did I miss these past few days?"

"First, where is my brother? Where is Paul? Why did I capture Thanias only to have Mithdrool free him and almost kill me?"

"I am uncertain how you captured your uncle and escaped. But it is probably by some intervention by an Order that spared you. Paul is fine. He is being taught his skills as they are rather difficult. Oh, yes. Who reversed your damage, Edwina?"

"Tatiana. I told her not to, but she got in my face literally. She took hold of both sides of my head and had this rather intense stare going. I couldn't look away or blink. She said some words and I went to sleep. I don't even know if I am still a Moon. Are my gifts gone Grandpa? Grandpa..."

Zanor left the question hanging and headed through the family room passing by his wife directly to Tatiana's room. He caught a quick glimpse of her as she made herself disappear. "Tatiana! My dear Tatiana…." Zanor knelt by the bed and wept. Kira and Myron rushed in.

Menosh appeared before them. "It is the child's choice. She wishes to not be found, but she is safe."

"Where is she old friend?"

"I cannot say. It is forbidden when an Order can not to be found."

"Is she part of the lost Order?" Kira interjected.

"I want you to hear me and understand what I am saying. Tatiana is bound by no one to stay here. She went in silence for reasons I am uncertain of. I do know she is safe."

Tomas entered the room. "I may know where she is. She wants to be recognized instead of being treated like a no body. I know how that felt, until I met your grandchildren. She went to where she feels important and where people truly like her. And if it is not in Treah or Ruan, then it is somewhere desolate."

Mithdrool sat beside Thanias as he did on occasion while his ally was recovered. He was searching for clues on how the girl captured Thanias. A brilliant display of falling leaves accompanied by falling snow swirled about the room. In the center a small child appeared before them, surrounded in a brilliant golden glow…

"I am here Uncle Thanias. You have much to answer for."

Thanias sat up in his chair. "Well now. What have we here? Tatiana of the Intervals."

"Thank you for showing me my chambers in Burwash. It was really neat. I wanted to show you what I have been learning, if that is okay?"

Thanias mused at this thought and looked at Mithdrool. "Well, let's see what you can do then."

"I can end lives and I can mend broken souls, just with the seasons."

Thanias smiled. "Very well, proceed."

"Not so fast. First, I want us to go to the Palisade."

"Why?"

"I have to retrieve something from there. It is most important."

"I will not take you there, perhaps Mithdrool…." As he spoke, Tatiana caught his arm and both flashed into the Palisade. "How did you…" Tatiana dragged her uncle behind while the Paladins stooped and watched in amusement. "How did you get so strong?"

Brenda M. Hokenson

"I harness all of nature, not just weather. Now… Oh yes, over here." Tatiana pulled Thanias into the building where Altus was left as dust.

"Where is he?" Thanias looked in disbelief.

"Uncle Lucien healed him, his spirit and bones were still strong."

"So he is only animated." Thanias mused.

"That is why I am here."

Altus appeared in the door, in a semi cognitive state but not whole.

"Sit down Uncle, and learn something. *Lumini a Altus, reparis a Altus, immendis la cerebre.*"

Several Paladins had gathered in the door and watched in amazement. Thanias watched as Altus returned to his former self. "You, Thanias, will be punished severely for what you have done." Altus spoke as he sat down. "Now it is your turn to receive your fate."

Tatiana stood in the center of the room. "Wait." She grabbed her uncle's wrist and the two disappeared in swirling mass of snowflakes and flower petals.

Thanias asked as the emerged from the swirling mass, "Why did you take me from Forest Mithdrool? Do your parents know where you are? What do you want?"

"Well, I am tired of seeing horrible things that are about to happen and I am tired of people getting hurt, especially my brother and sister."

"How do you plan on stopping it?"

"I don't know. I hoped maybe if I show you things, you will see…" Tatiana sniffled and wiped away some tears, "you would see that you are hurting your family."

Thanias did not say a word when suddenly Tatiana grabbed his wrist again and the two disappeared once more. They emerged in a past, when Mithdrool first emerged as a powerful evil. They were standing in the middle of Nagazthastar, where Lady Phallas had saved her people and family many years ago. The scene was replaying as Tatiana watched in horror. Thanias could see it greatly disturbed the child. "Why are we here, if it hurts you to see this that much niece?"

"I am here to understand, so that when I crush you and Mithdrool and his idiots and that crazy lady, I will know what power I will feel. All will bow to me, and there ain't nothing that's gonna stop me you pig."

"How do you? Why?"

"Shh. You can only watch. Watch and see the bad things Mithdrool did. You can only watch, just like me, through darn rocks like Uncle Lucien. Watch as Grandpa Zanor almost dies and watch as Grandpa Harold has to save everyone. Without Grandpa Harold, Kaprius and Ruan would be destroyed and the cultures dead and gone. Watch now as Mithdrool walks all over Mercurian and force those people to be like him, even the little people. What a punk. How can you be like him, Thanias?

"You are wise for your age little one. But sometimes power has to change sides to restore balance."

"I don't believe you!" With that, the two disappeared again. Thanias found himself in free fall, landing before Mithdrool's throne.

Mithdrool looked up in wonderment.

"How? What?" Thanias was confused. His forearm stung from Tatiana's grip during their trip.

"How in all of Kluanaria did you just fall through my ceiling Thanias? Who are you looking for?"

"My niece, Tatiana. She just transported me all over to include into the past."

"Interesting, now seriously, what happened?"

"I just told you. And her family is unaware of this ability."

"I think you need more rest Thanias. You were encased in that gem for some time you know. While you rest, I will look into this travel and time thing."

After releasing Thanias, she traveled to Treah, where Shadowblyts called home high in the peaks of the mountains that formed part of the barrier of the worlds. She glanced out and could occasionally see the Veil between worlds fade in and out. A Veil Guard bowed and walked past her as she made her way to the seat of the Shadowblyt. She was surprised to see Guilles greet her instead of Rithmas.

"Welcome Tatiana. Welcome to the home of Shadowblyts and Izmaa. I am pleased your journey was safe."

"I am glad you are here, Guilles. I need you to help me. I have this power and it lets me do things that no one else can. I don't know where it came from."

"Relax, Tat. Do you have a book or something maybe that taught you this advanced stuff?"

"No, maybe the Crystal Dragon taught me. Sometimes I learn this while I am daydreaming, but mostly when I am asleep. Can you help me?"

"No, but Rithmas may be able to. You must tell him everything." The two walked down the hall where Rithmas was seated at a table prepared with light snacks for three.

"Be seated, please." Rithmas nodded and the chairs slid outward for the two guests. "What brings you here Tatiana, daughter of Myron, grandchild of High Lord Zanor and Harold?"

"Thank you Rithmas. I know my family, and I also know Grandpa Harold is War and that he saved everyone because the Orders did not work together the first time."

"Where do you get your information from?"

"It comes to me, and I can see the past, present, and future. I don't want to but I can, through my seeing stones, like Uncle Lucien. But something else is bugging me. I found out that I can save people like my sister and Altus and go to different places and even different time."

"How did you save them?"

"I had a hold of their heads with my hands and stared them straight in the eye, then I said some words, but I don't remember, and poof they were fixed."

"Where did you learn this form? It is not even taught anymore, because it requires extreme focus and control."

"In dreams. Sometimes things happen and I learn while weird stuff is happening, like to my sister. Then one day I was out walking along and thinking about what it would be like to move as fast as the barn swallows and hummingbirds. Then the next thing I knew I was going really fast and landed in Kaprius. So it took me a time to figure out…"

"Do Malos or Menosh know of this?" Guilles asked.

"No, no one does, except you two. Kren, my zephyr or nymph I can't remember, knows also. Have you seen Alasha, my sprite? She said she was going to her homeland until I needed her."

"No child." Rithmas spoke. "Come with me. Irra and Onachala will be her soon, so rest. You have had a long day." He escorted Tatiana to the guest house where she found a soft bed and fell asleep.

Guilles, in the meantime went to the veiled mirror in which he scryed with Impresaria and Gareth. He did this as he realized why Tatiana had avoided her direct family and chose the safer route. He asked that Tatiana be protected, as the family has a history that can change everything for better or worse. He knew Impresaria could get Lucien to Tatiana quickly.

"Gareth, it is good to speak with you since our journey through the Veil to Earth."

"Aye, Guilles. This seems to be very urgent from the message I received before this."

"One of the Newlings has a most powerful gift, let's just say the Mithdroolean Legion already knows. Jaetoth is still in the mage prison as is Llylandra."

"Who, Guilles?" Impresaria asked as if she already knew.

"The young girl of Myron, Tatiana."

"I will send Lucien immediately. She will be safe here." Impresaria left her chamber and sought out Lucien, her husband.

"Well, Gareth, I believe we need to summon all of the Orders, both main and minor. Especially the Sprites. Alasha has vanished. Who knows what Mithdrool will do with this knew found knowledge? Especially since the Newling also has seeing stones."

Gareth thought for a moment. "We will hold the Council in Treah then. Are you able to hide the girl from all things magic?"

"Yes. I have requested Irra and Onachala return at once to keep her company and I have her masked." Guilles responded.

"Be sure to include all Orders, even those in Mercurian and Vale Kilowas."

"There is still resistance in those lands?"

"Yes, Gareth. Seek out Omiporici of Mercurian, an Interval responsible for sprites, zephyrs and nymphs, but right now is trying to restore his homeland. In Kilowas, you need to find Blayne she is responsible for the Veil Guards. Omiporici would be good to speak to about Tatiana. They have some of the oldest knowledge, next to Aantiri and Chrinthold."

"Do you foresee any issues with the Council?" Gareth asked.

"No, everything should go smoothly. High Lord Beryth will be here along with Lady Phallas. They may have some insight on Tatiana as well."

"What about Zanor and Harold. You know this may cause some feelings to be expressed."

"Relax, Gareth. Tatiana's true education from Kluanaria seems to be advancing, rather unexpectedly, however. There should not be any upset like when Harold permitted Iris and the family to leave permanently from Ruan to Weelin."

"Are you kidding? There was almost a civil war over that." Gareth added.

Guilles chimed in. "It is in the past. So let it be."

"Look at the 'let it be' we have now! Mithdrool was defeated, but he sure is back and I know several Orders are considering alternatives."

Rithmas added, "Do we know anything about this Llylandra who corrupted Thanias?"

"No. Maybe Edwina remembers something. She was held in vale Kilowas with the group for a while." Gareth added, "What happens if Tatiana leaves here?"

"I cannot say, but she will be visible to the enemy and vulnerable. For heaven's sake, she is only seven, as of today. She will be hunted until captured." Rithmas stated as he paced.

Tatiana was asleep when Irra and Onachala arrived. They sat at a table playing Crazy Eights while they waited for her to wake up. Her friend, Tommy, showed up with food his mother made for the group.

"Hey Irra and Ona! Is Tat up yet?"

"No." Onachala said as she got up from the table. "What a way to spend a birthday."

"Yeah, Tat is seven today." Tommy smiled and showed them the cake. "Her grandmas sent it. They said they had a meeting here somewhere. Anyway, mom sent some cookies too."

Zanor stopped by the guest house on his way to council. He entered Tatiana's room and closed the door. "Tatiana, wake up."

Tatiana stirred and jumped as she saw her grandfather sitting next to her. "Why are you here?'

"You caused a rift in the fabric of Kluanaria. I am here with all of the Orders to figure out how. Before you say anything, I know the why part."

Tatiana sat up and took her grandfather's hand. "Papa Z, no one is stopping any of this. Mithdrool is about to get the new lady out of the jail in Kaprius. He also has plans for the deadmage and Mercurian."

"Where have you learned of this?"

"It comes to me when I daydream or sleep."

"Where is your sprite?"

"She hasn't been around since Ruan. She said she was going home and she would come back when I needed her."

Zanor paced. "Are you absolutely sure, Tat?"

"Yes Papa."

"Thank you, Tat, now I believe your friends have a party planned for you."

Tatiana gave Zanor a big hug and ran out to the dining area. Zanor paused in the dining area and lit the candles for them and presented Tatiana with a gift. She opened it quickly finding several items.

"This is your official circlet, Tatiana." A familiar voice spoke from the entryway. She turned and saw her dad. "Happy birthday, Squirt!" Myron walked over, hugged his daughter, and presented her with another gift.

"What is this branch for?"

"That branch will shrink or grow to your height and age. It is important for when you need to defend yourself." Zanor said.

Myron added, "It is a staff and it will also help you focus your abilities and…"

"And they mean it protects you and makes your magic stronger." Onachala interjected.

The grown-ups left while the kids and teens enjoyed cake, cookies, and punch, which was a new drink for the Kluanarians.

After the adults were gone, Tatiana began wondering if the grown-ups were going to imprison her like Thanias was for a time. She paced and thought. "Onachala, do you have a way that we can sneak into the meeting?"

"Umm, no, but since I am the oldest of us four, I am gonna try and go in. I will stay as long as they let me and let you know what they are gonna do. Then you can decide what you want to do before they are done."

"I was thinking of just going and taking out Mithdrool. Jaetoth and the mean lady are locked up and my uncle won't dare hurt me."

"How? You are just one little kid like me." Tommy said.

"Your box thing, of course! Remember William and Fred said that it has special powers, not just different colors flashing. I think it is…"

Onachala interrupted, "It is called a prismatic prison. True Veil Keepers all have one. The darn dragon forgot that part. So, you would easily be able to lock Mithdrool up."

"I don't know how it works." Tommy said in a disappointed tone. "William said that in time I would know. Fred, the dragon, said not to be too excited because it will be hard to find a trainer for me."

"The place, Vale Kilowas, has a small town that has real nice people who are Veil Keepers. The Veil Guardians usually have a box like it too. We can go there and ask." Onachala added.

"But Ona, if Tatiana leaves here, the bad guys can see her again." Irra added.

"What's this about a Veil," a tall figure asked as he rounded the corner into the room.

"Uncle Lucien! I didn't think you would come." Tatiana raced over to her uncle and gave him a hug.

"Tatiana, tell me what is going on, please. Impresaria said this is very important."

Tatiana recounted every detail from Thanias breaking out to Edwina collapsing to herself healing her sister and Altus and dragging Thanias everywhere and ending up in Treah. Lucien sat as he processed all of the information.

"Oh, yeah. I forgot. My sprite is gone. She said she was going home and would come if I need her. I don't think she is a sprite though."

"Well, that is possible. Perhaps she is a shaepling. Talaharian could easily have had one of these about." Lucien pondered.

"Who is he?" Onachala asked.

"He is a deadmage. He converted Llylandra probably twenty years ago, in Earth time. On Earth deadmages are called necromancers."

Irra asked, "So you think that he has something to do with this?"

"More than likely. He led Mithdrool to a summoning place where Mithdrool could try to raise and control a horseman known on Earth as Death. William, Fred, along with Malificence and a small girl named Luly crushed the plan. Right now," Lucien paused and cast an over-protective spell over the four kids, "I want you to use your special power and go to Luly. She has your powers too and can help you. Think only about Luly. Now take this to her. She will know what to do. I will be there after the meeting." Lucien gave a small object to Tatiana.

"Are you telling the Council where we are? Tatiana asked as she hugged her uncle.

The Kluanarians

"No Tat. They would not understand. Oh, yes, a Veil Keeper is there along with a Shadowblyt and Izmaa."

"By Lucien," the four kids chimed as the clasped hands and focused on Luly. Lucien watched as a swirling wind of flower petals and snowflakes consumed the kids and they disappeared.

As the cloud dispersed, Tatiana immediately recognized her first camping area in Treah. She ran over and reflected on all of the events of that adventure. A tall, slender lady approached. Tatiana noticed a slight green hue of light surrounded the woman as she approached.

"I am Luly. Lucien said that I would find you here."

"Hi. I am Tatiana. These are my friends, Tommy, Onachala and Irra. Lucien said to give this to you." She passed a small object to Luly who held out her hand in anticipation. "I think I know what it is too."

Luly smiled in amusement. "What do you think it is child?"

"That is the pouch of endless pockets, and in it are three horsemen."

"It does exist!" Irra exclaimed. "I thought maybe it was made up."

"How do you know of it Tatiana?"

"Walther of the Palisade told me a bedtime story and it was in it."

"Very well. This is that very pouch. We have a bit of walking to do before we reach our destination. There are some special folks awaiting you along with your trainers."

The four kids followed Luly on an almost nonexistent pathway that wound up a steep slope, through a tunnel and into a grove. The small grove opened into a very desolate place with enormous peaks surrounding. The village they walked to was very simple and seemed disenchanted as compared to everywhere else on Kluanaria or Earth for that matter.

"Tat, where are we?" Tommy asked as he watched the residents go about their business.

"I don't know, and I am kinda scared. Uncle Lucien said he would be here. I won't stay the night here. Papa Z told me about a place like this. It is a very sad place and needs healed somehow"

"So you do know then?" Irra and Onachala chimed in at the same time.

Tatiana whispered, "It might be Bittern. Maybe Luly will know."

Luly was ahead of them speaking to a group who appeared to be in charge. Tatiana and Tommy jumped and screamed. They almost ran

Brenda M. Hokenson

down the path, but a pair of hands grasped their shoulder. "Calm down. Calm down. No need to rush off." Lucien whispered as he gripped their shoulder firmly.

"Do you think this place is like Bittern, only warmer?" Tatiana asked.

BITTERN

"**L**ET ME TELL YOU ABOUT Bittern." Lucien said as he took the kids to the small grove and sat down in the center with them.

"Back when Kluanaria had just begun to emerge with true strong villages and as you know Orders, who could be of any race on the planet, Bittern was a remarkable sight. Treah lay at the land's base. Bittern was somewhat isolated, because of its location. The races enjoyed the diversity but the Orders wanted to be separated out so they may learn from their own Order and not worry about the others trying to take their knowledge. The truly felt that their knowledge would be contaminated by other Orders' practices. The Shadowblyts and Izmaa once inhabited Treah and worked closely with the Intervals in maintaining balance in Kluanaria. They were very strong allies.

During this time, Shaeplings were rampant and bending the ears of many in all the Orders. There was a deadmage who wanted ultimate rule. He convinced many to join him. Mercurian became his stronghold. His parents were part of the court of the high seat. He knew of Mithdrool. His parents helped defeat the dark one before. This was even before the horseman ran rampant. This man knew that finding and restoring Mithdrool would make him very powerful."

"What was his name, Lucien?" The four kids interrupted.

"Oh yes, this deadmage had a name, Talaharian. The Order of the Star caught wind of his plan. They sent messages via zephyrs, nymphs, and sprites to all of the Orders. The intervals were first to answer. The two decided that there would have to be a meeting involving all of the Orders to solve this, as the fate of Kluanaria was in jeopardy. Messages were sent out from Bittern, the

stronghold of Intervals, or druids as Earth people call them. Responses began to come in and it was clear. Bittern would hold the Council.

Bittern at the time was the most pristine place on Kluanaria, except for the beaches of Mercurian. The elevation was such that forces such as the Truncheon, who were turned by Mithdrool and now by Talaharian, would not be able to reach it. The villages in the lower land of Treah had a passage to Bittern for safety. The buildings you see today have fallen to ruin. There used to be pillars leading to the grove. Before you got to the pillars, you would have to pass through the high seat of Bittern and given a blessing of passage. The structures were as white as the snow; the windows were always covered by frost. The land was cold, covered in snow and had amazing ice sculptures at many entrances to the village. The only location not covered in snow and ice was the grove. The hall was elaborate, adorned in ice crystals and the seats were of wood from Treah. The aisles, grass with flowers along the edge of the benches closets the aisles. The high seat was crystalline. As always, there were gusts of wind though the hall from zephyrs delivering messages. Every so often, flower petals and snow would intermingle in the air as Intervals entered and left the hall.

When all of the Orders arrived for Council, the hall was changed to accommodate all. There were at least ten representatives for each Order. Monitors were placed who could detect Shaeplings. Veil Guards also joined the meeting for the Protectors Report. Veil Guards, Chrinthold, Paladins, and Truncheon took part in this report. The serious business began and after the day expired, no results. The Orders retired to a special quarters designed for each specific Order, which was a first. This would become a standard over time. The next day, the Stars began to complain. Their rooms were dull and boring, it was frigid outside and it takes from their abilities, they did not want to b in a wasteland.

The Intervals, in hearing this through many channels and in many ways, decided to accommodate the selfish Stars. They asked the Shadowblyts and Izmaa for assistance in the grove. After an hour long prayer and meditation, a spell was cast. All of the snow dissipated, the ice, gone, the beauty that once was, was now bare. It took much energy to get flowers and grass to grow quickly to fill the barren area. Two Intervals were internally damaged from the intense concentration, one Shadowblyt lay on the ground, unable to utter another word. They were taken to a healing house, which also later became a standard

The Kluanarians

in villages, and the remainder returned to the Council, very sullen and quiet. The Stars accepted the gesture of unselfishness and were satisfied.

After the Council, the Stars left and offered no help in restoring the land. The other Orders helped, but it was in vain. The land after the meeting, deteriorated and some parts crumbled into dust as the Orders stood and watched. Many folk abandoned the land and went to Treah where their strongest friends accepted them. They spent long hours together researching the restoration of the once formidable land.

One day, not long ago, a group of visitors who came to Ruan from a distant place, Weelin, journeyed to Treah and made camp. A young girl, who wanted to see a druid, sparked the interest of all. The intervals heard her questions and thoughts. They provided what the group needed.

"They also brought Menosh and Malos to Treah, as an answer may have been discovered." Luly interjected. "You are by far, the most gifted Interval in a great while."

"Uh, hmm, as I was saying. This group ventured into Treah, have been protected by all three Orders, plus their families' Orders, and have no idea why. I believe, Tatiana, that once Bittern is restored, we can imprison Mithdrool. The Intervals need to be completely healed, as well as the Shadowblyts and Izmaa. Your mother is a Star; she can assist in fixing this devastated area." Lucien added. "You must convince her to repair this land with you."

"I still don't see why I have to be here." Tatiana scuffed her foot on the dry ground.

"Because I said so." Lucien said firmly.

"You aren't my parents and I don't care!" Tatiana ran off.

Lucien yelled after her, "No, but I am your uncle and protector at this time." He shot a glance at Luly, hoping she could stop her. As Luly extended her arm out to reach Tatiana, time seemed to freeze briefly. Is all Luly grasped was thin air.

Kren, the nymph who was Tatiana's messenger, appeared in the grove where Tatiana was running to. Tatiana, as always had her notebook, recording the events of the day and added details of the buildings and land. She counted at least fifty different types of trees in the grove.

"Kren, how am I supposed to do anything? I don't even know where these spells come from."

"Lass, you can restore this place. You know how already. Your mother is not needed, and I can help. See nymphs also have powers but we get ignored, like little kids do. The spell you placed on Edwina and Altus to heal them is the one that will restore here."

"How do you know?"

"I have seen it undone here and the spell is pretty much the same to reverse it. It took many Intervals, Shadowblyts, and Izmaa to turn this place like it is now. I believe Irra and Onachala can help too. You will need to know exactly where the ceremony happened."

"How will I know that?"

Kren responded with a deep sigh, "You just will child."

"Did you teach me all of this stuff?"

"No, that knowledge is special and was bound to your spirit since you were created. It is slowly awakening as is the knowledge in Onachala and Irra. Tommy will be strong. I am taking him to the Veil Guard after our meal and he will learn much."

"Can Luly actually help me? My mark hurts."

"Yes, Luly can help you. It should hurt, and if you look closely, it looks to be bleeding. That is not real blood, but it is representing the pain and anguish here in Bittern. It will do that every time you set foot here. Remove your shoes now, and let your body guide you to the ceremony's location of old."

Tatiana was unaware that the elders were observing her. Lucien and Luly stood by as she let her body be one with the earth. She closed her eyes and walked all over the place. Irra and Onachala joined her in procession, shoes off. She stopped, noticing a large group gathered behind her through her mind, at the other end of the village. A small empty pool about the size of a mud puddle dried up was in front of her. There were remnants of trees that she could feel their extreme desperation in the air.

"It is here, Kren."

"How do you know?"

"The trees, well the used to be trees have spoken. The dead trees spoke to me!"

While the procession was occurring in Bittern, Mithdrool was studying the past. He gleaned what he could from ancient texts and the history involving him. He turned to Thanias for more clues.

"Thanias, while you are awake, at least for the moment, tell me about your niece."

Thanias sat up in his recovery room and pondered. "Well, there is some history that you may or may not know. Her mother is a Star, her father a Truncheon, her grandparents are most powerful."

"I know all four of her grandparents. They saw to my downfall once and in a couple of them, more than once. There was one of their friends who thought I was an Interval."

"Who, pray tell?"

"The name, the name…eludes me. No, it was not Malos although he is strong."

"Could it be the dragon master, William?"

"Ah, yes, William, he has been my ancient enemy for millennia. Now tell me about the child. Can she control what she is doing?"

"I, I don't really see Tatiana as a threat."

"Well, then, I don't have to tell you that she is able to reverse Bittern's demise."

"There is not a Star to support her. After all they were the main reason it died. I heard tell that Iris is in a crystal carried by Menosh."

"Fool! Tatiana doesn't need any help; the ancient alliances are still strong between the three who share the land of Treah,"

"Ok then. When I first met Tatiana, she seemed sad and had many questions which to me were amusing. First was 'what do druids look like', then was can I meet them sometime,' followed by do they come down from up there very much.' Then Tatiana told me of things that have been happening to her at home, well her not true home on Earth, and also in Ruan. It seemed to bug her as her friends noticed some things.

When Paul broke his leg, thanks to Llylandra, we ended up in Burwash where she got to meet the healers, some of which were Intervals. Truance is one but her focus is healing and no threat. Soon after, the great ceremony was to take place, since my brother decided to return from self-exile to protect the darn Star to his post as Doyen to the Truncheon.

Before the ceremony, I was permitted to take the children on a tour of the receiving hall, where all Orders have a room especially suited to their customs. Tatiana did not know where to go, but I could see that the Interval chamber was drawing on her somehow. I took her toward it and told her she could look in it if she wanted. She had just entered the room when the room sealed itself. I was not able to pass through and all was hidden to me. Tatiana came out a couple hours later with a Sprite and a Nymph. So, in my responsible uncle mode, I asked Malos if that is where she belonged. He confirmed this. I helped her find appropriate attire in the massive wardrobe and Malos found the Circlet of Seasons." Thanias paused in reflection for a moment while Mithdrool received a report from Mercurian.

"Oh, yes. Continue, please Thanias." Mithdrool spoke as he read the parchment and quickly sent response."

"As the pomp and circumstance of the unseating of me and the introduction of the Newlings continued, the comet appeared. This to me was my sign that finding you and restoring you was upon us. The family departed back to Earth; Iris did not want any part of things and Myron had things to complete before his true return. The family had a vacation at Clamshoe Bay."

"How do you know all of this?"

"I was there for the most part. Llylandra, after retrieving me from the ceremony, ported us to Mercurian. We were able to gaze upon the family through a special mirror, like those seeing stones Lucien has. A massive storm was forming off the coast. Somehow, they found refuge in an old structure with lots of history. She somehow made the storm dissipate. I never saw anything like that other than from a more senior Interval."

"So, if I understand you correctly, with this information and the history I have compiled, I believe we will have an extreme battle if we do not end this swiftly. No one has any power of that magnitude at this time, except her. I believe she created the storm, unknowingly. She seems to need at least a bit of attention or things happen. We need to get her to see our side of the story. She is the ultimate tool."

"Are you serious? Do you know how crazy that sounds? Are you ingesting hemlock or something?"

"Thanias, I will tell you once. She thinks you are what she is supposed to save. So let her and in the process bend her."

Thanias pondered this for a bit and then lay down. He was still injured.

"Do you know anything about the Izmaa and Shadowblyt Newlings?"

Thanias yawned, "Can we discuss this later, please. Let my mind recharge. This discussion has drained me." He drifted to sleep as his sentence ended.

In the meantime, Mithdrool turned his attention to Mercurian and inquiring about all of the Newlings recently recognized by the High Lord, Zanor. Threads trickled in from Shaeplings who had infiltrated the Izmaa. A veiled herald of the Morket arrived.

"You must not disrupt Mercurian." The herald said. "You must restore order or face utter destruction."

"What will the once mighty Morket do if I don't?"

"I will smite you where you stand, deadmage!" Impresaria spoke as she removed the veil. "She raised her hand in preparation for the retaliation. "I have aide, this time." Lucien emerged from a behind Impresaria.

"Go ahead and try. You still have the Fraelochan problem and Talaharian to deal with, and they are for more vicious than I ever was."

"You forget we too have eyes everywhere. Leave the Newlings alone and surrender now. We may let you remain awake, or do you prefer stasis." Lucien spoke as a Veil Guardian approached with a prismatic prison.

Mithdrool snapped his fingers and vanished from his lair.

"Impresaria, what do the two Newlings have for knowledge?" Lucien asked as he watched his brother sleep. "What about the Fraelochs and Talaharian?"

"They were born with all their knowledge. They did not have to learn it like your nieces and nephew. Their powers dwarf that of their highest in their Orders. They can easily change balance as can Tatiana. The Fraelochs under Talaharian are ready to raze all the Mercurian lands."

"So, what does that mean to us?"

"It means these three will need a special spell of protection. Now let's get back to Bittern." The two vanished as the Veil Guard also departed.

Tatiana and her two friends knelt at the depression where a massive tree once stood. "This tree was most important to the stability of Bittern." Tatiana brushed back some tears, as did Irra.

"Let's be done with this." Irra said as she helped Tatiana and Onachala up.

Each Newling had a different part to do in the restoration of the land. Impresaria and Lucien arrived as the girls prepared.

"We need the Morket!" Onachala exclaimed.

Hearing this, Impresaria stepped forward. She removed a pouch and opened it. All knew some of the contents of the pouch, from lore. There was a glistening substance in a small vile that the Chrinthold sprinkled in the sunken ground of the mighty tree.

Onachala began. "*Mendos aspriti terrini. Mendos aspriti terrini!*" She then took a small pouch out and sprinkled a dark green powder around the sunken ground, but not in it. She then knelt by where an altar once stood.

Irra continued by removing a vile of water of the blessed earth and sprinkling it in the center of the hole. "*Mendos apsiriti flora! Mendos apsiriti flora!*" She then took her place by Onachala.

"*Mirris Edziza, mirris Treah, mirris Burwash, mirris Burwash. Mendis floras, mendis terrini, mendis intervae. Mendis!*" Tatiana repeated over and over as she circled the depression. "*Mirris. Mendis. Mendis, mirris Bittern. Restoris rime.*" She went into the hole and knelt. From the air she grasped a snowflake and placed it in the exact center. "*Flurris, flurries, mendis floras, mendis terrini, mendis intervae!*" Tatiana stood in the center of the depression and extended her arms to the heavens. As she lowered her arms a massive blizzard from the East began to roll in. The village folk went into the great hall and braced for the worst. William arrived just in time. He ran to the center of the hole as Tatiana continued her chant. Onachala and Irra rose and fell into procession repeating their chants. William removed from his jacket a small seedling and threw it down to his feet.

The tree immediately began to grow. The dead grove behind where the altar once stood began to recover. The buildings that once were dilapidated started to restore; they no longer looked like hollow shells with twig roofs. The snow deepened and Frostlings began to return. The Frostlings began to sculpt ice that hung down on pillars; some began etching patterns on the windows. Others went into the great hall bringing the chilling air in and restored the interior as the ice reformed.

Tatiana was exhausted, but continued on, along with her friends. William stepped out of the hole as the tree expanded and stretched its might branches into the air. William fell in procession behind Onachala and finished the ceremony. "*Mendis todis, mendis todis, hastae!*"

The four returned to the fully restored altar and emptied the remains of their viles and pouches into a small levitating bowl. The contents froze instantly and a Frostling whisked over and shattered the contents into small flakes, then in one motion dispersed the small flakes into the air. Bittern was saved.

A celebration began soon after in the great hall. William took his place on the High Seat. "Tatiana, Onachala, and Irra, we are most grateful for your generosity in restoring our and your lands. I did not know this could be done without a Star, so thank you! Please make yourselves at home. I understand you have much to learn and we will oblige this request which was brought forth by Lucien." William nodded at Lucien and Impresaria.

"William, I have one request, please," Tatiana spoke.

"Yes."

"You did not hear my question." She stood puzzled as she watched Menosh appear with her mother. She ran up and hugged both. The assembly applauded as Frostlings danced in the air.

"Where have you been? You didn't even say good-bye." Tatiana said as she watched more familiar faces enter through portals. "Edwina! Edwina! Dad!" She raced to them and held on tightly. "Where is Paul?"

"He is in training. I am not certain when you will see him again." Myron said as he picked his daughter up.

All of the kids' families were present for the fabulous ceremony that William hosted. Zanor arrived with Paul a bit later as the long procession was winding down. Tatiana ran up to them and hugged them. "You forgot your dragon," she whispered to her brother.

Tommy sat with his family and Tatiana's for the great Feast of Restoration. "Tat, Kren said that Wryn will not train me as he has never trained a Veil Keeper before. I will find someone in Vale Kilowas who will help me."

"Blayne is there, but you can't go there. Bad things are happening there."

"But I need to learn."

"There is another way." Menosh overheard this in Tatiana's thoughts. He sent a thought to her. "Tatiana, let it go. Tommy has a trainer here, just calm down."

Tatiana gazed up at Menosh who nodded his head. She nodded in return and refrained from speaking. She returned a thought to Menosh. *"Luly is in danger and Ruan can't hide her."*

THE MERCURIAN'S FUTURE

WHILE GREAT CELEBRATIONS CONTINUED, THE Orders' highest members excused themselves and met in an anti-chamber to decide how to save the Mercurians.

Gareth came forth with the Kluanarian map of all. It was basically a rather large atlas that had all key locations, routes and Veil Points marked. It was a special map as it also was animated. It was animated in a way that would show massive movements from large armies to include their path and projected path. Paul was permitted to sit in on the meeting as he was learning Aantiri, who have to learn everything about everything.

"We use computers in Weelin and it does the same thing." Paul spoke to ease the tension in the room. "Do any of the villages along the waterfront have large ships?"

"Aye, they do lad." Gareth responded. "What are you thinking?"

"Has there ever been a time in which you used your sailing vessels to help in a battle?"

"No," Zanor responded. "But that does not mean it can't be done, just never tried."

"I believe that it would save several weeks march across the continent since we obviously should not go through the frozen desert to get to Nagazthastar. I don't believe the truncheon use portals, but I could be wrong."

"Well thought out." Guilles responded. "We do have contact with Omiporici inside Nagazthastar. We can use a mass transport device…"

Impresaria stopped him in mid-sentence. "We are currently located between a darn rock and hard place. Vale Kilowas sits north of us on the waters and slightly to the north and east is the continent of Forest Mithdrool. So, I think we can safely port our Truncheon and everyone else who will be involved into Burwash. It is a safer place to launch from than Kaprius or here. The Palisades has a river, but it is not deep or wide enough for the vessels to get to sea."

Myron paced. "How many Truncheons are we talking about? Will there be enough rations available? The Mercurian lands are vast, and I know they need our help, but how do you propose accomplishing this? Our ranks are thin because of Thanias and his wasteful petty wars to prove something."

"If you would not have left in the first place, because of the Star, we would not be in this predicament!" Lunacerian shouted from across the room. "You left us all in jeopardy because your wife is too namby-pamby. She needs to either start fulfilling her duties in her Order or give up her darned powers."

Many in the room were in agreement with this. They called for her to be present for this meeting and Kren obliged and retrieved her.

"Why do you want me here?" Iris demanded.

"We have all agreed that you either start fulfilling your obligation to the Star Order or relinquish all of your powers immediately." Lunacerian stated. "You have been a detriment to our very survival by your antics. You cost us many Truncheons and Paladins. Our strength wanes while you remain hidden on Earth. Tell me, how long do you think Earth would survive if Mithdrool makes it through the Veil?"

"It is not my fault you are an inept Chancellor representing all of the Orders for the past century, Lunacerian. You brought this on yourself."

"No, Iris..." Malificence stood, "You chose to flee at a time in which stirrings of evil were rising. You gave poor Myron an ultimatum, his true duty or you and the kids. You caused this rift and now you must decide."

"I did not force him to leave. Myron, please tell them."

"No, Iris. I supported your decision all of this time. I must lead now. If I don't Kluanaria will not be able to protect Earth and it will more than perish. It will be absorbed by the evil here, and collapse. The planets will be gone."

"You... You don't know this. Who will take my place in the Order?"

Brenda M. Hokenson

"You are not needed," Malificence responded. "I am still here and there is a very strong Newling who is quite capable of taking your place." She turned and faced Iris. "I am sorry for this. *Confisci a satelli, confisci a ispiriti a Iris restori a comini ispiriti!*" A brilliant light shot from Iris and into the heavens. She collapsed to the ground, powerless. A Veil Keeper escorted her out and the Council resumed.

"Now, as I was saying," Impresaria continued, "the waterways from Ruan and Palisades are too shallow and very narrow. I believe that Omiporici has sent us a tally."

"Ah, yes." Harold said as he strolled into the room. He could smell the anticipation of the inevitable conflict. "I have to stay neutral in this, as I am not interested much in the outcome here as I am of what will happen to the Earth Realm. I will read the report and excuse myself. 'There are approximately six hundred of the Legion and one hundred twenty-two deadmages that currently occupy Mercurian lands. One thousand are enroute, via march from a small landing point, Krispin.' Is there even a Krispin on the map? I don't remember sacking it?" Harold paused and looked to Gareth for an answer. Gareth pulled out an older map and noted the location with a nod. "Very well, 'of the six hundred occupying, two hundred seven are in Nagazthastar and there are plans to break into the sand cavern stronghold of Beryth.

Guilles interjected. "Well, I'll be! What chance do they have against the sand?"

"I believe a very strong chance." Beryth spoke from the opposite end of the room. "Our powers are waning from keeping up the defenses for the past twenty years. This very Council never has done anything to support us, yet we have sent many to the wars leaving so few for our own defense. We lost Nagazthastar, not because of my rule or its defense, but because no one supported us when we plead for help. Now, we ask humbly of William, please allow us refuge in Bittern."

"There is room enough for you. Please let us assist you in your exodus from the dark sands." William spoke as he outstretched his arm to grasp Beryth's wrist.

Zanor continued where Impresaria left off. "We will need our skilled naval crews to prepare. I think we need to count our members before we go whole-hog first. I do believe at this time we should adjourn until morning, when we can resume after more collected thoughts. Council dismissed."

While the Council met, the Newlings were busy having their own discussion. Edwina was still recovering. Irra and Onachala noticed her and sort of hovered about her for most of the evening. "I don't suppose either of you can help me remember?"

The two girls giggled. "Of course, we can!" They exclaimed. Onachala practically dragged Edwina the entire length of the hall to get her into a very, very small room.

"Hold still Edwina!" Irra said as each girl stood to an opposite side of their subject. "Sit down."

After Edwina was seated, they placed their hands on her head one each to the forehead and one each to the very back of the head. In unison they began a spell. *"Mendis a memorae a di. Mendis a memrae a Edwina."* A deep purple mist filled the space they occupied. Edwina relaxed and closed her eyes. She could feel the mist moving through her nostrils and ears, eventually her mind. Her eyes watered as the mist repaired damaged brain matter and slowly regenerated nerve endings and restored lost knowledge. She watched the mist dissipate as she opened her eyes, her memory once stronger with the very last spell she used on the tip of her tongue and her last journeys fresh in her mind.

"Thank you, Ona and Irra." Edwina stood, "I think we need to get Mithdrool out of the picture, permanently." The girls nodded in agreement and told her to rest for a while.

Tatiana found Tommy staring at the random snow flurries. "Hey Tommy, are you okay?"

"Yeah, I just wish I had a way to help everyone like you."

"You will. You are gonna be an awesome Veil Keeper!"

"They don't do much."

"Yes they do. Grab your box." Tommy barely had hold of the box when Tatiana began pulling him down the hallway where Irra and Onachala were waiting. "Are you ready?" Tatiana asked of the girls. They nodded.

"Everyone take each other's hand and don't let go." They all braced with teeth gritted. "Focus on Omiporici."

"Why her?" Tommy said.

"Because Mithdrool is headed toward her house, and we can beat him there and take him down."

"Ok then!!" The three clasped hands tighter as Tatiana took them through a whirl of flowers and snowflakes, arriving immediately in the home of Omiporici.

"Don't be alarmed." Tatiana said as she peered through one of her seeing pebbles. "We will beat Mithdrool here!!"

"Why are you Newlings here? Who are you? Mithdrool is coming here?"

"I am Tatiana; this is Irra, Tommy, and Onachala. Yes, Mithdrool is coming here, to either recruit you or destroy you. And we are gonna stop him."

Omiporici tried not to laugh. "How pray tell, are you going to stop this deadmage?"

"You will let him in your house and let him talk to you. It is rumored he likes cheese and wine. Then when he is completely ok with being here, we will zap him."

"I have not yet trained you, Interval."

"Give me a chance."

Omiporici peered out the window briefly. "Very well." He cast an invisibility shield over the Newlings that also protected any spell they cast. He went to the door as someone was knocking. "Yes, who is there?"

"I am Mithdrool. I wish to speak with you about your gift. Let me in Omiporici."

"And if I refuse?"

"Let's just say you won't last the hour if you refuse."

"Very well. Come in, but don't touch anything."

"Forgive my intrusion. I have joined forces with Thanias…"

"Thanias. Where is he? He has not been here in many, many months."

"Well, he was injured. But any way, I am in need of an Interval to assist me."

"Assist you with what, lord?" He asked as he retrieved spirits and food.

Mithdrool was flattered by his kind gesture. "I need someone who can help me free a very dear friend from captivity."

"You have been on a long journey, please, relax and I will consider this assistance.

"Your hospitality is most appreciated Morket."

"Ah, I see you have an eye for rare races, or is this your first stop in searching for a loyal Interval?"

He laughed. "So, tell me, will you be able to assist me?"

As the conversation continued, the well-hidden Newlings prepared. Onachala and Irra did a small ritual of resistance as they knew Mithdrool has automatic blocks set up to protect him. The four surrounded the deadmage. Tommy recited words to open the prismatic prison a small Veil Shrike appeared on his shoulder. Not visible to Mithdrool or Omiporici, brilliant colors emanating from the box encased the entire room. Tatiana was stunned by what she was seeing. The four watched as the colors slowly consumed Mithdrool's body and were startled when the lid snapped closed. The invisibility lifted and the Veil Shrike flew down and provided a seal to the prismatic prison.

A small celebration broke out briefly, when Tommy asked, "So now how do we stop the deadmages and Mithdrool's Legion?"

"Talaharian is still here, somewhere. We have to stop him so the deadmages will go back to their own lands. The Legion should vanish since Mithdrool is defeated." Omiporici said as he looked out a window where plumes of mist rising from the fallen Legion were visible. He saw the deadmages and warlocks running away.

"We will never catch them." Tatiana said disappointedly. "They aren't from here are they? The deadmages I mean."

"Sure, we will," Tommy said. "That last little bit of my spell was for them. Their portals will land them in the Vale Kilowas prison, so Blayne should be very proud of me." Tommy nodded and crossed his arms in triumph. "What! The deadmages aren't from the Mercurian lands?"

"No, I am afraid they are not. They are Fraeloch. Llylandra is actually a Fraeloch as is Talaharian. They came from Phallas Minor, probably piggy backed the comet that passed through six years ago and probably have more enroute since it just passed again during your ceremony, Tatiana."

Impresaria said as she emerged from a portal opened and closed by a Veil Keeper.

"Thank you, Newlings." Omiporici said as he walked toward Impresaria. "Now we have much to do to heal the people of Nagazthastar and all of Mercurian."

"Truance and Malos are already working on that. The deadmages are contained, but we need to figure out how to send them back to Phallas Minor." Impresaria said. "Their containment is very, very temporary as their mind is stronger than the greatest Aantiri."

Menosh arrived with the Council and met the Newlings in the yard of Omiporici. "Well done young ones. You have fared better than I had expected. Tommy what a brilliant plan you came up with! Irra and Onachala, thank you for your blessings and Tatiana, thank you for being their vessel. You four have learned what the Highest of the Orders cannot comprehend, and I am proud."

"What did we learn Menosh?" Tommy asked.

"How to come together and work for a common goal of course. The Elders have never been able to do this, ever. You bring hope and more than that you bring the beginnings of peace and restoration to the whole of Mercurian and its people."

"But we gotta find Talaharian!" Onachala said.

"We will, in time. Perhaps you have renewed something in the Elders that will cause them to act decisively."

"We came because we didn't want any more people to get hurt." Tatiana yelled. "The big people keep ignoring the people who are hurt. Don't you understand?" She continued yelling as tears streamed down. "How can you be so dumb?" With that, Tatiana vanished into thin air.

"No! Tatiana. No!" Myron collapsed to his knees. "Don't run away. Don't run…"

Truance and Malos approached. "Tatiana will be okay." Truance said as she comforted him.

Edwina was with the Council. "How dare you say that Eupepsian!" Edwina started forming a small ball of light in her hands. "How dare you say that she will be okay! It is pretty clear that she isn't. Heck, you don't even know where she is or what she is capable of!"

"Edwina, stop." Zanor snapped. "Keep quiet while we meet."

"To hell with that!" Edwina snapped back. *"Tranisiti a Bittern!"* Tatiana however was not in Bittern. Edwina searched everywhere in the newly restored land. Tired from the mind healing and searching, she went to the Moons' chamber and went to sleep.

Ermenya took human form and descended to the bedside of Edwina. She reviewed all of the images that the Moon had stored for the day. She interpreted Tatiana's actions and that of Edwina. Ermenya placed a mark internally on Edwina to protect her, as the dragon knew things were about to get a lot worse. She then reappeared in Nagazthastar as her formidable self. Menosh was startled. He had not ever seen Ermenya before.

"What do you want dragon?" Menosh spoke as he raised his staff.

The dragon ignored him and took flight. She inhaled a very large amount of air and exhaled. The smoke rolled from her mouth as she circled the town and countryside. The Mercurians fell to the ground, consumed in smoke and gasping for air. The smoke cleared and all who collapsed, stood again completely renewed. She landed again. "Menosh let the Newlings and their families go to Weelin, now."

"How dare you tell me what to do dragon. I…"

"You have no power over any dragon, especially me."

The townsfolk and Council stood in awe as the crystal dragon noticed Fred descend. The Kluanarians could not hear dragon speak unless they were being addressed directly. The conversation to them looked like two dragons staring at each other.

Fred appeared. "Ermenya! Why are you here?"

"Yes Freiderich. I am here. Paul asked me to help. His training is progressing, and he is very strong in mind and soul."

"I see. Thank you for restoring the Mercurians. Can you tell me how to find Talaharian?"

"No, he is not of Kluanaria. I am unable to help you. The Fraelochs in town, however, are plotting, so you may consider acting."

"How do we return them?"

"First, we must find Talaharian, use Llylandra as a tool. We will have to consult Lady Phallas. She may have ancient writings on this. Her and Gareth."

Freiderich nodded in agreement. "Impresaria, can you arrange to have Llylandra transported here, and should we retrieve her?"

"She will be here within the hour." Impresaria responded.

Both dragons took flight and disappeared along with Gareth and Lady Phallas. They went to Bittern and had a smith prepare his forge for the finest metal shaping ever done. They then went to the newly restored grove and dropped a small sliverette of silver onto the frozen water in the leaf shaped basin.

An image formed very clearly. The Fraelochs and Talaharian had retreated to Edziza. They could see them attempting to communicate with their home world. The dragons and company were able to discern invasion plans for Earth.

"They don't want us. They want Earth!" Gareth exclaimed. "Oh boy, oh boy! How do we explain to the Earth leaders? They don't even know what truly exists!"

The dragons laughed. Ermenya finally responded. "We will explain it to them."

"How, they will just lock you up in some sort of cell in a far away unknown place." Gareth replied.

"Oh, believe me, they will listen." Fred countered.

Lady Phallas began asking questions. "What is so special about Edziza to these Fraelochs? They did not fight in the long, long battle there, no restore it."

"Didn't the horsemen pass through a long time ago?" Gareth inquired as he tried to remember all of the history for this land.

"They did, and one remains standing." Lady Phallas answered.

Edwina entered the grove where the four stood staring at frozen water. "The horsemen left this." She handed a brilliant, jeweled circlet to Fred. "They want this as it is used for summoning Shaeplings and other bad things. My grandma Malificence had it. I think you had her hold on to it, Fred."

"Yes, I did. I had no idea what it was for, but now I do."

"So, you two dragons know, if it is destroyed, they too will be destroyed." Edwina smiled.

"How...when...who?" Fred was dumbfounded with this information.

"I taught her all knowledge through the pouch of interchange. Her books had all of this information." Lunacerian interrupted. "And so you know, Tatiana is not safe."

"Where is she Moon?" Ermenya replied.

"She is searching for Paul and is currently at Edziza, unknowingly wandering into Talaharian. Look at the blasted image." Lunacerian departed, taking his protégé with him.

The four returned immediately to Mercurian. Ermenya made an announcement. "Mercurian is hereby declared safe. All Shaeplings and Talaharian have retreated to Edziza. There true target is not here, but Earth. Please all help each other during this recovery time."

Cheers were abounding. A great celebration spontaneously began. Merriment that had been depraved for so long was now bountiful. Food and drink started appearing on tables conjured by mages.

Menosh looked to be in shock at the news. He was uncertain to let the Newlings return to Earth with their families, but he did not want to appear weak. He paced for hours and the dragons took notice.

"Menosh let them go." Ermenya requested.

"If you don't, I will." Zanor said as he approached the group.

"You failed, Aantiri." Ermenya said.

"I have not failed. Harold and I have been working on this problem for a long time. We have decided that we will present this dilemma to the Earth Realm ourselves. After all, the humans there have always tried to kill dragons. You two would be no different. But the decision is ultimately yours, Menosh, since in all actuality you are the last creator that we know of." Zanor then walked off toward the celebration.

"Go back to Harold and make plans. We will join you soon." Fred said as he turned to Menosh. "Get those families to Weelin now!"

Menosh humbly went to the center of the celebration. "Please give me your attention. All Newlings to me." The Newlings gathered along with the Council. "I grant you passage to Weelin where you will continue training." Menosh opened a portal for the group and watched as they departed. He sent a Veil Guard with them who would remain for the duration. He then walked back to Lady Phallas and Gareth. "You two need to get to the Vale Kilowas and enter the keep. There is some knowledge there that we must have to win this fight.

The two nodded in agreement and were ported to the keep instantly by Ermenya. She sent a subliminal message to them. *"Look in the fire mantle of the great hall, the base of the stagnant pond in the lower level, and in the wall of the sky in the towers."*

Fred stared at the circlet now in his hand. He took human form so he could view it more closely. He was trying to remember why Malificence had it way back when. What made her so special? "Ah ha." He exclaimed. "Malificence is truly from there as well as all of the Morket. Impresaria and Omiporici are her daughters as is Iris. Llylandra must then be from there unrelated but on the same escape ship or comet as we are calling it."

The remainder of the group agreed and decided to inquire with the Morket.

RETURN TO WEELIN

As the portal closed behind the Newlings in Weelin, their families rushed forward with open arms. William was present as the families reunited. The Veil guard briefed him on the events that had transpired on Kluanaria. The two watched as Iris solemnly approached. They knew this would be difficult.

"Where is Tatiana? Where is my baby?" She asked as she looked around at the other families. With no response she went to her home and wept. She knew where Edwina and Paul were at, as they sent messages to her.

Myron came through a portal and spoke with William briefly before he went to his home. He found Iris kneeling before her Star shrine with tears streaming. He knelt beside his wife and tried to comfort her.

"Myron, where is Tatiana?"

"Well, she and her friends saved Mercurian and took out Mithdrool. She got a little upset because the Council was not acting on anything very efficiently."

"So what does that mean?"

"She got extremely angry and upset, then vanished. Ermenya and Fred along with Lady Phallas and Gareth located her at Edziza through the restored grove's basin."

"No, no. I will stop this now." Iris stood along with Myron and gave him a hug. "You go tend to the families."

"Uh, ok. I think? But I just want you to know, no matter what you are feeling inside, I want you to know that I would not change anything if I

Brenda M. Hokenson

had to do it all over again. It was the right thing, so don't be rash about whatever action you are considering."

"Just get out!"

Myron left rapidly, he knew something was up and thought William would be the best to answer. After the door closed behind Myron, Iris began her work. *"Transiti a Edziza."* Iris was gone.

The families were assembled around William when Myron caught up with them. "William, I need to talk to you about Iris," Myron whispered.

"What about Iris?"

"Well, she is up to something, and I know that Malificence and Harold were hiding her since she was born."

"How do you know this?"

"Let me get these folks going first, and then we will talk." William agreed and Myron spoke to the families. "Thank you all for allowing our Orders to train your children. We have never had so many Newlings with such great skill get introduced to trainers and their Order at the same time. The first thing on our agenda this afternoon is... Ice Cream!!" The children began to cheer, and the volume increased. "Get in the truck!" Myron yelled as the families were cheering. Chaos broke out as they raced to the old farm truck. Each individual was given ten Weelin dollars for their excursion. Then Myron added, "And a movie!" The kids were almost out of control.

Myron drove the old farm truck down the road. As it picked up speed it vanished, reappearing in a parking space near the center Weelin. A few people were walking by and staring. They saw the big truck fade in and out until it was solid.

"See Johnny? That woman wasn't crazy. Did you see it, did you?"

"Helen, it is impossible for a farm truck to just appear. Maybe you were really looking at the funhouse poster which distorts reflections from the parking lot."

She slapped Johnny. "Look. I have it on digital camera. I was still recording from our historical walk."

"Ok, then. Let's settle this once and for all." Johnny dragged Helen to the truck, which to the touch was solid. "So, the truck is solid, Helen. Now let's just talk to the driver."

"No, they might be of the Occult or something."

"I have seen them here for a while. I doubt they are Occult.

Myron heard the entire conversation and did his best not to laugh as he walked toward them. "Good afternoon, Johnny. How are you today?"

Helen grabbed Johnny's arm and whispered, "He knows your name."

Myron rolled his eyes as Johnny spoke. "Hey Myron. This is Helen, my wife."

"Nice to meet you, Helen." Myron extended his hand.

"Nice to meet you as well. How long have you lived here?"

"We have been here about nine years. We moved from Los Angeles because we were tired of the crime, weather, and lack of nature. My wife, Iris, picked this place out. She is sort of a geography nerd and loves this area."

"Where is she at?"

"Oh, she left earlier today. Her mother is ill, and she wanted to go help her out."

Helen ran out of questions.

"Well, it was nice meeting you. Say, Johnny, I wanted you to look at the truck for me. Can I bring it by your place later?

"Oh, sure thing. Just drop by any time."

"Ok, I will see you later then." Myron walked off, still trying not to laugh at the whole experience.

William caught up to Myron as he was exiting the parking lot. "Iris never was a Star, was she?"

"No, Myron. She is a Morket. So she is not in an Order. Her abilities are natural, just like Impresaria, Omiporici, and their mother, Luly." William paused reflecting. "Their homeland had been overtaken by the Fraelochs and Shaeplings. There was no other choice for the Morket. Thousands took a risk after monitoring comet for thousands of years. Their science did not build machines that waste precious resources and pollute the environment like you see here, on Earth. They went a completely different route. They went smaller. Since all Morket have natural abilities, they planned an escape. The spell that Edwina used to capture Thanias can be cast by each Morket, with a different result. It encapsulates the caster only. Once encapsulated the individual is able to cast another spell and basically teleport to a near object or location. The comet that comes from Phallas Minor passes extremely close to the planet, within 250 Earth miles. So during its transition across the planet, thousands of Morket encapsulated themselves and used the comet for transport, not knowing where they would end up. Many perished during the journey as the comet does heat up and its tail was solid once, so you can imagine the loss over many, many light years to Kluanaria. This is not a comet seen by Earth, but it is possible that some Morket drifted through the Veil between the worlds." William paused as they walked into a small coffee shop and seated themselves.

"So, then I assume that the Fraeloch can do the same thing?"

"No, the Fraeloch are very, very powerful. They can just cast a spell and end up wherever they want. That is what is wrong right now. Their communications is all telepathic and thus, more deadmages transition in and out of here. Those that Tomas captured are already back in their homeland, with exception to Llylandra. The prismatic prison blocks her powers. So Impresaria will not permit the seal to be broken."

"Ok, enough history. Let's enjoy the great coffee here."

"Where is the tea? This stuff tastes horrible. It tastes burnt."

Myron laughed. "That is because it comes from a bean that gets roasted and then ground."

"What is wrong with simple ways Myron? Tea is from dried leaves, not burnt like this stuff. You left your homeland because of Iris. She had forgotten that she was not a Star. She became a Star. I noticed the majority of your Orders have similar incantations."

"Yes, we do, but the foundations are based in the Orders creation and how and when they are used. One spell for one Order may not do exactly the same thing as another Order, with exception to healing and transport."

Omiporici decided to join the group in Weelin. She entered the coffee shop and sat next to William. "Father, you have not told him all yet."

"No, Omi, I haven't?"

"What is this more, Omi?" Myron asked.

"Well, pretty much all of the Mercurian folk are from or descended from either Morket or Fraelochan lines, some are intermingled as they learned to co-exist peacefully here. The deadmages' arrival is a very bad thing. It means their worlds will soon die because Phallas Minor has what the Earth folk call a supernova and they are in direct path of it."

"So, do they want to preserve their culture and beliefs here or bend everyone's ideals to theirs? Or perhaps, Talaharian is unaware and is just trying to gain control." Myron mused on these thoughts for a bit. Ok enough business; let's join them for a movie."

"Movie?"

"Ok it is something I can't explain well, so you will have to see for yourself." Myron escorted William and Omiporici to the theater where the main feature was from way back. "This is called a Western, and I am sure it will make no sense to you for a bit."

The families were already seated with ice cream and popcorn and plenty of laughter when an announcement came over a loudspeaker. "Your attention please. Please proceed to the nearest exit. The ushers will escort you …" There was a pause. Loud crackling noises came over the loudspeaker followed by a crash with more loud crackling. Then silence.

The Newlings and other kids began screaming and running. The background noise included more thunderous rumblings and cracking. The parents caught up to the kids and got hold of their hands. Another thunderous crash resonated in the theater, this time it sounded closer. The ushers quickly got their patrons down a set of stairs and into a large room that was built like a bunker.

Myron and William went looking for the manager. They found him at the entrance staring out at the street. The roads in front of the theater looked like a plow was tearing them up and rendering them unusable. The two stepped out the doors and surveyed the scene. Another crash emanated in the near distance along a ridgeline. They watched as another mountain collapse in on itself as the trees on the outer edges slid down the slopes.

"This is not good! Can you get Fred to fly over and see if he can tell what is causing this, without the drama he sometimes causes?" Myron asked William as he began to walk up one of the undisturbed slopes for a better view. "I wish Tatiana was here; at least she could use seeing pebbles."

"Fred is already doing that, along with Ermenya. Do you have any clue from this mess as to who or what is doing this?"

"No, but it reminds me of Clamshoe Bay, with the massive storm that came out of nowhere."

"I know who has the power to do this. Your daughters plus Jaetoth, Llylandra, and Mithdrool."

"Well, Tatiana just did the majority of the healing of Bittern. Edwina is recovering… Omiporici may know."

"I am unsure. I have never seen, let alone witnessed mountains collapse and a road get torn up in this manner." William paused as he noticed something in the air hovering over the area. It noticed the Kluanarians. It raised its left arm into the air, which caused lightning bolts to be hurled toward them. As it closed its right hand tightly the ground trembled. Then opening its hand quickly, the ground split between William and Myron, knocking both of them down.

"Who is that William?" Myron asked as he got back on his feet. "That was wild."

"It can't be." William focused on the hovering thing as Fred landed and took a human form. "It looks to be Jaetoth. But that's impossible. He is in a prismatic prison."

Myron squinted, hoping to see the object better. "That's Tatiana on a horse! What in the world?"

Fred grabbed Myron by the arm and made sure he didn't trip as he stared at the sky while they walked back to the theater. Fred went to the PA system and made a statement. "Please return to your homes and the local authorities will give you further instruction. The roads are damaged; some are drivable, while others are not. Proceed out of the theater with caution." He then assembled the Kluanarians. "We must get to the bottom of this. Where is Iris?"

"Last I knew I was talking to her about all that we had gone through and that I was proud of everyone; then she started yelling and told me to get out. That she had something to do." Myron answered.

Iris appeared as Myron finished his sentence. "Fred, you need to know something."

The dragon turned toward her, the fire usually in his belly could be seen in his eyes, which meant anger.

"The Council areas in all major cities and outposts have been completely destroyed. All of the Orders' chambers, with exception to Truncheon, Interval, Izmaa, and Shadowblyt have also been ruined. There is a great fissure now where the Latana Spring Bridge stood."

"What do you mean where it stood? We repaired it." Myron interrupted.

"The fissure is twice as wide as that bridge was and twice as deep as the small gorge that was below it. Thanias has taken over the Palisade with some rogue individuals.

Fred paced and then briefly looked up as Ermenya joined them.

Myron spoke to Iris trying to understand. "Why did you leave? Where did you go?"

"I had a feeling chaos would be not too far behind since the work done at Bittern and the lands of Mercurian was successful. Tatiana from what I understand, as I was not there, was overwhelmingly upset. Anyone capable of doing the majority of the healing of a completely destroyed land as Bittern is quite capable of causing just as much damage as the healing done, if not more."

Ermenya spoke. "She is not destroying the people, only things around the people, which happen to be things in Weelin that Kluanarians use most. Your small community has been obliterated. All of this is directed at the Orders."

Tatiana drifted to the ground on the horse Kira had given her landing on a nearby remnant of a mountain, clearly tired. Iris went toward her but was stopped by the dragons. The Newling turned toward them as if taunting them. She rode her horse toward them. She then returned to the dragons and the others gray colored Brabant with silver colored eyes. It had moon glow that surrounded it and no bridal, which surprised Iris. She approached both, to the irritation of Ermenya and Fred, and examined the horse closer, not paying attention to Tatiana who looked very, very angry. Iris telepathically asked the horse to raise it hoof, and it complied. She examined each hoof, making sure there were no issues with the shoes, as she discovered highly polished ones and neatly cared for hooves. She then examined his teeth carefully, noting no problems. She checked out its eyes and ears and found no infections. She stroked the horse along its main, which she mused as Tatiana had braided it. The tail was also braided and rounded into a bun. As she finished, she looked at Tatiana, "Would you like help down?"

Tatiana jumped into her mother's arms and cried. She raised her head as her mother still carried her in her arms and pointed at the group. "You are the most stupid old people! Sorry, Dad. You have no idea how bad Kluanaria truly is because you ran away, Dad." Tatiana said as tears ran down her face and she paused for a breath between the yelling. "And just so ya know, the Fraeloch and Morket don't have a home world any more. Their sun devoured it!"

"Whaa… How do you know that? Myron asked. "Where did you learn…?"

Brenda M. Hokenson

"Oh, that. I just know it like everything else I just know. Sort of like how I knew how to fix Edwina and Bittern and Walther and…" She paused as Ermenya turned her gaze to Tatiana. "Anyway, I have transcended into what my true duties are. I am not a kid anymore." Tatiana spoke as her voice seemed altered. "I can see far off places, and I can go anywhere I choose."

"How is this possible? Myron asked of Fred and Ermenya.

William answered, "This is beyond our comprehension. I have never seen or heard of anything like this from Intervals. I only know of one who can possibly do these things."

"William." Ermenya spoke in dragon to him. "Menosh has passed. As her mentor, I believe he gave her everything she 'just knows.'"

Fred responded to Ermenya in dragon speak. "He has not passed yet. I do believe, however, that he is giving her this knowledge."

William looked at both in bewilderment as Tatiana responded to their musing in their tongue. "William, I did know Titans spoke dragon." She smiled. "Menosh is not dead." The dragons looked at her. "Yes, I can speak all languages of the universe on both sides of the Veil." Tatiana snapped her fingers and Thanias appeared. "Uncle Thanias, you have to promise to stop hurting people." Her eyes peered into his deep enough to hear his thoughts. "I mean it Thanias. You will not walk away from here if you cannot promise this to me. I will be your end."

Thanias said nothing and walked toward Myron. "What in the world is going on with Tatiana?"

"We don't know. Why did she bring you here?"

"Don't know, but she healed me. Where is…"

"Enough questions, Thanias! Make your choice now!"

"What makes you think you have any power, little girl?" Thanias turned and looked at his niece. "It seems that someone granted you powers that can only be imagined and yet you don't know how to control them very well, do you?"

"It doesn't matter. You need to choose now!"

"Don't raise your voice at me you little twit! You are just as much a pain in the butt as your mother."

Tatiana snapped her fingers, taking the life from Thanias. "Game over! Now, if the rest of the darn Orders would have taken care of everything the right way, I would not be bound by my duty to fix it all." Tatiana mounted her horse and as she rode toward the mountain something miraculous happened. The mountain began to reform with all of its trees as if nothing happened. As she traversed the road, it too began to mend along with broken buildings. Tatiana's horse levitated with her and they circled the town and the outlying area, healing everything except the small village that Myron had designed on the edge of Weelin. It was not so lucky.

Kira and Zanor showed up in time to see the end of their son and their granddaughter disappear. They stood in horror as Myron picked up his brother and walked toward his parents.

William spoke to Ermenya and Fred. "We must go to Menosh and we must get control of that girl. I don't know how to find her."

"Her grandfather, Harold or War, can find her. And she will need to be bound." Fred said.

"What will we use to bind her, the circlet, the seeing rocks…?" William said.

"No, we will use her horse's brush." Ermenya said.

"Are we going to be able to remove her powers, so she can be normal?" William asked

"I hope so." Fred pondered this after what he had seen.

The two dragons shifted into their true form and flew invisibly toward town.

Myron placed Thanias on the ground as he comforted his parents. "This is very bad for our family. I don't know what can be done to restore us. I don't know what to do."

"It is not for you to know or do, son." Kira added as she hugged Myron. "We will weather this together."

Zanor was stronger. "Tatiana will be punished for this and for all other destructive behaviors."

"How will we find her?" Kira asked. "What will the Council do?"

"I don't know, and the Council has limitless options, as Thanias, even though turned, was still a Truncheon. Myron, I can't protect her."

"I understand. Her heart is too big to hold back anything, so I am not even sure that the dragons will find her."

Kira opened a portal and the four went through, emerging at the High Seat of Burwash.

THE BREAKOUT

As THE RULING FAMILY OF Kluanaria prepared for the funerary ceremony, Vale Kilowas was having major issues to deal with. Trincotts circled the prison, shrieking and waling. Shades prowled the outer lands surrounding the prison. Only the worst acts violating Kluanarian law could land anyone here. The worst that had to be contained in prismatic prisons were several levels above the surface in the opaqueness of the sky with crystalline floors. Veil Guards and Veil Keepers were responsible for the security of this magnificent building. The containment cells in the upper floors were smaller. At the back of each 10 by 10 room, there was a pedestal on which rested an occupied prismatic prison. These boxes were made of many different metals with different designs. All had similar repelling spells cast on it as well as binding spells.

Jaetoth was housed at one end of the floor and Llylandra the other. Mithdrool was kept in an undisclosed location to protect all. During the restoration of Bittern and for a few days after, the prismatic prisons of Jaetoth and Llylandra began to tremble. The Veil Shrikes holding the seals telepathically spoke with their owners. A keeper and a guard approached along with Blayne. Blayne was the unofficial overseer of the entire Vale Kilowas and prison. Blayne sent a sprite to Omiporici and Impresaria to warn them of the impending "escape". "No worries, guys. There is no way to contain them here. I am surprised they have lasted this long in our boxes. So, we now need to have someone do an immediate portal as soon as they breach the seal, back to Mithdrool's seat.

A sprite returned with three Newlings. Onachala and Irra looked

The Kluanarians

around as Tommy spoke with Blayne. The two agreed and asked the Izmaa and Shadowblyt for help. Blayne spoke frankly. "Newlings, our prison is in need of your assistance. The prismatic prisons were not meant to hold Fraelochs for very long. These two contain Llylandra and Jaetoth. Once the Shrike detaches from the box, we need a portal that would basically remove them directly to Mithdrool's land and away from here, where they could do no damage here."

"That is possible." Onachala thought for a moment. "For a price, we will do this."

Irra looked puzzled and nodded as Onachala spoke to her telepathically. Blayne smirked. "Ok, what is this price Newling?"

"Tell me what you know of the Krosslaen Site."

"Oh. Hmm." Blayne thought for a bit. "After you do this task, I will take you to the great library which may have your answers. Krosslaen was before my time. I know that there was much hostility amongst the Orders and multiplied with incoming Fraeloch and Morket ideas it was a very bad time."

Onachala took a little bit and processed what she was told and nodded to Irra. Tommy interjected. "Wait, the Krosslaen Site. Isn't that under Edziza? Didn't Walther teach us that in one of our lessons?"

Irra answered him. "Yes, Tommy. The Krosslaen Site is also what the deadmages are searching for. My grandfather told me a story once about its origin. So now I will tell you." Irra paused and reflected on her grandfather. "Krosslaen was a beautiful village at the base of Edziza. Many worldly and other worldly things got stored there. This included something of the Fraelochs most powerful order, the deadmages. It was of course another rock." She paused as Tommy rolled his eyes. "Yes, another darn rock. But this was very important to them as it would allow them to rebuild their world if necessary. A young Fraeloch a long time ago was here on Kluanaria as an explorer. He wanted to keep the rock safe until needed. His was kind of like Gareth, but he traveled much further to here to seek refuge for this stone. Anyway, this traveler asked the dragon queen if it could be placed in the hoard for safekeeping until such a time was needed for it to be used. Well, it was agreed and not long after the placement of the rock, a civil war erupted amongst the Kluanarians. The dragon queen took Krosslaen in her claws and transported it beneath the Mountain Edziza where knowledge would remain undisturbed."

Brenda M. Hokenson

"I guess I should have asked you Irra." Onachala replied. "I am asking because that is where the deadmages are gathering. They are at Edziza looking everywhere for something. So, let us help Blayne and the see the library. I don't want to end up in deep trouble like Tatiana is in."

"Tatiana is in trouble?" Blayne inquired. "What could she have possibly done?"

"Well, I was not there, but Kren sent word that she had done a couple bad things. That is all I know."

The prismatic prisons vibrated harder. The Veil Shrikes were awakening and slowly getting ready to unlatch. Onachala ripped sliced the very fabric of the air and spoke to the tear. *"Transitae a Forest Mithdrool nus Jaetoth uns Llylandra."* As the two prismatic prisons opened, the individuals were immediately taken through the portal.

"So much for a true break out, though it would have been ugly," Tommy said. "Will I be permitted to stay and learn from you, Blayne?"

"Yes, young man. You may sty, if your parents are ok with it. Now, let us go to the library."

Irra made sure the tear closed before the group left for the library.

At the center of the large building was a great opening. There were 8 wings to the building and at the very center was a columnar library that was along the edge of each floor of the structure and extended to the height of each ceiling. Special floating baskets were available for use to get to the needed area. The group climbed into the baskets and Blayne requested, "Krosslaen." The basket shot down 4 floors, about 80 feet in no time flat. It then shot straight across to the appropriate section and a yellow light illuminated the section of interest. As Onachala studied what she wanted to know a small Shrike shot down to the basket and alerted Blayne of an attempt to escape.

"If you will excuse me, I must see to the breakout. I will return when containment has been restored."

An explosion reverberated through the prison. A black mist filled the halls and crystalline walls cracked as the shockwave passed through. Shrikes that were in the Learned (pronounced learn- ed) Wing were mobilized. Veil Guards and Keepers came in droves. They met on the fourth wing of the fourth level at the fourth block, where a rather large pit remained. The prismatic prison lay on the edge of the pit, melted open from the inside. Blayne had the Shrike that sealed it taken to the healing house near the entrance.

"Blayne, this was no random act." Irra said as the three kids approached. "Do you know who was imprisoned here?"

"I don't have all cells memorized Newling. I just know that this is going to affect more than Kluanaria. Are you sure you are only 7 years?"

"Earth years. Here it is more like 15, ya know." Irra responded. "This prison was that of Chorlanda. She was the first!"

"Irra, say no more. We must speak with Rithmas and Guilles. Only they will know what to do." Onachala sliced the air and spoke, grabbing Irra as the tear enveloped her; they disappeared.

"So, Tommy, we have much to learn quickly about this Chorlanda. Let's go to the library while the Veil Guards take charge here."

An hour later the Shadowblyts and Izmaa entered a tear in the library of the prison. Guilles approached Blayne with a large scroll and pointed out the history of the Chorlanda.

"Thank you for coming so quickly. I am not given much information on who is actually kept in prison here." Blayne said as she studied the parchment.

"Let me give you a quick Fraelochan history then," Rithmas said as he observed the scuttling about of Shrikes, and Veil Guards. He continued watching the corridor as if something was about to happen.

"I got it Rithmas." Guilles said as he sprinted down the hallway with Onachala.

Blayne was confused. "What are they after? Chorlanda is no longer here from what I can tell."

"Look here woman, Chorlanda is about twenty of Mithdrool and Llylandra combined. She is the first." Irra replied as she watched a small Shrike flit about.

"Chorlanda is the first Fraeloch to leave the Phallas Minor star system. She was accompanied by a crystal dragon. They arrived here many thousands of years ago. Prior to their arrival, some other folks began inhabiting Kluanaria and some were crossing between the Veil separating this realm from Earth. Your Titan, Enygminite, and green dragon came from far off locals as well. The four horsemen, as the Earth folk refer to them, cross between the realms as it is necessary for the balance. Your

High Lord is one who helped quash their running amok here with the aid of these folks. Unaware of the ulterior motives of Chorlanda, the group caught up with the horsemen and captured them, save one, War. He fancied a lady named Malificence and made her his wife. He would take leave and stir things on Earth as required and would return. He adopted the name Harold to be formal amongst the Kluanarians and win over their trust. Chorlanda did not approve of his meddling and sparked wild rumors and accusations across the land."

"What about this crystal dragon?" Blayne interrupted.

"She desired a home world for her brood. She took shelter at Mount Edziza and asked the Kluanarians to preserve their artifacts as to her you should never forget the past."

"Did something happen in her past that would cause this?"

"Yes, but my focus is Chorlanda. Chorlanda convinced the Orders, both major and minor, that Harold was about to unleash his true powers and devastate the land, bringing it to war. However, this was untrue, as he was overseeing a skirmish on Earth, in which Malificence had already spoke to the Orders about. Nevertheless, Chorlanda was successful. There was not a High Lord, or any lord, at this time, and all Orders marched upon each other. As the battles began, Chorlanda continued twisting the Orders. She sent forth sprites, nymphs, and zephyrs about the powerful armies marching through the lands. Most of the folk did not ever use their powers, so they took up arms. She convinced them that at Edziza, they would find the truth and that the most powerful of the Orders were there and that none would be left." Rithmas paused for a moment as the Izmaa returned.

"In the meantime, the crystal dragon carefully guarded the artifacts that had been entrusted to her. She sent a plea to Freiderich, the green dragon, for aid as she was also caring for their brood. The two flew about Edziza and encapsulated the focal point of the attack, Krosslaen, and pulled it deep within the mountain. The two remained in the Mountain and came out when the battle approached. As the warring Orders merged at Krosslaen, the dragons took to the skies, circling the fighting factions. In cowardice, the Orders met in the middle and stood in awe as these mighty beasts landed and took a less frightening form. They introduced themselves as Fred and Ermenya. Flowers and snowflakes fell from the sky. Once the masses were calmed, Fred explained the true nature of the war. He helped build a great monument on the valley walls where many hundreds of thousands had perished."

"What about…" Tommy interrupted.

"Chorlanda made her presence known during the placement of the sacred well on the grassy knob on the side of Edziza. She started to curse the whole of Kluanaria when Ermenya found her and as she reached her dwarven arm toward Chorlanda; the crystal claws came out and picked the chanting woman up. Caught by surprise, she stopped chanting. A Shrike was circling and helped the dragon encapsulate Chorlanda in a crystalline prison. Fred arrived shortly after and also bound the prison inside of a secondary containment made of a rare mineral here. When this was done, the Shrike found this to be an inviting location to preserve peace. If you didn't already know, Shrikes look menacing, but only seek peace. So, he bound himself to the crystal prison."

"So, my prison, was established by Veil Keepers and Guards, with prisoners contained by Shrikes?"

"Yes and no. The Orders built this prison together. It is the first time they had ever worked together and ever since, they held councils at varying locations to keep the communications open. They appointed an Aantiri to be the High Lord as they are the most powerful, well, until now."

"So, with Chorlanda free…"

"Times will be much, much worse. I am uncertain if the Shadowblyts and Izmaa will survive this round. That woman singled our Orders out and made full mockery of us. She said we had invaded Mercurian and Treah. When we had worked in harmony in both locations and established strongholds with other orders. We were the first to do this. It turned many strongholds against Nagazthastar and Bittern several times. She enslaved our high orders, killed the first-born children, and razed what is now the Sand Caverns. It sunk on its own to heal, as it was once a very prosperous location, mostly occupied by Intervals and a few Shadowblyts, Izmaa, a Moon, and a Fraelochan High Priestess and her husband who was basically a Truncheon. She will no doubt use Talaharian, Llylandra and Jaetoth as her weapon. Mithdrool was captured by you, Tommy. He will not survive in the prison as he is of this realm. So, he is no longer a threat."

"I beg to differ on some of your information you possess." Chorlanda said as she entered the room. The group stared at her as she approached. The clothing was nothing like they had expected from an imprisoned Fraelochan mage of some manner. She seemed to buck the trend of most mages. Her clothes were a silver-grey color that were leggings tucked into white boots, the top was long-sleeved and more form hugging than most attire worn on Kluanaria. Her head piece was similar to a head band worn by little girl except for it was metallic, not cloth, and had a strange device that ran from her ear to her mouth that could be moved out of the way. She wore a white belt that held some devices on it "It is true. I was the first; the first to leave Phallas Minor. The dragon, well the dragon just happened to be vacating for reasons that are her own to divulge. I am not your enemy as you think."

"Why were you imprisoned if you are not here to destroy the very humanity of Kluanaria" a familiar voice asked as she walked in the room.

"Lady Phallas." Chorlanda knelt. "I have been detained for a rather long time. I fear the star system is destroyed by now. You know I was sent here to observe the prisoners."

"Yes. It is. Ermenya confirmed this for us a few days ago." Lady Phallas took Chorlanda to the side. Some of the Fraelochans have been corrupted here because of the inferior armaments and defences. The dead magi are rampant and Llylandra are here. The woman corrupted a prominent man who was in charge of the Truncheon, the foot soldiers to us, and together they did an unspeakable horror and raised or woke Mithdrool. This Mithdrool was powerful and brought almost complete annihilation to Nagazthastar, where we had established an outpost and I met High Lord Beryth, once and the second round was their aid and it almost cost me my daughter, Rynn. Is your assistant of any use? I know he is young, but I was told he has knowledge from the Earth Realm concerning some advanced sciences."

"Yes, Lady. He has also progressed with his Order to a point where they are comfortable in letting him accompany me to many locations that we have interest in. They feel he will make a wonderful ambassador for the Earth Realm and Kluanaria. Also, Talaharian is no threat either. He is a son of Regence and still on Earth."

Tommy was intrigued by this conversation. "Do you fly then? Who is your assistant? Do we know him? Is it…?"

Paul entered the room wearing a silvery grey tunic with matching leggings, white belt and boots... He too had a band holding a device near his mouth. "Hi all. Grandpa Zanor said that it would be in my better interests to learn as much as possible from Chorlanda as there are some very troubling things underway."

"Paul, Paul!" The Newlings shrieked and ran up to him and hugged him. "Where have you been? What did you see? Did you get to ride on a dragon? Did you fly in a machine?" They continued in unison.

Paul took the other Newlings off to the side and chatted while Blayne, Chorlanda, and Lady Phallas discussed repairing the prison and containing the dead magi. "I want to tell you all what is really going on. The elders don't want you in the loop for your 'protection' but I think I have to tell you since you all are making names for yourselves already." Paul paused as the group found a seat at the center of the room. "Tatiana is in deep trouble, Edwina, well, Edwina is working on something with Grandma Kira."

"What do you fly with her?" Tommy asked. "Is it a dragon?"

"Come on, I can show you." Paul said as he led them out of the prison and to a small clearing. The Newlings stood in awe as they stared at a semitransparent object. "On Earth, we call it a spaceship. In Phallas Minor it is called a Warp Travel Explorer."

"What does it do? Does Kluanaria have any?" Tommy asked as he walked closer to the extended stairs.

"Well, it flies and goes really fast. It can take the people on it almost anywhere. Kluanaria does not have any to my knowledge."

"Do you fly it, Paul?" Onachala and Irra chimed in.

"Umm, no. I am an assistant to the navigator."

"What's a navigator?" The three Newlings asked in unison."

"Well, he is like Gareth. However, he is only responsible for studying maps of the area where the ship is going. Gareth is responsible for the maps and all the studies of the areas he goes."

Paul showed them the inside of the craft as they talked amongst themselves. Lady Phallas, Blayne, Rithmas and some of the Veil Keepers joined them as they talked about the flying machine.

WEELIN UNREST

As Tatiana destroyed the land, the folks who were not in the theater and bustling about the small village ran for cover. Several took pictures and video clips on their cell phones. The police captain himself went out and watched in horror as the slopes around his town. He saw in the sky a figure that appeared to be riding a horse. He called the Pend Oreille County Sheriff for assistance. The onslaught seemed to last forever. After fifteen minutes by helicopter, the Sheriff arrived. The sheriff brought a videographer with him to record the chaos and destruction. He had deputies approaching in squad cars, along with a multitude of fire engines and ambulances. Dust filled the air. There were rumblings from the ground. As the entourage made its way to the police department, the windows exploded. The very road they were on ripped wide open, the videographer fell from the tremors. Another thirty minutes passed and the small figure landed. The sheriff and police chief started walking toward a small group who the figure landed in front of. They could hear the dialogue. It wasn't very pleasant. The figure dismounted and was actually smaller than the law enforcement officials thought. It was a child! The videographer continued rolling. They watched for ten minutes when the child mounted her horse. As she ascended, the ground began to repair itself. The slopes were reformed and everything that was destroyed was in order once again.

"Sheriff Dylan, I don't know what to do. What do I tell my townsfolk? There are a lot of witnesses, and they will want answers. I can't very well say that it was their imaginations, as so many have proof of it."

"Ron, I don't know what to say. It something beyond our control and

I am at a loss for words. The cameraman will not release this to the press until we get to the bottom of it. Hopefully Spokane will be preoccupied with their goings on and ignore anything that floats in to their news stations."

"I hope so. How do…"

"My name is Fred, this is Ermenya." The dragons approached in human form as they interrupted the discussion. "We would like to talk about the happenings in the last two hours."

"Well, now. Fred is it. What can you possibly tell us that we didn't see with our own eyes?" Ron asked. "I am Police Chief of this beautiful town and in all of my twenty-five years on the force; I have never seen or heard anything like this."

"This is called a twelve-year-olds temper tantrum." Ermenya spoke as she shook the officers' hands.

"That child is not twelve. She looks more of six or seven."

"On this world she is six or seven. In ours, she is about twelve."

"What the heck? What do you mean our world?" Sheriff Dylan asked. He turned down his radio as the group spoke. "You know she killed a man?"

"If she did, where is the body?" Ermenya inquired, knowing the official was right, but wanted to test the waters.

"We watched his neck break. We watched him collapse on the ground before this child. She will be taken into custody."

"First of all, Sheriff, where is the body?" Fred inquired. The group walked toward where the child had landed and interacted with other folks. "I see no body, and I was here. Perhaps you are mistaken.

"Let's review the footage that your cameraman took." Ron said as the scene began to feel more intense.

As the five walked back to the police station, they were interrupted. "I told you so, Ron. Johnny and you are both idiots. I told you they were Occult! I told you and you shunned me." Helen screamed. Now my home is completely leveled. What do you have to say now? Honestly, why are you even still the Chief? They are all possessed by demonic entities." Helen was almost in hysterics.

"Ah, this is Helen, and her husband, Johnny." Ron introduced the two as they approached. "She believes that anyone who moves into town and doesn't socialize frequently or attend one of the churches here are Occult. Pay her no attention."

Helen slapped the chief across the face. "It is true. They even a have a truck that appears out of nowhere."

Johnny spoke up. "My wife is a bit paranoid, sure. But whatever crumpled this town also demolished our home. Yet the town is fixed, and our home is not. How do you explain that?"

"I will send a couple officers, deputies, and firefighters to assess the damage, if that is ok with you Ron." Sheriff Dylan answered.

"I am thinking something else is going on and you two please go with the officers and they will work with you and take your statement." Ron also replied and nodded to the couple.

The group entered the empty police station and had the cameraman roll his video in the conference room. "You see, right there. That man had his neck broke." Sheriff Dylan exclaimed as he jumped out of the chair. "Enlarge this image and play it again Sam." The cameraman nodded and re-ran the video enlarged.

"Ah, I see." Ermenya responded. "Let me first explain some things to you that will be rather eye opening."

"Sam, stop rolling and join us," Chief Todd said as he started some coffee. "Well, young lady, what do you have to say that will open our eyes?"

Ermenya nodded at Fred who agreed with what she was saying in dragon. "Very well, thank you for hearing us out. Fred and I first and foremost are not humanoid. We are from a distant land in a star system that has just recently gone as you would say on Earth, Supernova. Our world is gone. You have a small group of folks from a world that is parallel to yours. They are in a way protector of your world as there is a group who used a space vessel to reach their homeland and they who have traveled have been corrupted by some previous travelers."

"What the hell are you saying? How do you expect us to believe that?"

"If I may…" Fred interrupted. He extended his hand and as he did, so his dragon forearm shown. A sphere grew in his claws which eventually took both of his hands to support. In the sphere was an image. It showed the first explorers leaving Phallas Minor, the discovery of Kluanaria, and the Veil between Earth and Kluanaria. It flashed through images on Kluanaria like a slide show up through the most recent events, to include the settlement in Weelin and the destruction and resurrection of the town. The image ended and Fred retracted his hands from the sphere, and they went back to humanoid form.

"Your hands..." The sheriff paused as he recounted the video. "Your claws..." Sheriff Dylan was dumbfounded. "Those places... Where?"

"I am a dragon, as is Ermenya. We are technically from Earth until we started being hunted by your ancestors. No, you are not from apes. We have been here longer than most. Some of retreated to a far-off place like Phallas Minor, which you saw in the sphere. Others stayed here, hidden amongst you and beneath the earth." William spoke frankly and gave pause to Ermenya.

"Your town has been most hospitable to the folks who have crossed the Veil. They have fit in for the most part well, except for today. The folks are from Kluanaria. It is the world was shown after departing Phallas Minor. Kluanaria has always been with you as have its people. However, the people of Earth are power hungry and since Kluanarians value peace, they choose not to cross as they possess great gifts of the mind that you of Earth regard as magic. The family who moved here some thirteen years ago came here to be more like you and not use their gifts." Ermenya saw a board and drew a map for them showing the paths to Kluanaria from Phallas Minor as William took over.

"You see, Earth children, there is some very grave dangers unfolding on Kluanaria. What you saw today was a child, being more gifted than any on Kluanaria, upset with the lack of decisiveness on the part of the Elders which permitted many atrocities to occur there. This young child has restored a lot of the damage with help of her friends and her being upset, especially with her family who settled here, caused this episode you witnessed today."

The police chief and county sheriff stared at each other in disbelief. Looking perplexedly back at the two dragons, Ron spoke. "So, if we are to believe you, how do we relay this to well, the rest?"

"I am sure in time, your pictures will what Paul says 'leak' out into the world and at that time Ermenya and I will address the supreme ruler."

"We don't have a supreme ruler over the world. We have a President and Congress who will laugh and scoff and mock us. They can't even fix our immediate problems at home. They will take you as prisoners more or less and test you like animals."

"Well, let them try." Ermenya replied. "We are not afraid."

"This Veil thing; can we go though it?" Sheriff Dylan inquired as he jotted down the map on the whiteboard.

"Yes, in some instances like the summer festival in Ruan, but generally NO for the folks of Earth do not believe in as you say magic and thus the way is mostly locked." William replied.

"So, what do we do with the hysterical folks," the police chief asked.

"Let it be. It will work itself out, as nothing is destroyed."

A knock on the conference room interrupted the discussion and Ermenya quickly erased the whiteboard. The group who examined the demolished house had returned. "Enter, please." The Chief responded.

"Sir, we have done a thorough investigation of Helen and Johnny's home. We found that the rumblings in town had nothing to do with the house's collapse. The fire chief found a faulty valve on the gas line going into the home and the energy from the shaking actually caused the valve to rupture completely, which more or less saved the occupants' lives. The insurance company should be able to cover it in full as we took pictures of the valve and everything. Helen is in the office trying to contact them now."

"Thank you. Is there anything further on this that needs to be discussed?"

"No sir. The bank has offered them use of the old Laramye homestead for however long they need."

"Well, that is good. Please work with the two and help them gather whatever is salvageable." The investigation team departed and the discussion that was interrupted continued. "Now where were we? Ah, yes, how can you say let it be? Do you know what media is like? They are a thousand times worse than blood hounds. They will not rest until they learn the truth…" Ron was interrupted.

"Or they make up their own conclusion. We will be the laughingstock of the country and the world. What is very strange about this conversation, Sheriff, is that it isn't disturbing." Ron chuckled.

"Well, we can confiscate the media devices and put everyone in lock down, or we can go back to business as usual," Sheriff Dylan added. "Is the hotel here still in operation? I think we will stick around a few days and see what else shakes out."

"It shuttered last season. But this could be the new hub with all of the stuff going on. If you want, the apartment upstairs here is vacant and fully furnished. You can set up there. I will see if I can get a couple folks ready just in case calls pour in."

Ermenya and Fred spoke in dragon, deciding the best way to deal with this mess, if it becomes larger.

"Now, Ron, we don't want a circus, so let's see what the day brings. Maybe it will all remain calm." Sheriff Dylan said as he scratched his chin.

"What do we do about the outsiders?" Ron asked under his breath. "If they go how do we know they are truly gone? What happens if they bring more in?"

"You should not fear those who are here. There are far worse things that will begin attacking the Veil if the Kluanarians fail. You will be defenseless." William paused as he looked at Ermenya. "You need to return to Krosslaen. They should be almost ready."

Ermenya nodded and vanished. "What is almost ready? Are you preparing an attack on us?" Police Chief Ron inquired as he paced in the conference room. As the chief turned around, two individuals appeared in long silver robes adorned with symbols of the Moons. "I knew it! We are done for!" The chief drew his weapon and chambered a round.

"I am Kira, this is Edwina. She is my granddaughter and lives on the edge of your hamlet. Your weapon does not frighten us." Kira snapped her fingers, and the pistol grip became colder than ice. "Place it on the table before you get frost bite." The chief did as he was prompted and then sat down stupefied. "We have knowledge that should be of use on both sides of the Veil."

"I am Sheriff Dylan; this is Police Chief Ron Todd. How can we help you?"

"You can't. I am trying to get control of a situation first, and then we will focus on defenses here."

"Whoa now, are we going to be under attack?" Sheriff Dylan asked as he nodded to the videographer in the other room.

"Kira, you need to go now!" Fred said. "We all need to go now." He barely finished his sentence when several officers entered the room with rifles drawn and handcuffs at the ready.

"Fred, destroy our home. We will meet you in Krosslaen." Kira said as she vanished with Edwina.

"Where did…What…" Chief Todd tipped his head back and roared in frustration. "What the hell do we do now?" Thirty minutes passed, then an hour. The phone in the station rang. "Weelin Police."

"This is Jenna Samson from Spokane. I was wondering if we could come out and do an interview with you concerning today's events."

"What events are you speaking of ma'am."

"First, with whom am I speaking?"

"I am Officer Lawrence ma'am."

"Earlier today we received video footage of your community being decimated. We were seeking clearance to enter the disaster zone."

"You can enter, there is no disaster here." Officer Lawrence looked at the chief who nodded in agreement. "Perhaps someone has superior skills in editing footage."

"So, you are you willing to review the video for yourself and …"

"No, we will not review footage that is clearly a hoax of some kind. There is absolutely no damage here. This is Police Chief Ron Todd speaking, for your reference. Now thank you for your concern and have a wonderful day." He walked back and forth at the front desk. "Now we have mayhem on the way! This is just what we need! I am calling Immigration! Surely, they can deal with this."

Sheriff Dylan had an amused expression as he leaned on the table. "So, Ron, just what pray tell do you think that Immigration is going to do with true aliens? How do you think they will react? Do you want to be put in a psych ward? However, I do have a number that may be able to assist us. This was given to me by the mayor of a small town south of Spokane. They had issues with floating objects on the edge of town and then with the satellite that came down, activity escalated. Maybe it is all related."

"How do you know this guy from Las Vegas will actually show?"

"This seems up his alley. We have the footage."

"Well, what can we lose? Go ahead Sheriff, call." Chief Todd gazed out the window. "Oh, no. Not now! Not now!" The media had arrived.

Kira and Edwina had translocated to the Moons' Temple. The Council had already gathered and there was much discussion. Kira spoke first. "My fellow Moons, we are too late in the hopes of a peaceful coexistence with the Realm of Earth. We will need to find a way to seal the Veil. They have enough technology, given the knowledge that Paul has shared with Zanor, to be a threat in the future. I am uncertain of how far in the future, but it is only a matter of time. Please take heed, Talaharian has already established an outpost."

"Where? When?" Lunacerian asked. "I thought the deadmages were retreating to Krosslaen?"

"They have a small village underway across from Mt. Edziza. There are plans in the works for either movement through the Veil or finding a way into Krosslaen." Gareth said as he entered the room.

"Ermenya has Krosslaen under control. William should be here soon, and Fred is taking care of our outpost in the Earth Realm," a familiar voice spoke as the Enygminite materialized. "I have disturbing news that will affect all orders and possibly the realm of Earth."

The council turned toward their guest as Gareth spoke. "Greetings, Menosh. You have traveled a great distance to relay this news. Did the High Council discuss this already?"

"Thank you, Gareth. No, this somehow relates, however. The sprites have rebelled against the High Council." The room became energized with chatter and steadily raising voices. "IF I MAY," Menosh said telepathically. "The sprites have sided with Talaharian. They have also found a weakness in the Veil." Menosh walked to the other side of the room in thought for a moment. All eyes were on him. "If Sprites decide to exploit the weakness, it will cause a rift, not a simple tear that heals. This will spread until the Veil is almost gone. While this is occurring, the two worlds will merge."

Gareth began looking through a rather large book of Kluanarian history. "Kluanaria and Earth will collide or merge."

Kira responded, "Gareth, the answer is yes and yes. The collision is more like the…"

"Gravity fields of the two realms will be forced together with the Veil gone. There will be massive electrical discharges in the atmospheres." Paul said as he entered the room with Zanor and Chorlanda. "The gravity fields of both will start tugging at the physical properties of the opposite realm, and there will be much destabilization and particles and large masses will start drifting off into the outer atmospheres."

Chorlanda added, "We are not sure how the merge will physically change the realms, but there will be massive extinctions." She drew a chart on the board at the side of the room. "We have diligently been searching for a habitable realm for Kluanarians and those of Phallas Minor."

"Do we know anything about this weakness in the Veil the sprites discovered?" Gareth inquired.

"Yes, we do." Alasha said as she emerged in a swirling wind of leaves.

"Thank you for gracing us with your presence." Lunacerian said as he studied the small being. "Why are you here?"

"I am here to help you with some quite serious indiscretions on your part and to share a bit of my knowledge. Now, where is Tatiana?" The room roared to life. Yelling and gestures from all Orders began instantly. The sprite utilized a rare gift. She closed her eyes and the room shook. It knocked everyone down and silence filled the room.

Kira almost snapped. "Tatiana is in serious trouble."

"What could a Newling possibly have done to cause this much energy in a room? It's not like she killed someone or brought a house down. She doesn't possess that knowledge of have strength enough to control it." The room was still, a grain of sand could be heard falling in the hourglass. "What exactly transpired?"

Altus began the long briefing. "After your departure to deal with Sprite issues, the Newlings bonded, which is the first in a very long time, and became close friends. Edwina was taken prisoner by Thanias through a tear created by Llylandra to Vale Kilowas. The younger Newlings did something crazy. The Shadowblyt created a tear and she and several Orders went through the tear in a rescue." He paused and Lunacerian continued.

"Edwina escaped on her own, bringing with her Thanias, who she had imprisoned in a gem. The group departed Vale Kilowas and returned to Weelin. The Newlings continued their learning with members of the Orders. Mithdrool had Llylandra and Jaetoth searching for Edwina, starting in the Palisade. They practically killed Altus, actually he was dead."

"Mithdrool grew impatient and searched with his mind for Edwina." Harold said as he joined the Orders. With a heavy sigh, he continued. "Mithdrool used his powers and cracked the Veil enough to see where

The Kluanarians

Edwina was. Once she was found he snapped his fingers more or less. Edwina collapsed to the ground and Thanias was freed. Kira mended her as best she could. This is when ..."

"Tatiana became enraged." Myron jumped in. "She healed her sister with the aid of Irra and Onachala. They then went to Bittern at the request of Impresaria, with Tommy for further training. They did not know it was a test. The Newlings with the help of a couple Orders restored Bittern to all its glory. The Shadowblyts and Izmaa returned to their pact with the Intervals and began healing the lands. Tatiana and the group then set their sights on Mithdrool, who they were successful in capturing with help from Omiporici."

"My... my granddaughter..." Zanor took up the last bit of the happenings. "She vanished. She found Thanias and dragged him all over the place showing him the great suffering and imbalance he brought. They stopped in the Palisade, and he watched as she restored Altus. Then she demanded he repent for his crimes and if not. Well let's say, a few days ago she got a hold of him again. With her great Brabant, she pulverized Weelin and the surrounding area, landed and in the presence of her family snapped her fingers, and Thanias who was with her at that moment collapsed, dead. My son is dead by my granddaughter."

A thin, grey being enter the room. "The High Council is discussing this very matter, Zanor. Do not be troubled." Menosh spoke. "As for the rest of the Orders, the High Council will convene at Bittern and you are hereby commanded to be present."

"What would they care about the plight of Kluanaria, the Earth Realm and of the deadmages from Phallas Minor?" Gareth asked in a tumultuous tone.

Alasha thought for a moment, seeing the tension between the Enygminite and the Orders. She then spoke, "Menosh, it is not the High Council's business what transpires here. I was at the same meeting with you and they are still indifferent. The one Earth folk revere didn't even show up to discuss this. How will Earth take this? There is an invasion planned by the deadmage, Talaharian. Llylandra and Jaetoth are planning on sacking Krosslaen, as they know what is inside. Ermenya and Freiderich are attempting to move Krosslaen as we speak, but they will need the help of the Star."

Brenda M. Hokenson

"We don't have a Star. Iris, we found out is Morket and can do many things. This Star we need is not amongst the Newlings either." Harold responded.

Alasha provided an answer. "The Star is present; you just don't know the name. Have you ever considered looking to Thallas?"

"Thallas of Ruan?" Zanor responded.

"Aye, Aantiri, it took you long enough."

"That is right! Stars do not wish to be found. He may not even know himself."

"Alasha, I will retrieve him." Harold spoke.

"No, Horseman. You will need to go with Freiderich to the Earth Realm along with Blayne and Malos."

"HOW DARE YOU, SPRITE! How dare you tell the Orders what to do!"

"Be silent Menosh. You were the High Council member responsible for overseeing Kluanaria. You failed them. You allowed them to be invaded. You allowed the deadmages to run rampant. You allowed two previous Stars to walk away."

"You insolent…"

"You have no power here, Enygminite. After you left the High Council to 'intervene' I provided the truth, as Sprites cannot lie. You have no power, so sit. Sit and be silent!" There was a gasp in the room. Confused looks between the Orders and rumblings began. "I will depart at once along with those I named. We will get Earth's cooperation, or they will be extinct rather quickly."

"What about the Veil and its weakness?" Gareth and Altus asked together.

"That is far off. The rebelling Sprites know what it is but have no way to achieve their goal. I will continue to monitor this. As for the loss of Thanias, I am sorry for the loss of a son, but you must remember, you reap what you plant." The departure group gathered at the center of the room. *"Transitae a Stockholm, transitae a hastae!"* The group vanished and translocated to Stockholm.

"Where are we going, Alasha?" Malos inquired as he looked at the structures.

"To see the King and he will speak with the King of Norway. Then we will ask for a summit amongst the Nordic lands."

"This is far from Weelin. Are you sure they will help?"

"Yes, they will. After all, we have 'Thor' with us and Ragnarök is around the corner."

"I…"

"Yes Harold. You are their Thor, so deal with it." Malos laughed as they continued to the castle. "The King will love to meet you."

"I…"

"You pack that overly large mallet with you everywhere, so how could you not be." Freiderich added.

"Oh, ghadzuchs. Why not…"

"Stop whining and pull it together Horseman." Alasha snapped. "If we can get Sweden and Norway to hear us, we then have to work on Denmark's Queen. She may be more difficult, and we won't bother with Finland."

"Whoa. Why do we need to stir all these pots?" Harold asked.

"They are all Norse and they all need to remember history, for it is about to get very nasty." Alasha said as she paced about.

Blayne spoke up. "Alasha, my Shrike has sent word."

"What is it, please?"

"The authorities in Weelin have requested their higher governance to act, asking for something called 'Immigration' to help them."

"We cannot deal with Weelin right now. Talaharian has put pieces in motion. We must convene with the Norse Lords first. Myron is tied up with funerary details for his brother. Zanor and Kira are in morning. It is the logical choice right now. Freiderich, is your broody ready?"

"Aye, Ermenya is present with them. They should hatch any day now. That will seal the venerability of the Veil."

IMMIGRATION AND INVITATIONS

"You have reached the United States Customs and Border Patrol Office in Spokane, Washington. Press 1 if you know your party's extension otherwise, please remain on the line for the next available agent." Sheriff Dylan held on the line for about twenty seconds. "U.S. Customs and Border Patrol, this is Agent Patriksen."

"Umm, yes, this is Sheriff Dylan out of Pend Orielle County, Washington. We have some very strange occurrences out here in Weelin. There are aliens who are not registered and are dangerous. Would you or someone in your office be willing to come out here and review our evidence?"

"Weelin, you say? That is very isolated. I will see if I can get a team together and assist you. Do these aliens have weapons and are they threatening the citizens?"

"A girl killed a man…"

"Well, that in itself is threatening, so give me a couple hours and we will be out."

"Thank you, Agent Patriksen. We will be waiting for you in the Police Headquarters."

"Agent Dunwoody, is your schedule clear today?"

"Yes sir. What do you have for us?"

"Get your gear and find Agent LaCluae. This could be an interesting case."

"What is it?"

"Just get LaCluae and the car. I will brief you on the way."

LaCluae brought the car around front and the three proceeded toward Weelin. "Ok, you two." Patriksen spoke. "There is a situation in Weelin. I thought it be best we take a look at the evidence collected by the town's police and county Sheriff. It seems a death occurred and some other actions warranting us to look into this."

"Is there a morgue doing the autopsy?"

"Not sure, Weelin is so remote, hopefully the road is passable." Agent Patriksen said as he gazed out the window of the Pontiac. "At least there isn't rain in the forecast. We need to go through Metaline Falls and take the gravel road. The gravel road turns to packed dirt after the pass on Gypsy Peak. Then we climb another hill and drop into the river valley. If this is extremely serious, we will have to work with the Canadians. There is not an airstrip, but helicopters can be used."

"What do you think we will find." LaCluae asked.

"No idea, but it will be interesting. Now watch for deer crossing; this stretch of road is dangerous."

They stopped in Metaline Falls for lunch, where they dined at 5th Avenue Bar and Grill. Agent Dunwoody inquired about the route to Weelin when she got an earful. "Agent Dunwoody, is it? I am so glad you are here. My name is Helen, and my husband and I live in Weelin. We have some photos you may be interested in." Helen reached in her handbag and pulled out an envelope that had multiple photos date and time stamped. "I hope these will be of use."

"Thank you, umm, Helen. Can you tell me which road we need to take to Weelin? We have never been there." Agent Dunwoody returned to their booth with directions and photos which they examined while they waited for their order.

"This is terrible. I wish Sheriff Dylan would have called sooner. Everything is in ruin!" Agent Patriksen said as he examined the photos.

"Yet, how much do we know about Helen? Does she stand to gain something in this? Is it a hoax, the photos I mean?" Agent LaCluae responded as he too looked at the pictures.

"We need to go soon," Agent Dunwoody commented as their meals arrived. After they were finished, Dunwoody drove to the turn-off and began the slower journey via gravel road. There were many switch backs and steep grades as they approached Gypsy Peak. The road coming out was more dirt than gravel as they continued, with more twists and turns. Dunwoody had white knuckles and pounding heart when they reached the valley floor. She gave control of the car to Agent Patriksen. As they approached the town both Dunwoody and LaCluae compared the photos with what they were seeing. "Nothing seems out of order like this photo shows. Do you think that Helen modified pictures?"

"No telling, Dunwoody. That's why we are here." Agent Patriksen said as they rolled up to the Police Station.

Chief Ron Todd raced out followed by Sheriff Dylan and a mix of deputies and police officers. "Thank you for coming to our aid. It is of national security. But where is the Immigration Service"

"Good afternoon, Chief Todd." Agent Patriksen responded. "Immigration is for folks who want to become citizens. Sheriff Dylan contacted our office because it is a security matter. We will have to brief Homeland Security at the conclusion of our investigation."

"Ah, I see. So we are hoping we will have enough evidence to get some much needed help."

"We don't see any distress." Replied Agent LaCluae as he pulled out photos. "We believe you are trying to stir things with these photos." He handed the pictures to the Sheriff Dylan. "Now where exactly are these locations?"

"Well, they were taken downtown, right here. When this girl leveled the place and then rebuilt it."

"You expect us to believe that hooey?" LaCluae responded.

Sheriff Dylan stepped up, "I think you need to watch what we have on film, from several cameras used for surveillance around town, plus the material from the conference room down the hall." He led the group inside the room and together all watched the accumulated happenings of events. "This is a matter of national security, so what do we do now?"

"Well, can you tell us much about this Helen person?"

"Ah, Helen, she believes they are Occult, which clearly they are nothing like that. What floored me was the little 6-year-old girl and how she just snapped her finger and her uncle died instantly. Of course, we can't prove it as there were no cameras pointed at where the incident took place." Chief Todd responded.

"We know that. What about Helen? Do you think she is in league with them to save her own bacon?"

"No, she is a God-fearing citizen and never misses church or associates with unfamiliars to here." Chief Todd paused a moment. "Her husband, Johnny however may have more knowledge of them. And we can take a drive up to their small area at the edge of town. I have been there on occasion and found nothing out of the ordinary."

"Very well, let's take Johnny with us and we will see what we see, I guess." Agent LaCluae responded.

Before the group left the building, a flash of light and purple mist filled the conference room. The occupants drew weapons pointed to the center of the room. A young voice said, "If you use the weapon, you will only kill your friends." The individual speaking remained invisible to the humans' eyes and continued to speak. "My name is Edwina, I am of the Moon Order from a sister planet and with me are two of my closest allies, Irra and Onachala. Please hear us out before you do anything, shall we say rash."

"Why should we believe that you will not harm us? A little girl killed a man earlier today." Agent Patriksen said as he placed his pistol on the table.

"Who was killed?" Edwina asked as she had not heard anything of this.

"A man who the girl called 'Uncle' and proceeded to raise her voice at the adults." Patriksen responded.

"Thanias. Uncle Thanias." Edwina could be heard weeping. "I could have saved him."

The three removed the invisibility from themselves. Onachala spoke up. "Edwina's family, Myron, her dad, Iris, her mom, and her brother and sister moved here probably 13 or so years ago. They came to escape, as bad things were beginning to happen, and Iris wanted the kids protected."

Irra continued, "They returned to their planet through a Veil, which isn't visible really, and spent quality time there until bad things started happening, so they returned here. Then a second journey home, brought more bad things and several other families chose to go with them and cope, and try to fit in."

"Everything my family did was within the laws of your land, everything was paid for in American dollars and earned, because my parents had to learn to fit in and what true work was."

"Your family failed to file a green card for each of you and state the length of your stay." LaCluae answered. "We can take you in as illegal aliens."

"You can, but how will you transport us?" Onachala smiled wryly.

"We can render you unconscious and everything will go smoothly."

Irra caught a glimpse of a police officer with a taser. She shielded the group and all vanished. She said behind the invisible shield, "We would like to help you as there is a far worse thing than Tatiana here on this planet that can wipe everything out in about an hour, if he is mad enough."

"If you would like us to help you use this stone at the center of our learning lawn." Edwina said as the three translocated to their semi-destroyed home at the edge of Weelin. "It will take them about an hour to get here, so let's salvage the important things and make sure the learning lodge is vaporized. The houses have no magic and no trace, so they are safe."

"We are sorry for your loss, Edwina. We are sure you could have changed things." Onachala spoke as they visited each room in the rather old looking learning lodge. Once cleared, the Shadowblyt and Izmaa cast a spell that imploded the building and removed all evidence it existed. Grass was growing in its stead. "Ok, we need to get to Ruan, since that is where your dad will be, Edwina." The three vanished.

The authorities arrived about twenty minutes after the departure and began looking for evidence that spoke of 'illegal' aliens. The group stood in wonderment, staring at this stone handed to them.

Alasha, Malos, and Harold made their way to Drottingholm in hopes of speaking with the King of Sweden. Alasha had fond memories of visiting here when Thor was more active. She also remembers visiting each new King of each country when they came to power. "I will speak first." Alasha said as they went through the gates without being seen. "We can stay cloaked until we are inside."

"What?" Harold said as they approached a pair of guards. "Why can't we be cloaked inside?"

The Kluanarians

"Because, you, you buffoon, cast an anti-cloak spell in each castle so that they would not fear us." Alasha retorted.

"I..."

"Yes! Now be quiet."

The three found themselves in a grand entrance. The cloaking was slowly waning as they walked through to the secret door to the antechamber where Harold noticed something. "This requires the King's signet ring to open."

"You don't say." Alasha spoke as she went toward the atrium where she noticed the King seated by a fountain. "Good day, Your Highness. Do you remember me?"

"Come closer. I am assuming since the guards have not chased you or your friends by my antechamber, then I must know you, or you have some kind of invisible spell to cast."

"I am Alasha. I return to you on this day, lord, that I might bring news of the return of Thor and to inform you of…"

"Thor? It can't be."

"There is only one way to find out for certain."

The King immediately rose and almost sprinted down to the antechamber. He rushed past Harold and Malos and inserted the signet into the reading device, which was designed by Gareth in each of the Royals' palaces worldwide. The doors were very intricate they opened first as normal sliding doors part, and then when half way open, they split in the center and sunk into the ground or raised into the upper frame.

The four entered the room and sat at a table designed long before the current King reigned. The King was frank in speaking to the group. "I don't know if you are full of wine, but I have seen some of the workings of Thor in use today. Tell me, why should I believe you, Alasha? You promised that Ragnarök was averted, and from my readings I can see that you have said that to every King who has walked in Drottingholm. Where is my proof of Thor? What is bringing about Ragnarök?"

"Allow me." Harold said as he stood before the King. "This is my mallet. If I am correct, it will open the sacred vault that Gareth built and in there, we will have this discussion." Harold walked to the wall where a small vase shaped object sat on the ground encased in dust. He removed his mallet from his back and allowed the King to examine it. "You see, these are original markings that you have in here, hidden by the dust on this vase, caused my departure for your world." The King returned the mallet, and Harold placed the handle into the vase forcefully. A cracking sound echoed in the whole of the castle. "Sorry, it may cause panic above." The vase sounded like it shattered, but it was intact. Another door opened in the same manner the outer door did. Harold went inside and found what he was looking for. "King, I command you request the presence of your Norse brethren, as there is much to discuss."

The King seated himself at an oaken desk that had automatic writing in runes on special parchment. Once the invitations were completed, he marked them with his signet that he never knew opened until that moment. After they were marked they disappeared. After about twenty minutes passed, several royals entered the antechamber, where Malos greeted them.

"How was your journey, Son of Norway and Daughter of Denmark?"

"Fast," replied the Queen. "I was unaware until the letter arrived that there was a special vehicle for this journey."

"It will also return you when we are finished." Harold added.

"How did you get the doors pried open?" The King of Norway asked as he examined the mallet and the open door. "Do we need to wait for anyone?"

"He didn't pry them open, I did. And, no to your second question. Please enter and sit at my table." Harold entered and pulled out a very aged alcohol and some small goblets of oak. "Drink this, my children. Drink this and let truth come to you in the next hour." The royals drank the tart beverage and learned of the Veil. "Malos wishes to speak now."

Malos stood before the group. "You will not know me as well as Thor, but I am an Interval, a druid in your realm, and I practice healing and oversee training of the Newlings. Newlings are rare and once discovered we try to train them and mold them to fit in to their proper Order. This land we generally stay at is on the other side of the Veil. There are guards and Keepers that protect crossing as much as they can. However, there is a group not from our realm, or yours. They recently lost their home planet in a supernova and have been here, on your planet, not long after Thor departed. They are called Morket and have an exceedingly advanced technology that allows them to traverse space in a short period of time.

The Morket are generally peaceable, except the ones that crossed through the Veil recently. They are deadmages, led by Talaharian."

"Deadmages?" The Queen of Denmark inquired.

"To you they would be necromancers. This particular group almost destroyed Kluanaria, which is our home world, through the Veil."

"How do you think we will be able to assist you? Our technology is not that advanced, save a few things that are well, unknown to the public." The King of Sweden said as he stood to pace the large room. He studied the artifacts from when Thor was more present in their history. "You know, Thor, much has changed since you left. There are so few who are willing to trust their officials, let alone crown royals like us, I am not sure if we are the right ones to ask."

The King of Norway spoke. "So, if I interpret you correctly, we have true alien races on our world, some of which are hostile. Will they attack people or meld?"

"We are uncertain at this moment. But there is an outpost they established is on the far north islands of Svalbard. There are no known entities that they can resurrect to the best of our knowledge." Alasha said as she watched two Kings now pacing.

"The United Nations will want extreme details, as they are the only governing body that represents many of the world's countries. I am not sure how this will go over. How do we address it?" The Queen of Denmark said as she joined the pacing kings.

"I will do it." Harold said as he walked to the altar at the far end of the room. "This room is where very hard decisions are to be made. Can you tell me how to send an invitation to the security side of this United Nations?"

"I will send it as urgent. There are several countries on the panel and they should bring sway to the rest." The Swedish Monarch said as he went to the oaken desk and picked up a phone that miraculously still worked. "I will start with a few monarchs in our area who are not currently present, and then we will go from there."

"This will be faster." Alasha said as she created a small whirl wind and one by one about twenty-four more monarchs entered through the wind. They represented all monarchies to include those whose country became a republic, or other form of government.

Those present in the room were stunned as everyone arrived. The room expanded as did the table and number of seats about it. Each also had a goblet at their seat that and appropriate titles and names for each guest. The guests mingled about for ten minutes or so and then were seated for a very long discussion.

In Weelin, the sheriff, police chief, and government officers scoured each building. All the rooms were furnished, just like any normal place in the country. Pictures were present, most were paintings in styles of Monet and Manet.

"Ok, Johnny, how much do you know about this Myron?"

"He is a good man. He moved here around 13 years ago. He works downtown at the garage. He is a most excellent metal specialist; not sure where he trained, but he got a license from the State of Washington for welding and such. He also does his own restoration projects, in fact, that there farm truck, he fixed up last summer and the families here all come to town together once in a while in it for ice cream and movies."

The authorities inspected the truck and found all to be in order. They examined all of his tools and found a small forge in a side room. The examined the tools in the room and found nothing out of the ordinary. They examined some of his works in progress and left.

"Well, now, that was a quite a neat shop. How often does he take on bigger projects?" Agent LaCluae asked.

"Well, not very often. Sometimes he asks me for help. We built the fountain downtown, as I am a stone mason. He spent about a year and a half on the sculpture, which he did using his forge for each intricate detail and a very small soldering tool to weld the pieces together."

Agent Patriksen found a door in the side of a small hill. He opened it and the group went in. "Well, this seems to be normal, a cellar for vegetables. Nothing looks out of place." The group then went to the rock in the center of the yard. "Are you certain she said this rock? It appears to be a large sundial, which is cool."

Agent Dunwoody reviewed her notes. "Yes sir. Edwina said, 'Use this stone', the one in your pocket, boss, 'at the center of our learning lawn.'" She paused and found it to be the most central lawn.

The Kluanarians

"Very well. Let's see what happens. LaCluae and Todd, you two will have cameras on the whole time. Stay back about 20 feet or so, just in case." Patriksen approached the rock and took the small stone out of his pocket. He held it up trying to figure out what would happen. While he was fumbling with it in his fingers he dropped it. "Darn rock!" He exclaimed as he stooped to pick it up and cracked his head against the tall stone. In his fumbling, he found a small piece missing from it and saw that the small stone he had just recovered fit perfectly in it. All at once, when he placed the stone in its rightful place, a brilliant silvery light surrounded the area. "Are you recording? Are you recording?" As he finished yelling, the group vanished.

Meanwhile, Edwina and the other Newlings had transported to Ruan, where they ran as fast as they could to the Great Hall. There they found Thanias lying in state. He was in his official Truncheon officer garments with his favorite sword and shield at his feet. Edwina knelt as did Onachala and Irra. They cried together, hugging, and after ten minutes they stood. Myron and Kira entered the room, followed by Zanor. "I am sorry daddy." Edwina mumbled as she hugged Myron and her grandparents. "I will have revenge."

"No, child." A voice whispered in her mind. "It is supposed to be this way." She recognized the voice as her deceased uncle. "Everything will work out, I promise. I should have been more attentive to your actions in you trying to save me in Vale Kilowas."

Edwina nodded and walked over to her uncle and hugged him. "Daddy, Uncle Tha…"

"I know; he seemed to have a certain thought left for each of us. Don't be afraid and don't seek revenge. Your sister is following the path that chose her."

Kira took the three girls in her arms. "My Newlings; you have done so much for Kluanaria and even the Earth Realm. We are forever grateful to all who have done such things to restore our home world to its true state. There is much to do still. But first we all must move past this grief. After the ceremony tonight, there will be a clean state and a renaissance if you will. Much has changed here while you have been studying. Come now, let's get you to your homes so you can prepare for tonight. I want you each to rest for a while and eat with your families. Then come here in your

Orders garb. It is required of all Orders. Menosh has been put in a state of silence and currently William, will preside over our Orders." The girls looked confused and accepted it. Their parents joined them in the Great Hall where they escorted the girls to their homes.

Kira fell to the ground. A vision entered her mind. It was a scene playing out. *As she opened the door to her cottage, two shades which resembled opened umbrellas which were flattened came from an upper corner in the hallway and rushed out past her into the road. There they transformed into two individuals. The first individual was a slender woman with fair hair and wearing a white leather tunic that went to her mid-thigh. It had red lines that ran horizontally across the front center about 6 inches to each side with a gold cord surrounding each line. The line ended on both sides with small spades pointed outward. Her leggings were a white leather as well. She appeared to be a mage. The second individual was a taller man, about 6 foot or so. He had grey/white hair and sharp blue eyes. He wore a robe, appearing to be a silk or something similar that was black. It was striking. There was a flame in the center of the chest that seemed to flicker. The trim around the neck and sleeves was silver. Between the shoulder and the neck, there were openings on each side that were oval. They extended down from the shoulder about 3 inches to the front and three inches to the rear.*

He turned and walked toward a bridge where she noticed the back had an opening above the waist in an ovular shape encased with silver also. She went toward the bridge in her vision and got to the bridge, where they had crossed. As she set foot on the bridge, she observed it. It seemed to be of driftwood bound many times, or possibly dragon bones as it was as wide as the chest of a dragon. The water under it had stopped flowing long ago. When she looked up another person came into the scene. He wore very heavy armor. His helm remained on as he looked at her. It was not a standout helm. The face plate completely wrapped around and there was tuft of white hair from a horse's tale protruding from the top. His shoulders were slightly tarnished, with leather bindings and under garment with a tunic under it. The belt was leather with a small pouch on it. His leggings were leather with tarnished plate as well.

As she put her foot on the bridge, the woman and man in the robe began casting. The woman let loose white bolts from the sky, resembling how folks draw arrows on paper. They came in clusters of 6. The man in the robe, was almost done with the incantation, when the man in armor said, "No she is mine." He approached the center of the bridge and in Kira' mind, she, walked toward the center. The man began to charge with sword drawn. Kira defended her ground with all of her spells she has learned since she was a Newling. After what seemed to be a ten-minute battle, it seemed to pause. Then the man charged again, and the same battle occurred for another ten minutes. As the pause occurred again, Kira watched the other two while they sat at the side, observing. The man returned to the center of the bridge as did Kira. As she prepared to defend herself, the vision ended. Kira sat stunned, not knowing what to make of it.

"Are you alright Mother?" Lucien exclaimed. He had been supporting her head since she had fallen. "I thought you too..."

"My son, we are together forever. Nothing can separate us. Myron, I had a vision." Myron and Zanor approached. She recounted every detail of the village and the bridge and the folks in the vision. "I don't know what it means. Is Iris here or Lady Phallas? Maybe..."

"I am here." Rithmas said as he approached the scene. "At least you missed the mud puddle." He smiled as he knelt beside his long-time friend. He levitated her and basically pushed her to her home and into her bed, with her family following them. "Will you recount your story to me, lass?"

Kira smiled, "Yes, friend, and maybe Gareth later." She didn't have to speak. Rithmas placed his hand on the back of her head and closed his eyes. *He saw all of the details that had unfolded the past two days and then the vision which was very suspenseful. He saw the village seemed to be rustic and buildings were of wood with small stairs leading up to each door. He saw the sky was a brown, gray color. The sun seemed very dim from air. The trees had no leaves, so he assumed maybe autumn. The lack of water under the bridge concerned him.* Kira slept for some time as Rithmas continued viewing the images still sharp in her mind. When he finished his viewing, he released Kira's head gently.

"So, what did you learn Rithmas?" Gareth asked as he walked through the door.

"Well, I have not seen Talaharian before, but I think the man in the robe may be him." The area is very familiar. It is what Bittern looked like two hundred years ago. There was no snow, there was no water. There was a bridge at the Northern end where the path winds out of the village toward Monti dei draghi. This vision of hers could be from the past or the future."

"Well, let me check the parchements stored in Bitterns great hall." Gareth said as he opened a small pouch that had many scrolls in it. "Ah, here we go. This is a past vision. But you know how history is."

"True. Lunacerian will want to know of this. Also perhaps a certain Palisade Keep will have some clue as to thes individuals." Rithmas said as scratched is short strawberry blond beard. He asked a zephyr to take a message to Lunacerian and also Walther.

The zephyr reached the Palisade quickly. He went into the linrary where he found Walther working on about four different scrolls. He observed Walther's work. The zephyr noticed he wrote a paragraph an then moved on to the next . "Walther, I have a message from Rithmas and Gareth."

As Walther received the note, the zephyr disappeared and reappeared in the antechamber of Lunacerian's library. "Lunacerian. Rithmas and Gareth request your presence."

"In regards to what?"

"Kira has had a vision of the past. They believe history may repeat itself but would like aide in determining the individuals who are in this vision."

Lunacerian bowed. "Thank you, I will depart at once." The two both vanished, reappearing in Ruan.

As the Kluanarians studied the vision and the delegation in Sweden worked on explaining everything to all the monarchs, ruling or not, the authorities from Earth who used the stone at the center of a learning yard emerged in a land unknown to them. The group of five found themselves standing at the base of a snow capped mountain. It appeared to be late autumn where they stood.

"Well, we are somewhere, I guess." Chief Todd said as he looked around the immediate vicinity. "It doesn't look so bad and we haven't died, so the air must be similar." He found a small building that looked like it would accomdate the group. He entered it and looked around. There was a small desk in a corner and there were three bedrooms, two with hand carved bucks and the third had a large bed to one side and one that was about half the size in a built in nook that seemed to be changeable. He tried his radio. "Chief Todd to Base, do you have a copy?"

"This is Base, we copy. What is your six?"

"We are not in Weelin anymore, over."

"Do you need support?"

"Not yet, please keep this channel open, over."

"Roger. Base clear."

"Well, at least we can communicate, I guess." Chief Todd said as he wandered about the room. Well, I thnk we should go out and see what we can see." The group agreed. "Sheriff, since the US Government is represented, I say we give them point."

"I agree. Agent Patriksen, please lead the way. We will maintain comm with Base. Agent Dunwoody, please see if the camera and video work."

"You can't tell me what to do ..." Dunwoody was cut off.

"Just do it, Dunwoody. Or give it to LaClue, now."

The group began their wanderings. They followed a path that led them down into the Treahan Forest. They gazed upon sculptures that lined the path as they were closer to a village. The village was even more remarkable. The buildings were solid wood with intricate carvings on the door frame and along the roof. The windows all had small gardening trays where herbs and flowers grew. The village center had stone walkways that met and formed a circle around a silver fountain that had a sculpture of a dragon and a rather tall man.

"Are you recording this?" Patriksen asked of Dunwoody.

"Yes, so long as the batteries don't die."

"I got spares." Agent LaClue replied. "Let's see what is going on in there." He steered the group to a pub. They entered the building and the room that was buzzing with noise became silent. A tall slender man approached.

"Welcome travelers. Edwina of the Moons said you would be here. Please, join us for food. I am Guilles of the Shadowblyts. We reside in this land along with Intervals and Izmaa. We have lodging for you as well."

"Thank you, Guilles. I am Agent Patriksen and they are Agent Dunwoody, Agent LaClue, Sheriff Dylan, and Chief Todd. We are trying to determine your purpose on Earth."

"You are not on Earth, so you will abide by our law until your true intent is discovered. We were told that you tried to place our most revered

Brenda M. Hokenson

friends in captivity. So any object you have that will harm us here need to be left here, in this box."

Agent Patriksen looked at the group and nodded his head. "We will accept your request. All weapons and cuffs go in here, now." The group complied.

As the last objects were placed in Guilles closed the lid. A Shrike came forth and sealed it. The newcomers stood in awe. "Do not ask, as I know you will not understand no matter how simple of explanation we provide." Guilles said as he seated them at a table amongst some of the elders of all of the Orders. "Now, if you don't mind, I must return to Burwash. Truance will give you a tour after you have supped."

The group was treated to organic food. Deer steaks, fresh vegetables that were steamed and garnished with herbs grown on the window ledges, and fresh pressed apple juice. The plates were silver as wewere the utensils.

"I thought we weren't supposed to eat with silver utensils." Agent Dunwoody said.

"These silverware and plates have been used for centuries. No one has gone mad or became ill from it. We do not add chemicals to our kitchenware and tableware that we use. I do believe that your realm does, but you also no longer use them for eating, and only for decoration. The goblets are carved wood, just so you know." Omiporici said as he helped place the food and drink. "My name is Omiporici. I am an Interval. Your realm calls me a Druid. Truance will not be joing us this day. I will be most honored to show you about our lands. Are you seeking anything specific?"

"We are seeking a man who died in Weelin. A young lady named Edwina gave us a small stone that she said to place in the center stone. We arrived at the base of your great mountain and chose to take the path to here." Agent Patiksen said. "This meal is wonderful."

"We do not keep supplies like we have seen in your world. It is unnatural and will eventually cause the downfall of your realm. The chemicals should have never been created."

"How do you know so much about us and we so little about you?"

"Patriksen, what a strange name. Anyway, we have lived amongst you on for 13 years. However, our friends, the dragons, have lived in your realm since the earth cooled from its firey beginning. Your kind have hunted them almost to extinction, then they found the Veil. They came

The Kluanarians

through the Veil and have found peace here. The two we know traveled from a distant place far beyond your stars to get here. Dragons choose not to enter your realm any longer. All we need to know about you has been recorded since the first dragons began an exodus to here. They were given peace and in turn they helped us by teaching us about your kind. As an Interval, I found it imperative to know what was on the other side in instances of your kind's transit through the Veil. Please keep in mind, your devices work here, but the magnetics crossing back will distort images you have captured. So I hope you can draw."

"Well, Omiporici, we have no reason to harm you, just to bring an individual to justice for a crime committed in Weelin."

"Mr. Patriksen, there is no evidence in your village to support such a wild claim."

The discussion went back and forth for hours with no ground gained by the invitees from Earth. As the tension amassed Omiporici gave the visitors a parchment that was a brief history of Kluanaria and a letter of invitation for the realm of Earth. The moment Agent Patriksen accepted it, Omiporici opeend a tear and pushed them back through to Weelin and resealed the tear.

The group found themselves on the edge of Weelin where the 'aliens' had once resided. As they looked around, they noticed that there was nothing remaining except for the stone. Dunwoody reviewed her footage and found garbled recordings. They walked to their vehicles and went back in to town.

In Burwash, Kira was recovering from her horrible image. Guilles had joined Rithmas and Gareth as they discussed the content of her vision. Zanor entered the room and sat at the head of the table. He clapped his hands and a small feast appeared on the table. The men ate as they continued there discussion.

Zanor finally said, "I cannot say what this means, but it is reminiscent of the horsemen invading Ruan from the slope to the West. This reminds me of William revealing himself along with Malificence and others to gain control. We were fortunate that Harold was sensible and aided us. WE were also fortunate as he helped restore the Morket through his unity with Malificence. However, this vision seems to be in the future. Perhaps we can have Chorlanda and Paul take this image and put in in their computer and see if Earth has a place similar to it."

"That is a great idea!" Gareth exclaimed. "I wonder if they will let me go?"

"Of course, Gareth." A familiar young voice said from the doorway. "Chorlanda said I would find you here." Paul paused as he entered the room and hugged his grandfather. "I am sorry about Thanias. If I would of known Tatiana..."

"It was meant to be, Paul. You should go pay your respects."

"I already did Grandfather. His mesaage to me was that I need to seek Walther in the Palisade, he wil have important things for me in the defence of Kluanria."

"Then sit and eat with us, lad. You must be hungry." Gareth said as he pulled a chair up to the table for Paul. "So Paul, where has your training taken you?"

"Well, I was invited by Chorlanda to learn mapping. Not just a certain area, but entire worlds. I have been given advance classes in physics that explains many facets of interstellar travel. I also learned about fueling nothing more than light. And that it doesn't have to be a bright light to do it. Dark matter emits light as it is consumed and since space has an abundance of it, there is a limitless supply." Paul paused and filled his plate. "I have also been learning Aantiri stuff. It is really hard and requires total focus. I can only hope to be half as good as you,Grandpa."

"You will be very powerful, Paul. That I am certain." Zanor said as he watched his prodigy eat. "The ceremony for Thanias will be at sunset."

Chorlanda entered the room. "Sire. I have word from Malos." The group turned toward her as they continued eating. "The invitation to the Earth's true rulers was well received. He reports that all invitees are in attendance and are slowly becoming more receptive of the events. They are aware, as a whole that they have been watched over for millenia and are working on a way to convey this to the othe leaders."

"That is very positive. Is there word yet when we will send an entourage to their worldly meeting?" Gareth inquired.

"They are working on the details of how to best present this. I am told that they will represent their own countries and not someone else who will leave out details."

"Thank you Chorlanda. Please feel free to join us, or depart." Chorlanda left the room and went to her home which had been unoccupied for some time. She found it still impeccably clean and the garden well kept in her absence. She found and invitation from Malos, requesting a large ship and the entourage to rendezvous at Drottingholm in seven days. She asked a zephyr to deliver the note to Zanor as she relaxed on her lounge chair.

In Weelin, the group made their way into the police station where the footage was reviewed very carefully. At the request of Agent Patriksen, the FBI and CIA sent specialists to assit in restoring the footage. All video recordings at the station were downloaded and made into one file. This included the investigation at the edge of Weelin and as the video rolled on, the images of passing through the Veil were recorded as well. Two specialists worked together and were able to restore what was taken in Kluanaria.

Patriksen waited patiently and at last, all the pieces came together. "Gentleman, what we have here is a serious world problem. A problem that is potentially lifechanging to every last man, woman, and child. The question now becomes how do we address this with the world leaders?"

THALLAS OF THE STARS

THE CEREMONY FOR THANIAS STARTED at precisely sunset. William was present and had been to visit Thallas earlier in the day. He asked permission for Thallas to join him at the Stars' Altar which was most important during the ceremony. During the ceremony Thallas held the large tome open for William and as the sun began to set a bright light resembling the exact details of Thanias when he was alive. William read several incantations to release Thanias and grant him passage as Zanor and Kira stepped forward. The starlight generated by William took on Thanias' shape it moved forward and knelt before the High Lord, Zanor, his father, and also owed to the Orders. As the last bit of sun sank in the horizon, the starlight forming Thanias walked into the sky and then at the blink of an eye shot into space. Starlight and moonlight lit the Great Hall. As Thanias vanished so did all of his material belongings, except for those he left to Tomas.

William spoke after the sunset ceremony. "We have lost a good Truncheon leader. He will not be forgotten and has taught us all that even the strongest can be bent by evil. This man, young in years, will not be forgotten and his strength will live on in Ryatt." Everyone looked back and forth amongst each other. The news startled his parents. "Ryatt wed Thanias two years ago in secret with the blessing of Freiderich and Ermenya. Their child will be born in six moon cycles."

"This is very troubling." Zanor said as he walked to the center of the room. He knelt beside where his son had been laying. "Ryatt will need much support. Where is Ryatt?"

"She is with Ermenya in Krosslaen where she is well cared for."

"We, as Thanias' family would like to care for her." Kira said.

Confusion was rampant in the room. Zanor faced the group. "This is most upsetting to all of us. Perhaps, if circumstances were different, we would be celebrating the wedding of Thanias and Ryatt and rejoicing in their soon to be child. Take this with you as you depart to your homes. Thanias was turning back to the way of the right and Ryatt was his companion through this. We will support Ryatt. Think of your children and the turmoil that face them. Would you support them or shun them?" With that Zanor and Kira took William aside. "William can Thanias be restored? Is he truly gone?"

"We will need to speak to Truance of these things. For she is a healing Interval and has great knowledge."

The three departed to the Healing House where they found Truance pacing before two patients. "I know why you are here. What you will ask of me is most difficult. It delves on the edge of being a deadmage and playing God."

"Truance, umm. I just want to..." Zanor started. "I know this is difficult to consider, but is this even feasible?"

"Yes, Lord. It is feasible, but I will need time to prepare."

"How much time? What do you need? Do you need specific herbs? Will he be whole to include in spirit?"

"You need to ask yourself if you are prepared for what returns. It may go perfectly or it may go very wrong. I also need to know if you have a Star available, for that person is an integral part to this?"

"Well…" Zanor was cut off.

"I will take no part in this ceremony, Zanor." William spoke. "I have to go through the Veil and assist Malos and Alasha in their endeavors with the true kings of Earth." He paused briefly. "However, I am on my way to speak with Thallas. He is a Newling Star. He has advanced knowledge from what I understand and this may be the challenge he needs."

"How old is he?" Truance said as she checked he patients.

"He is about 13. Or as Tatiana would say 'On Earth it is 7.'"

"Hmm. Does he have a trainer?"

"Yes. He has me and I am certain this will be fine. I however won't be here to assist. Will that be an issue?"

"It might be. Do you have time to review the tome covering this with him or is that asking too much?"

"I can take care of that. He is studying the older history that covers this right now. I will be instructing him for the next week, and then I must depart for Drottingholm."

"Be sure he knows his place. It can go very bad if he does not." Truance said as she escorted the men to the door. "Now if you will excuse me, I need to attend my patients."

Zanor and William departed and made straight for Thallas' home. Thallas saw them approaching and raced out to meet them. "I remember you. You are Tatiana's Grandfather, Zanor. This also makes you our High Lord."

Zanor hugged Thallas. "Thank you, lad. William has said that you are a Star?"

"Yes sir. Just so you know, last year, when Tatiana was visiting you, I wasn't trying to make fun of her and the butterflies. I was kinda trying to ignore my own stuff."

"That is okay. I told her that not everyone understands what happens to their friends when they are relaxed or anxious. Tell me, how much have you learned?" The group went into Thallas' home. Gwendolyn was seated with her mother learning how to sew. "Mama, High Lord Zanor is here."

Constance stood immediately and curtsied. "My lord."

Zanor bowed. "How are you this fine morning?"

"Well, we are all quite well. The day is young, and I am wondering if William will be schooling Thallas tomorrow?"

William responded almost immediately. "I will school him tomorrow. He has done well in his training and I would like to see if he is willing to try something challenging."

Thallas perked up. "What is it? Do I get to try to capture a moon beam with a sun ray yet?"

"No, that is very advance, but this is something almost as advance, but it is more difficult as it has to be done precisely. There are only three lines, but they are at exact times when working with an Interval."

"Really? I really get to work with an Interval? What will we be doing?"

"Saving a life that should be spared."

"Interesting. While you are here, this tome arrived though the book exchange pouch. It has some spells that I would like to learn." Thallas showed William the tome. "It is these two here."

"Ah, yes. The second one is the one I am referring to. If you will notice, your part for the incantation is very brief but this gives details on how to do it."

Zanor interjected, "If I may ask, why you want to learn the Words of Retrieval? It is a very difficult undertaking, from what I am told."

"Well, Tatiana did something bad, and I want to fix it."

"How do you know she did something bad? And why do need to fix it?" Zanor asked.

"Well, Tatiana was here briefly and said she took out the problem. So I figured it had to be bad. I went to the Palisade and asked Walther if he knew of any books that would help me to learn what Star Order people are supposed to know. This is one of the tomes. Altus is in charge of the library, and he gave me this pouch of book exchange."

"And…" His mother added.

"And, Walther said I need your guidance before I do anything with either of them. So I am asking if I can learn these from you next."

William thought for a bit. "Ok, you will need to relax and clear your mind completely for both. Tomorrow, I will test you on your knowledge and then the following day we will start with this one here." He pointed to the Words of Retrieval.

Thallas was excited. He ran to his room and pulled out a small notebook that reminded Zanor of Tatiana. In it he put a check mark on one of the items on his list. Zanor mused, remembering Tatiana and her list of clues as she worked on solving puzzles and learning new things.

"Lord Zanor, would you look at my list, please?" Thallas asked as he stood perfectly still with his book extended toward the Aantiri.

"Of course, lad, and please, don't be so formal. I am after all just another person. I don't need to be treated special." He smiled and pulled the boy up onto his knee as he reviewed the small notepad. "My, some of your works here are very detailed. Your writing is exquisite! Tell me, what other things have you written young man?"

"Well, let me think." Thallas hopped up and ran back to his room. He brought with him some drawing books and full-size notebooks. He

Brenda M. Hokenson

first gave Zanor the drawing books. "This is my very first drawing, right here. See?"

Zanor smiled, "Yes, I do. Will you tell me about this picture?"

Thallas hopped back up on Zanor's knee. "The dots are some stars I would see over and over again in my dreams. The outline... Well, the outline is kind of like a place where those stars live. This here, the dark line, it is the route a comet takes that cuts across here, in front of this bigger star every 3500 years."

"Do you know what this area is called by chance?"

"Well, as of lately, I have not seen these stars in my dream. I think that the comet crashed into the star that some planets go around."

"Wow, now tell me about this picture here."

"Well, Zanor, it is a drawing of a flying device. I think the people on the planets by that comet and star used them to get away. What do you think?"

"Well, Thallas. I believe you are exactly right. How long ago did you do this?"

"Umm, it is my very first drawing, other than when I was little and made stick people and funny animals."

Constance added, "He really got started drawing, to include that picture about 2 years ago."

"How interesting." Zanor replied.

"Show Zanor the other drawings you have done Thallas." Constance said as she handed him the more recent sketch pad.

"Yes mom. Zanor, this is what started about the middle of the summer before people started going to Weelin." He pointed out some key components, a large crack and remnants of a bridge, a star system with ejections coming from the star nearest it, and a lightning bolt and a table with folks gathered about. "This is kinda bad, but I think it is or has happened somewhere."

I have this cool guide called Mansakren. He is small like a Sprite, but he glows like the stars. He said I am seeing the past and present for three realms and that William may be able to explain why the lightning bolt in the table is important for here and the Earth Realm. Do we share the same deities?"

"Well, these sketches are very accurate. That one with the bridge is what has happened near Treah on the road from Ruan. The star system did in fact happen not long ago and that is why there are a great number of Morket here. The last one, with the lightning bolt, yes, we share a same deity type figure. Here he is a horseman, on Earth he is known as Thor. He is there right now trying to help get containment of the Deadmages and Talaharian. This reminds me, I need to depart for there soon. William, will you stay with the lad and school him, please. I will take your place for now and send a zephyr if I need to be replaced by you. Also, I have to go check on Ermenya. I believe that Edwina will be there shortly."

"Thank, Zanor. I hope I will be as good as William someday." Thallas said as he hopped off of Zanor's knee and ran over to William. "You will train me, won't you?"

"Yes, young man. Bu first, you need to eat some dinner. We will continue in about an hour or so. I will return here after two errands I must take care of." William said as he patted the boy and let himself out the door.

"Zanor, you do realize he is highly advanced?"

"Yes William; and I know that you are the only Star in this area who can train him. Your Order is rare and since there is no other means..."

"Yes, my lord. I will see to it. But is it necessary for the Words of Retrieval? We were able to contain all of Thanias, spirit and all. Nothing was lost and I do not feel comfortable that a boy so young in years should have this very difficult task placed upon him."

"You know it takes two Stars to do the ritual along with an Interval, which Truance agreed to, and one dragon."

"Freiderich will be difficult to sway in your favor my lord. How do you plan on that?"

"Ermenya will do this for me."

"What of your grandchild who started this mess?"

"Tatiana will be dealt with swiftly."

"You say that now old man. There is no way of knowing where she is. Her skills are more advanced than any Interval I know and not even the Enygminite can track her. Speaking of, where is Menosh?"

"He is at Krosslaen with Ermenya. He is a dragon healer, and the clutch is about to hatch. He left for there after the ceremony for Thanias. And don't call me old. I believe that your years are greater than mine."

Brenda M. Hokenson

William and Zanor parted ways at the center of Ruan. Zanor disappeared, translocating to Drottingholm. William went to the Palisade where he found the three he was looking for.

"Walther, Lunacerian, and Altus, it is good to see you on this chilly autumn day. I need your assistance. I have a young lad who is very advanced for a star…"

"You speak of Thallas." Lunacerian responded. "He is far better than all of the Stars I have had to work with, well except for you. What do you need?"

"Do you know where his vast and deep knowledge is from? His sketches come from dreams; some reoccur. But they are very accurate; even more accurate than Gareth's drawings."

"He is a true Star. This gift is the first we have seen. There is something unique about this entire class of Newlings. Each one of them has advanced knowledge and skills. I believe that the High Order, which Menosh and Alasha are a part of, may have better information than me." Lunacerian said as he escorted everyone in to the library.

"I have looked for signs in the skies myself." Walther added. "As usually I can pull a tale or two from the birds and winds and night sky. This is different. I have had no tales to record other than the Morket, Deadmages, and the marvels some of the Newlings have accomplished thus far."

"I too have sought answers in meditation and scrying. There is nothing to find."

"Very well. I am to instruct Thallas on the Words of Retrieval. Ermenya hold the key to its success. I am uncertain it is wise." William said as he looked at the shelves.

"Zanor misses his son and if Ermenya has truly captured all of his essence, spirit and flesh, then there should be no need to fear." Walther countered.

"You are aware that the most powerful warlock on Kluanaria went through this process? How do you think we should react? Zanor might be letting his feelings interfere with life." Altus added.

"I don't want that Newling to be hurt because of an old foolish leader." William sat in a chair and tapped his fingers in rhythm to a song of old that filled his mind.

The Legion treads upon the shores.
Ten thousand strong, no way to hold.
Mages cast; Truncheon poured,
Through the gates of the Krosslaen lords.
Chrinthold charged to pierce plate;
The Legion held as many blades break.
Ten thousand strong, no way to hold.
Bittern lost, Treah in flames.
Intervals healed, Paladins wield;
Shadowblyts shield as the casters aim;
Ten thousand strong, no way to hold.
Mithdrool reigns as Burwash yields.
Dragons soar with wrath and pain;
Beneath Edziza, Krosslaen spared.
Ten thousand strong, no way to hold.
A horseman with fiery blades
Cut them down, one by one.
A priestess too, with a slivery staff.
One by one she cast them out;
The Legion falls, Mithdrool yields.
A sentence to him: a lost soul
Kept in hoarfrost, millennia to pass.
A monument built as tribute to
The reigning lord. Who in turn
Saved us all.

Lunacerian, Walther, and Altus found themselves singing with William.

"I do not believe there will be any issues. However, I will be present just in case, as I can assist in this matter." Lunacerian said as he remembered learning about the battle of Edziza. "Take this charm with you. It is actually a Star relic and might help focus the boy's abilities. I will be along shortly to help you."

"What kind of help will I get from a Moon?"

"Well, since we are opposite, he can cast at me and such. I have minor spells that I can use toward him when you feel he is ready for that."

265

Brenda M. Hokenson

"This is going to be good Walther." Altus smiled slyly. "This kid could prove to be more than Lunacerian can handle." He began laughing.

William departed, taking a horse from the stable and the long way round, along the stream which as he meditated gave him serenity and focus. He arrived at the gate only to see Thallas at the ready. He extended his arm to the boy and the boy took it. In a matter of seconds, he was seated on the horse and headed to the Stars' hidden grove. William removed his shoes as did Thallas. He then snapped his fingers and the sky directly above the grove darkened with only star light filtering in.

"First you must meditate, Thallas." William prepared three seats near a small pool of water. "I have a gift from the Moons' Order. They have kept this relic for just such an occasion." William removed the small neck piece from his pocket and placed it in the water. *"Purifi a satelli, purifi a satelli."* A bright light came from the sky and struck the relic. The tarnish was removed and a new symbol representing Thallas' house was etched in it. Lunacerian appeared and took the relic and blessed it for the Moons. He then placed it around the boy's neck. "Face the water but look up. Your focus comes from the stars above you." William said as the three sat in meditation. The meditation lasted an hour. "You are ready lad. Lunacerian has chosen to be your target, though I am not sure it is necessary."

"Come on lad; let's see what you can do." Lunacerian said as he walked to the far circle in the grove. It was inlaid with what appeared to be specific constellations.

"Ok Thallas. I would like you to test out the spells you know. If you are not comfortable with one, we will work on it together." William said as he took his place on the near circle. "For demonstration only, I will…"

"Please, William, may I?" William nodded and let Thallas stand on the circle which had a nebula etched in it. *"Remuer a lune, remuer a lune!"* Lunacerian was hurled off the far circle. William looked twice at Lunacerian and his young pupil and nodded.

"That was lucky, Thallas." Lunacerian said as he returned to the circle and set a protective shield about his body. "Again."

"Remuer a lune, remuer a lune!" Once again Lunacerian was flung like a rock off of the circle.

"Try something else, please." William said as he chuckled under his breath.

The Kluanarians

"Ok, *'Potre de étoile à lune!'*" A brilliant beam of light struck the circle where Lunacerian had just vacated. The plate smoked and sparked.

"Well, now that is impressive. How long have you practiced this spell?" Lunacerian said as he approached.

"I have studied this stuff for a couple years now. I never actually got to cast them until today. I was reading a book from the Palisade's library that taught me technique. So, I would mouth the words and copy the forms that were in it. I have even learned the Words of Retrieval, but I get confused on a part. Is there supposed to be more than one Star in the ceremony?"

"Yes." Lunacerian spoke as he sat on the ground near the boy. "William will do…" Lunacerian pulled out a parchment and scribed the words on to it, "will do this part that is underlined. The parts that are boxed are for the Interval to do and the dragon, well, that is this garbled up stuff here. Did Zanor say when?"

"No." William replied as he too sat down on the ground by Thallas. "I think we should do it sooner than later."

"Can we get to her?"

"Yes, I think she left the passage clear for us."

"Are we gonna see a dragon?" Thallas asked of the men.

"Yes lad. Yes." William responded

"Let's wait for Zanor to return here, as he always does before he crosses the Veil." Lunacerian said as he assisted William up. "Young Star, you are a force to be reckoned with. My shield was no match."

The three returned by horse to Thallas' home just as Zanor was walking down the path. He saw three and changed direction.

"The clutch will arrive in a few more days. Ermenya sends her regard and has witnessed young Thallas' powers in use. She has said that he is strong and should be more than ready."

"We agree, Zanor. We will depart at once. Is Truance prepared?" William replied.

"She is already at Krosslaen and has set up the area. I shall open a portal for you." With that Zanor cast a portal that the three went through and emerged in the heart of Edziza.

The dragon was in true form, albeit a smaller version, when they entered Krosslaen. "You are a much-disciplined Star, young Thallas. Please approach, I wish to read you." Thallas walked in front of the dragon, and she took her sharp claws and extended them toward his head. She gently rested one claw on his shoulder and one on his head. "I see no malice, ill will, or negative feelings within this Star." As she lifted her claws from him, Ermenya gently placed the tip of one in the center of the top of his head. Thallas felt a small charge of icy and hot energy course through him briefly. "That is a special gift from me that will protect you from all evil and corruption Thallas. The spell we are about to do is delicate, so watch for our cues to you, Lunacerian will give them directly to you. "Truance here are the essences to be placed."

Truance stepped forward and received the essences from Ermenya. She then placed them at the altar and took her place on a circle etched with the four seasons. Lunacerian escorted Thallas to his circle which was etched with a nebula.

William took his place and began the ceremony. *"Récupére a Thanias, récupére a Truncheon. Répare a Thanias, répare a Truncheon."*

Ermenya used her dragon's breath to break the seals containing Thanias' essences. Truance poured fire water into a small basin next to the essences and the dragon again breathed fire upon it.

Lunacerian nodded to Thallas. *"Allie a Thanias, allie a Truncheon. Répare a Thanias, répare a Truncheon."* Thallas then walked toward the altar, where he placed Thanias' signet. *"Rendre a Thanias, render a Truncheon."* He then returned to his circle.

Ermenya again breathed dragon fire upon the altar. Truance placed an oaken branch upon the altar and returned to her position. William continued, *"Récupére a Thanias, récupére a Truncheon. Répare a Thanias, répare a Truncheon. Récupére a Thanias, récupére a Truncheon. Répare a Thanias, répare a Truncheon."*

A whirling wind with ice and flames surrounded the altar. As the wind dissipated, a person emerged, Thanias. The dragon approached cautiously and Lunacerian placed a shield about him and Thallas. Ermenya placed her claws on Thanias as she did on Thallas. She studied him external and internally. "Your mind, body, and soul have been restored. Your essences never left Kluanaria; therefore, I was able to have these most valued Orders help me in restoring you. What do you remember?"

"I...I remember everything. Why Tatiana struck me down at that time, I don't know."

"You, Thanias were struck down by her as in her eyes, you mindlessly allowed evil to corrupt you and are responsible for the deaths of many innocent lives. You are only revived because your work here is not finished, which your father had acknowledged. Ryatt is with child and the Deadmages have gone into hiding somewhere near Krosslaen. Talaharian has crossed the Veil and has set up a remote village on an island north of Norway."

"Thallas, is that you?" Thanias said as he scanned the room.

"Yes."

"Thank you for seeing the good that remains within me. I am unsure as to why I did what I did, but I am glad you were a part of this. What can I do for you?"

"Well, sir. I don't know what you have left to finish, but your family has been devastated so I would like to arrange a feast in the honor of your family. I assume your line comes from High Lord Burwash who founded this land and created a seat in the village of Burwash."

"Yes, we are on father's side. Have a seat, I will tell you the story."

"First, I will tell you a story that has been written for millennia and is now unfolding." Thallas whipped out his sketches and sat down on the floor. Thanias and the others joined him. "This is all from my dreams, but I know it was done a long time ago. *In a far distant planetary system...*"

"You use such big words for being so young, Newling." Truance said as she looked at the sketch he was holding up.

"Ahem... In a far distant planetary system, a massive explosion was about to occur. Many adventurers left the system in hopes of finding refuge for everyone. Some came here, to Kluanaria and some pierced the Veil unknowingly. Other went into Orion and Scorpio, some yet went two the spiral galaxy next door. All of Phallas Minor soon headed the call to vacate quickly as the nearest star began sending radiation whips across the heavens. Chorlanda was first in mapping the systems, now she has help of an Aantiri named Paul. Everyone on the lone planet escaped just in time.

A terrible explosion as the star went boom, echoed through the far galaxy as the shockwave tumbled space vehicles off course. Many more came here and some to Earth. As the Morket landed an evil began to grow. Talaharian came along with Llylandra and destroyed Mercurian and enslaved its people. The Truncheon lords were complacent and lazy. The evil crept through the ranks and the leader fell.

He helped orchestrate death and destruction, the rising of the 'Soulless' and siege of Treah. But before he knew it, a Newling came, restoring Bittern and reclaiming Mercurian. Her friend too took Mithdrool. Tatiana smote him and now he is restored. Welcome home Thanias."

"Well that was a very good tale and very accurate. Now I will tell you about High Lord Burwash, as only Ermenya will know this. *Before the folks from Phallas Minor arrived, this land was at peace and the Veil had not been discovered. The land and its people were in turmoil for many years prior to the peace. Mithdrool had rose and fell twice in that time. Burwash, my Great Grandfather, took up arms and got some of the Orders to back him. The first major siege ravaged the land of Mercurian all the way along the coast to the Mithdroolean Forest. Great ships were used between the two as battles raged on both sides of the sea. Burwash led a vast army of Paladins and Truncheon into the heart of Mithdrool's Legion on the edge of the forest. He was joined by a Fraeloch Priestess named Lady Phallas. She is the one who is still with us today. At her side were High Lord Beryth and his army of Fraeloch and Morket mages and priests. Together they formed a strong alliance and were able to defeat Mithdrool.*

The peace that ensued lasted 30 years. They had placed Mithdrool in a deep sleep and monitored him. They did not believe in death as the soul will live forever. After the twenty-fifth year, the people were becoming complacent and more and more Fraelochs and Morket were arriving as their star was dying. A Fraeloch named Talaharian found a way to release Mithdrool, but he needed help. The land of Ruan was right for the taking. He found a way to summon horsemen who would destroy the land and possible point him to Mithdrool. He was mistaken. After he summoned the horsemen, the one called War took the pouch of many pockets from Talaharian before he was able to finish the binding spell. The four rode off, leaving Talaharian to his own devices.

The Battle of Edziza started not long after the horsemen were rampant. All artifacts were stored at Krosslaen. The evil that was building in the West knew this. Talaharian had corrupted many Orders and many folks without gift. He turned them to the point of rebellion. Under his command he marched his army to Krosslaen and began laying waste to the outer wall. Ermenya was aware of this and south aide from Burwash. But he was unable to respond. A rogue zephyr took the last breath from him. His daughter, Matelina, a very strong warrior who was also schooled by dreadmages and priests, answered Ermenya's plea.

Matelina brought with her warriors who were skilled with both the blade and shadow magic. She secured the perimeter with her army as Ermenya and Freiderich translocated Krosslaen well below Edziza in order to protect the artifacts. Talaharian and his troop were hunted for ten years. At this time, Matelina decided that a stronghold need constructed to better aid villages far away from Ruan. She founded Burwash, in honor of her father. Lady Phallas and Rynylla monitored the horsemen and Talaharian; but lost track of him when he went into hiding. Years past and Matelina had wed and had two children.

Another generation grew up and Matelina remained in the High Seat at Burwash. She gave the land of Mercurian to the Fraelochs and Morket as they had enjoyed a life by the sea. She invited all Orders to build a chamber at each of the cities' Great Halls and ceremonies took place alternating between them. Rumors began to spread as the solstice of sun progressed. In what would become Ruan, the elders who were very complacent and not heeding the governance took matters in their own hand. They decided together that there would be one church in the middle of town and in it a secret lower level where the old ways would flourish as needed but the main focus was on having one deity to worship. They did not believe in the abilities of the Orders anymore. The townsfolk followed the elders' word and practiced as they were taught.

At this point in time, the horsemen were still loose but not really stirring things. That is when a small child noticed them at the edge of town on plateau overlooking the area. The horsemen noticed the small boy and decided peace had been reigning too long in this very city and they peered in the hearts of the people and saw the discontent focused toward the elders' poor governance and lack of basic needs."

"I know, I know!" Thallas said as he jumped up and down. "Walther told Tatiana the story and she told me. This is where they go into town, and the people go in the church and then through the secret door, and a small boy turns out to be…"

"Yes." William said. "That was me in disguise, trying to restore the old ways as the elders eroded everything and destroyed much history in the process. I think our adventure paid off as we did recapture the horsemen, save one and."

"Well, there went the rest of my story," Thanias said as he smiled at Thallas. "Anyway, Matelina's four children from her marriage to Wilhelm Truaxx, a dwarf, were Dezire the heir to Burwash, and her son Regence who inherited Ruan. Beryth, inherited Mercurian after the first round of Mithdrool. Zanor received Burwash when he finished his training for his Order, the Aantiri as Dezire would become Supreme Ruler. Regence also asked Zanor to govern over Ruan as he did not want his children dealing with the governance but would be supportive of the Order and their missions. Regence was actually the first Kluanarian to cross the Veil. A few other families joined him. They were located not far from Weelin, near Salmo Mountain. There are still Kluanarians there to this day and left completely alone."

"Ok, so we know your family now, Thanias. What am I supposed to do?" Thallas asked.

"Well, William will train you."

"He is far advanced, Thanias. I believe he needs…"

A grey mist formed in the air followed by a low male voice. "This child and the other Newlings are all above your Orders' abilities. They will be the next to be on the Council of Orders." An entity began to emerge. He was grey in color and stood about 6 feet tall with slender build. His hair was silvery, and garments were also silver in color. A circlet and sash about his waste were pearl. "Protect you Newling Aantiri, he is in grave danger." The entity stepped back into the mist. "I will see the Newlings soon." He vanished.

"Who was that William?" Thallas asked.

"That was a very powerful individual who is one of eight who govern the whole universe. Menosh sits on the High Council with him and Alasha. Alasha is a Sprite here who helps us out occasionally, but she also governs many worlds beyond here. Menosh is an Enygminite who in theory governs here and several other worlds. His powers seem to be waning and there will be discussion soon concerning this."

"And…"

"Well, young man, you are of the Star Order and very powerful. William will help you learn to control your abilities. I think you will have a very important job to do on top of what you have done for me."

"Wait, watch this!" Thallas focused, *"Transitaea a Ryatt, transitae a Ryatt!"*

A few moments later, Ryatt emerged from the scrying pool at the center of the room. She raced to Thanias and hugged him. Emotions of sadness and happiness and elation filled the chamber. Then it happened.

"It is time!" Ermenya said as she looked at William. "Please, go now. Get Freiderich! Our clutch!!"

Small squeaks and hiccups and cracking filled the air. Ermenya in her dwarven form sprinted down the hall and transformed into her normal self. She used a claw to help the hatchlings as they emerged from the shells. She counted them over and over.

"Can we see, Thanias?" Thallas asked as he kept himself from racing down the hall.

"Not until the dragon invites you. Never ever enter a dragon's chamber without being invited." Thanias responded.

Truance however, was special. "I will give you a report Thallas. I must check their life force and overall condition." She entered the room and assisted Ermenya in collecting the empty shells into a special pouch made of mithril. "Ok, Ermenya, I have collected all the bits and pieces. Freiderich approaches." Truance removed herself from the chamber as the dragon entered his roost and joined Ermenya. "Dragons…"

"The Star may enter," the deeper voice of Fred boomed. Thallas grabbed Thanias by the arm and dragged him to the entry. "I guess Thanias may enter as well. This is a very rare special thing you have done and are also witnessing, Newling. Take care not to get cocky and end up as Thanias did. There is no saving a Star."

"Yes sir. I was told that the Veil will be restored, or umm have its weakness found and repaired."

"Yes. That is correct and it will be again up to you and Edwina and Truance to do this for us. William will take you to Burwash where Thanias will be presented with Ryatt. Then you will perform this…" Fred placed a claw on Thallas' forehead and new incantations flowed into his mind. "You will know the one to use when it is time. I have much to teach you as well. For now go and I will remain here with my Ermenya and brood."

William created a portal for Truance and Thallas to cross and escorted Thanias separately. "Thanias, we will need to exercise caution as there is

Brenda M. Hokenson

still great evil inhabiting the Orders and common folk. They will be glad and afraid of your restoration."

"I will be cautious. Is Edwina recovered? I know she was gravely injured by Mithdrool."

"She is not fully recovered, but I must give credit to Tatiana for reversing most of the damage and Izmaa and Shadowblyt for assisting her with brain function. She mourns for you more than anyone knows."

"I see. I think we need to port to where she is and go from there, if you please, Master William."

THE DROTTINGHOLM REQUEST

ALASHA HAD ADDRESSED THE MANY nations' true rulers openly. Malos was able to pinpoint on a map the location of the Fraelochan establishment on Svalbard in the Arctic Ocean. She paced as did Malos and for that matter Harold/Thor. An unexpected visitor arrived just before the questions began. All eyes turned toward the door that slowly opened as the Pope entered the room.

Silence was deafening for a moment. "Welcome and thank you for joining our most important and historical meeting." We were uncertain if you would be willing to participate since this is not in your normal area of expertise." Alasha said as she found a space at the table for their newcomer.

"I must say, I was in shock when I received this unique invitation. I was uncertain if this was some sort of farce to get back at all of my views or something truly curious. As with any leader, I believe it is important to have all of the information before I can decide fact or fiction, so here I am."

"Well, Alasha, is it, please go over the timeline of events. We don't need intricate details, just the timeline, please," the Queen of Denmark demanded. "I want everyone to have this exact timeline and facts, so nothing is missed that is crucial in deciding the fate of our countries."

The Swedish King pulled a lever and an opaque cube that could be seen from every chair with clarity appeared. Young Paul entered the room and stood to the rear of the room and used a keyboard in which the words appeared on this cube for all to read.

"I am Paul, son of Iris, who is daughter of Harold/War. I am of the Aantiri Order and have been asked to do this portion." He paused as the royals looked about at each other commenting on such a young person with such great responsibility. "I may be young, but on my normal realm, all children are taught responsibility and manners. We have some archaic ways as you would say, but they are ways that lead to respect, which is seriously lacking everywhere on this realm, especially in the United States." He paused as the group chuckled.

"Now for the serious part. The first Kluanarians crossed the Veil I would say 50 to 60 years ago and settled by Salmo Mountain. They wish not to be disturbed and have had no interaction with the true Earth inhabitants. About ten or so years ago, my mother brought us through the Veil and Dad took an Earth job in Weelin, saved up and bought a large tract of land where he built a small offshoot of Weelin for others who wanted to escape. The Fraeloch and Morket, who are not of our realm, crossed probably some thirty years ago, when my Great Grandmother Matelina was still ruling Burwash. Talaharian has a village on Svalbard with about 300 occupants, maybe more."

"That is it," the King of Spain said, "what is the problem then. We deal with not so nice people every day on this very issue. We have had troops in many, many countries fighting this battle for the past 100 years. I think since we know about it now, we will have to send an emissary to Svalbard on our behalf and see firsthand what is truly happening."

"I agree, but who do we send?" The King of Sweden responded.

"I think we Norse should go." The Norwegian King replied, "And drag along our lovely Queen of Denmark."

The Pope was very intrigued by what he had learned from Paul's presentation. "Say, Paul, if you have a minute might I speak with you in a less crowded location as they discuss the entourage?"

Paul nodded and had Harold accompany him. "What is it sir?"

"I am curious as to how you have pulled off this great charade. You have all of the true monarchs convinced that this Talaharian will decimate this land in time. Yet there is no proof of such a place as this Kluanaria, let alone new races. The sovereigns have been hoodwinked by you and your tall tale. You speak of Thor. I will have you know young man, that is a false god and you are asking for trouble. Christianity has been part of these countries…"

"Since it was forced on them." Harold responded. "I am Thor, and

Ragnarök is inevitable. The only way you received an invitation, Pope, was because of the sovereigns of Europe saying that you are included. So, you can either work with us or return to your Swiss Guards."

"How dare you. I hereby excommunicate you, Harold."

"You can't. I am not a Christian, Catholic, Muslim, Buddhist, or any other religion of this planet teeming with violence. I serve as War, one of the horsemen here."

"I…I think you have had too much to drink. I think you are hallucinating and need mental help."

Harold replied calmly. "I am terribly sorry if I am one of their 'gods'. I am not truly a god, but I sure have helped them over many millennia and where is yours?"

"There is no evidence to support your existence."

"It is called mythology. And most myths came from legends which came from true deeds. Plus, every so often I happen to show up here and tweak things that the good Norse are unable to do without intervention. I do listen and I do respond."

Paul watched as the two squared off and finally said, "So what does Harold need to do to prove he is Thor?"

"He can't do anything. A false god…Well he cannot do anything to prove himself…"

"Ok then." Harold thought for a moment and said, "This should do it." He took with him from the room one of the artifacts that remained in the hallway. "This is a small stone to you, but to me, it is a gateway to Kluanaria where I am also an observer, but more so a horseman than here. Come with me, you too Paul." The three walked into the garden in the center of the castle where the king had been seated. "This here is the very thing that will prove to you once and for all." Harold took the stone and raised his hand high above his head. He then forcefully threw the stone straight down. Thunder and lightning filled the sky and a brightly colored road appeared. "Let's go." He grabbed the Pope by the hand and stepped on to the road along with Paul. The road instantly vanished along with the three who then reappeared in the Palisade.

"You are supposed to go to Asgard."

"Well excuse me. I happen to be an observer and horseman here. So now maybe you will BACKOFF!" He took the stone and again tossed it down,

277

taking them briefly to Asgard's gates and then again to Drottingholm. "So don't tell me I am not real."

The Pope was humbled by this and decided to move back in line with the reigning sovereigns to get the matter addressed. "Forgive me. I am in awe at this time and need a few moments to digest what I have just observed with Harold here." He excused himself to the drawing room and accepted a nice shot of brandy from the Queen of England. "I would of never... Not in a million..."

Alasha was pacing with Malos when Kren appeared with a message. "Alasha, we need to get Paul out of here, now!"

"Why?"

"I just left from Freiderich and Ermenya. Llylandra is about to tear the Veil here and take him."

Malos nodded and summoned the young Aantiri. "Go with Kren to Fred and Ermenya. They will protect you." Paul nodded and the nymph took him through a portal of multi-colored leaves that swirled about. The room of sovereigns watched in awe as the swirling leaves quickened and the two vanished. "Well, now that safety has been restored, what is your decision?"

"We will be sending three emissaries, those being one Norse, one Belgian, and one from Liechtenstein. I am hoping you will have some sort of protections available just in case." The King of Sweden answered.

"Yes, of course. And do you have a ship that will transport you there that will hold you and your own guards? We will supply the necessary muscle, but we would like to ensure you have trusted guards to venture with you." The three nodded. "So then, tomorrow we will start making arrangements."

"Agreed," was the consensus of the sovereigns, and then the inevitable questions begun. "Are we all remaining here until their safe return? How long must we stay in Drottingholm? What is for supper? Do you have rooms enough for us? Harold, may we see Kluanaria?"

The host stepped forward and used a horn of old to silence the group. "There is plenty of room for all in my Castle. I will inform the staff to prepare oh, what is the count now, 20 rooms and a great feast will follow in about three hours. Does anyone need to contact their homeland?"

"Not necessary was the main response." Most pulled out cell phones

The Kluanarians

and called the significant other with the news and sent for them in the specially designed ships with a pilot/chauffer.

"Tack så mycket Alasha. Du är skyldig mig fruktansvärt för detta." The Swedish host said as he smiled for the first time in a long time when it came to hosting so many guests.

Alasha grinned as she went into the next room with Malos. "We are so close to resolving this! My only hope right now is that Paul is safe enough."

THE CUSTOMS REPORT

AGENTS PATRIKSEN, DUNWOODY, LaCLUAE, AND the Sheriff and Chief of Police stood in awe as they got their bearings. The quickly radioed Police Headquarters and reported their status and then drove back to Weelin.

"So, Agent Patriksen," Sheriff Dylan began, "what do you think we need to do at this point? Obviously the majority prefer not to be here let alone interact with us, yet there is some urgency in what they have said about this Tala..Tala… oh whatshisname."

"Well, this is a major, major problem and I don't have any answers other than 'They do exist!' So how we relay this to our superiors is the bigger problem." Patriksen responded.

"If we go public then there will be major scoffing." Dunwoody added.

"Wait just a minute. That report has video footage and if Spokane airs it you know they may consider sharing it with their sister cities." Chief Todd interjected.

"Well, it is possible, but she only knows the road and town was decimated, not that it was restored. We can't give her evidence until we get it sorted out through the proper channels." Patriksen retorted.

"I don't know then. But since I still have that darn rock, we can have some scientists and our supervisors and such out to study this. The footage is recorded on the cameras throughout town. Plus if we can verify our evidence was successfully saved on our little jaunt…" LaCluae added.

Dunwoody took the video camera and still camera into the small evidence room that had a good playback device. She uploaded everything she had recorded on to the system and began reviewing the images. She

The Kluanarians

also put it up on screen so the group could see it as well. The IT specialist helped cleanup images and saved all of the before and after fixes. "Well, the place sure looks similar to here except for the lack of roads and the buildings. This is like going back in time. Everything built was quite elegant, even the attire."

"Thanks for your opinion, now can you tell me if the dialogue with those people turned out?" Patriksen asked as he hovered behind the IT specialist. "Do we have dialogue from when they were in here?"

"Yes sir. And I think we can submit all of this in chronological order to the higher levels in government as evidence. I also believe that we can get a team of scientists and such here rather quickly."

"What makes you so sure of this?"

"Well, because I have been undercover in this town for ten years. There were anomalies in the geomagnetics that run through the ground and get distorted for earthquakes, slides, building, and from what I can tell with my current data, teleportation via that stone at the center of the habitation Myron built. Yes, I know Myron and he shared information, especially since this threat has started."

"Whoa. Back up a minute." LaCluae interjected. "You mean to say that you have been monitoring this for ten years? You didn't tell us anything. Who do you work for? And what the heck is your name?"

"I am Agent Albrecht Weisjord and I work with your CIA and FBI through a special United Nations agreement set in place when Myron asked them for help in a very closed session."

"Ok then Agent Weisjord, where are your credentials?" LaCluae was getting irritated.

"Back off LaCluae." Patriksen responded. "I believe him. He is wearing his badge." The Customs and Border Patrol senior agent pointed to it. "And besides, he briefed me when you and Dunwoody were arguing earlier. The question is, is there enough evidence to support our claims?"

"I believe so sir." Weisjord replied. "I am not too concerned over their being here, but about the threat of these folks not from Kluanaria. Myron was uncertain as to where they would enter our world and how many. We have a very small team that monitors these anomalies as I have been doing here, but the 'Veil' works differently, and I think there could be a pattern to detect it. You see, as you drive north from Weelin, there is a section that seems to be always misty or foggy, depending on temperature, but never clear. Many folks go on vacation through that section and return just fine. I think that stretch of road is where we need to get scientists to."

"Agreed."

"But what about the stone?" Dunwoody inquired.

"That darn rock is not the Veil. It is a translocation device of some kind and doesn't disrupt the Veil." Weisjord replied. "Oh yes, and they possess very advance space vehicles."

"Whoa now!" LaCluae began to speak but was cut off.

"Yes, but the Kluanarians don't use them. Some of their new settlers have them and we are not sure how many the group Myron is worried about has."

"Do you have enough for the UN to look at?" Dunwoody asked as she sat down in thought.

"Well, they are already aware of the presence of Kluanarians. In fact there is a treaty in place that allows them to come and go as they please so long as they are not hostile."

"How long has that been in place?" Patriksen inquired as he refilled his coffee cup.

"I have a copy here. If you will notice that it is almost sixty years old."

"Where is this location listed in the document?"

"North, and east. You travel along the same road as the Veil is theorized to be, but after crossing Mount Salmo, you would take the left fork to their village. They are the watchers I guess."

"Well, let's go pay them visit then." LaCluae said as he picked up his jacket.

"First let me send all of this data to the team and they will analyze it. You know, you are the first to enter through the stone. I am truly surprised any data you recorded was even usable. The Veil destroys it."

"How far is it? Oh, it is 15.2 miles from the Forest service road you used to get here. And of course, the time it will take to get there is more than your normal commute. It is all Forest Service Road and with the light drizzle, could be slick, but at least the dust will be down."

"Ok, let's move out then. We should take two vehicles, one with supplies just in case." Agent LaCluae said. "Maybe a tent and sleeping bags, I doubt they have hotels."

The Kluanarians

"Good call." Now get in the SUV." Agent Patriksen said as he and Agent Weisjord, Sheriff Dylan and Chief Todd loaded into the first SUV. The second vehicle carried Dunwoody, LaCluae, a deputy, and a police officer.

A light fog added to the drive as they sauntered along through the drizzle that was night quite a light rain. Their visibility was approximately a half mile which was a good thing. Several elk crossed in front of them and a deer further down the road, where the slope to Mount Salmo started. After about an hour of winding and dealing with slippery roads, they reached the fork in the road. As they made the corner they could see a small village in the distance.

Patriksen radioed the second SUV. "Dunwoody, make sure everyone is on alert. We don't know how our presence will be received."

"Yes sir. Do you want us to bring extra weapons with us when we exit the vehicles?"

"No, that shouldn't be necessary. Just make sure you run the camera, LaCluae forgets how to turn it on."

Dunwoody chuckled as she got a glare from across the seat.

About fifteen minutes passed when the group arrived at the village. An older man who looked to be in his 50s approached. He had long grey hair that was braided and a very neatly kept thin beard. He wore leather leggings and a tunic of sorts. "Welcome visitors to our village. I am Regence, the founder and signer of a treaty formed long ago. Is there a problem?"

"That depends." Agent Patriksen started. "First off, I am Agent Patriksen, and these are Agents Weisjord, Dunwoody, LaCluae, Sheriff Dylan, and Chief Todd. Can you tell us anything about a possible invasion by," Patriksen flipped through his notes, "Fraelochs?"

"Fraelochs?"

"Yes. I understand they were on your world first and I was hoping for some insight. A fellow who lived in Weelin, Myron, had alerted Agent Weisjord to the possibility of attack by these beings."

"Well, I can't say I ever had the pleasure of meeting a Fraeloch. Have you sought guidance from the Council of the Orders?"

"No. Who are they? Are they here? Is there a way to contact them?" LaCluae asked as he grew impatient as always.

283

"They have regular meetings in Kluanaria, though I have not ever attended one. My sister, Matelina, forced the Orders to work together and hold council to discuss major issues of the land. I left when our parents handed the High Seat to my sister, mostly because I want to keep my family safe and out of the limelight, I suppose."

"We have had a long drive. Do you have any where we might stay?" Agent Weisjord inquired.

"Yes, of course. We don't have many travelers from your side, but we do keep a nice inn." As the group walked down the path and into the inn, it began to pour. The deputy and police officer had already gone inside.

"How much will it cost for us?" Dunwoody asked. "Do you take credit cards?"

"No. Credit cards and currency are not used here."

"Well then, how do we pay?"

"Lodging and meals are free. It is the Kluanarian way. So please make yourselves at home. There is a room for each of you and if you need there is also a meeting room." Regence answered as he walked toward the innkeeper. "Samuel, please make sure our guests are well taken care of. I will see if I can get someone in Kluanaria to help these folks."

Sam nodded and began showing everyone to their rooms. He had a deep booming voice and spoke slowly and clearly. "Supper will be served promptly at 6. There is a bathhouse, or as you would say hot tub and sauna room, just out the back door and to the left. We also have a room of tranquility where you are welcome to go to meditate, which is out the back door and to the right. If you have any problems, please come to the front desk at any time." With that, Samuel went back to the front and arranged for the evening meal.

Regence meanwhile left the building and went to his home. He and his wife, Emilae, poured water into the scrying pool for the first time since it was built over 55 years ago. They carefully recited the words, long kept from use and the pool swirled and then cleared. There was an older woman who appeared in the image. "Dezire, is that you?" Regence asked in stifled excitement.

"Yes, dear brother, it is I. You have not spoken to me since you and the families departed. I was hoping to visit, but there was so much turmoil at the time and now there is an even greater problem that may affect you."

"You sound so tired Dezire." Emilae added. Would you like to come here for a while? I am sure Zanor and everyone can handle it. You have done so much for Kluanaria already."

"Thank you, sweet Emilae. But first I need to help you."

"The people of Earth have sought us out. They have been monitoring Weelin, where Zanor's son, Myron, established a small colony since they arrived. He has shared bits and pieces about us, and also something about a possible attack by 'Fraelochs.'"

"Well, it is about time. Maybe Myron will return to Kluanaria and take his rightful post. The Fraelochs, well most of them, are peaceful. They came here with the Morket and melded mostly with those in Mercurian. Mithdrool returned, but I do believe the Newlings took care of him."

"The Newlings. Are they the ones prophesied so long ago by Freiderich and Ermenya?"

"Yes. Mithdrool had gained support from within the Orders and from Fraelochan deadmages and one or two Morket. They have a figure head, supposedly Talaharian, and from the report I received today from Drottingholm a base so to speak in Svalbard. Harold has returned to get support from the sovereigns and see what exactly is happening. The Fraeloch and Morket have very advanced vehicles, weapons, gear and the like. Chorlanda will have a vessel there to take them on this journey."

"Talaharian was never a deadmage. He is my son, you know that. Would you like us to go? What of the true sovereigns of the Americas?"

"No. Let Alasha deal with that. We will give your visitors as much information as we can. The American true sovereigns are already in agreement with us and have sent an envoy prior to this meeting in Drottingholm. Results will be forthwith I believe." Dezire paced for a minute. "Perhaps in the morning or afternoon I will translocate with the Newlings and see what we can clear up."

"That would be most excellent. I shall prepare more rooms in the morning then."

Dezire smiled. "As you wish dear brother. Take care and I will see you tomorrow. Keep in mind I am old, but not as are you, and our memories may need time."

As the scrying pool cleared, Regence walked back into the inn and joined everyone for the evening meal. He wondered how the Veil hardening was going, along with the ceremony for Thanias, his beloved Nephew. How he longed to witness both. He planned. After the meal was served to the special guests and members of the village, he took Emilae aside and told her of his plan. She agreed to it, albeit unwillingly. Regence departed once again to the room of tranquility hastily which caught the attention of LaCluae, and thus was followed.

"Agent LaCluae, how may I assist you?" Regence asked as he lit some candles and went to the center of the room where he intended to enter a meditative state.

"Well, you see, you are being observed as you just whispered to your wife and ran out of the room."

"First of all, young man, I always whisper to my wife on things of personal matters. Secondly, I did not run. I walked out at a hasty pace because I will be joined in here shortly for meditation. If you wish to join us, then do, but keep your lips turned off and your mind cleared of all thoughts, or you will be more confused than you already are."

"Me, confused?"

"Yes, I mean my god man, who dresses you, your little niece who is eight?"

"How do you know?"

"Oh, I know all about everyone who enters our village. It is a special privilege I have with the treaty. And I know your niece does not dress you, she lives in Motone Rock out beyond the Cape Loop Road on the west side, right. And she thinks that you are too much of a smarty pants. Very bright child I must say."

"Look…" Agent LaCluae was cutoff as several villagers and his team entered the room, which seemed to expand as it filled.

"Welcome all. Tonight, we have amongst us some special visitors from the Earth Realm. They have been granted permissions to watch as we will to ceremonies that are to take place on Kluanaria. I know we vowed to not meddle in Kluanarian things, but this is special, as there will be both a Veil hardening, which has not occurred in thousands of years, since dragons first came to us and also a recognition ceremony for Thanias, who as you know was restored." Regence paused as he and two more men went to the center of the room and created a large orb that was transparent at first. It also rotated and remained levitated during the proceedings. The folks of the village watched in real-time the events at both Burwash and Krosslaen.

First the ceremony for Thanias began. The entire ceremony was done in silence. *A great procession of the Orders along with the Newlings, filed in, followed by the commoners and then High Lord Zanor and his family. Truance called for each Order to send forth a representative, in which most sent two, an Elder and a Newling. Freiderich, the dragon entered in full form in a slightly smaller scale followed by Edwina wearing her favorite Moons garb who was accompanied by Tomas, the Chrinthold who had not been seen or heard of in months. Paul entered with Chorlanda, both escorted Thanias, which was a great surprise for Edwina.*

Thanias stood before the dragon and his people. Tomas brought forth a new sword with a platinum hilt embedded with pearls representing each member of his family. The blade was forged by the great blacksmith Kent of Ruan. Ryatt, his wife, was then escorted to the center of the room, in which the dragon presented her with a special ring forged from dragon ore, a precious metal only found in one location.

Finally, Thanias approached his family and knelt before them. Edwina presented to him a new shield carved of green moonstone from Kahs, Kluanaria's satellite. She had used her powers to etch in a couple of significant points into the shield. Paul presented him a cloak made of silk emblazoned mithril with symbols of the Orders of his house along the neck. His parents, Kira of the Moons and High Lord Zanor the Aantiri, stood as he bowed to them. Freiderich placed a circlet of the Truncheon upon Thanias' brow. The Truncheon who stood in rank knelt before him. After this, the people in stands made room for the Truncheon to be seated as the Veil Hardening had been moved just for this occasion.

There was a pause as the folks watched the procession. Tears were wiped away. "And now for the Veil hardening." Regence said in a somber voice, which quaked as he had just witnessed the true restoration of Thanias, his nephew. While they waited, LaCluae had passed a note to Patriksen, in which he got the 'how dare' you look from Agent Weisjord.

The Veil hardening commenced. Thallas began as he had been instructed, "Redonne a voile, redonnea voile!" He paused as he removed the finely crushed dragon shells from a pouch and made a circle in the center of the room. "Redonne a voile. Redonne en fortifiea voile! Redonne a voile. Redonne en fortifiea voile!" As he repeated this, Truance had taken water from the scrying pool and sprinkled it on the circle. "Redonne a voile. Redonne en fortifiea voile!"

"Pour la force de Kluanaria en Earth, redonne en fortifiea voile! Pour la force de pueple, redonne en fortifiea! Pour la force den draegn redone en fortifiea!" Truance said as she finished sprinkling the water.

A bright light engulfed the rooms, both in Kluanaria and in the village at Mount Salmo. As the brightness faded spectacular colors could be seen dancing in the night skies at both locations. Both rooms had ceilings that opened to the night sky for just such an event. Freiderich nodded at Thallas, and to William who had been standing apart from the rest during the ceremony.

As the folks wandered about from the stands at Burwash, and greeted each other and congratulating Thanias, his wife, Truance, and Thallas, the folks in Mount Salmo's shadow too greeted each other and welcomed their guests.

Regence went off to bed, taking his wife of sixty years along with him. The rest mingled about and tried to answer the visitor's many questions. "You will have more clear answers to your endless questions tomorrow, lady and gentlemen. I bid you good night. First meal is an hour after sun rise." Sam bowed as he left the guests for the night.

In the meantime, the vessel for the entourage to Svalbard arrived a few days early, which was a good thing as the seas were become very rough. Chorlanda entered the meeting chambers and escorted those on the journey to her vessel. The group of what amounted to be ninety boarded and she cast off. Once the vessel was clear of the harbor, she took it skyward. The sovereigns were given a tour of the vessel and the troops sent along were given chambers to rest and enjoy themselves complete with a full-service kitchen.

Harold spoke briefly. "I am not the captain of this vessel, but I do know we have about an hour to get to Svalbard, so don't get too comfortable and dose off. I expect to be meeting the true sovereigns of the Americas at some point between now and then. They will join us on this vessel for briefings. I have heard nothing but good responses so far, and I feel we will have the same."

After twenty minutes had passed, a smaller vessel latched onto Chorlanda's and many ancient cultures exited. Light snow began to fall as the groups converged in a large room to discuss the findings. Chorlanda kept the vessel on course as winds pushed against it.

In the room, Harold took charge. "Welcome all. I am pleased to see that everyone could be present."

"Thank you for your hospitality. Our journey has been long, and I believe successful." A small woman from a South American tribe spoke. "The village you are going to is very small, with only thirty people there. A Talaharian is there but is in poor health. He is not sure how his people have survived but would like to go to a place called Mount Salmo in Washington State. He has family there who will welcome their group."

"He is bringing with him, deadmages and others who are going to destroy the whole of the Earth!" The King of Sweden responded. "For Alasha has told us, in Europe, this and that is why we are going there, for the truth."

"I have given you the truth. They may be necromancers, but they do not practice. It is used only in defense. "The small woman said as she stood before the group. "These folk are looking for a place to live in peace. A lady had driven them from their newly established village near Krosslaen. I am unsure where this is, but it is the truth. This lady had also helped restore an ancient evil there, something older than a 'Mithdrool'. It lays in wait. There is a celestial transition to take place before it. We as a world need to support these people, as they are refugees seeking our aid." The woman then sat down.

"Thank you. Is there anything to be added?" Harold inquired. "If not, Our European envoy will disembark on Svalbard with some physicians to tend to Talaharian. We will communicate with Mount Salmo and see how to prevent this great evil awakened from crossing the Veil and starting Ragnarök. I do not want a massive war that has to be fought on two planets. However, we need to brief the United Nations."

Back at Mount Salmo, LaCluae hung out at the small bar across from the inn. He was joined by Dunwoody and Weisjord. "So, how do we write this in a report for Customs and Border Protection, which you know will get routed to the higher ups in Homeland Security? Do you realize this is career ending?"

"It is not career ending, LaCluae." Weisjord answered. "But it makes the special program that the U.N. had established 55 plus years ago more important than ever. I will have the program head request all reports directly from you as it is of more importance to them right now than Homeland Security."

"I don't know. You have met Agent Patriksen, right?"

"Yes. He has." Agent Patriksen said as he pulled up a chair with the agents. "And I believe that I will call our branch chief and direct her to the U.N. special programs manager right away. These people mean no harm and by law, they can be here, but we need to make sure Weelin is included in a treaty. Now we don't know what will happen tomorrow since Regence's sister will be arriving. So I suggest get some sleep."

As the group walked back to the inn, a heavy snow was falling. Two inches had already fallen in the time they were talking. Dunwoody noticed the dead calm, which always meant something. She was the first into the inn and was amazed by the tranquility. A loud thunk coming from the far room grabbed her attention and she moved forward as if to clear the room before proceeding.

FROZEN CHAOS

BITTERNESS

As Agent Dunwoody started to make her way to the rear of the inn, the other agents followed her lead. Two veered left into the next hall to secure the spa while Dunwoody and LaCluae entered the spiritual sanctuary. As they crossed the threshold of the door, a brilliant blue light filled the room. Two beings stepped out of it.

"Darned brother. Why did he have to pick such a mediocre place to set this up?" A short lady said. She was clad in plate and had a rather large sword for her stature. "What are you gawking at? Haven't you ever seen a short person before?" The woman said as she walked right past the two agents who were in shock. "Come on lad, we don't have all evening, this is supposed to be a surprise, though I don't know why."

"Because, Dezire, you want to set things right," replied the tall stocky male escorting her. "Regence indeed will be surprised."

"Excuse us. Do you mind if we ask you a few questions?" Agent LaCluae said as he stepped in front of them.

"We don't answer to you. We know all about you. So get out of the way or this blade will remove you." Dezire responded.

"Is that a threat?"

"If you want to take it that way boy," Dezire got in LaCluae's face. "I dare you."

"Pardon me." The man with her responded, "I am Tomas. This is Dezire Truaxx, current Supreme Ruler of Kluanaria, in her mother's, Matelina of Greystone, place. In case you are wondering the blade is real and she is capable if inflicting much pain at the snap of her fingers."

Brenda M. Hokenson

Agent LaCluae refused to let the action go. "If you don't mind, you are on my planet now and you will answer my questions. Let's start with why you are here at this hour?"

Dezire Truaxx turned toward the agents and raised her hand and arm as if she was envisioning herself lifting LaCluae off the ground. Suddenly LaCluae found himself dangling in midair being held up by an invisible hand about his waist. Her steel grey eyes stared at him. "Perhaps you didn't hear me the first time, Agent LaCluae." She flicked her arm toward the wall and LaCluae was flung into the wall. Dunwoody helped him recover and as they went into the hallway to catch up, but the visitors were gone. Dezire and Tomas used a stealth spell and made it to the inn keep who handed them a room key and they vanished.

"What the heck? Who was that nasty little woman? What is up with tossing people?" LaCluae was rambling. "Someone needs to knock her down a peg or two."

Agents Patriksen and Weisjord sprinted down the hallway as they had heard the exchange of words and the thunk of LaCluae first hitting the wall and then the floor. "What is going on?" Agent Weisjord asked? "We are visitors here and their culture must be respected."

"Tell that to the angry short woman who just left here. What piece of work." Agent LaCluae answered sharply. "I only asked some direct questions."

"Well, not exactly, LaCluae." Agent Dunwoody filled in the rest. "As we got to the door of the spiritual room, a brilliant light filled the air, and this small lady and tall man stepped from it. They were walking right past us like we weren't even there. So LaClueless starts in by jumping in front of them to make them stop so he could ask questions. Anyway, his tone was very unprofessional and spiteful. This small lady got in his face briefly and well, you know how LaClueless gets with the personal bubble thing. So, she somehow picked him up and had a short sentence for him and tossed him like a bad apple."

"You met her!" Agent Weisjord responded. "I can't believe she is actually here."

"Who, Weisjord?" Agent Patriksen asked as the four went toward their rooms.

"Dezire Truaxx. Her brothers are Regence, who resides here, and

Zanor, who is High Lord of Burwash, who also lives near Weelin. She also has another brother, Beryth, who is the restored High Lord of Mercurian. I know this as it is in the report that was furnished to UN's special council for Kluanaria. Zanor and Beryth I think are on good terms, but Dezire expects order and respect, and does not tolerate people getting in her face as you just did."

"What ate her cereal then? Is all she had to do was answer a question." LaCluae interjected. "Who is that tall kid, Tomas?"

"He belongs to the Chrinthold. A Newling, like the little girl you are looking for." Regence said as he walked down the hallway. "My sister is highly offended by your demeanor, so I would wait a while before trying to approach her. She has great skill with the blade and darker magic that accompanies the blade. She is much like her mother, Matelina. Goodnight, lady and gentlemen."

"Why does she?"

"Their customs dictate that a Chrinthold escort the Supreme Ruler. So far that has been to everyone's benefit. Her mother had an insatiable drive for utter destruction of all enemies, not just making peace. Dezire is the same as her mother. Both very short tempers and wicked strength, both physical and mental." Agent Weisjord added. "Now I think we need to get some sleep. Tomorrow will be very interesting."

"Why is that?" Agent Dunwoody inquired.

"Dezire will be dealing with her brother, and they are complete opposites and have a history of not getting along. Well according to the information the UN special council was provided."

"Alright, hit the rack. It will be a long day." Agent Patriksen said as he opened his door and went inside.

What was unknown to everyone at that time, a major winter storm was dumping snow at the rate of 3 inches an hour. There was already a foot and a half on the ground. The wind whipped through the tall trees. The temperature plummeted to below zero as the village slumbered. Dezire woke and looked at her window after 4 hours of sleep. "At last, endless winter shall be present in this forsaken land." She thought as she went back to sleep with a grim smile upon her face.

The morning sun was blotched out by the massive blizzard. The agents' vehicles were almost completely buried. A couple of men used unknown methods, to the agents who were looking out their room windows, to clear snow from the major paths of the village. Each paced in their room wondering what would happen today. They remembered the short angry woman and were hoping she would be more relaxed after her rest. Agent Patriksen went to LaCluae's door and knocked gently. The door opened and he entered. "Well, we are cut off from the outside for a while it looks like, so please, please keep your extra reactions in check. These folks can be extremely dangerous, as we saw during that 'restoration' of the guy who was killed by the girl in Weelin. I have not decided about this 'Veil' thing yet."

"Well boss, I think we need to go our separate ways here and have discussions with different people here and see if we can learn more about them. They seem peaceful. Well, except that woman from last night."

Patriksen laughed. "Well, you sure know how to welcome folks don't you."

"She just had to…"

"Here you go again. Your ego is getting in the way ad you need to get it in check."

"But…"

"Today, your job is to see if the internet works and get into the UN special council for this great mess and dig up everything you can, especially about this nasty lady." With that, Agent Patriksen went and walked to the end of the hall where he watched the wind whip through the trees. He smiled as he watched some men clear the paths and then another use some sort of spell to create a clear tunnel to walk through which kept them open. He thought, "I wish we had that in the real world." Patriksen then went down to the dining area and sat at the counter.

Sam brought him coffee and a steak and omelet. "How was your rest sir?"

"I slept great. That was the most comfortable I have felt sleeping in a very long time. This coffee is wonderful."

"Thank you, sir. Do you have a first name, or is it not allowed on business?"

"Oh, yes. My name is Jon. Thank you for the meal. Are you sure you will not take money?"

"It is against everything Kluanarian, Jon. Please don't feel bad. We are

The Kluanarians

happy to have visitors. Normally your people turn at the top of the hill and go through to Ruan. This has been a great experience and maybe you will tell your friends to come visit."

Patriksen smiled. "I think I will. But be careful what you ask for. Some of our people are not so courteous. Would it be ok to ask you questions later, as your dining room is starting to fill?"

"That would be fine sir, Jon. If you would like, you can help me in the kitchen."

Agent Patriksen agreed and headed in the kitchen where he could ask questions and be able to help. His conscious bothered him and thought this would help. As he handled the toasting of breads, shredding fresh potatoes and mixing eggs, he began his questions. "So, Sam, how long have you been here?"

"I came here when I was thirty, which is about fifteen in your years. My parents were in Orders that were imploding, and they needed something better than themselves. They knew that Regence came through thirty years prior to them considering this and sent a zephyr to Regence. He was most excited to have our family arrive. About two families a year have been migrating here."

"That isn't too high of a rate. Where does everyone live?"

"After work, I will give you a full tour, if that is ok." Sam responded as he placed more and more food on the service counter. "Would you mind running these out. The servers are swamped?"

Patriksen smiled and went around to the front, only to find the meals he was serving went to his agents. "Not a word, LaCluae. Not a word." LaCluae nodded with a smile. "Just eat. See Dunwoody is even managing that. Where is Weisjord?"

"Don't know boss. He isn't even one of us."

"He agreed to join us in this case. So, he is mine."

"Technically agent Patriksen, you are mine." Weisjord said as he took a small table in the corner. "Here is the latest from the UN special counsel." He handed copies to the agents, "As well as the entire history." He then provided a copy of the historical documents for them to share.

"Agent LaCluae, this is your assignment for today." Patriksen handed the historical documents. "Dunwoody, hang out with anyone who is willing to talk. I am not sure what to look for, but something doesn't feel

Brenda M. Hokenson

right." She nodded. "Weisjord, just do whatever it is you were tasked with and please, let me know what we need to focus on." He then walked back in the kitchen and continued assisting Sam.

The rush passed and the two left the kitchen and strolled about in the sheltered garden. They could see about three feet of new snow since dawn. Sam showed Patriksen the herbs and spices they would be harvesting and the vegetables that would be harvested by two more folks a little later. They returned to the inn only to find Regence, Emilae, and Dezire seated by the fireplace.

"Let's sit down and relax a minute, Sam." Agent Patriksen said. The two seated themselves in some cozy chairs with cups of tea and tea cakes and observed everything.

"Thank you for visiting us, Dezire. We are delighted you are here. Did you rest well?"

"Get off of the tourist crap, Regence. Mother is concerned in the stability of her people, which means I am naturally concerned for your wellbeing, along with that of the other emigrants. Tell me, why did you uproot and come here? Mother is still feeling the stinging pain from your departure."

"You know darn well why I left, Dezire. Do you really want to walk down that path again? Do you really want the Kluanarians to have to rewrite history because your lie lived on and was recorded to be true? Do you really want Mother to know what really happened with the mess in Ruan twice now? Can you live with losing your 'Supreme Ruler' title?"

"How dare you."

"You know Dezire, I can end you here and now, so I would suggest watching your tone. Besides I have guests from this realm who don't need your drama. I am also aware you cast one into the wall for asking questions. Tread lightly."

Emilae interjected. "So, Dezire, is there any word on this potential invasion by the dead mages of Phallas Minor? Someone has commented a few times that our son, Talaharian is their leader."

Dezire responded as she stared into her brother's eyes. "Yes, Talaharian has been named as their leader, but I believe that this has been resolved on Kluanaria. Emilae, how are you doing? Is your family in Ruan well?"

"I… I don't know."

"Hmm, perhaps Regence has kept you from them. Perhaps he wants everyone here to be cut off completely." Dezire stood up and paced about. She waved her hand and the air in the room chilled by ten degrees even with a fire going. "Maybe he wants to start a revolution." She said as she leaned on the chair Regence was seated in.

"Why did you truly come here, you vile creature?" Regence inquired as he stood. "Perhaps Mother is tired of your lies and deceit? I am glad I left. You are planning to let the horsemen free in our lands. They are not a normal occurrence, except for Harold. You are the cause of the death of many, many villages and the start of two wars, not counting Llylandra, unless you are actually working with her, which would not shock me."

"Well, Llylandra is a great pawn. She has no idea what was in store." Dezire smiled wickedly.

"You ass! Why would you have most of the Mercurian villagers murdered? What could you possibly gain? Heck, you started the first major war against Beryth."

Emilae leaned to her husband and whispered. "Your mother is dying. She wants full control. She was given the title but no real authority, which she just realized. She…"

Dezire cut off her words by raising Emilae from the chair by her neck like she had tossed LaCluae across the room. "Silence," She then released Emilae so she fell to the ground unconscious.

Regence stood up and cast a spell about Dezire. She was unable to cross the ring. As she raised her sword and summoned a shade for assistance, Regence snapped his fingers and she was encased in a crystal prison with her summoned shade. "Sorry about that, Mr. Patriksen and Sam. I had afterthoughts after I spoke with her early yesterday evening. I had no idea she would do this, not here."

"We all have one in our family. Do you know how to stop her plan?" Agent Patriksen inquired.

"No. I am not even sure who she has as pawns. That is what we need to find out. Our son, Talaharian, moved to a remote island, Svalbard with about twenty folks. They were seeking peace and tranquility. His group has very powerful abilities and I think we should go there to ease my mind at least." Regence responded as he carefully propped his wife up against his chest and made sure she was still breathing.

A small girl raced into the dining area. "Uncle Regence, you have not met me, but I am Tatiana. Zanor is my grandpa."

"Tatiana, everyone has been looking for you for some time now. Do you know what is causing this endless snowstorm?"

"No. It is pretty much like that all over Earth right now. I have been visiting places that have spiritual significance here in hopes to control my temper. A tall thin grey man in long robes with long hair came to me in a dream and said to go to those places. He said I will need as much tranquility as possible to help stop the coming battle."

"Did this man send you to me?"

"Yes. He said you are by far the most tranquil I will ever find and that you would be able to help me harness my emotions and use them properly." Tatiana couldn't help looking at Emilae. "I will fix her for you. She has been squished by that lady pretty bad. *Restori a Emilae, restore a Emilae.*"

Emilae took a deep breath and slowly opened her eyes. "Thank you Newling. Where did you come from?"

"I am Tatiana, granddaughter of Zanor."

Agent Patriksen came forward with some water for everyone. Sam brought finger sandwiches, and everyone sat at a table. "Tatiana, I am Agent Patriksen. Are you okay?"

"Yes sir. Your world is in great danger, and I need to find my brother, Paul. He is in even worse danger. The grey man told me that Dezire will raze this land."

"Well, Dezire is the lady in the crystal. I will shrink it and then we need to go to Svalbard. Talaharian will know what to do." Regence responded.

"He is not with Llylandra?" Tatiana said with a confused look.

"No, he is your older cousin. Dezire doesn't have kids and you have met Beryth, I assume?"

"Yes. His children are a lot older than me."

"Yes. He is the oldest, followed by me, then Dezire and then your grandfather, Zanor. So when would you all like to translocate?"

Agent Patriksen decided to say something. "Is this open to Earth as well or just Kluanarians?"

"Of course, you may join us. It might help you understand the balance we try to maintain."

"I will not be going." Emilae said. "I will remain here and can communicate to you if there are any more surprises."

The crystal began to crack. Tomas was attempting to free Dezire. Tatiana used a small burst of air to break his focus. "Tomas, don't she is corrupted!"

"Wha… Tatiana, where have you been? Dezire is the Supreme Ruler."

"It is only a title, Tomas. She has no authority; she gave it to grandpa."

A brilliant light filled the room and Edwina stepped forth. "Tomas, Rynylla needs you to return to Kaprius. She has a special project."

Tomas acknowledged the message. "How have you been Ed? Are you ok? You had us all worried, but I was in training and couldn't…" Tomas embraced Edwina tightly. "I will see you again." With that he vanished into thin air.

Edwina used a smaller crystal and pulled Dezire and her shade into it so Regence could release the large crystal. "It is time Uncle."

Regence placed Sam in charge and cast a translocation spell for the group. They arrived in the center of Svalbard where they were greeted by Talaharian. "Father, what brings you so far?"

"Dezire has started this mess and it is going to get terrible. You know her skills and abilities. Well, there are many more just like her, and for that fact your grandmother. They are using the Phallas Minor deadmages as a diversion for their true quest."

"I had true sovereigns from the Americas here not more than two days ago. They left before the storm which is unrelenting."

Tatiana stepped forward. "We have much to discuss according to a tall, thin, grey man. Can we go inside?"

Talaharian smiled and nodded. He motioned for the group to follow him into the inn which was very similar to the one at Mount Salmo. He had food and drink brought for everyone.

"Tatiana, this tall, thin, grey man, have you seen him before?" Talaharian inquired as he helped her into the taller chair. "I heard there was some stuff that happened in Weelin late this summer."

"Yes sir. The man came to me in a dream. But I don't know who he is. I kind of destroyed the town, some small mountains and Thanias. I don't even feel bad about Thanias."

Brenda M. Hokenson

"Don't worry Newling. Thanias is restored and knows his true purpose."

"But how? I watched him fall. I made him fall."

"Ermenya was there, and she captured all of his essences, spirit and body. Your friend, Thallas performed the ceremony at Krosslaen. He also did the Veil Hardening at Burwash." Talaharian said.

"How do you know all of this?"

Talaharian snapped his fingers and became the man from Tatiana's dream. "Because I am that person from you vision. This is my true appearance. My mother is Fraeloch and dad is well, you know my father. We Fraelochs can be many shades of grey to almost white, if this eases your mind. I am also preparing a special council that you and the Newlings will be part of since the Council of the Orders does not work at all. Menosh is on my high council along with Alasha and William. The dragons are invited, but rarely show."

"What are we gonna do to stop the war?"

"First, I know there is a group of folks heading this way. I need to meet with them first and then we will figure this out together. Don't worry about Paul for now. He is with William and the dragons where he is safe."

Agent Patriksen was very interested in the coming group of people. Who were they? Why did Talaharian meet with true sovereigns of the Americas? Could these folks be true sovereigns from Europe or somewhere else?

In the meantime, all news media across the globe were reporting the same thing. *"The snow has been falling steadily since last evening. There is a current accumulation of 3 feet in Tokyo, 3 feet in Sydney, 2 feet in Kabul, 4 feet in Seattle, New York, Chicago, and 2 feet in Atlanta. There is no predicted end to this event. Is this a sign of global warming? There is no word yet on how this will be handled by world leaders. Emergency shipments of blankets, tents and clothing are being sent out to countries in need. No word on how it will be delivered to the masses." You are being advised to keep inside. The snow will not be cleared until the storm weakens significantly. Please stay tuned to your local station for weather updates.*

"Edwina, release Dezire, please." Talaharian requested as he placed a special ring about the center of the room. Edwina entered the circle and placed the crystal in the center. Once out of the circle, she cast a spell and Dezire was free.

"Talaharian, how are you?" Dezire said as she studied those in the room with them. "I see you found dear, sweet Tatiana. And Edwina, our most precious Moon. How was Llylandra?"

"Now is your time to answer questions, Dezire." Talaharian said.

"Maybe, maybe not. If they are the right questions…"

"Who are your contacts?"

"Wouldn't you like to know?"

Talaharian closed his hand partially, which moved the circle inward toward Dezire. "You are aware of what happens if this ring gets too close to you?"

"Yes."

"Then answer the question."

"I will never tell."

Talaharian again closed his hand a little more.

Dezire watched those around the room. She summoned her shade again which tried in vain to break the circle. "Why do you want to know?"

"We are going to stop you." Agent Patriksen interrupted. "Maybe you will talk to me."

"You are an interesting person. What makes you so special that you think I will talk at all?"

"Because you just began the conversation. Tell me, what is your purpose here, on Earth?"

"It is a land in great turmoil, and I will see that turmoil end? You all are oblivious in the fact that the people just like me are already here and are already winning. They also have aid…"

Talaharian moved the circle closer. "Who are the contacts?"

Dezire smiled. "I have many who are already here, just waiting for the right time. You see, I have control of the Trincotts, shades, Shaeplings, and some others you have not met yet."

"Answer my question!" Talaharian shouted. She stood in the center of the ring smirking; knowing that she had the upper hand, at least for the time being. "What is wrong with you? Your mother gave you control over everything, and you gave it away. Why do you want to destroy this realm and ours?"

Brenda M. Hokenson

A brilliant bolt of light struck the ground, right in the middle of the ring where Dezire stood. Two stepped from it. She became uneasy as the snow in the immediate area melted and flowers bloomed from frozen ground. She summoned her shade to help her.

"It will do no good, Dezire." A small child said as he walked toward her. The shade advanced upon him and tried to knock him to the ground. But the boy was resilient. He batted at the shade with his arm and the brilliant light surrounding him destroyed the creature. "I am Thallas of the Stars."

Dezire back-pedaled away from the boy, only to run into William. "What is your purpose here, Dezire? Matelina has sent us, as you have disrupted something that has been in balance, but she would not say what."

"Isn't it obvious? I want to destroy it and Kluanaria, control the masses and have total domination."

"It is more than that. Your powers are very strong. Your mother was strong, but she chose to not use them." William said as Dezire moved away from him as well.

"You don't stand a chance against what has been woken. Prepare to meet your doom!" She extended her arm and reached toward Agent Patriksen. As she closed her had a larger shade tossed him in to the circle. "And you will be my first." She unsheathed a large sword that seemed almost bigger than her and prepared to cut him down. As she swung, Patriksen rolled to his left and then tumbled behind Thallas. "You are too weak, human. You will taste this blade."

A crowd had gathered as the commotion was exaggerated by Dezire's dark booming voice that seemed to carry for miles. A blizzard was upon them again. Thallas cast a light spell that dissipated the snowstorm however, only briefly.

"Give up, boy!" She said as she watched William and Patriksen. "You will not win this day." She disappeared and reappeared right behind Thallas. She used the hilt of her sword to knock the boy unconscious and began trying to open a gateway.

William ran toward them, casting blinding rays at her as he took hold of the boy. He shoved her in the portal and cast a spell so as she could not enter the Earth Realm using the same spell. "Thallas…Thallas" William remained fairly composed and called upon the stars to heal their Newling. Talaharian entered the ring. "We meet again."

Talaharian nodded and took the boy from William, "Let us go into the great hall, it is warm and dry. We will need to heal him quickly. We need to notify his parents."

A long procession followed them out of the weather. The European envoy was preparing to exit their vessel. A couple of the new world sovereigns joined them as they approached the great hall. Shrikes were present around the village along with the Veil Guards.

Thallas was being tended to by William and Talaharian when Harold approached. "What happened to the lad?"

"Dezire! That monster!" A female onlooker said as she went to find blankets for the boy.

"What is the meaning…"

"Harold, you know as much as we do now. This is Talaharian, he is truly not evil like we were led to believe, and in fact I have been working with him on the Veil Hardening that Thallas completed. So now, please let us get the boy to a stable state. Agent Patriksen, over there, can fill you in." William said as he tried every spell he knew to save the lad.

"Riparare a spirito a Thallas, riparare a corpo! Reparare a cervello!" A grey mist filled the area in which Thallas was being worked on. The woman returned with blankets. *"Riparare a spirito riparare a corpo! Reparare a cervello!"* Thallas stirred for long enough to see people staring at him and then closed his eyes again. *"Riparare a spirito riparare a corpo! Reparare a cervello!"* The woman shouted. The ground at their feet trembled and the fountain in the hall began to flow. Flowers sprang up around it and around Thallas. *"Riparare a spirito riparare a corpo! Reparare a cervello!"* The woman knelt by Thallas' head and supported it. "Bring me dragonsbreath and twillium, Harold."

"Where is it?"

"By the fountain. It only grows herbs that are needed for healing specific wounds. You should know this by now."

"Oh, shut up. Just because you're your father…" Harold paused and reflected on the last great battle he had. "Anyway Rynylla, are you able to help him?"

"Yes, he is healed, but it will be a while before he will get to do anything.

I suggest the stasis chamber on Chorlanda's vessel. Two Chrinthold gently placed Thallas on a stretcher and the three vanished into brilliant light. "There now, I have requested his parent presence on the vessel and now we must discuss this new threat Dezire has brought to our doors and the doors of the Earth realm."

Agent Patriksen paced as he observed everyone. He paid particular attention to Rynylla. Why was she the only one who could stop the internal bleeding? What made her so special? Whose side is she truly on? The agent did remember that one of hers was with Dezire when LaCluae was tossed into a wall.

"Why is she so hateful?" The King of Sweden asked. "What have we ever done to her? Now there is this war coming. We do not have flying ships capable of what yours can do, or the magic you all possess in some manner. What made her so bitter?"

Harold took the King aside. "Vi försöker lista ut innan vi planerar vår flytt. Snälla ge oss en chans. Detta tar oss alla tillsammans att lösa."

The King nodded and returned to the other royals who were being shown magnificent chambers for their stay. A large oval table with many chairs was in the dining hall for the guests. A massive feast was being prepared.

SNOWBOUND

WHILE THE EUROPEAN ENVOY FINALLY met with Talaharian and some of the Orders, the rest of the world was reeling from the snow that had been falling for a couple days. Some areas hadn't seen snow in millennia. Parts along the equator were fairing a little better, while many northern and southern areas were up to 5 feet. Schools were closed and some governments set up a delivery system for food and other goods needed. Many countries were experiencing a high death toll from the weather. In the past hour the snowfall lessened, and the temperature remained constant. Shipping lanes were slowly icing over, and all air traffic had ceased. Trains were being taken from storage and put on tracks to help the masses get around.

Through the Veil in Kluanaria, the people were dealing with the massive amounts of snow better. They had a means to keep paths clear and food on everyone's table. The people were used to large amounts of snow during the winter. The Council of the Orders was meeting to see what needed to happen to keep everyone safe. Lunacerian led the discussion. "Thank you all for attending this most pressing meeting. As you know we are going through an unnatural storm along with our friends and family across the Veil in Weelin and Svalbard. We are adept in dealing with this as are our folks in the Earth realm. However, there is much destruction as you can see." Lunacerian had a similar sphere that the village by Mount Salmo used earlier. It showed many different places on Earth and the devastation. "I feel it pertinent that we dispatch as many Orders' members as possible to help with this crisis across the Veil."

Guilles volunteered the services of the mapmakers and historians, to help educate the land across the Veil. The Izmaa and Shadowblyts volunteered to split up and create tears in the Veil to allow easier passage for the Orders who are on this humanitarian mission. The Eupepsians, Paladins, and Chrinthold took up the cause and recruited many Truncheons to help. Intervals would be used to clear major routes and help establish food points. The Aantiri, Zanor, decided that it was time to speak to his mother about the situation. First, he sent word to Freiderich and Ermenya about the frozen lands on both sides of the Veil.

Zanor went to the furthest cottage in Burwash. It had a stately path to the home. A stone wall about 3 feet high separated the domain of Matelina from the grass that filled the center of town and extended to each family's domain. He observed the home was in need of some work. The stately design had some minor cracks and roof damage from the howling winds. As he walked up the steps, he noticed how lifeless the land seemed. "Mother, are you home?" Zanor called as he knocked on the door.

"Yes, my son, please come in." Matelina, being one hundred five, moved rather briskly to the door. I hear there are some problems that you need guidance to understand better."

"Mother, you know I would not be here unless I felt the situation was out of hand or worse."

"What is worse than out of hand?" Matelina walked with him to her sitting room. The walls were covered with items from her many battles defending Kluanaria. "Please sit and have some tea."

"It is about Dezire. She has somehow manipulated a spell, which I have seen you use only in battle once. It is causing a relentless snowstorm both here, in Kluanaria, and through the Veil in the Earth realm. Their people are dying by the thousands. Many of their lands are impoverished nations and nations in self-turmoil. Others are stubborn and won't ask for aid. Lunacerian and the Council are sending our people to help them as much as we can."

"She truly has cast this frozen chaos?"

"How... How could she do this to her people and the ones she has never met? What is the point to this?"

"I am very glad that Dezire gave you control of Burwash. Things would be much darker if she had not."

"What does that mean?"

The Kluanarians

"It means, Dezire is like me, battle hardened and the lust for war grows in her. I do know she has put things in motion which will lead to a great battle. She has played the Fraeloch and Morket. Llylandra is one of her victims, but she too would like to see control of this land. The only way she could have cast this spell is if she was able to gain favor of the lord of Riftan."

"That place is a mere legend."

"No son. It is not." Matelina pulled out her book and showed him the spell that Dezire used. "For both worlds to be in such peril, she had to find Arkronde, the liaison to the lord, in order to gain favor."

"What does Riftan have to do with…?" Zanor stopped to think. *How did that bridge truly break when Paul fell to meet serious injury midsummer? What caused the massive storm at Clamshoe Bay through the Veil near Weelin? Llylandra would not have known anything about the family without help from the inside.* "So this place, Riftan, it allows those with favor of the lord to go anywhere and return?

"Something like that. Riftan is a land built into the very fabric of space and time, and very difficult to locate. It sits in the very mist of the Veil and resides nowhere, but everywhere. I am aware that she has amassed a great army that is hidden within Riftan and has a few spies in both realms."

"Why is she doing this? Was this your idea?" Zanor asked as he poured more tea for them.

"No. I have only used my powers, which are still stronger than hers, to protect our lands. I have also used my diplomacy to secure friendships in the Earth realm."

"How do we stop her?"

"I am afraid it is too late, son. She has set the cogs of war in motion and only after a true victory will it end. Just to let you know, the violence and upheaval on Earth feeds her thirst for war and domination. She is recruiting some anti-people, types across the Veil and has been successful. I am aware that Alasha and an envoy are meeting with Talaharian."

"This is true mother. Do we have enough in motion right now?"

"I will need to help you in this endeavor."

"But your age."

"You are forgetting; I was born with this unnaturally long life as she has been. The older we are the stronger we become. So, I should be a key instrument when it is time. So for now, I believe that I shall remain here as an onlooker until the time is right to put an end to Dezire and her plans."

"You have no army, well a strong enough fighting force, to command."

"Trust in me. I can conjure more than she and I also have favor with the actual lord of Riftan. We will weather this together. Let us walk." The two left the cottage and made haste though Burwash.

No one had seen Matelina in a long time. She wore her plate, which when looking at looked like thick white leather, but was a thousand times stronger, her blood-red cape, and circlet. Her favorite sword was strapped to her waist. The ruler watched the snow as it came down. She saw the fear in her people. She paused in the center of the town and decided to cast a magic free zone about the entire city, which allowed the spellbound snow to dissipate immediately. "Come along Zanor, you must translocate us to my other villages."

Zanor agreed and cast the spell. After arriving at Treah he asked, "So how many more are like you? Would they be willing to help Earth as it has more people than here?"

"There are thousands of us, hidden in plain sight and most do not practice. I think once I have finished clearing this land, I will take you with me to our stronghold." She looked up at the high peaks of the once magnificent Bittern. "I have gazed upon the once great center of my Order. Interval, Shadowblyts, and Izmaa were amongst us. Who restored it?"

"Your great granddaughter, Tatiana, her friends Irra and Onachala, and a couple other elders in different Orders restored the village. Then the Newlings followed after Tatiana and her friend, Tommy captured Mithdrool."

Matelina mused. "Why have I not met this child?" She was wondering if any Newlings were of her Order. "I would like to meet all of the Newlings."

"Mother, you are…"

"Too old, too weak, too mean" Matelina said sarcastically.

"No, I was thinking too busy with clearing the villages."

"Well, I will have you do an immediate summons for them, once we get to Bittern."

Feeling defeated, slightly, Zanor agreed. "Yes, mother." He sighed as any son who had plans dashed by a parent would.

Treah had already been cleared to Matelina's surprise. It was the same magic free zone spell that she had used. She could tell by residuals in the spell that caused the zone to slightly expand and contract. She pondered about the caster. Zanor translocated them to Bittern after her mother had finished studying the cast. She had a slight smirk.

"What is the silly grin for mother?"

"I know the caster quite well. He is probably in the citadel here."

"What citadel? I don't see…"

"Shh. *Avsløre porten. Åpne kammeret*" Matelina spoke in a very deep voice and raised her hands up and out to the sides slowly.

An opening appeared in the middle of Bittern's walking path. It was steel grey with a large Shrike emblazoned across the doors. The two passed through the gate and it closed behind them. Sconces lined the hall which lit as they ventured further into the citadel. A room off to the left drew Matelina's attention. It was well lit with a few people seated at a table. She then looked to the right and noticed the map room was full of activity. She approached the main room in which there was a throne made of granite where a polearm was thrust into the backrest.

"Welcome home, Matelina." A tall slender man spoke as he advanced toward them. "We have been expecting you."

"Rellos!"

"We have found the one."

"Truly? Where? How?"

"The clues were most puzzling. However, we will need to translocate to Mount Salmo."

"What can possibly be there other than my son and some others who chose to remain 'normal?'"

"The land there is in peril and Dezire has a profound friendship with Arkronde. In other words, the lord of Riftan will give her anything she wants, because of her friendship with his liaison. She has requested the assistance of our Order, and you know how we are."

"Yes, but I am telling you, do not do this. We have an agreement with their lands already. It would mean the utter destruction of the Earth realm."

A few moments later many members of the Fraust gathered in the halls and sat patiently on the benches. Zanor did a summons for all Newlings, which pulled even those who had no idea they had special gifts. "Matelina, ruler of all Kluanaria, these are your Newlings. He introduced all to her individually."

Matelina waited impatiently to meet the Fraust Newling, and her great granddaughter. She greeted each child with open arms welcoming them to the New Council, which would be based in the Fraust Citadel. A small child about 6 in Kluanarian years stepped forth. "I am Nicolai, son of Blayne. Mom raised me in Salmo, now she is serving as the head person in Vale Kilowas. Father is Omiporici and is an Interval, but I don't know much of him."

"I will take care of that for you." Matelina said as she studied the boy. "How many of you Newlings are without one or more parents?" The kids looked around at each other, several immediately stepped forward as Rellos recorded names. A few minutes passed and another five children joined their peers who stepped forward. Rellos recorded them as well. "Aantiri, you know what to do." Paul cast a summoning spell on the children and parents were immediately brought to the chamber. "I have summoned you into the Chamber of the Fraust for a specific reason." Matelina glanced at the parents of the children. "Many of you have chosen to not be part of your child's life, so I am telling you right now, you are too late. These children belong to me now and the elders of the Orders will provide them with everything they need, to include love and respect. I have three great grandchildren here and two or three more who are a bit older who are trying to help end the frozen chaos that is gripping Kluanaria and Earth. Your beautiful children have great gifts, and I will use those to restore order." Matelina paused as the parents looked amongst one another and observed the elders and the entire legion of Fraust. She then turned her attention back to those who were seated on the benches. "Thank you for doing wonderful things with and for your children. My hopes are that we will defeat this new enemy and have new allies on Earth. I realize some of you have jobs that take you away from them, so I have set up special privileges for you to meet with them more frequently."

With that Matelina walked toward the Newlings. "Do not be frightened. You all have room here to train and no one can harm you. Shades guard everywhere and will guide you if you are lost." She took time and hugged them all. "Down this hall," she said as she escorted them on a brief tour, "are two sections, one side will house the girls, the other side is the boys. Each of you will have your own room and a Shade for a guard. If you need anything, your guard will help you. Now, I must return to the others, so please follow Rellos."

She arrived to loud confusion and many hostile words. "BE SEATED! ALL OF YOU!" The group immediately became quiet and sat down. "I am ruler of this realm. I have maintained peace, at great cost to my Order and myself. I have built grand cities from the ruins of war and you folks' laziness. I had rules in place, and you did not follow them. So, for now, please join us in a great feast to honor your children. They will rejoin us in a few moments after Rellos finishes their short tour. Once the feast is over, you will be returned to where you were at and you will change or there will be severe consequences."

The Fraust used their powers and generated carved ice tables in the center of the rooms, Shades gathered chairs and the other Orders conjured great quantities of food. Everyone took seats with their children. The Orders intermingled with the Fraust, who usually remain isolated from the rest. Many tales were exchanged, and some histories were corrected and recorded. The families looked around nervously. The Fraust all wore armor like Matelina's and seemed to be preparing for a battle. Truncheon arrived at the gate and Shades welcomed them. They were then followed by an escort of Chrinthold, Paladins, Intervals, Stars, Moons, Shadowblyts, Izmaa, William, and Freiderich, the dragon in his humanoid form. More tables and food were prepared.

Meanwhile, snow began to fill the skies again. Frostlings darted about Bittern and entered the chamber, leaving etchings on windows and mirrors. They danced about the children's heads as if to bring a bit of ease to the rigidness of the Fraust Order. Zephyrs and Nymphs also prance through the gates and exited.

Kren approached Zanor. "Sire, the snow has returned, which means that Dezire has left Riftan. I fear she will strike Earth first."

Zanor nodded. "Which of the Newlings will be both mentally and physically strong enough to go with you to Svalbard?"

"Why Svalbard?"

"Talaharian is there, and I know he is trying to come up with a plan to help Earth. I need you to tell him the Orders are in motion and will reach Svalbard in the next day or two." He paused and motioned to Irra.

She ran to him as her parents watched in horror, thinking the worst. "Will you create a tear for Kren to enter Svalbard, please? He needs to be there so he can start sending messages."

"Once he is there, the tear will close, sir." Irra replied.

"I know, dear. Once he is there, his remnant will be on this side and can communicate with us."

"Remnant?"

"It is like a thought, and it will be kept in this." He showed her the fountain near the throne. "There will always be a Shade near it who will inform the Orders."

"Ok, I will do this for you. When does Paul have to go back to Krosslaen?"

"He leaves after this ceremony. Luly was also moved there. I am still uncertain why she is in danger, as I believe everyone to be. Now, let's get Kren to Svalbard."

Irra meditated briefly and closed her eyes. Everyone stopped eating and watched in amazement as she raised her left arm in the air and slowly extended a finger and lower her arm as if she were using a nail to rip through the very fabric of air. As her arm lowered to her side, a fissure of brilliant colors with a dark center began to open. She then took both hands and stretched the sides a bit. "There you are Kren. Please take this. It will be needed by Harold."

Kren nodded and held the small object tightly in his hand as he went through the tear, appearing in the middle of the great hall. Rynylla was there and received him. "Thank you Kren. Harold is over there, pacing. He feels devastated that Thallas was well."

"I understand. It is imperative I speak with him." Kren bowed to Rynylla and rushed to Harold who was pacing as the meeting with the Sovereigns was about to begin.

"Kren! What brings you here?"

"This object, from an Izmaa does. Irra said it will be very important to you soon. I am to remain here and send reports as they will be sending reports to you."

"The Fraust granted access?"

"Yes and offered their refuge as sanctuary for the Newlings. Luly and Paul are there right now which can bring great peril. However, Fred is present. The snow has begun to fall heavy again. The Fraust are using no-magic zones over the villages on Kluanaria, which is helping. Also, the council met and Zanor has enlisted all Orders to come to Earth and help as best they can. The latest Eupepsian report says millions have died here, on Earth the past day or so. The Morket have a great vessel in the sky circling this planet that is monitoring."

"How are you to report? You came through an Izmaa tear."

"I left a remnant at the fountain. I did not have a Newling travel with me, as I think they need more time."

"That is understandable. Come join us. I will open this discussion and you can tell them these plans. Do you have a map?"

"Of Kluanaria, yes. Of this realm, no, but I am sure Gareth can get me one if I can get him on the Morket ship."

Gareth heard the comment and came running. "A map you say. I can make any map you want. What would you like?"

"One of this realm please. I have some points that need to be discussed."

"Well, now, that sounds like a challenge. How to get this map…"

Rynylla approached them. I" will get you to the ship. Chorlanda is still here, she can coordinate with them."

"Do we have enough supplies? The water here is much colder…"

"You will be in space circling."

"Uh, I have never traveled in a floating vessel other than a boat. I have visited distant worlds but never by vessel."

"This is your new calling then." Harold snickered. "Get to it Rynylla, we don't have time as the snow is coming down heavy here, I can only imagine in other places.

Patriksen approached the group. "I need to check on my agents. How do I do that from here?"

"Where are they?" Rynylla asked.

"The village at Mount Salmo, inside the inn trying to learn about your culture."

"Talaharian can get a message there." Harold answered. "We need to know what the weather is there and if possible, everywhere here."

"Why?" Patriksen asked looking puzzled.

"The small angry woman who tossed you is going to freeze you of

Earth to death or to the fringe of death in which you will beg her to stop, and pledge loyalty to her." Harold responded.

Patriksen nodded. "Weisjord will need to speak with the UN?"

"UN?" The Orders chimed together.

"United Nations. It is like your council of all your Orders. It is a council of the many countries of the world."

They nodded and Rynylla summoned Talaharian and explained what needed to take place.

Many of the sovereigns had gathered at the windows and stared in amazement at the rate of snow fall and wondered what was happening, since they were of Europe, their subjects were in grave danger.

"Excuse me." The King of Norway said as he walked toward the Orders. "We would like you to bring the remainder of our party to this location and from here; we will take your flying vessel to the UN in New York. It is our decision, as these are our people."

Harold nodded in agreement. "This will also get us a map. I am thinking survey fairly quickly and transport everyone into the UN." At this time Rynylla communicated with Chorlanda telepathically.

"Maps cannot be rushed." Gareth said. "They take time, there are many measurements…"

"Which are now done on these brilliant devices that the Morket have and the Earth folk use for other things." Chorlanda said as she entered. "Let's get everyone on board, as the village is completely buried. Then we will go to Drottingholm and do the map for Kren to discuss with the Earth sovereigns."

When everyone was on board, Shrikes escorted families to their rooms and the sovereigns to their chambers. Folks peered out the windows as they lifted off the ground. The snow became more intense as they moved south and eastward. The frozen lands of Sweden and Norway were completely white. There were no signs of villages anymore. Larger towns had all but vanished in the whiteout conditions. Monarchs cried, seeking consolation in each other.

Alasha arrived on board the vessel several miles before Drottingholm and met with e monarchs. "Your people are safe, for now. The Fraust Order and several others are here to protect the large cities. The outlying villages… We did not make it to every single one yet. I fear there will be many dead. The European continent below the North and Baltic Seas are almost as bad as here, we have thousands of Orders who are trying to aid you as we speak. There are thousands in North and South America. We also have more headed to Africa, Australia and Asia. Your people of Earth need to know that if they interfere with our help, we will not help that particular area as we do not have time to waste on the vain."

"Excuse me. The map is ready!" Gareth said as he entered the room with Kren and Talaharian. He stretched it out on a table that slowly rose from the floor. Kren marked specific locations on the map.

"These points here, in North America, in particular Yellowstone in the United States and Tuya in Canada, will be attacked. One is a nightmare waiting to happen and if our sources are right, Dezire, who just left Riftan, will try to disrupt the true cycle of these volcanoes. She has help. There are reports of her armies..." Kren was interrupted.

"What armies? Dezire doesn't have armies." Matelina said in a concerned voice.

"I beg to differ, Matelina." Gareth added. "She has acquired Llylandra's deadmages, Mithdrool's warlocks, shades who are not within Fraust, Trincotts, Shaeplings, and some of the Fraust who want adventure. They however now wear crimson armor and call themselves Bloodbreakers. Although Mithdrool is quite dead, this time, Jaetoth and Llylandra are commanding legions on Earth. The lord of Riftan has granted them privileges to open small voids to allow their forces to cross. As it is snowing quite heavily, Dezire is more than likely headed in our direction."

"I...I don't understand. She...She..." Matelina broke down. The room grew quite frigid for the folks witnessing this event. Her shade emerged and attempted to calm her. "She..." Something struck a nerve. Matelina stood up straight and stoic. Her voice deepened, which was shocking to all except Agent Patriksen who had heard Dezire using this tone. "She has betrayed me. She has betrayed the Councils. She will die by my blade!" Any sign of weakness or fragility was completely gone. Her full strength had completely returned. She snapped her fingers and the snow falling stopped. "Let's get to this New York, now, Chorlanda!"

The sovereigns who had joined them in the chambers were in awe. How can someone snap their fingers and turn off a snowstorm? How can her voice be so deep?

Brenda M. Hokenson

Chorlanda increased the speed by double, shortening the time considerably. The lower decks were translucent, and the folks were looking in wonder at the large metropolis below them. Agent Patriksen pointed out a few things as they began to descend onto a heli-pad. "Won't this be conspicuous?" Agent Patriksen asked.

"No, the machine is invisible for the most part and with the material it is made of, Earth solids can pass right through it, so they will think they are hallucinating." A technician on board replied. "What will be conspicuous is when we port everyone at once into that room in the center of the building. Did everyone bring what you call… passports?"

The sovereigns looked about. Patriksen finally was able to use his satellite phone. He attempted to make contact with Agent LaCluae and Dunwoody. Weisjord had gone from Weelin to New York in a special transport. He had just started to brief the special committee as everyone appeared at once.

The room in which they stood had a podium and numerous rows of seating with a long-curved writing bench before each row of seats. Several members were busy reading notes and taking notes. A recorder was to the front near the podium to take notes of all committee dealings. The room appeared circular due to the seating arrangements.

"How much snow has fallen in this place?" Matelina asked in her deep voice as they materialized on the committee floor near the recorder.

"Who are you, Madame?" One of the committee members asked as he stood up. "What is the meaning of this…this invasion? GUARDS!" Many guards flowed into the room as an alarm button had been pressed when they appeared.

"Pardon me." The Queen of Denmark said. "We are European sovereigns and need to have an alert for the entire world. This storm encompasses the entire world plus the land these kind folks are from. They have some abilities that they are willing to share with us in order to preserve whatever life remains."

Agent Weisjord attested to the committee that the folks present were in-fact legitimate. "I sent you several memos, did you read them?"

"Yes, we have read the compelling information. We do not feel it a legitimate problem at this moment in time."

Agent Patriksen stepped forward. "Excuse me, sir. I am Agent Patriksen with Customs and Border Protection. I was curious if any of you had taken the time to watch the news in the past oh, say three days? Right now, there is more snow on the ground in New York than there has been in the past decade. So, if you don't mind, please listen for once."

The chancellor for the committee rolled his eyes. "Do you expect me to believe you just because you have...?"

"I am telling you, right now, Simione, take action." The Queen of Denmark said as she approached the podium. "Open your laptops and type in world news. Then maybe you will change your minds." Simione glared. "I hereby exercise my limited authority and remove you from Denmark's council to the United Nations. And we the true sovereigns invoke our rights to take full control of our countries as they are in grave danger and the current politics are preventing action."

The King of Sweden looked at the others. "Can we do that?"

"I don't know, but it needs done." The King of Norway replied with a smile. "This should change the world more so than anything else."

"Excuse me, please." Matelina said. "I do not know what a laptop is, but if you will notice the accumulations here are great and vary all over the world. Millions have died and many more are on the brink. This is an act of war, which has begun and must come to term. We have already dispatched our advanced Orders to aide in the salvation of your people. There are some orbitals that will provide housing for the survivors until we get control."

"Orbitals? You mean flying saucers?" The chancellor inquired.

"What is a flying saucer?" Matelina retorted. "If you mean flying ships, yes, but they do not resemble saucers. Now if you don't mind, where is the main military body here?"

Agent Patriksen answered, "For the United States, it is not that far, but each country has its own."

"Very well, we will go there next, while the sovereigns tend to the matter of coordinating search and save for their countries. They can also get their militaries on line as this will need everyone."

The sovereigns took over the UN building and started coordinating evacuation points for all countries. Agent Patriksen took Matelina, Gareth, and Chorlanda back to the heli-pad. "Does this have a pod that can take us south?"

Brenda M. Hokenson

"Chorlanda nodded and had a pod from a bay materialize. "This should work for what you need."

Patriksen's phone rang. He answered in his normal business tone. "Agent Patriksen."

"Boss. This is Dunwoody; we are unable to locate Weisjord. LaCluae and I have been in the library researching, but when we turned around, Weisjord was gone."

"No worries, Dunwoody, he is here with us. Our current location is in flight headed to the Pentagon. I am not sure how the reception will be there, however. Is it snowing in your area?"

"Yes, but these folks have a neat system of keeping the walking paths open. The road is completely blocked. The radio says there will be more snow with no end in sight. What is going on?"

LaCluae grabbed the phone from her. "Hey boss, the short little angry woman just showed up. She has a small force with her. She is marching them toward the crest of the hill."

"How long ago?"

"That's why I grabbed the phone. The small rock in the middle of their square lit up bright red. They are wearing blood red armor like the short angry lady."

"Ok, see if you can find a place to hide out. She really has it out for me and you two. She is extremely..." Patriksen was unable to finish speaking, as static came from the other end.

"Crap!" Patriksen restrained in the pod's harness restricted his movements.

"What is wrong?" Matelina asked.

"Dezire is at Mount Salmo with these so called 'Bloodbreakers' and I just lost contact with my agents."

"I see." She took a small stone from her pocket. She placed it in front of her eye and it took her across the continent in an aerial view. She counted about 500 Bloodbreakers forming up on the crest of the hill where they could either march on Ruan or somewhere close in Washington State, most likely Ione. "We can't do anything about this yet." Matelina responded as she placed the small stone back in her pocket. "They have two choices, marching on Ruan or somewhere here, like the small town of Ione. It is hard to determine at this point, but it is clear the threat is real. You have

320

The Kluanarians

the full support of the Fraust and all of Kluanaria. I do believe that they will advance on any military or governmental facility to disrupt security."

"Why has Dezire chosen to call them Bloodbreakers?"

Chorlanda answered as Matelina was in deep thought. "They are called Bloodbreakers, as the spells they can cast are mostly of absolute cold, which causes blood to break down in their targets, so the enemy does not stand much of a chance. This unending snow is a result of their combined 'Bitter Winter' spell. There are only handfuls that can break this very powerful cast."

"I see." Patriksen said. "I think it is time to put this bird down and seek out General Thomas. He will be the most open minded and is a trusted ally to my team."

The pod landed softly in the courtyard of the Pentagon. Chorlanda cast invisibility on the craft and them so they could get to General Thomas quickly.

Patriksen led the group down a special passage that entered to the rear of Thomas' office, where they found him answering his phone which had all the lines full. "General Thomas." Agent Patriksen said as he walked toward the general.

"Ah, Agent Patriksen. What brings you here today? I hope you have some better news."

"You don't seem surprised to see us, sir."

"No, the UN got through on the red line and said to expect you. It seems as the once ruling monarchs have returned to power to help resolve this international crisis."

"Yes, the monarchs are extending their power in an effort to stop this nightmare. But right now, their sole purpose is salvaging every life that can be saved. My people are supporting them with evacuations and whatever else is needed." Matelina answered.

"Who the hell are you?" General Thomas stood as he looked at the lady standing before him wearing leather armor. "Where are you from?"

"I am Matelina, the ruler of all Kluanaria, which is a world out of phase with yours. We share some same points where our world's overlap and people can transit between. This endless snowstorm is a result of one who wishes total domination of both worlds."

"What do you intend to do to stop this? Many, many countries do not have the correct materials to survive this for very long."

"That is why everyone is being evacuated. We have space in our crafts to accommodate everyone. We will then begin to stop..." she was cut off.

"Craft? Like spacecraft?"

"Yes." Agent Patriksen chimed in. "Matelina has been kind enough to provide the world refuge on her spacecraft. It is not so outrageous. There are thousands of vessels a few for each country, so that all the survivors will have food, clothing, and shelter, while we figure out how to stop this attack."

"Why is it so easy to believe this...I wonder. How long have your ships been coming here?" General Thomas inquired.

"Only since last night, we fully abide by the treaty your world leaders have signed with us, and one of those provisions is to support you world when it is in imminent danger from our side of the Veil. Omiporici and I will accompany Ermenya to Riftan."

Omiporici nodded, "Shall I summon her?"

"No, she is here already." Ermenya said as she appeared in the center of the room.

General Thomas watched as she went from a small crystal dragon into a humanoid form. "Whaaa..."

"Yes, General. I am a dragon. We are here to save your planet and ours. We have a common enemy who has gained favor of Arkronde, the gate keeper."

"What does he do?" The General asked as he paced back and forth.

Omiporici spoke. "Sir, he can open a portal to basically anywhere in Kluanaria and here, on Earth. Nebulos is the ruler of Riftan and has been kept in the dark for the past few months. He was busy in trying to deal with a battle on our world. Mithdrool reigned chaos with Llylandra and Jaetoth. It was quite a relief to see Newlings handle that trio with very little help."

"Will they be able to assist us?"

"We have our elders working with your many countries right now. The Newlings are in Bittern receiving specialized training to deal with the Bloodbreakers." Omiporici added.

Agent Patriksen interjected. "Now the reason we are, General, is to request the support of all of the military in evacuating areas that are near these five points." He laid a map out with circles around key locations.

"Yellowstone and Tuya? What is their significance?"

"Well, sir, if Dezire can dump enough snow on Yellowstone, she could potentially trigger a major eruption which would as you know set us back several years and kill millions. I am not sure on Tuya. It is a volcano." Agent Patriksen overlapped the Kluanarian map. "And Edziza, in Kluanaria somehow matches up with Canada's extinct volcano, Mt. Edziza. I believe they are trying to cause a rift between the two worlds which would cause a mass eruption on both sides of the Veil." Agent Patriksen kept staring at the map. "It also has a couple other potential volcanoes, one in Russia and one in South America that look to link up to a significant location in Kluanaria." He thought to himself. "*This is the end of the world. This is going to be the end of everything.*"

GARETH, GUILLES, AND THE NEWLINGS

In the Hall of Fraust, the Newlings were being taught how to combat cold snaps used by the Bloodbreakers. They listened to Rellos cover the history of the Fraust and how Bloodbreakers came to be. Several Fraust separated the Newlings by their Order and instructed them on how to break various cold snaps, as the Fraust and Bloodbreakers, named their spells. Each Order had to be trained differently as some were more vulnerable than others. Paul had been returned to Krosslaen where he was in counsel with William and Freiderich.

Tatiana approached Guilles and began asking questions. "Where is Paul? Where is Edwina? Where are mommy and daddy? Why don't I need to do this dumb cold repels?"

"Young one, you don't need these spells as you already have mastered them. Paul and your friend, Thallas, are now in Krosslaen for their protection. Rynylla decided it would be safer for Thallas than Chorlanda's ship. Edwina is with the Moons already on Earth, saving lives. Your Aunt has unleashed a very bad cold snap with her friends over both Kluanaria and Earth. Right now, your mom and dad are helping there as well. Your Grandmothers, Kira and Malificence are waiting to see you."

"Ok. So, what am I supposed to do? I did kill Thanias and I didn't even apologize…"

"Don't worry about that. Thanias understands why and has accepted it. He is whole again and will be your main guide. He will be with you during this battle, as he had a lot of experience in fighting the Bloodbreakers."

"I don't want to hurt anymore people."

The Kluanarians

Kira and Malificence nodded to Guilles as they entered the room. They both hugged Tatiana.

"Together we will be able to stop them. But you have to be strong and do what needs to be done." Kira said. "So, please, just do what you are told, when you are told. That will go a long way."

"Yes Grandma." Tatiana said. "I will do my best."

Malificence added, "Oh, your Uncle is here to see you. He is over there." She pointed in Thanias' direction. "So, hop to it lass. Apologize and you will feel better."

Tatiana nodded and ran toward Thanias. I slight wind picked her up and she barely slowed before running in to him.

Kira and Malificence then turned to Guilles to discuss the role of the Newlings in this massive battle that was unfolding before them.

Guilles laid out a map with the common points marked. "Ermenya and company will be seeking counsel with Nebulos. He is unaware of Arkronde's present involvement with Dezire and her Bloodbreakers. We need to hope they will be in time. We have a shade in Riftan who reports to us daily of the Bloodbreakers' movements and it is quite alarming." He placed small crimson beads on the map where the enemy was forming up.

"Well, this is of interest, eh, Malificence?"

"Yes, indeed, Kira. Indeed. They look to be preparing to exploit the volcanism of the Earth and the remnants of Krosslaen, err, Edziza."

"Yes, ladies. That they are. I am suggesting that we place Veil Guards there, as they are unstoppable and can lock down the Bloodbreakers, one by one."

"There are too many to do that." A weary voice said as his body emerged.

"Zanor, what happened?"

"Well, you know how things go with the high counsel, with the local Orders, and of course, with countless little rug rats. We are going to need to act now."

"But how, we aren't enough. Our people are scattered across Earth right now trying to save them. The Newlings…"

"The Newlings are ready. I have seen them do too many things, unthinkable things, for me to say any different would be a lie. Now if you

Brenda M. Hokenson

don't mind. I am headed to Riftan. Ermenya and her group will meet there within the hour."

"What of Arkronde?"

"Kira, don't worry about him. A shade has his full attention for the next while and all will be just fine. Trust me."

"Last time you said that, Harold became part of the family through Iris."

Malificence smiled. "Very true. So, I say we go tend to the Newlings and check with the Fraust to see how the cold is working for the kids." The two ladies departed as Guilles met with Zanor.

"Sire, it is prudent we move at once. They are still vulnerable." Guilles paused as Rellos approached. "Rellos are the Newlings…"

"Yes, they are ready. I have not seen such strength in any individual as I do in these fine children. You do realize that the Fraust will not let them go alone into battle?"

"No. No we were unaware." Zanor responded.

"It was Matelina's last order to us. To ensure the safety of the Newlings while this massive battle carries on. I am hoping to stifle it before it starts however."

"Agreed." Guilles said. "Shall we go now?" He scratched the air in front of him creating a small tear for the three to get through. As it opened fully, he and the other two stepped through, and then the tear closed.

As the portal opened, Gareth welcomed them. "Welcome to Riftan. Ermenya is here with the group from Earth."

The group looked around. Riftan's threshold to the great seat was very open. It seemed devoid of energy. The ground had numerous boiling pools of different colors. Trees line the walkway. They appeared to turn toward the winds but not shed leaves. As they approached the final step, a fierce wind blew through the cavernous opening. It was neither hot nor cold. But it seemed to be disturbed.

"I think Arkronde has damaged Riftan." Gareth spoke in a low voice. "I have been here several times and know that this isn't normal."

"Normal or not, we need Nebulos." Guilles reminded them. "Ah, Ermenya. I hope your journey went well."

"Yes Guilles, it went well. Now let us press on while the Rift Lord is still about."

The group reached the high seat of Riftan and found Nebulos studying a map. He did not look up when he spoke. "Ermenya and the Orders. How lovely to have you here. I am assuming this has something to do with a lost child of Matelina's?"

"Yes, lord." Zanor knelt with the other Orders. "We need your aid."

"Of course you do. But I cannot help you at this time."

"Why?" Ermenya asked calmly. "Are you aware Dezire has moved Bloodbreakers to Earth and has devastated the majority of that world?"

"I am quite aware of this activity. But I still cannot assist you."

"Again, I ask why."

"Because this is my land and the only time you are ever here is because you need my help. I am an Order and I have things that need dealt with. I was nice in helping the Newlings earlier."

"You. You helped the Newlings."

"Yes. A small child about 13 in our years, named Tatiana, visited me for more than two months. She has quite a powerful gift." He opened his hand and the image of he and Tatiana visiting appeared in the palm of his hand. "She will be the future leader of the High Counsel. Oh yes, Menosh is also here."

"Tatiana was here."

"Is that so shocking, Zanor? She is the only being I have ever found to be thorough in tracking down folks and asking tough questions. Oh yes, she needs a new notepad, before I forget."

"You gave her lessons?"

"Of course, I did. She is the only one worthy enough to ever receive training from me. Tatiana will be your key. When my time comes, I will have that small Interval take over Riftan, as she is fair and very wise for her age."

"You do realize she killed Thanias?"

"I am quite aware of what every single person in each Order is doing everyday all day. Opening rifts is nothing. She has given me hope that the evil will quell itself."

"Nebulos. What are you exactly saying?" Ermenya spoke as she advanced toward him with her crystal claws ready.

"Easy, lady dragon. I will aid you, but only if Tatiana is willing to also help. She is having problems right now in deciding which side is right."

"How can that be?"

"Dezire met her and explained her side of the story. Well, you know she is very power hungry since she gave up her claims to the thrones in Kluanaria. She made up this long drawn out story about how it really wasn't and Tatiana is slowly digesting what she was told by her aunt. I am sure she will be fine in a few more days."

"She is with Thanias right now, so hopefully he can help her." Gareth said.

"Either way, you are wasting my time. Tell me what you need right now that will aid your cause?"

"Nebulos. We need you to open the rifts that were opened for Dezire and use the Winds of Retreat."

"Hmm. I haven't had to use that yet. I will think about it. In the mean time. Please join me for supper." He clapped his hands and a large table filled with food and lined with chairs materialized. "Well, don't just stand there, sit down; eat up."

The group obliged their host and joined him for supper. They discussed the last two counsel sessions and the visitors in Treah. They talked highly of Tatiana's decisiveness and thought processes.

While the group dined with Nebulos, the Newlings in the Fraust citadel were honing newly found skills. Skills that would protect them in the inevitable battle that was upon them. Thoughts ran rampant. *'Where will the battle be? Will we succeed? How many will die? Will both planets freeze forever? Will the people of Earth attack us?'*

Many members of the Fraust saw these questions, as they had been through many wars, but not as children. Rellos then required that the Newlings be assigned a Shade. Shades would be able suppress all thoughts that would cause the children to worry and lose focus. The Shade assigned to each Newling became a guardian in battle and in peace. It is the first time ever that Shades were allowed to accompany non-Fraust Orders. Rellos sent his Shade to Matelina with this information. She however, was not pleased. After her meal with Nebulos, she decided to end the visit.

"Nebulos, we have been allies for many, many years. I understand that you believe Tatiana will be your replacement, but it is too soon to tell. She has so much more to accomplish in her lifetime before she chooses her path."

"Matelina, she will be the decisive key in the war that is on our doorstep. She has listened well to Dezire. Has she given you that courtesy?"

"I will have your cooperation, Nebulos. Arkronde has betrayed you and you still sit upon your throne with no clue of the totality of his deception." As she finished speaking, she looked at Guilles who immediately opened a small tear and the group departed.

Once they were in the Fraust citadel, Gareth spoke. "Matelina, our true leader, we must make the first move. It is recorded in our history that every time we wait, we lose that battle."

"What are you proposing, Gareth?" Guilles inquired as he walked with the group toward the battle planners.

"Well, seeming that we have many of us already on Earth, trying to save their people, we may have an advantage. The Zephyrs and Sprites are neutral for the most part. We can use them to determine the necessity for us to support certain areas more, allowing more favorable results in saving the people. At the same time, as they travel so quickly, they can report where the Bloodbreakers are staged. We can use this to deploy the Fraust, Chrinthold, Truncheon, and Eupepsians in. We will request that Shadowblyts and Izmaa join us."

"Hmm. I believe that the dark orders will accept your request. Please allow us to do the transport, as we have ways through the Veil that are less damaging to it, especially since it was recently restored." Guilles responded with a smile. I will send word to Rithmas who will send word to their leader."

"Where is she?" Matelina inquired. "She has not been seen for 20 years."

"Well, she passed and the Shadowblyts never bothered to replace her."

"So tell me who will make the decision to involve them?" Matelina asked as she walked closer to Guilles.

"Well... Umm..."

"Enough. As Supreme Ruler, I command all Orders to assist in the ensuing battle. It will cost many lives. You, as representatives of your

Brenda M. Hokenson

Orders, will support me, as the Fraust and a handful of folks have protected you for some many centuries now. We are bound to protect our world and that of Earth. The Bloodbreakers must be stopped at any cost!" Matelina paused, swirled her hand in front of her which created what looked to be a blizzard in a whirlpool. From that emerged all leaders of the Orders and higher-ranking members as well. "You heard my message. Gareth will now deploy the Zephyrs and Sprites. This will be our only window of opportunity."

Gareth nodded and sent out the Zephyrs and Sprites. "We will need to be ready for immediate redeployment of the vessels circling Earth. Simmons will communicate directly with Kren who is aboard Chorlanda's vessel, since the Zephyrs and Sprites are reporting directly to him. We will be able to send forces rapidly to meet the Bloodbreakers head on." He spoke very loud and was gesturing as if obsessed with the upcoming battles.

"Calm down Gareth." Rellos spoke as he entered the room. He first knelt before Matelina. "The Newlings have Shades who will be with them through this ordeal."

"Who authorized the use of Shades in this manner?" Matelina leaned forward in the seat she was in. "We never have used them for this purpose."

"I believe it is in the best interest of all, to use them both as a mentor and protector. Yes, our Fraust did an outstanding job in the Newlings' training. However, the Shades are far more mobile and have some special skills that we do not, which will be beneficial."

"Very well; I will let this pass. If it truly works, we will use them in this manner to enhance our abilities."

Gareth interrupted. "Matelina, the Bloodbreakers have a main base in a fairly remote location, south of Mount Salmo in some rolling hills. The town is almost non-existent, other than in name, Elberton."

"Is there a place we can form up without being conspicuous?"

"I am looking now. Hmm. That area is farmland, two buttes, and a string of mountains to the east. So I am thinking here." Gareth pointed to a raised but of land directly north of Elberton. It does not appear to be occupied and would give us a slight advantage. We will be able to look down towards the Bloodbreakers."

"Very well. How many are in their group?" Matelina inquired.

"Approximately 100, I am sure there are more on the way."

The group examined the map for some time. Guilles and Rithmas approached Matelina. Rithmas spoke first. "Your Excellency, I would like to extend the support of all Shadowblyts. We have received word from a Zephyr who said the snow has stopped falling across all of Earth. I believe right now would be a bad time to advance. Their focus is moving troops when the snow stops. We have seen it during many of the wars where the Fraust would be relatively quiet, as in no blizzards, while they did two things. The first was regenerating all the spent energy and the second being moving troops. You should be aware of this, as you are Fraust."

"True, very true. It has been some time since I have seen battle. I fear this shall be my last." Matelina returned to her throne and sat down again. "Prepare for battle. I want a minimum of 75 Fraust, 100 Truncheon, 30 Chrinthold, 20 Eupepsians, and about 45 Shadowblyts and or Izmaa for this. We will go in and use extreme force. Leave no one alive. I will request Shades to retrieve the deceased as this battle progresses." The Council looked back and forth at each other, unsure of what to say or do next. "What is the matter with all of you? This is war and you need to suck it up and send your people to battle. The keystone in the Fraust citadel will be the rendezvous and departure point for Elberton. Now get moving! Our window of opportunity is very brief."

Everyone leapt out of their seats and frantically contacted their members for immediate action. The Newlings awoke at the witching hour and heard raised voices echoing through the long corridors. Unsure of what was going on, Irra and Tatiana poked their heads out a door. They tiptoed toward the commotion and hid in the shadows. Curiosity overwhelmed them when they saw the Orders in full battle gear. The two moved closer toward the keystone and watched as the Orders formed into small groups, all equally balanced with the different abilities.

A Shade spotted them and spoke to Kira, who then approached Matelina. The two women walked over toward the pillar and grabbed the girls. Kira spoke first. "Tatiana, you know better than to meddle. It is not yet time for the Newlings. I want you to return to your rooms at once!"

Tatiana glared at her grandmother. Matelina added, "If you don't get there within the next minute, you will become one of my statues!"

The two girls squealed and ran like lightning down the hallway. The heavy oaken door slammed shut behind them and a Shade was placed as a sentry to monitor movements of both dorms.

Meanwhile in Earth's orbit, Chorlanda and her vessels continued rescuing folks. The Orders already in place did their best to save everyone. General Thomas paced as the snow stopped falling. Agent Patriksen was able to get through to his agents.

Agent Dunwoody answered the satellite phone. "Agent Dunwoody."

"This is Patriksen, what is your status?"

"Our status, where are you?"

"Hovering above the Pentagon. Now update me."

"The short angry woman is here. There is word of a formation in a small abandoned town south of here probably 100 miles. Probably 2 hours from Spokane. Not sure on time, as I have never ventured south of the city. Arkronde, not sure who he is, arrived this evening and unsure of the next …"

Agent LaCluae took the phone from her. "Hi Boss. I hope I am not interrupting, but I just came back from supper and well, the angry woman and a man were in the lounge."

"And she didn't fling you into another wall?"

"Well, no. I apologized and was asking questions."

"And…"

"Well, since you had me research their culture, I took that approach. It appears this angry short woman is exacting revenge on her brothers, all 3 of them. They somehow got all of the powers granted by the Supreme Ruler and she got nothing. She also is aware of our planet and its many thousands or more cultures. She has pretty much laid waste to the entire planet. During the no snow periods, her troops are resting."

"Thank you LaCluae. Keep up the questions. We need to…" The satellite phone died. "Darn it."

"Well, if you would have gotten to the point faster it wouldn't have died."

Agent LaCluae turned around. "Well, it sure wouldn't have anything to

The Kluanarians

do with them standing in the doorway either, now would it, Dunwoody." He looked at Arkronde and Dezire with a sheepish grin.

"Boy, you are asking for so much pain right about now." Dezire said as she entered the room. "But no matter. Your efforts are fruitless; we already have begun the purging of this planet, starting with Ione. We are called Bloodbreakers because of our cold spells. We can slowly freeze our enemy from the inside out, causing the blood to separate in the veins and arteries. Then our enemy's hearts beat faster and poof, no more enemies. What do you think, hmm, LaCluae?"

"I think you are a sick, twisted, angry short lady who..." Dezire cut him off in mid-sentence as she physically tossed him across the room.

"Do you want to die by polearm or broken blood?"

"I prefer neither."

Dezire found the satellite phone and immediately crushed it with her fist. "No more phone calls." Arkronde followed her out of the room. "Watch them closely Arkronde. I do not trust them.

Emilae was cleaning the last dishes of the evening when Dezire returned. She tried not to notice her pass through to exit the building. She knew something terrible would happen. About a minute later there was an explosion. The two government vehicles had launched into the air about 75 feet and burst into flames. The vehicles crashed through the Kluanarian equivalent of church and burst into flames in the explosion. Emilae shook her head and prayed for help.

Next, Dezire walked up the hill to the Veil and forced a staff into the ground at the exact location of the Veil. Electricity filled the area around the Veil point. The Veil seemed to shake momentarily. A passing Zephyr noticed this and immediately returned to the Fraust citadel.

LaCluae and Dunwoody stared in awe at the flaming church with two cars sticking partially out of it. "What do we do now?" Dunwoody asked. "How do we escape?"

"I think it is too late for escape. We need to survive. Luckily for you, I found a secret hiding place."

"Oh really? Just where might this place be."

"It is under the bed. There is a trap door. Emilae showed it to me when we checked in, for just in case. She said no magic can enter it."

"So how do we get in there?"

Brenda M. Hokenson

"Carefully. Follow me." LaCluae low crawled and reached under the bed. He found a small latch that opened the hatch and the two crawled into the space. It was a rather large space, but that was expected as the Kluanarians were well versed in magical rooms. "Wow, this is massive. It seems to be solid. Look two twins and everything else we could need."

"Just how long do you think we will be stuck here, hiding from that short lunatic?" Dunwoody said as she paced about the room with her arms crossed.

"I don't know, but I am going to make the most of this time. Maybe write my will…"

"Shh, someone is above us." Dunwoody interrupted.

The two became very quiet as they listened to the footsteps and rummaging. "Darn it. They are gone, luggage and all."

"They couldn't have gone far with their cars lodged in the spiritual center and burning." The intruders left.

"That was close. Where is our luggage?" LaCluae mused.

"Oh, I moved them down here while you were looking around, right before you sealed us in here." Dunwoody said. "By the way, I still have Weisjord's sat phone."

"He gave you his sat phone?"

"Yes, do you have a problem with that?"

"Yes…Err, no. Just weird, that's all. Are you dating him now?"

"Where did that come from?"

"Just asking."

"It isn't your business. Right now, we need to see if we can call Patriksen." Dunwoody responded.

"Well, I think you are chasing a man out of your league."

"Let it go LaClueless. Ahh here we go." The satellite phone had a tone finally. She quickly dialed their boss.

"Agent Patriksen."

"This is Dunwoody, you need to tell someone in charge that that little woman just launched the cars into the air, and they landed on the spiritual center here with a massive explosion. LaCluae opened his mouth and got flung across the room…"

"Where are you at?"

The Kluanarians

LaCluae took the phone from Dunwoody. "Thanks a lot! Hey boss, Emilae showed me a secret hiding place and so far, it seems to be ok."

"Well, stay low for now. Is there food in there?"

"Yes, it seems to 'materialize' on schedule with the timing of the meals at the Inn."

"Good then, sit tight. I am not sure how long you will be in there, so I won't tie up the phone. I will call you when we are able to get you out."

"Ok, good luck boss, and watch out."

"For what?"

"Well, on top of the cars and church, she also wedged a staff in the Veil contact point. It arced and sparked and then she walked off."

"Good to know. I will let the Kluanarians know." Patriksen hung up.

"It's just you and me for a while now, I guess." Agent LaCluae said as he paced about.

"Yes, it is." Dunwoody said as she settled in to her part of the room, unpacking her belongings and finding a book.

Dezire had moved on to Ione. Her Bloodbreakers decimated the sleepy town on a scenic route within five minutes of arrival. Everything froze in place, people collapsed from severe hypothermia. The snow advanced ahead of them on their route. From Ione, Dezire's troop split going both westward and southward. Arkronde created a rift for the groups to go through to get to the next two destinations more quickly.

ELBERTON

Dezire left her two groups to their own devices to carry out annihilation as they crossed the state. She and Arkronde journeyed to Elberton, a town with a church and collapsing buildings surrounding it. She mused remember passing through Bucyrus, South Dakota thinking the same thing, 'What a great place to be and not be noticed.' She had the 100 Bloodbreakers assembled there reconstructing the collapsing buildings and rebuild the ones that had fallen. "This will be our Seat of Rule! This will be the new 'Founders' Day."

Her Order applauded her and quickly got to work on the rebuild. They were very resourceful in materials. Arkronde created a rift to Treah, where they could quietly take trees from the far side of the land and not be noticed. Shades were present and could make themselves rather large, so they handled bracing the support beams and roof structures while the Bloodbreakers hammered.

The day was clear and no snow was on the ground in the area. She noticed the old rail station remnants and decided it would be good to restore this. She personally took on the rail station. After six hours of work, food was served in the newly established inn. The tired turned in after supper. The next day would be peaceful, as Dezire had a schedule that had a rest day in between difficult days, except during war.

As the men and women slept, Dezire asked Arkronde if it was possible to see Elberton as a whole, before it was deserted. He poured water into a small scrying bowl. "Be patient, this is very old and not sure if any will make sense to you."

The image played out on the water. *Elberton, in its prime had a substantial population for the area. Two mills along with the railroad helped shape its future. It started dying in the 1930s and a fire that destroyed the majority of the town pushed more folks out of the area.* The image sped up to present day where it showed a few outlying farmsteads and a confidence course. The image ended and the water evaporated. Dezire knew at that moment that this will be the site of resurrection and revitalization. She decided that her leatherworker could help design their Order's crest.

As Dezire and Arkronde turned in for the night, Rynylla led the Orders to a small ridgeline overlooking the town that had been raised from the dead. They set up a camp, with patrols, while the rest bedded down for the night. Rynn and Wryn were part of the observation force. Rynylla spoke to them briefly. "I realize Dezire is your aunt and this could be difficult for you…"

"It is ok, we have accepted this a long time ago, when she first started turning. She slowly turned many, to include our cousin, Thanias. The laws of Kluanaria will be upheld and we will save as many people of Earth as we can." Wryn said as he paced.

They heard a familiar screech coming from the town. "They brought Trincotts." Rynn said as she halted the patrol. "We need to stay under complete cover. Do we have a Moon, Shadowblyt or Izmaa with us?"

"Yes." Phoelicia responded as she walked into the moonlight. "I am the head of the Izmaa, and I will secure our zone."

"When did the Trincotts join them?" Gareth asked as he arrived at the base camp.

"Well, I am thinking that since the Bloodbreakers are inherently evil, the Trincotts easily joined them." Rynn answered.

"But, how do they communicate with the Bloodbreakers?" Gareth asked.

"They don't have to; they probably were near a rift and went through with the Bloodbreakers." Rynn responded.

"Well thank goodness the Newlings are far from here. This would be a bit much, especially after the rescue of Edwina from Kilowas Vale. Those wonderful girls from the Shadowblyts and Izmaa were very well versed, but not strong enough. They are going to be very powerful within their Orders." Gareth added.

Wryn posed a question. "If Trincotts are here, I am sure that they have Shades, but do they have deadmages and Mithdrool's warlocks?"

"Only time will tell." Rynylla responded. "Tomas will be joining us in two days. He is visiting with his family and friends."

"He is too young!" Gareth said in a loud whisper, so as to not draw the Trincotts. "He is not much older than Edwina."

"He is of age and has volunteered. He is doing this for Edwina, for he is connected with her in some manner and wants to end this."

"Did he train with the Fraust?"

"He had advanced training with them over the summer before I sent him as the Chrinthold escort for Dezire. He is why we have the knowledge we have now."

"Does Dezire know?"

"That is an unknown at this time. What we do know is that she believes his family needed him for crops and the store." Rynylla responded. "I suggest we get rest, or we won't be prepared in body."

The encampment consisted of about 40 tents with floating cots and a stove that used rocks heated by dragons, which did not cool for weeks. Each person had a footlocker and table with washing bowl. There was a stream to east of the site where fresh water could be collected. Since it was winter, the stream was frozen solid, so the small army became resourceful in collecting the water.

Rynylla used a small scrying bowl to peer into Elberton and see what the Bloodbreakers were doing. She found the streets mostly covered in grass but could see the construction going on. A message came to her through the scrying bowl, so she placed her finger in the water to attune to it. It showed the staff at Mount Salmo in the Veil contact point with electrical energy surging through it. It was beginning to make sense. She went to Rynn. "Your aunt is creating a new Veil contact point here. I am not certain how this will play out, but it potentially means that her armies near Mount Salmo can easily get here, and from Ruan."

Rynn sat up. "Thanias said this was being tested and that is why the

Veil was so weak over the past 7 months. That is why Thallas did the Veil strengthening in Ruan. We need to warn Ermenya."

"Warn her of what?"

"When I was captive in Mithdrool's dungeon, Thanias did not know I was able to get out of the prison and wander about. I found this." She removed an object from the base of her arrow quiver. "I think this can be used to destroy Krosslaen."

Rynylla took the small object from the older Newling. "It is more than that. It is a key to another place. If taken to Krosslaen and if the correct incantation was used, it would open up another dimension, the dragons' home world. This has been lost since the Battle of Edziza and maybe before then."

"What do we need to do now?" Wryn asked as the whispering stirred him from his sleep.

"We need to get it to the dragons of Krosslaen." Rynylla replied. "For now, keep it in your quiver until I figure out how to get it there without a lot of folks knowing about it."

The twins nodded and drifted to sleep. Rynylla returned to her floating cot and removed a small stone from a pouch. She placed it against her forehead and directed her immediate thoughts to Lucien. *'The dragons' gate has been recovered. We must get it to Krosslaen. Trincotts are here.'* She then returned the small stone to the pouch and went to sleep.

When dawn broke, Rynn was in the command tent speaking with Lucien who arrived in the late hours. She told him of how she came of it and told him of the room in Kilowas Vale where it had been removed by Mithdrool. She spoke of Jaetoth, who had access to many secret rooms. She spoke of Thanias, who was kind to her even while she was imprisoned by his cohorts at the time. She spoke of her escape with Thanias aid and of the map, also in her quiver. "We must not let them have this. The dragons guard this and will fight to the death to protect it."

"I understand. You will accompany me to Krosslaen and we will more than likely have an important task." Lucien answered.

Rynn agreed. She gathered her belongings and spoke to her brother about the events taking place. She and Lucien departed through Wryn's portal to Krosslaen.

In the meantime, the encampment slowly woke from peaceful sleep and Gareth had arrived to record everything imaginable. He also had an observation lens which allowed him to see the happenings in Elberton. He had gone to the museums in the county and gleaned as much detail about Elberton as possible. Gareth had Paul assist from afar on anything recorded on computers. He noticed the buildings erected were as they were in the prime of Elberton's days. His attention turned to electricity in the air around the old railroad depot. "Darn it!"

"What is wrong Gareth?" Rynylla said as she approached him on the grassy knoll.

"The depot, more exactly the train terminal, outside, is the Veil contact point. It is set to be where the folks would have tied their horses or pulled coaches up to it on the entry side. So what that means is that Dezire wants to bring folks here, like in Ruan, but I am thinking for their destruction. But only time will tell."

"Tell me this Gareth, why is there a normal amount of snow here but everywhere else, to include Kluanaria, it is completely buried with few survivors here?"

"The Bloodbreakers stronghold, and it gives them immediate access to both Mount Salmo and…And I don't know where the actual connection in Kluanaria will be. Once that is established, she won't need to keep Mount Salmo's contact and will likely raze it. Why the difference in snow, I am afraid to know. Very few have that kind of power, if any still exist."

"We need to get Regence and his community out of there, now!" Rynylla said almost yelling. "And start working on the snow issue!"

Gareth had a communication device that would allow him to speak with the vessels in orbit. "Chorlanda do you read?"

"Yes, Gareth."

"Mount Salmo will be razed. Evacuate the village. Repeat, evacuate the village."

"Understood, Sentinel is enroute to Salmo."

Dezire woke to a bright sunshine coming through the window. She walked over and looked out at the construction from the previous day. Much had been done already. She had a special meal prepared for all of the

The Kluanarians

Shades and Trincotts. She then turned her attention to the still slumbering Bloodbreakers. A spell was cast so that as each would wake, their meal would be ready for them, like breakfast in bed. She worked them hard in the reconstruction of Elberton and wanted to do something special.

She then went to her floating cot and pulled out a small seeing stone. She homed in on her two companies that were marching southward and westward. She watched each town fall rather quickly. She was contented as no blood was spilled, just frozen bodies. She pulled out her scrying bowl and spoke to the two leaders. "Regroup on the west's flank to work through the larger cities. It is imperative that none survive. Do check for gifted children, as they are Newlings and don't know it. I want them trained in Kluanaria." She then ended her communications and prepared her meal.

Arkronde arrived at her quarters a short while later. "My lady." He knelt as always. "How was your sleep?"

"Restful. I am glad I chose this location for the contact point. It is very peaceful and out of the way enough to not cause prying eyes."

"I must say the construction is magnificent. I walked the grounds this morning and found no trace of the enemy. But I think it is only a matter of time…"

"Until what dear?" Dezire stood and walked to the window where Arkronde was standing.

"You know they have an uncanny knack for meddling."

"I have something in store for them. I know they are on that ridgeline, by the way the Trincotts kept circling it. They will not like the results if they interfere."

"Ok, what is the plan then?"

"Mount Salmo has already been razed, first of all. I had that done last night. I am not actually setting up a contact point, just wanted to draw their attention away from my razing of Salmo Village and of the deaths in all of the towns in cities headed westward and southward. It was the perfect diversion."

"Most excellent. What do you need from me?"

"Mostly, I need your support. I cannot do this alone and I trust you. I never ask for help as you know, but this, this is going to be very difficult, and I am not strong enough alone to handle all of the aspects."

"Thank you for your confidence in me."

"No, it is I who is thankful to you. I would not have gone this course without your support. We will be as one." She smiled and hugged Arkronde. "We are as one. This will be our home. This evening I would like you to open a rift so that our forces may retreat back to my keep, which will greatly confuse the Orders. The town will stay. I think we will change plans slightly and finish it today. After our great feast, we can all venture through the rift."

"Very well, I will speak to the Bloodbreakers on your behalf, Dezire. Rest for now, work will begin within the hour." Arkronde walked off and found them gathered in the depot eating their breakfast. "Today, Dezire has asked us to change the schedule up, as the Orders are watching. She would like us to finish this build today, and after supper, I will open a rift in which we will return to the keep for rest and visitation of the families. Trincotts will return also. This is to keep the Orders guessing as to what is going on. Please raise your hands if you have an issue with this request."

No one raised their hands, but cheering broke out. Dezire entered the room and more jubilation radiated from her Bloodbreakers. "You all have been a wonderful asset to me. So, starting tonight, spend time with your families and friends. I will send word when we start the assault. I have two companies advancing to the west. Last night the southward company made it through Garfield and has rejoined the westward unit. They are sparing the Newlings hidden amongst the towns and they will bring them to the keep once they march to the sea. We are leaving the sovereign nations alone on this continent, so it is not completely wiped out."

"Why them?"

"They were here first. Is that good enough for you?"

"Well, it is how wars work. The weak get assimilated."

"Which is why the weak in this war are being annihilated, and I am returning the lands back to the people who respect it."

"I think you need to consider something as this progresses. The Orders see your destruction as open war upon everyone. The march to the sea will take out most of the northwest of this land. We only have so many Bloodbreakers to do this."

"That is why they will have rest for a while. It allows the Orders to withdraw, and it will give me time to assess the damages I have already inflicted."

"Yes, but the continents on or slightly above and below the equator, their populations have been decimated instantly by the cold snaps and massive snow fall. I think the Orders spared a few."

"I am not done yet, Arkronde. I still plan on using some volcanism to quash the resistance."

"There will be no resistance if you go through with this."

"Let it play out. I don't really care about what happens here. I am more interested in seeing what the Orders will do."

"Dezire, my dear, they will strike all Bloodbreakers, deadmages, and warlocks down. We will be purged as we have done in the past to preserve Kluanaria."

"Yes, but I have Riftan behind me. Mother has nothing other than her precious Orders who can't work together for extended periods of time. I want it to be known on both realms that I am the true Supreme Ruler."

As the conversation ended, the two strolled out and watched as the Bloodbreakers and Shades finished one building at a time. A scribe was out documenting each building and recording the number of workers and length of time it took to make whole again. He had composed a note for the County Commissioner of the restoration of the small town and asked that it be occupied as soon as possible. He also drafted letters to the newspapers and had included photos. He then turned to Dezire, "How would you like me to get these to their destinations?"

"Trincotts can deliver them very efficiently. I think that will be all. Spokane has not been frozen yet, so there should be someone there to receive the notes. As for west of here, that is a very different story."

"Why did you spare Spokane?" The scribe asked.

"It is a temporary thing, but they have what they call news media that will be to our benefit shortly."

"Understood." The scribe returned to his documenting.

Gareth became antsy on the ridgeline overlooking Elberton. He had a bad feeling of things to come. "You know, Rynylla. Things are too calm over there. I think we missed something important somewhere along the line."

Brenda M. Hokenson

"I agree, but I am not sure where to start."

"Sir, it's a message from Regence. He is with Chorlanda recovering folks."

"Well, let me see." Gareth and Rynylla raced into the command tent and looked into the scrying bowl. "What is it man? We are observing Dezire and her Bloodbreakers."

Regence looked terrible and his voice sounded worse. "They…They are all dead…My village is gone. The folks were all…" He choked up worse. "Burnt alive as they slept."

Gareth looked at Rynylla in awe. "We have been watching them…"

"Are you really that stupid Gareth?" Regence asked. "Dezire split her forces. She purposely led you to Elberton. In fact there is probably not much happening in Elberton. We have passed to the west of Mount Salmo…" He choked up again. "The Bloodbreakers flashes froze everything west of the village and have converged near a great river. There is nothing left north of these rolling plains. Everything is iced over."

"I am still searching for an answer to the frozen iced over bit. Please be patient. We have never encountered this before." Gareth said as he waited for a command response from Rynylla.

MATELINA'S LEGACY

Rynylla, after Regence closed the scrying, had the encampment return immediately to Fraust Hold. She found the Newlings training with the Shades and Fraust and that Matelina was seated on the throne at the center of the room tapping her fingers on the arm rest. Gareth returned to Chorlanda's vessel to give a report.

"This makes no sense to me, Rynylla. Why did Dezire raze the village? Tell me what is truly happening."

"Matelina, I fear for the worst for the people of Earth. She has frozen the land almost completely yet sparing certain areas. I am thinking she is trying to re-establish Earth back to a more peaceful era. The communities are all continents apart and she seems to be sparing the true sovereigns lands. She seems to be eliminating people she feels are a threat, so all reports must be analyzed."

"That is not helping me! I will vanquish her and imprison her. She has crossed the line."

"How will you stop her? You are very old." Thanias said as he entered the room. "How, Grandmother, will you possibly stop her?"

"I am going to pass knowledge to you."

"Why?"

"True Fraust are not found amongst the Kluanarians. The chosen are given the knowledge and skills from the elders, and well, since I am the Elder, I will pass this to you, as you have seen death and have been restored. I believe that you possess the ability to control your emotions, as they affect the abilities of all Fraust."

Brenda M. Hokenson

"And if I say no?"

"You won't. Someone has to succeed me on this throne." Matelina paused walked to a reflection bowl accompanied by Thanias and reflected on her legacy.

The trees of Treah bloomed as the snow fell to the ground. Matelina of Greystone enjoyed learning healing form the Eupepsians and accompanying the Intervals though out the land. She spent hours studying various Orders and how they came to be. Matelina had friends amongst all of them and would go on adventures, hoping to discover what she would become.

Frustrated with being 'normal', Matelina embarked on a journey that lasted almost three years. She packed one evening in secret, after the evening meal. She said good night to her parents and went to bed. Two hours before dawn, she woke and escaped through the window in her room. The air was heavy with mist and no breeze to be felt. She learned a spell to light her path from an Interval which she used when she reached the edge of Greystone. After a couple hours of brisk walking, she reached the Palisade, where her father was for training.

"Just where do you think you are going Matelina?"

"I am leaving on my adventure, to discover who I am supposed to be."

"Time will tell you who you are supposed to be. You should not go rushing into this, as this cannot be taken lightly."

"I don't understand, Father."

"You have a very important destiny, and your true Order will reveal itself in time. It is not one to take lightly."

"You speak in riddles."

"Matelina, you are only fifteen. You are not ready, but I will not stop you on your so-called adventure. Promise me you will take these seeing stones and this rock of return, for my sake. I am an old man you know."

"I will, father." She bowed before him. His men came to attention and bowed.

"Hail Matelina of Greystone. Hail Matelina of Greystone." The men repeated many times. She could hear it echoing in the valley where her small boat floated on the lazy river, toward the sea.

Matelina paused briefly and observed Thanias mesmerized by this image. She then continued.

At the mouth of the river there were no villages or folks to speak with. She had to rely on all her camping trips with her family and friends. She would have to rely on all the skills the Intervals taught her and many of her other friends. Alone on the sea, at last; she mapped the coastline for several hours and documented formations. Matelina found a small inlet where she navigated her small vessel and set up camp for the night.

The evening was eventless, she wrote in a journal recording her travel and the encounter with her father. She paused and took a seeing stone from her pocket and gazed upon her family. She could hear the conversation between her parents.

"Edgar! How could you let her leave? Are you in your right mind?"

"She is old enough to go off on her own without us hovering over her like she was newly born. She has a very strong presence and I think this will give her a sense of purpose which she is so desperately seeking."

"She is just a girl. She can't do things without…"

"Well, she did and you have to live with it. She is your child, stubborn, pig headed and very moody. Now let me finish my supper woman."

Her mother sobbed. Matelina wiped away a tear as this memory was the dearest to her. *She then placed the seeing stone back in the pouch her father had given her. Her tent was set, and all of her belongings were already placed. As soon as she dowsed the campfire, she pulled the boat amongst some tall bushes and shrubs and then retired to her bed. A small light illuminated her space as she jotted a few more things in the journal and then as she closed her eyes, the light dissipated. The image of her mother arguing with her father the departure amused her.*

Matelina reflected, quite amused by her memories. She went to where Menosh became known to her, and then to her homecoming

As Matelina rowed back to the embankment near the Palisade, her father and some of his Order approached her. Her father spoke to a man who appeared to be a year or so older than her and the man came forward. He pulled the boat to the shore and offered his hand to her. "Welcome home Matelina. We are glad to see your return."

"Do I know you?" Matelina said as she walked past him to her father. "How did you know I would be here?"

Edgar responded, "Matelina, this is Demitri, he is going to be an Elder of the Fraust soon. I asked him to assist you, so you will mind your manners. You

are a lady. And for the second question, I too have seeing stones. At any rate, welcome home. I trust your long journey was to your satisfaction."

"No, it was kind of disappointing, although I have brought some better maps back with me. And there was this creature; he called himself Menosh, who said it was time for me to know."

"Menosh." Edgar began grumbling. "That creature has no business interfering, I don't..."

Demitri approached, "Sir, she can hear you."

"I DON'T CARE! I DON'T CARE. SHE DOES NOT NEED THIS BURDEN! AM I CLEAR?" Edgar shouted toward the formation of the Fraust behind him. "DEMITRI. You take her to my wife. Stay with them until I dismiss you."

Demitri nodded. "Matelina, please come with me. I have a horse ready for you at the stables." He again extended his arm to her. "The Fraust will gather your belongings and transport them."

"The Fraust?"

"Yes, your father is head of the Fraust Order and also oversees Greystone and some other areas.

"So, Demitri, why do you have to stay with my mother and me?"

"That I am not certain of. But if it makes you uncomfortable, I will post outside your home."

"Oh, no. That will be fine."

"Where did your journeys take you? I know your father had kept close eye on you, but he never said where or anything."

"Well, I ended up going around the coast of our lands once, crossed the waters and landed on a sandy beach. I found a very dark forest. Something about it makes me uneasy. I keep having images."

"Well, if you want to talk, I will listen. Oh look, the stable. That was faster than I thought it would be. Here let me help you up, lady." He helped Matelina mount the steed. "I just want you to know that I was required to follow you and study your interactions with the folk of this world, both hostile and friendly. You have the balance necessary to be a Fraust. And I think this is what you father is upset about. I will join you in a moment, please ride ahead."

Matelina teared up as this was one of her treasured memories. She decided it would be okay for Thanias to see the family dynamics. She looked at her Grandson, who smiled, and then she continued.

It was late afternoon as Matelina rode up to her home. Demitri was nowhere to be found. As she dismounted and began walking her horse to the stable, he appeared in front of her. "How did you do that? Where were you?"

"A spell that the Fraust use. I had to gather your belongings and get them to your home."

"How…Why?"

"It is part of Fraust culture. Since your father is the head of the Order and he assigned me to you, I, out of obligation carried out my duties."

Matelina looked furious. "How dare him! How dare you! What is going on?" She began rambling under her breath with tears. "I don't even know what I am supposed to be."

Demitri was not sure what to do so he put his hands on her shoulders. "You are to be a Fraust, your mother does not know but your brothers and sisters have known a long time."

Matelina began to cry and Thanias went to her side and put his arms around his grandmother. "Gramma, this is too painful for you. Please stop."

"No, I … I want you to know how we became who we are now. And I want you to help me find him. He promised." She sobbed harder, "he promised me. Demitri is your grandfather, and I just know he… He is alive."

"I know, Gramma. And I will. How much more do you want to share with me?"

"There is quite a bit more, but you are right. I… I need to rest for a bit. Would you help an old lady to her quarters?"

"Yes Gramma." He escorted her to her room and helped her as needed. He saw a sketch of her and Demitri on the dresser. "Why did you go on the journey? What happened when Grampa Edgar got there? How long has Grampa Demitri been missing"

"I went to see if I could make it on my own. My mother sheltered me; my father let me learn, so he would sneak me off to the Palisade occasionally to be around others of all ages and different Orders. I kind of didn't want to return to Greystone, because I was free, and no one could tell me what to do. Mother was materialistic and wanted me to be that way. You see, my father ruled Greystone and a couple small settlements up to the border with Ruan. Then Mithdrool went through and annihilated

Greystone. Those are the ruins you see on the far side of the Palisade. Anyway, that sort of covers what I would have you see in the vision bowl. There is more for a later time. Father told mother how it would be and, in the yard, did a ceremony for Demitri to become an Elder, as he spoke more Fraust arrived, and all of the other Orders were present. Then he announced that I would be the next ruler and he had Demitri began the ceremony for me. Father had this old table, which is over there in the corner, in the middle of the yard. He began to share knowledge with me, which was very overwhelming."

"So, Great Grampa, he was the Fraust Lord before you?"

"Yes, he was, for an extremely long time. I was married to Demitri about two days after my return and Demitri assumed my duties until I was able to learn my place and learn my duties as a Fraust. My father taught me everything and Demitri taught me a bit more. Mithdrool was a very powerful, devious adversary. The Orders did not trust one another, and it almost wiped the folk off the map. Father perished in the battle and mother was devastated. She found the Veil and was the first to use it. She never returned."

"What happened to Grampa?"

"Well, I know he is alive and is being held. I just don't know where. He is a very strong man and I am sure one day he will return. I just know he will."

"Do you need anything else?" Thanias inquired.

"No, just know that you are a very strong person and what you have overcome has made you who you are. A Shade will accompany you and begin explaining things to you as you sleep."

"Why as I sleep?"

"They can plug into your mind and feed you a lot of information while you are at rest. Now go. Go to sleep and take care of your wife, Ryatt."

Thanias nodded and departed Fraust Hold. He found his wife asleep and covered her. His mind raced with what Matelina could possibly add to what she had just showed him. It couldn't be good. A Shade appeared near Thanias' door and requested entry. It was granted and the Shade had already prepared for the barrage of questions.

"Master Thanias. You grandmother wants you to know her journey took her through Mithdrool's lands, Mercurian, the Sand Caverns, Kaprius,

Krosslaen before the Wars, Vale Kilowas, and various other recorded in this." The Shade handed Thanias a map. On its reverse there was a description of each village and composition of townsfolk. "This journal goes with it. She still writes in it and will until her end."

Thanias took both from his new companion. "I will return the map to her, but please, return this to her now as I think she may have something she wants to add."

The Shade departed with the journal and returned later as Thanias slept. *"Överföra minnen till honom. Överföra kunskap till honom. Överföra förmågor till honom."*

Thanias' mind was flooded with new thoughts and ideas that seemed overwhelming. He tossed and turned for hours as he tried to sleep. Ryatt awoke to him sitting straight up and saying, "I understand." And then lying back down. Thanias slept through breakfast and dinner. The Shade woke him before tea at Ryatt's request.

"Good afternoon Thanias." Ryatt said as she brought him some tea and fresh baked bread. "Your grandmother is in the front room. She looks very serious, so this can't be good."

"Thank you dear. I will change into…" He looked out the window, "The day is over half gone! That was some wild dreaming."

Ryatt nodded. "I will take your drink and bread to the front room then." She left and joined Matelina, who was staring out the window.

"This was our home once. I hope you don't mind me giving it to you and Thanias."

"No. No, ma'am, not at all. We are grateful for your generosity."

"Generosity. Posh. I am doing it because I care about the future of my family, and I have more than enough places to reside. Thanias loved coming here as a child, so it is only natural that he gets it."

"What happened to him yesterday? Thanias came home late and then tossed and turned for hours. Now he is at peace, which I have never seen before in my entire time of knowing him."

"He is a Fraust. Yesterday, I started giving him a lot of family history and last night, a lot of knowledge was given to him. He should be at peace the rest of the time you know him."

"He… He is a Fraust?"

"Yes. Why does that alarm you so?"

Brenda M. Hokenson

"That is the most powerful order, followed closely by the Aantiri who are even rarer. I am not sure how."

"Ah, you doubt his loyalty to me and Kluanaria after this past summer and autumn? Well, I assure you, he will be fine. And he will also be taking special care of you and the small one growing inside you. I will have him as my replacement, and I need him to find something for me."

"Something or someone?" Thanias asked as he entered the room. He hugged Matelina and sat beside his wife. "I only heard the last sentence."

"Quit being nosey, young man," Matelina snapped. "Your duties right now, from this day until I say otherwise, it to be with your wife and unborn. Think of it as my first test of you." She snapped her fingers and disappeared.

"What was that about, Ryatt?"

"She was telling me a bunch of stuff and seemed very distracted. I think whatever you spoke to her last about is bothering her."

"Well, then I need to find my father and have him give me some guidance."

"Does Zanor know you are Fraust?"

"Well, if he doesn't, he will know in a little bit. Would you like to go with me to the Great Hall?"

"Ok, mind you I am a bit slower right now."

Thanias nodded and helped his wife. Ten minutes later they walked through the town center of Burwash. As they approached the Great Hall, they could see a long line of people waiting. The people turned toward them and knelt. Thanias looked around and then to Ryatt. She smiled.

"Your grandmother did something, but I am not sure what."

The two entered through the main door, where they found Zanor at the High Seat with Kira. "Father, Mother. Please give me guidance."

"My son, I have to tell you something of importance first." He paused as Thanias acknowledged him. "Your, your uncle Regence, who went through the Veil, may want your aide. His small village on the other side of the Veil, near Mt. Salmo, was razed by your aunt and her newly formed Bloodbreakers. The lands are frozen, and that parallel planet is in dead winter."

"Oh, well…How can I help them Gramma?"

"Yes, my mother is very particular about how everything is done. Now she also tells me that you are Fraust. That is good and can explain a lot of things. So, now let us walk and Kira can take Ryatt with her to a more comfortable place."

"What is everyone lined up for?"

"They are waiting for you to walk through this door and announce yourself the new ruler of Kluanaria."

"But I am not."

"I know and your grandmother is already waiting for us out this door."

"Father, she wants me to find Grampa. She said he is still alive and is being held, she just can't see where."

"Interesting. Anyhow, since you will be her replacement, you might as well go with me to the armory for the proper gear. There are some terrible things occurring across the Veil, and we need to stop it. Harold is in awe at the devastation, which is saying something."

"How long do we have?"

"I plan on departing in the morning, against your mother's wishes. I am thinking my mother will have you accompany me, but it is too soon to tell. Myron and Lucien have control here. Paul is at Krosslaen and Edwina is at Kaprius with Malificence and Impresaria. Lunacerian will be joining them. I have Beryth, Omiporici, Blayne, and Malos at Mercurian. The Newlings are still in the Fraust hold under Bittern, which is a good spot for now."

"Do we know of the enemy's movements yet?"

"Dezire retreated through a Riftan gate two nights ago with most of her troops. I believe that extensive use of the cold spells has drained them, and they are recovering for the time being. Ermenya has located their stronghold."

Matelina entered the room. "Are you plotting, Zanor?"

"No, Mother. I am updating your eventual replacement on the status of the other world and of our movements."

"Very well. Carry on then. But I will have you know; I will take Dezire myself."

"Mother, she is very powerful."

"I know, but I have a few tricks up my sleeve. Come on you two, move faster than me. I am the old one. You need to hurry up, Thanias! Move along! Your gear is waiting." They entered the hall where the Orders chambers are located. Matelina dragged Thanias into the Fraust room and pointed him to a solitary table. "Place your left hand in the center of it."

Thanias did as he was told, and a great chill filled the room. Shades began appearing all around the room advancing toward him. Matelina stood with her arms crossed, observing his reactions. He relaxed a bit and the armor that was on the table disappeared. His jaw dropped. Something warm wrapped around his entire body. He looked at his arm and found the leather armor already in place. "This isn't normal."

"Yes, it is, at least for Fraust. We fight hard, so it is a blessing, it also comes off by placing just your right hand on the table."

"Gramma, what are my first orders from you?"

"Your first order as a Fraust is to escort me along with Zanor to the Great Hall. Then you will be going through the Veil to assess the Bloodbreaker damage. Your Shade will assist you and help you record the appropriate information. It will be a very terrible scene and I believe that you should be able to port to Chorlanda's flying vessel."

Thanias nodded, and after he attached his weapons, he extended his arm to his grandmother. As they exited the Fraust chamber, the Shades began to fade and Zanor approached. "I see it was successful. Let's get to the hall, a bit faster. *Expediame a trio, expediame a trio.*"

The group teleported to the Great Hall. The room became eerily quiet as Matelina stood to speak. Zanor and Thanias took seats.

"My Kluanarians, I am here to tell you, I am still the Ruler of all Kluanaria. Zanor oversees Ruan and Burwash. Beryth oversees Mercurian and Regence had abdicated his rule to Zanor. Thanias is a new Fraust." There was a rumbling amongst the crowd. Matelina raised her hand and the rumbling ceased. "He has gone through much inner turmoil for a very long time. Fraust are not born into the Order, they slowly stumble to the path. My journey was different than his, but he had no one to guide him, until now. Thallas of the Stars found him worthy to be restored and this sign caused the Fraust to take notice and study all of Thanias' journeys."

"What are we doing to get the newly formed Bloodbreakers in check? They have devastated our parallel world, Earth, and have strong ties to extreme evil." Lunacerian said as he stood toward the back of the crowded room. "Will we be able to put an end to this new menace before our world suffers too?"

"We are still working on the issue." Matelina said. The room became loud again.

Zanor stood up and placed a hand on his mother's shoulder. She sat down next to Thanias as Zanor spoke. "People, the Bloodbreakers are a very new Order who we need to learn about before we can gain control."

Lunacerian began to walk forward. "How can you choke those words out? They have killed millions and have destroyed a planet for the most part. To my knowledge, with your sister being closely tied to Riftan, the end is coming. It only takes one misstep to cause a catastrophe greater than anything we have ever seen, almost on scale with the supernova which destroyed Phallas Minor."

"That is not likely. The only thing that could cause that would be for her to have a rift open on the Veil itself." Zanor felt weak at that moment, as the grave realization began to sink in. "Lunacerian, you are right. How could I have been so blind? I would like the Elders to meet now to assess this grave situation."

The folks in the room began to talk amongst themselves. Matelina took charge of the masses and sent Thanias with his father to the Elders' council. I am going to remind you of all that has been done for you under me and my father, so be silent and sit down."

A large sphere descended into the center of the hall. "Let's start with my father, shall we." An image of Matelina's Morket father appeared along with her mother, Minervene. *"Greystone was just being established, with about five families from Phallas Minor settling there. There were Fraeloch who were excellent builders and mapmakers, Morket who were skilled in farming and mining, and the Kluanarians who originally inhabited this vast every changing landscape of Kluanaria. The Kluanarians shared knowledge of healing, and conservative land use, to preserve the lands. The Morket and Fraelochs taught their hosts about their world and of the vast other worlds that could be seen from both Kluanaria and Phallas Minor."*

Matelina paused for a drink of water and then continued. *"As the village expanded, many decided to set up what started as outposts and became thriving cities. My father arrived in time to see that the cities were not successful. There was mass corruption and mistrust amongst the people. We lived in Bittern for a very long time and with the civil unrest, he decided to do something about it. He found the epicenter for corruption was Greystone and moved our family there. He established Orders, based on the skills of an individual and what caused their abilities to intensify."* She paused to wipe away a tear or two and then continued.

"He was voted as ruler for Kluanaria, and the Orders established guidelines for the world to survive and sustain a balance with nature. Everything was wonderful until the four horsemen ravaged the land. It was a short-lived set back and the people learned from what had happened. Twenty-five years later, when I turned 15, I took a journey to discover who I was, and was unsuccessful. My spouse, Demitri, explained why I was having issues and eventually I found my Order. Flash forward 6 years, and Mithdrool came to power. He is a Kluanarian Warlock who made his home in Forest Mithdrool. He wreaked havoc on the surrounding area. By then, my brothers and sisters were in power at various locations and prepared an assault on Mithdrool's lair. My father led the assault. Many lives were lost in this battle. The warlock was captured and placed in a stasis, since Morket and Fraeloch technology permitted it. Elders of the many Orders perished as they were the first line to attack. My father was lost in this battle. Greystone was razed in the process and Mercurian became a great port. Ruan was established by the founding families of Greystone.

Matelina paused again. *"Demitri helped me finish training and establish a stronghold in Bittern that can be used by anyone. Our Order is not selfish in that way. We raised three sons and a daughter together. In that time span I had to take overrule. Four horsemen arrived a couple times and we did battle as best we could. The last invasion by the horsemen produced a key ally in their group, Harold. He was key in helping my son, Zanor, get the rest contained.*

She paused for more water and glanced about the room. *"The dragons arrived from across the Veil a long time ago. I met Ermenya on my journey. She taught me about Phallas Minor, which is where they came from, and about the people on Earth. I established contact with the people of Earth, just in case crossings became a routine activity. I set up Vale Kilowas to hold our prison, which is still operational, and the castle there was controlled by the dragons to retain all the histories of the peoples of the three worlds united by fate. I found beings that were always about the Veil and gave them the task of protecting the Veil and assisting us in times of need."*

Matelina cried briefly. *"I ask of you to look inside of yourselves and say what I have done to aid this war that didn't need to be. Demitri is out there, and I will find him. I will also end the Bloodbreakers siege on Earth and here.*

It is time for my legacy to begin to wind down. If you want to know more, come see me; just don't think you were abandoned."

She closed her eyes and vanished, reappearing in her quarters where she laid down to rest. Her eyes were sore and her throat, raw. Her Shade closed the curtains, locked the door and stood watch. She dispatched a mind message to Zanor as she fell asleep.

A NEEDED BREAK AND THE UNTHINKABLE

Upon vacating Elberton, Dezire and her Bloodbreakers returned to their newly completed stronghold. Arkronde had a fortress built at Warroad, located on the opposite side of the island that Mercurian resides. Its walls appeared crystalline with great sculptures of various Orders throughout the atrium in the center of it. Sparkling pools were in many of the large rooms and a waterfall at the rear of the fortress was incorporated into the design so as to not disrupt nature's path. Arkronde escorted the Bloodbreakers to their quarters which were like 3-bedroom homes. Their families had been relocated there and made comfortable. Gardens were located in the northeast section where the ceiling was crystalline, and the waters flowed in specially designed channels. There was a section for children to learn and for Eupepsians to practice healing.

As the tour continued, Dezire paid attention to the details and found the hall exceptional. She retired to her quarters, which was very empty. There were sketches of where she grew up and a few of her and her siblings. She took them down and placed them in a drawer. After reflecting for a short while, she asked her Shade to see if she was able to glean information from Burwash. Displeased with the response, Dezire dismissed her and crawled into bed where she slept for over a day.

Arkronde returned to Riftan and spoke with Nebulos in regard to the Bloodbreakers. "My Lord, I have aided the Bloodbreakers in their goal."

"Their goal is the goal of only one, Dezire Truaxx. She is strangely deluded and misguided. I am uncertain as to why my gate keeper would choose to support the actions of one that jeopardized the survival of many."

"I chose to, just as you chose to entertain the Orders and their belief that everyone can get along."

"Arkronde, you are as delusional as Dezire. What happened to you?" Nebulos said as he swirled about.

"You have wasted so much time in Riftan; you don't even know what is out there. You have no idea of what truly transpires."

"But I do, Arkronde. I do. You my gate keeper are no longer necessary. Please leave at once."

"You are too late, Nebulos. You cannot stop Dezire's plan."

A Shade passing through caught hint of this demise and left to warn the other Shades of the impending doom. They met in secret to devise a way to save their Fraust who were bent by Dezire. One went to Zanor immediately to seek refuge for those who followed Dezire blindly, and their families.

Zanor immediately returned to the Great Hall to consult Matelina, but she was already gone. He returned to the Council of Elders and explained the state of Riftan. "If we do not act, many families will be destroyed. If we do not stop Dezire and Arkronde the worlds will collide. Is all she has to do is convince him to open a rift in the Veil at one of the contact points."

Gareth had just arrived from Earth with a report and added some more details to that thought. "If the rift opens in the Veil, both planets will be pulled into the Veil and the electromagnetism of both will interact and the compositions of both planets will slowly break up and create a dust and debris column between the two. Gravity will either be reduced or increased. There is a record of something like this happening in a separate area of the universe and only records survive. The people who recorded it were actually the settlers of Greystone; amongst them were Matelina's parents."

"And us." William and Freiderich said in chorus. The two took a seat amongst the Elders. William asked the anticipated question. "Where is Menosh?"

"We have not seen Menosh in almost a year. We were hoping that since he communicates with dragons more frequently, and sometimes Titans." Gareth piped in smiling. "Perhaps he can answer the snow question."

Zanor looked at Thanias. "You need to go to your grandmother and see what she thinks."

"Why not you? I have no say."

"Then we will go together. You said she thinks Demitri is alive." Zanor said as he stood.

"Demitri alive? Impossible." Gareth responded.

"She believes that she can see him and that he is being held captive somewhere but can't tell from the images."

William responded. "I think we can do an image extraction, if she is truly seeing this. My fear is however that it is a remnant stored to remember him. Fred should be able to discern that before we extract the image."

Zanor agreed and the four ported to Matelina's home and Thanias knocked on the door. It was eerily quiet. The door was locked, and her Shade came through the door. "How may I help you?"

"Is Matelina well?" William asked directly.

"She is resting. As Thanias and Zanor departed the hall to the chamber, she ported here, and I secured her home. She is very exhausted after the long speech she gave today."

Zanor moved past the Shade, "Well since she is my mother, I will go check on her." He walked down the hall and entered her room. He found his mother staring in a seeing stone. "Mother, you need to rest."

"I...I can't until my Demitri is home. Oh, please Zanor, find him."

"Fred and William are here. They can help us find him."

Matelina nodded in agreement and the two entered the room. Fred, in a smaller form, took the lead. "Lady Greystone, please use the seeing stone as you had just done. When it is the image you keep seeing, let me know."

"Oh, okay." Matelina's age showed some as she reached in her pouch, removed the seeing stone, and placed it in front of her eye. Her hand quivered as she gazed into the stone. "This is it, the image I keep seeing. Here Freiderich."

The dragon moved behind Matelina, placed a claw at the top center of her head, and closed his eyes to review the image she was seeing. He was able to zoom in closer, which caused the aging ruler to well up with tears, as Demitri could be seen much better. As if on cue, Demitri used his hands to communicate a location which the dragon acknowledged. They saw Demitri collapse, fast asleep, his ordeal somewhat calmed. Fred backed away from Matelina and Zanor helped her to lie back down. "Zanor, I know where we need to search for your grandfather. How he got there, I am uncertain." The group left Matelina with her Shade and Thanias. Zanor and company returned to the Elders with the new information.

As the folks in Burwash were in discussions of the potential threats, Arkronde had left Nebulos to his thoughts. He wandered to the heart of Riftan where Demitri had been hidden from everyone for many years. "Demitri, we are about to witness the end of two worlds and the beginning of a new one." Demitri was unresponsive, physically and mentally drained from all of these long years. The bindings were wearing, very slowly. The spell on them was too strong. He at least knew that his message was finally understood, as he could see Fred's great eye peering in to his mind and observing the surroundings. He sat up on his knees briefly to respond to the gate keeper. "Arkronde, you will not succeed, not so long as I draw breath and the Orders in Council."

"You are a fool, as is your family. So much has changed since your capture and you won't be able to bear its weight!"

"We will see. I believe Nebulos will erase you." With that, Demitri collapsed on the floor in an almost dead sleep. His Shade stirred, which was a first in many years. It remained out of sight and vanished to Matelina's quarters.

Arkronde paced back and forth. He had tried to torment his captive over at least thirty years, only to be mocked at every turn. He mumbled, "And your precious family! I had hopes of winning over Dezire, but she is too powerful. I had hopes of your Thanias, but he is dead. Perhaps I can sway Tatiana still. She is easy prey. But I will say Demitri, Dezire opened a bees' nest by destroying most of Earth." He stooped over the collapsed man, "I will have to finish the job." Arkronde walked to the center stone with two artifacts. The center stone controlled all Veil points, and he took these artifacts and used the center stone to port him to Ruan. He nodded to the passers-by as he visited there frequently. He walked to the edge of town where the mist began and placed an artifact on a small decaying tree stump, he then placed the second one on the opposite side of the Veil. *"Combinar estos dos mundo! Combinar estos dos mundos!"*

Brenda M. Hokenson

The land began to shake violently. All forms of weather pummeled the Veil's edge. In Warroad, the Bloodbreakers were alerted by Shades, who helped return them to Burwash, to include their families. A young member of their Order went forward, asking the others to remain in the chamber as he sought out the Council. Once he found them, he interrupted. "My lords, I am Tyrias. We, the Bloodbreakers, were deceived by Dezire and wish to return to Fraust. We will accept any punishment, but I am asking this happen as Arkronde has done something. This violent shaking was his cause. Let us help your efforts."

"Tyrias, your words are heeded, and we gladly accept your assistance. Where is Dezire?"

"She chose to stay at Warroad. There are Bloodbreakers on Earth who are as bent as she is however. A great river is where to legions were meeting, called the Columbia. Their goal is to march to the sea on the west side, annihilating everything in their path. They will eventually go to Tuya and after that, Yellowstone, where Arkronde will be there too. They will use the ice casting along with Arkronde's electromagnetic casting to unleash a super volcano and a dormant volcano that has been amassing magma for a very long time."

"Warroad? I thought that it was abandoned." Zanor said as he began to pace. He snapped his fingers and all the Bloodbreakers and families were ported to the Fraust Chamber where their gear was restored."

The violent shaking continued, along with the weather extremes. The electromagnetism could not be far behind. A Zephyr entered the room, "Elders and Fraust, I have grave news. Treah has been swallowed. Mercurian has massive tidal floes destroying it, and Omiporici bubbled it. The village is slowly being moved to higher ground... Ruan has lost two bridges and half of the Palisade has fallen to the ground."

"Understood, we will set up shelters immediately. Please seek out Ermenya." Zanor answered.

As the Kluanarians dealt with the Veil shattering, on Earth's side, Chorlanda had received notice of the event. She got on the com and relayed one message. "All vessels, prepare to mass evacuate. Repeat mass evacuate. The Veil is shattered." Her vessels responded, acknowledging the order.

Harold, being on board decided to take some action. "Chorlanda, can you port me down so I can assess the..." A massive electromagnetic discharge released under the craft causing it to lose power and descend violently. Harold noticed on through the window they were near where the Bloodbreakers were forming. "Not to add more issues, but the true Bloodbreakers are below us and have seen our plight!"

Chorlanda struggled with her crew to restart the vessel. "Harold, tell Alasha about this. She will need…" A large explosion came from below the bow. "They are targeting us. They are freezing our main lines!" She turned and looked at the Fraust. "DO SOMETHING NOW!" Screams were heard throughout the vessel. Kluanarians secured their guests and braced for impact as the vessel spiraled down out of control.

Harold closed his eyes, focusing on Valkyrie, hoping they would aid them as it was not time for the people of Earth to pass on the vessel. They heeded him and were able to protect the ship from further damage. The vessel was in freefall after many attempts by Chorlanda. Paul had returned to the vessel and was repairing the main line with some help from Kren. The engines fired and as the ship spiraled all systems returned. The navigator took control and throttled up as he adjusted the decent rate and leveled out.

Chorlanda was as white as a ghost. She sat silently in her command chair, staring at the screen. "What place is that? Gareth, pull an Earth map up on the screen."

Agent Patriksen stepped forward. "That was Wenatchee. It looks to be frozen over. These Bloodbreakers, they aren't marching, they seem to be in some sort of space warp to move at this speed." He paused for a moment trying to grasp reality. "Hell, they are dividing here! Into three large groups." Harold and Chorlanda stared in awe. "We have to stop them. How do we stop them?"

Harold watched and studied the Bloodbreakers' movement. "The largest is turning south, second largest west and the third is toward, oh, the country… Canada, according to your map."

Kren spoke as he entered the room. "I am a transmitting this information through my mind. I have an image in the Fraust's domain where Matelina is currently waiting for a response. Please watch the screen. As they watched, Zanor appeared on the image. *"Harold, if you are receiving this message the unthinkable is occurring. Please know that we have found Dezire's stronghold. It is at Warroad, which is also a contact point on Earth,* in Minnesota at a place with the same namesake. Those Bloodbreakers at Warroad were only engineers and builders. We have since transported them here and they are aiding us on this side." The message paused as Zanor braced during massive shaking. *"Arkronde has used an artifact at Mount Salmo and at its sister point here, Ruan. Ruan is lost! Stop the legion going north. We are sending support to this Yellowstone on Earth. Good luck."* The image faded from the screen. Kren returned to his post and sat staring blankly.

Agent Patriksen stood in awe. "What can these people do to a dormant volcano? Better yet, how do we stop them from reaching Tuya?"

"Arkronde will need to be in position with an artifact from our oldest war. It was used to disrupt electromagnetism on our world which caused him to lose his powers. If he wields this weapon, he will temporarily lose his abilities and at that moment it will dissipate to the nearest holder of the artifact's base, which will trigger a massive eruption." Gareth explained.

Below Bittern, the Newlings honed Fraust spells and listened to the history of the Fraust. Edwina became bored and then suddenly realizing her experience with a shade, raced to Kira. "Grandmother. I have figured a few things out just now!"

"What is it child?" Kira motioned to Malificence to join them. "The trip to Ruan. It was no accident. Father planned it. Then the Shade that attacked our home and I killed. It was Dezire's. Wasn't it? And I don't think that is was a coincidence to have Malos, Truance, and Thanias arrive. Dezire was planning this all along based on what Dad did." Edwina paused and looked at her grandmothers. "She can see through Dad's mind!"

Kira and Malificence looked at each other and responded at the same time. "We must find Myron."

Malificence snapped her fingers and the three were transported to Myron. He was in the Great Hall at Burwash pacing as terrible news streamed in from many Zephyrs, Sprites, and Nymphs. "What brings you three here during this dark hour? You are to be in Bittern with the Fraust."

Kira closed her eyes as she faced her son. With tears she looked at him and blinked. Myron fell. "Quickly Fred, save his soul." The dragon behind Myron used his magic to encapsulate all essences of Myron. Truance had arrived shortly after and preserved his body in a special case which was shrunk down to fit in Kira's pocket.

"Grandma… I didn't…"

"Child, without you putting these pieces together we all would have perished. Dezire is now blind to our movements." Malificence responded as she hugged Edwina. "Kira, take the High Seat. I will seek out Demitri. This is more than a war."

At Warroad, Dezire walked down the long hall where the waterfall flows. Behind the waterfall and linked to Riftan, a small chamber where her special prisoner awaited her arrival. "Tell me, Father, why will you not surrender your knowledge to me and be free of this place?"

"Tyranny is not the way, Dezire. I will never yield to you and your plot is being unraveled as we speak."

"You know nothing, old man. You will die here. Don't you feel the great lands quaking under us? That is my doing, not your precious Fraust."

"Are you aware, young twit that I can leave whenever I choose?"

"You're bluffing."

"If you say so but know this. Good will always triumphs over evil and your plan is slowly backfiring." With that, Demitri closed his eyes and vanished.

"NOOOOOOO!" Massive ice shards fell from the sky in Warroad as she screamed. Her greatest pawn in her game disappeared.

Malificence had ported them to Edziza, where one of the greatest battles took place and was recorded on all the valley's walls. They made their way up a steep winding slope, where they waited in a very small grove. Demitri had ported himself to this exact location as the three were looking around.

"It has been a long time since I have seen your face, Malificence. Who is this young girl?"

"This, Demitri, is your Great Granddaughter, Edwina. She is a Moon and has had firsthand experience in dealing with some major issues, to include Dezire's Shade." Malificence responded.

"Edwina, you are most skilled if you were able to defeat her Shade. She selected it out of the many millions because of its strength and power."

"Thank you, Grandfather. How do we stop Aunt Dezire's rampage on two worlds? I was raised on Earth near Weelin. They cannot handle this sort of attack. None are of magic, and none are advanced in spacecraft."

"Time will heal all things, as I have learned from the great battles fought here a very long time ago. We must retrieve the artifacts in Arkronde's possession first."

"We will do that. You need to go to Matelina. She has mourned your disappearance long enough. Go now. Be with your bride you were robbed from."

Demitri nodded and as he disappeared, he said "Mali, you know how to reach us."

Edwina and her grandmother made their way to the base of Edziza. They studied the large stone carvings as they walked through the long valley, noting the artifact in use. At the far end of the valley was a brook running down into the ground. Here the two paused for meditation.

"Edwina, I am a Morket, and can wield many powers. I chose the most powerful to share with you, as Moons are capable of handling all powers with their own. Please relax and think of this brook."

As Edwina relaxed, her mind was flooded by images the brook contained. It had scars from the many battles fought over this area, which was once Krosslaen. It showed her artifacts in use that did many different things. As Edwina was seeing the brook's scars, Malificence began transferring all of her spells.

Ermenya emerged from the sunken Krosslaen and sat in solitude next to them. She too had scars from the battles but chose to not share them. After a couple hours, she saw the girl collapse in sleep. Ermenya looked at Malificence. "Is it done?"

"Yes Dragon Queen. She has all of my knowledge and spells."

"Very well, I shall unleash our forces upon Earth and Kluanaria. I do realize that humans have not seen us for millennia, but we will save them. My brood has grown considerably, and the others are awakened on Earth."

"Will they be enough to stop Arkronde?" Malificence asked.

"Yes, they will suffice." A grumbling, wispy voice spoke as a figure emerged from a rift. "I will help your cause, Dragon." Nebulos knelt before Ermenya.

"I accept your offer, Lord of Riftan. The Fraust and other Orders will slow the Bloodbreakers."

Nebulos nodded, "I will need ported to Chorlanda, please."

The dragon in her attempt at a smile picked him up between two claws and he vanished in a swirling mass. "Good luck old man of Riftan." Ermenya took on her smaller form and sat with Malificence. "The girl absorbed much. She will need to rest. Let us go to the new Krosslaen where we will be protected." Malificence nodded and vanished with the dragon and Edwina.

On the ship, Paul finished with the main line repair and saw the Valkyrie were standing by. "Grampa Harold, they... the Valkyrie are still here."

"Yes lad, they are awaiting further instruction from me. I have never had to use them in this manner. I am uncertain on the outcome if they intervene too much."

"We don't have enough forces to stop all three prongs of the Bloodbreakers. Perhaps they could take the southern group. There are many millions headed south that can be spared."

"We are not to meddle in wars." A Valkyrie spoke as she knelt before Harold.

"Dismiss them but be on standby to retrieve souls. This will be a massacre." The Valkyrie acknowledged the request and had the host move to an observation distance.

"We have to do something. Everyone will perish under the ice casting." Paul spoke in a very emotional tone bordering on hysteria. "Very well, since you won't, I will!"

INTERFERENCE OF THE TRUE AANTIRI

PAUL PORTED HIMSELF OUTSIDE THE vessel. The lands below were not frozen yet. He walked forward and off the craft as it circled the separation point of the Bloodbreakers. Most appeared to be resting from the distance he was looking from. He glided down using his powers as brakes to allow for a swift descent. As he reached the ground, Paul decided to stay hovering slightly to appear bigger. The leaders of the groups noticed him and advanced with caution on his position.

"Step forth no more, Bloodbreakers. This is your last chance to spare the lives of your masses."

"Who will stop us? You? You scrawny silhouette of a man. You will draw your last breath here."

"I doubt it." Paul extended his arm toward his enemies. "I will smite you where you stand."

"You are not Chrinthold."

Paul opened his hand and slowly began to close it. The three leaders felt the air around them become denser and denser.

"Your tactic does not scare us, Shadowblyt."

"I am not Shadowblyt." Paul shouted. "I AM YOUR DEMISE!" He closed his hand faster.

The troop awoke to this loud ruckus and surrounded the four. "You are outnumbered little man. Give up now and we will let you live."

With all emotions blocked from his mind, Paul chose the largest man in the formation directly behind him and controlled his mind. The

Bloodbreaker charged toward the three leaders and split the skull of one, who fell lifeless. "Surrender now or you will be leaderless."

The commander nearest him used an ice spell that did nothing to Paul. *I am not on the ground you simple monkeys.* He squeezed his hand closed. The two commanders slammed into each other, both landing unconscious on the ground. "SURRENDER TO ME OR PERISH!" Paul shouted.

Harold was watching from the vessel with a host of Fraust. "What are you waiting for? Get down there and protect that boy!" Harold shouted at them.

"You are not going?" Chorlanda asked.

"I… I can't be involved in this conflict as it is between two worlds. I am not permitted to side." The Fraust acknowledged Harold's dilemma and ported to the ground followed by several other Orders.

Harold went to the true sovereigns who were in one of the designated rooms. "My grandson is saving your planet as we speak. I am unable to go to battle at his side as I also serve as War, the horseman, for many of your cultures and that of Kluanaria. Therefore, I cannot participate on either side.

"Who is this grandson of yours? Where is he from?" The King of Norway asked.

"His name is Paul. His other grandfather is the highest order on Kluanaria, and Paul has inherited all of his powers."

"He will surely perish. There are thousands surrounding him. Just look out the window." The King of Sweden added.

"He will be fine. The Order that those who are fighting him broke off from are there to protect him, along with others of great skill. Allow me to join you as this plays out."

Back on the ground, Paul spoke telepathically in Aantiri to his group. *"I have these two; please keep the rest off of me."* He returned his gaze upon the two commanders who were still lying on the ground and then looked at the masses. Telepathically he communicated to his foes. *"Surrender now and we will spare you! Lead us to Dezire. End your siege or fall without honor! I know this is one of the Fraust virtues, which you made an oath."*

One of the commanders rose to his feet and cast a spell toward Paul while his back was turned. Paul sensed the casting and was able to absorb it and redirect the energies of it. He directed it at the ground about one hundred feet from his group. The power unleashed when the energy hit that location knocked everyone to the ground. Dirt and rocks flew into the air in all directions.

Paul was the only one standing on the ground. He took advantage of this and cast a spell that weeded out the worst of the Bloodbreakers and brought them before him. He then had the Veil Guards bring out the prismatic prisons. Tommy was with them. This made good practice for him. The Shrikes upon the prisons closing, bound themselves to seal them forever.

As the remainder began to stand, he sat and focused inward to regenerate his energies. A couple of the Fraust joined him as his defense. "Rest Aantiri, you are well guarded." Rellos said as he sent up a frost-free perimeter. He took charge as Paul recovered. "BLOODBREAKERS, SURRENDER NOW! YOUR MOST VIOLENT ARE GONE. YOUR LEADERS WILL NOT ANSWER. LOOK AT THEM. PITIFUL!"

"I will respond, Fraust. I will destroy you." As Rellos turned to face the commander who was speaking, the other cast a frozen voice spell. Rellos was speechless.

The remaining Fraust used ice shard to decapitate the commander who harmed Rellos. "FACE ME, BLOODBREAKER. YOU COWARD." The smaller Fraust shouted. "HOW DARE YOU CAST BEHIND SOMEONE'S BACK!" She had ice shards floating around her as she approached the remaining commander. "SURRENDER YOU CLUMSY OAF."

"NEVER!" The commander began casting a spell. The Fraust countered and took the voice away from him. However, he could cast using his mind and she absorbed it. Paul stood and saw what was happening and snapped his fingers, instantly killing the commander.

Paul knelt by the fallen Fraust. "I can save you. I will save you!" He focused his mind on her injuries and began healing the internal damage as quickly as he could before the cold snap could spread further in her body. Chorlanda was monitoring from the vessel and once Paul stepped back, she transported the Fraust to sick bay.

Paul refocused on the remaining Bloodbreakers. "RETURN TO YOUR HOMES. BE WITH YOUR FAMILY." Another electromagnetic discharge occurred knocking everyone down again. "DO YOU KNOW WHAT YOU HAVE STARTED?"

There was a great ripping sound that was deafening. Everyone turned their heads to the sky and could see brilliant arcs amongst the clouds. The ground began shaking violently. While everyone was fixated on the sky, the Bloodbreakers vanished.

Chorlanda lowered the vessel so the Kluanarians could enter with Paul. "The Bloodbreakers vanished, Paul. They have some sort of object that allows them to move unrestricted throughout the worlds. I will guess that they are at their separate destinations. How do you wish to proceed?"

"I will go to Tuya with one third of each Order along with Rellos. The rest will need to divide up and head toward the south and west. I would like to request Rynylla to lead one group and Rithmas with Guilles for the other group. Is it possible for Shrikes to be invisible? I am thinking I can use one to get the artifact from the Bloodbreakers while they are encamped." Paul paused as he paced.

Gareth thought for a moment. He pulled out some old parchments describing various battles and the study of Shrikes. "Yes, young master. If you can get Blayne to part with a few, I would suggest sending some with each group as I think there are artifacts in each that will awaken these volcanoes that seem to dot this side of the country."

Agent Patriksen watched as everything started to fall in place. "My agents were in the inn at Mount Salmo in some sort of protective room. Is it possible there are survivors? I know I am no match for these things you are chasing down, but I would like to take a recovery team to Salmo and Weelin."

Harold nodded. "I will go with you. The Valkyrie will go with us as there will need to be soul transport for those who perished. Take my arm."

Agent Patriksen grabbed Harold's arm and they levitated through the vessel where a great steed awaited them. "This is the fastest way?"

"Well for you yes. I don't think your body would like to travel through subzero no gravity darkness. So let's go." Harold said as he pulled Patriksen up on the steed behind him.

As they headed east toward Weelin and Salmo, Paul and Rellos recovered from the battle. The Shrikes were arriving, and the group leaders were meeting with Gareth and Chorlanda.

"I will send my marksmen with each group, Paul. It is all I can offer right now. It will be a very bloody battle on all accounts, and it can fail. So, you and your leaders need to be cautious. I have never seen the spells the Bloodbreakers are using before."

"I wish I was stronger in my abilities. I have only begun learning this."

"True strength for your discipline comes from your mind. It is kept recessed and hidden only used to fix true wrongs. Zanor did not have to use that extra ability." Rellos said as he sat down with his back against the wall. "Allow me to open your mind."

Paul nodded and Rellos placed his left palm on the back of Paul's head and closed his eyes. Coldness surrounded the teenager, and his mind felt the brain freeze he would get eating ice cream too fast. He felt massive heat and electrical zaps every so often and as Rellos removed his hand, he felt at peace.

"Thank you, Rellos."

"You are most welcome, lad. Now it is time for us to do battle. Dezire more than likely will be at Tuya since Arkronde will be at Yellowstone. The Shrikes will work perfectly as they are both invisible and can shrink down to the size of a gnat."

Blayne emerged from a portal on the vessel. "I have given all my Shrikes and some special assistance to your teams. They will both come in handy. Gareth has provided me with the details, and I have briefed my team members who will separate and go with you, undetected of course."

"Thank you, Blayne. You are a fine Warden." Paul nodded and walked out of the vessel to meet the groups one last time. "I ... I am not good with speeches, so I will keep this simple. Thank you to everyone who is aiding our efforts to stop the mergence of two worlds. If you did not know that was occurring, you do now. These Bloodbreakers are ruthless killers who will stop at nothing to please their leader, Dezire. We will meet them, and we will be victorious!"

The groups were given tears to move through by the Izmaa and Shadowblyts. They emerged ahead of the Bloodbreakers, who had set up camp. It was dusk and patrols were dispatched along the camps' perimeters.

The south team found Bloodbreakers on the edge of Bend, Oregon.

They studied the landscape and determined the many volcanoes were all a possibility. Rithmas spoke. "We need to set up camp here. It should be close enough to the Bloodbreakers to monitor but far enough to be undetected. I will cast invisibility on us before we retire. Once in your tent, do not exit the tent until dawn. The Shrikes and other helpers will deploy when ready. I pray they are successful, as there are at least thirty artifacts here."

"How do you know this Rithmas?" Tommy asked.

"I have witnessed these artifacts in use before. They are extremely dangerous. Pray for our helpers."

Tommy nodded. He then went and watched as his favorite Shrike dance about in the air before becoming invisible and off on its mission. The group sat down for the evening meal and discussed the strategies for the next day. The elders made light of the upcoming events and tried to encourage the Newlings who were just recently ported to the south team's location.

As the south team was bedding down, the west team was advancing on their adversary. The Newlings accompanying this team were older and had been using their abilities for a much longer time. Wryn and Rynn were part of this cadre. Thallas, although younger, was sent along as a true Star was needed to break the ice cycles that were undoubtedly going to be used to extinguish the lives in western Washington and northern Oregon. Blayne was accompanying this team at her discretion. The Fraust along with the Orders took a small path above their adversaries. After an hour, the team was far enough ahead of the Bloodbreakers that they could set up an ambush which would allow the Shrikes and other helpers to remove the artifacts.

Blayne had the helpers who stayed back a bit in hiding to capture the Bloodbreakers in prismatic prisons. Several were also with the Shrikes already deployed further on the path of their quarry. Wryn had placed deliberate obstacles to slow progress. His sister found an observation point which she was levitated to. Thallas was ported to Rynn where they waited patiently.

The Bloodbreakers were aware of the prisons and were able to evade their captors. They quickly moved to their next point as they cast a blizzard spell as a group. The great swirling mass had wind speeds of 35 miles an hour with heavy snow falling once again on an already frozen landscape. The ground continued to creak and groan as the magnetism of the planet was distorted by Kluanaria's crossing the Veil. It was now visible by the remainder of the people of Earth and both planets were losing portions to each other's gravity. A great siphon appeared between the two where the planets were eventually going to collide. Dirt, rock, buildings, flora, and fauna flew through the air on both planes. The spaceships moved out a great distance from the two planets as everyone on board was able to watch the devastation.

On Kluanaria, the folks were watching as their world pierced through the phase veil and into Earth's gravitational field. The majority were able to make it to Bittern where they sought refuge in the great halls of the Fraust. Matelina had returned as Edwina recovered in Krosslaen, to find Demitri on the high seat. "Matelina, the dragons are needed now."

Matelina nodded and sent a Zephyr to Ermenya. "How did you escape?"

"You forget that I trained all the Fraust, to include you. I always leave some knowledge out for things just like this."

"So you were able to leave on your free will?"

"Yes, but I chose to stay to see what she was up to. Kren was instrumental in getting messages to the Orders."

Meanwhile, on the spaceships the Kluanarians comforted those from Earth. All watched out the windows to see the battles with the Bloodbreakers and the Orders. They also watched as Kluanaria came into view. Thousands were crying, others were in hysterics as the Eupepsians collectively decided to close the viewing windows for the time being.

Harold had managed to get a hold of the intercom which could broadcast to all the vessels in every known language. "People of Earth, I am Harold, some of your people know me as Thor and my realm calls me War. We are doing our very best to stop Kluanaria from passing through the Veil. It is visible out the windows of these vessels. My people have rescued as many of your populations as we were able to locate. We have also salvaged as many of your flora and fauna species that we could get to. The Bloodbreakers are a new Order which we have never dealt with before. They have frozen your lands, for what purpose I do not know. Please remain calm while we work through this nightmare together. All of your leaders are gathered and will speak with you in time." Harold ended his speech abruptly as a Zephyr whizzed by relaying a message: The dragons are here. He had the Eupepsians raise open the viewing windows so that those of Earth could witness this great sight.

On the ground, Paul continued with the Orders, chasing the Bloodbreakers as they could find them. Their enemy had the advantage in relocating instantly. Dragons descended and took the Kluanarians to the sky. They communicated telepathically as the pursued the most destructive force they have had to face since Mithdrool and his Legion.

Arkronde had made his way to Yellowstone National Park. He found the center of the super volcano and descended, releasing an artifact. After ten minutes or so steam rose from Yellowstone Lake, the ground was softening, Arkronde could see it happening. As he hovered above the ground he watched as some of the surrounding hills sank into the magma chamber. The geysers spewed molten rock into the air. An evil grin came across Arkronde's face as he translocated to Tuya. Dezire was already there and had placed the artifact. The two recited an ancient incantation caused the already quaking ground from the mergence of Kluanaria to shift. The ground became soft and viscous. Surrounding hills collapsed and Tuya grew. The Bloodbreakers in that area caused more winter storms. The group after witnessing Tuya's awakening, translocated to Taupo caldera in New Zealand, where they placed another artifact. They repeated their translocations to the Aira caldera in Japan, Toba in Sumatra, Etna in Sicily, and Nysiros in Greece. The Bloodbreakers continued casting blizzard spells as they moved from point to point.

Matelina and Demitri were not able to keep up, but they were able to stifle the winter spells. Eventually Paul and the dragons caught up. "Grandmother, what do we do now? Is this happening on Kluanaria too?"

"Young man, it is up to the dragons at this point. Our best chance is on the vessels of the Morket. The dragons have the powers to stop this."

Matelina answered as she stood in awe at all of the destruction caused by Dezire's new Order. "She is no longer Fraust."

Demitri hugged his wife. "Paul, I am your Great Grandfather, Demitri. I have some knowledge that I need to share with you since you are Aantiri. Please come here."

Paul stepped forward. "Before you do let me fix you." Paul placed his hand to the back of Demitri's head and closed his eyes. *"Repari a Demitri, Repari a Demitri."* Paul thought for a minute as he stepped back. "How did you know I am Aantiri?"

"Lad, I have been on this land for a very long time. Aantiri carry themselves differently from everyone else. You are the third I have met. Your grandfather, my son, Zanor, is one and before him there was one who was or is all powerful. He took care of both of these realms that are colliding. The dragons are only part of the answer to saving these worlds." With that, Demitri had Paul sit down and meditate. He placed his hand on top of the boy's head and closed his eyes. Electricity danced about them as Demitri transferred specific knowledge.

"I need to find this first Aantiri?" Paul inquired.

"No lad, he will find you." Demitri responded. Probably in a very short time. Let's get to Bittern and hunker down there."

Matelina grabbed them both by the elbows "It is too late. Look." She pointed at the complete emergence of Kluanaria through the Veil.

Demitri shielded them as massive electrical discharges shot up into the sky. The ground shook violently and the three fell to the ground. They could see similar electrical discharges from Kluanaria joining those of Earth. The moon of Earth was pushed out to a greater distance and fell into a similar orbit as Kluanaria's two moons.

"Grandpa, the worlds are stabilizing each other!"

"Yes lad. They seem to be balancing out now."

"Is that even possible?"

"You are the science boy as I have been told. You tell me?"

"In theory yes, but we have no knowledge of planets out of phase."

Matelina interrupted. "The planets are no longer out of phase. We need to get to safety." She said as she translocated them to Bittern. "Dezire has been successful in disrupting the magnetism of Earth and in disturbing its volcanoes. I could feel the floes under my feet."

Paul spoke up. "We need to stop those volcanoes, or the people of Earth will have no home world to return to."

Phoelicia entered through a tear. "We were unsuccessful my lady. We could not stop them. We lost thirty-five of our best Izmaa and Shadowblyts. Your Fraust survived and the Chrinthold. The Moons were decimated. We sent a recovery team to Talaharian's village."

"Was there anything to recover?" Paul asked. "There were some humans there that were sent to investigate us."

"Paul, the village was razed. We are trying to open a special capsule that may hold survivors." Phoelicia responded. "But don't get your hopes up. Emilae survived but is in terrible shape. I asked Truance to see to her personally."

"It is better than nothing at this point." Paul said as he paced. Thallas and William arrived. "Well, how was your objective?"

"We were able to imprison several in prismatic prisons. Our group lost about ten of varying Orders." William responded. "The Moons were useless to our cause. I am not sure why however."

"It has something to do with Dezire's Shade. My sister fought it in our home and won. Perhaps it took knowledge of this with it to Dezire."

"Perhaps...I wonder?" Matelina mused. The grounds of Kluanaria shook just as violently as that of Earth. The three were barely able to stand as the traversed the high seat to the scrying chamber. Matelina placed a small stone in the basin and observed with Demitri and Paul.

Earth was covered in a thick layer of heavy snow. Several large volcanoes were erupting, spewing large amounts o ash, rock, and gases miles into the atmosphere. The vessels had moved in to the orbit of Kluanaria and the leaders were amongst their people trying to take in the stark reality of having nowhere to go. They observed the village near Mt. Salmo hoping they would see survivors from the special room emerge. The gaze turned toward Kluanaria. Ruan was completely gone. A great ravine had devoured the village. Treah had smaller ravines running through it. Forest Mithdrool had sustained almost no damage along with the Sand Caverns. Burwash's larger structures crumbled and Nagazthastar sat higher than it had previously. Kaprius' citadel had crumbled to the ground, and they could see Lucien and Impresaria surveying the damage. The dragons flew past, so their gaze now followed the dragons.

The dragons flew past the orbiting vessels where all could see them clearly.

They crossed what used to be the phase Veil and entered Earth's space. Ermenya led the way. She homed in on the village near Salmo and quickly descended. Several dragons surrounded the preservation capsule which was almost welded shut from the heat of the fire that razed the inn. A tall slender figure approached from the wood line. "This is the Aantiri, Paul." Matelina whispered as they watched.

The man, wearing clothes made thick fur with a large staff and a short sword walked to the center of the dragons. He greeted them and looked at the preservation capsule. He took the staff and placed it in a small indentation on the capsule. With his free hand, he drew the sword and pointed it at the Moon. A massive beam came directly to the sword, through the man body, into the staff and finally into the indentation. The capsule illuminated and at least fifteen folks were visible in this light. The capsule disintegrated, but the folks in it were unconscious. William stepped forth and Freiderich breathed fire upon them, followed by Ermenya with frost. The folks slowly awoke from their deep sleep and found themselves in the claws of dragons, being transported to safety.

William was seen on the ground near Agent Patriksen. There was an exchange of words and then the two were teleported to Chorlanda's space vessel.

"Who is that Aantiri, Grandmother?" Paul asked.

"We don't know his name. We are just now he has been here since the beginning of time, and he will always be here. He is of all of the elements of the planets and cannot be destroyed. I am uncertain what he and the dragons can do to return Kluanaria to its place or if anything is safe." Matelina responded looking more despondent and aged. "I have seen too much in my lifetime and you, you helped find Demitri. I have nothing left to give this forsaken planet." She walked off, feeling tired and powerless.

"Grandma said that Thanias will take her place as the Fraust…"

"He will once he has earned it. Right now, I guess I must step up as the lord for now. Matelina is very tired. We are both very old."

"I know. I didn't mean any disrespect."

"I know. For now, let us see what can be salvaged. The Moons are not fit for war, but for healing and dark crafts on occasion. Stars on the other hand, are very good with wars and I think our slumbering Order has been awakened, so we will hope they and the dragons are enough to stop the Bloodbreakers." Demitri said as the two walked out of the scrying chamber.

The Kluanarians

"I would like to help in this war. Surely that Aantiri will accept my help."

"We will go together." A familiar voice from behind spoke.

"Grampa Zanor! Grampa Zanor!" Paul turned and ran toward his grandfather and hugged him. "Are you okay, where have you been?"

"Well, someone had to get Tatiana and her friends on a special assignment and send Edwina to Ermenya. Tomas is waiting for her at the stables, so not much longer now. You put up a good, strong fight with the Bloodbreakers, Paul. You need to rest before we go to the Aantiri. Come let us eat and drink."

Zanor embraced his father the first time in three decades at least. "My son, I thought I would lose everyone. Thank goodness for our descendants' perseverance and determination!" Demitri said as tears streamed down his face. "Your mother is not doing so well."

"I will see if Malos will help us with her." Zanor said as the three entered a rather packed dining hall.

LORD OF RIFTAN

NEBULOS HAD MADE HIS WAY to the Fraust in Bittern. He had watched as the two planets balanced each other and saw firsthand that the materials from each planet were no longer being pulled into the atmospheres. He passed through the great hall and nodded as folks paused briefly to greet him. He took his place on the high seat and waited for the Orders' primary leaders.

Tatiana saw him seated on her great grandparents' seat and raced up. "You cannot occupy that seat lord of Riftan. It belongs to the Fraust." She spoke as she continued walking forward.

"Little girl, don't speak out of turn in my presence."

"I don't answer to you!"

Nebulos laughed. "What can a small creature possibly do? Cry?"

Tatiana snapped her fingers and took Nebulos' breath away. "The question should be how you will stop me. She snapped her finger again to release the hold. "You're lucky I am not mad right now."

"So you know how things work, during crises like this, I am always on this seat, or any high seat depending where the troops rally, so I can open a rift to get them there quickly. Your great grandparents provide the strategy, the Orders agree or argue until they agree, and I transport them to the site. I am here until the battles are over and everything gets fixed as good as it possibly can."

"Grandpa Zanor has a special mission for me and the other Newlings"

Nebulos mused as he knew what the mission was already. "You won't like the mission."

"Why is that?"

"He isn't letting you go to Earth like you think. He is sending you to Warroad in search of something."

"How do you know this?"

"Passage can only be granted to the true destination, no matter what you say or believe it to be, the Council has already arranged passage."

"So, Grampa Zanor… he tricked us?"

"Sort of, I guess, young lass. This item can be found behind the waterfall that flows through Warroad's fortress. It can be anywhere where the water flows. The fortress was designed to not disturb nature, so the river and falls were built into its design."

"What exactly are we looking for?" Onachala asked as she approached the high seat.

"It is an object made of a blue-green metal. It is small enough to fit in your hand. But to carry it takes a strong mind. Any bad thoughts or fights or arguing causes it to grow heavier. And the more hope and cheerfulness there is, it will grow lighter in weight and also radiate a brilliant blue-green light from it." Irra said as she approached. My family designed it a very long time ago. It was brought from Phallas Minor by the Fraeloch and Morket. The dragons know its purpose; my family just had to carve it into a certain design."

"Well, now we are getting somewhere." Tatiana replied, "Nebulos, when do we depart?"

"When the Orders say so."

Tatiana and Onachala walked off toward the dining hall. They spoke quietly, which caught Nebulos' curiosity. He became a wisp and followed them as they spoke.

"Ona, I think we need to get Tommy and Irra, and head out soon. You know how bad the Orders screwed up last time."

"Yeah, let's sit with them and discuss it."

"Ok."

Nebulos reformed in front of them. He took each by the hand and escorted them to Kira. "These two are planning on not following the direction of the Orders. I hereby request they be placed in hold until further notice."

Kira responded, "Tatiana, do you remember what happened last time you chose to ignore the Orders wishes?"

"The Orders had no wishes when we did what we did! You all were too busy arguing and not helping anyone or with anything! That is what we are seeing now!"

A flash of light filled the room as the ground continued to heave violently. Paul had arrived. "The Bloodbreakers; they were successful." He said as he caught his breath. "My mind and body are so tired, but I have lots to do. Grandpa Zanor sent me here. Earth's volcanoes are very active, the planets seem to be adjusting to the different gravity, but Earth is denser and eventually will destroy Kluanaria. Worst yet, from my many different learning sessions, Kluanaria is Earth in the future. It doesn't really affect us, since we are from Kluanaria and migrate freely, but it will hurt them. Future advancement of the humans will be stifled unless we figure out a way to get Kluanaria free of Earth's gravity and somehow reestablish the Veil."

Kira quirked an eyebrow. "Do you know how extremely difficult that is going to be. I…I don't even know if there are enough Orders left, let alone dragons. The dragons are the key to the majority of this."

Nebulos stepped in. "Perhaps not necessarily."

"How so?" Paul asked.

"I rule Riftan and well, I have the ability to fix quite a lot of this mess, but first…"

Nebulos was cut off as a burly man in fur, packing a short sword emerged from a tear. "Well now, isn't this just like the Orders? No order, only chaos, frozen chaos this round, however. You should not have encouraged Earth folks to cross the Veil."

"Who are you?" Paul inquired. "I know you are an Aantiri like my grandfather and me."

"I am much older than your grandfather, Zanor, and you have much to learn."

Nebulos interrupted. "We have much bigger things to deal with right now. I volunteered to assist because someone opened my eyes to the deception of Arkronde. So, ALL OF YOU 'IMPORTANT' ORDERS TAKE A DEEP BREATH AND PUT ON YOUR BIG PEOPLE PANTS! THIS IS GONNA BE AN UGLY PROCESS."

The senior Aantiri nodded, "I agree, set a rift for Menosh and the ancient one."

Nebulos nodded. The rift appeared and the two stepped through arriving on a small orbital that circled a pulsar.

Menosh recognized them and approached. "I warned you of the intermingling of the two worlds! I warned you…"

"Shut up, Enygminite. You left the Orders in disarray for the last time!" Nebulos was in the process of casting a small rift that would send Menosh to the far reaches of space and time but was stopped by the Aantiri.

"He needs to help fix the mess and we still have to find the ancient one."

A whisper filled the air. *Look to the heart of the problem.*"

"Well now we are getting somewhere," the Aantiri said. "We need to get to the Fraust citadel. The heart is actually in two places so we will go by closest one first, and we need to keep that small Interval from poking in where she ought not be."

Nebulos nodded in agreement. "Menosh knows too well of that small girl's heart."

"Wait, heart. Darn, the ancient one means literal heart." Hurry up, you know how she is. She will destroy the girl." The Aantiri responded as he pointed at the lord of Riftan.

"Which 'she' are you referring to?" Nebulos said as he ported them to Riftan.

"The one in the heart of Earth. She has said many times to me that the girl is too much of a renegade and should be neuamn

tralized. Either by death or removal of powers. You do realize that we are not to use powers of that magnitude on Earth? Only some teaching is permitted. What she did…"

Menosh interjected, "She is a child with a name."

"I am aware Tatiana is a child. Tatiana is also aware of the rules. I visited with her after the destruction of Weelin and Thanias. At this moment, she and her friends are plotting to stop everything."

The Aantiri looked on in awe as he saw the damage Riftan had received. The seismic shaking continued. "Well at least she is doing something."

"And what is that supposed to mean, Zachariah?"

"Well, lord of Riftan; you should be able to control some of this seismic activity. You should be able to direct the energy into one of the void dimensions. I can use an interpulse to maybe reverse the gravitational pulls of the planets. Menosh, I will need you to prepare the dragons for a new Veil and get it up. If we fail…"

Harold entered the room, "The nuclear plants on Earth have released all of their energies. Volcanoes are active and the people are safe on the ships." He bowed to the most powerful of the Orders.

"Harold, the Earth beings still call you Thor, yet you have been away for millennia. Perhaps you can use your hammer and fix their darn rock." Zachariah said as he acknowledged the new arrival.

Nebulos nodded in agreement. "Have Chorlanda open the view screens for all Earth folk so they may see you have not left them. Talaharian is ready to assist you in this. The true sovereigns are all in the command posts of the vessels. Go now, this is our time."

"How do you figure this Riftan lord?" Zachariah asked.

"I am the heart of Kluanaria. The girl will be held by Matelina's Shade until we get this process started, at which time the Shade will take her and her friends to Warroad. I will meld with the Rift Queen of Earth, she is already waiting." The shaking was more violent. "Go now! I have to do this alone."

As the group departed for their stations, Nebulos entered the sacred Chamber of Void. He spoke telepathically with the Rift Queen. Together they entered the Void and stood looking at the chasm that passed through the Void. The Queen spoke, "There is much damage here and at the other end is the black hole of the Spiral Galaxy. We should try a different Void."

Nebulos agreed and the two stepped through the wall of the Void, entering into an adjacent one."I think this is the Void which leads to the Crab Nebula."

"Let's use it. It seems much more stable than the other."

Together they knelt as seismic energy filled their bodies, "Dargyfeirio ynni hwn. Ei throsglwyddo yn hyn, at y Cranc. Dargyfeirio ynni hwn. Ei throsglwyddo yn hyn, at y Cranc. Calm y tiroedd treisgar. Leddfu'r mynyddoedd fudlosgi. Cymerwch egni hwn o realms hyn." As the two slowly rose massive amounts of energy shot through them in blue and grey bolts of light. They were in fact a temporary pulsar as the energies were taken from the planets.

"I hope Harold hurries up. We will not survive for more than an hour of this extreme radiation."Nebulos said as he watched the Rift Queen gain more strength.

"Nebulos focus on one stream of light and use it as a shield. Earth is a very violent rock and the core is very active. This will take a long time to recover from," the Rift Queen said.

"We have a healing house that you may recover in."

"Thank you. But we must survive this first."

Meanwhile, Harold did as he was instructed. Talaharian met him on Chorlanda's command ship. "Talaharian, how do you wish to proceed?"

"It is good to see you Thor." Talaharian said as walked amongst the true sovereigns.

His very pale skin and long white hair was an image he created for them. "I hope my assistance will be of use." He created a sphere of both fire and water. "We first much stop the volcanism. I will flood the Earth as I have before."

Harold caught on to the religious reference of the biblical flood. "Then permit me to work with you since you are in charge now." He knelt for effect.

The two floated through the wall of the vessel as all beings of Earth watched. On the ground were many intervals, and casters who could conjure or move water, just out of sight of the onlookers.

While all of this was taking place, Tatiana tried her hardest to escape the Shade. She found no hiding place, no refuge. "Why must you do this to me?"

The Shade responded telepathically, "The worlds are too dangerous for Newlings to solve this. The heart, the soul, and the flesh of the planets will work together and heal each other. You do not understand what I mean, but in time, you will. So quit running and I can show you and your friends the efforts of many."

"We must hurry!" Talaharian said.

Harold held the hammer above his head and massive clouds formed.

Lightning danced across the sky. The ground, very frozen by the Bloodbreakers, began to thaw. Rain fell in torrents. Yellowstone was below them. The ground conjurers amplified the rainfall. Talaharian raised his staff to the sky and the rain intensified more.

"Are you sure we can stop a volcano like this?" Harold asked.

"Do you have any better ideas?" Talaharian answered as lightning danced across the skies.

"We need to get all of the seismic energy to dissipate."

"That is why it is worse now. Nebulos is channeling the energy. Hopefully someone has figured out how to cap these things." Talaharian replied. "But this will give Thor and the new god here kudos."

"Menosh is there!"Harold pointed to a figure flying with the dragons and Veil Keepers.

"We still have an issue with the gravities of the two planets and their moons." Talaharian said in a disappointed tone. "There is so much in the works here."

Zachariah and Zanor began their monotonous task of separating the planets. The two were visible to the onlookers circling the planet.

"Talaharian, how exactly is this going to work?" They are only two mortals.

"They are Aantiri. They can summon large things to aid them, although in foresight, it might be a bad choice."

"Why?"

"It will open a dimensional wormhole in which things will come through and once their assistance is no longer needed, will potentially cause even more havoc."

"Both planets?"

"Yes."

"Oh, great!"

"This will be worse than the Giants you fought."

"Well, Nebulos..."

"If Nebulos and the Rift Queen survive, they will be very weak and may not be able to open a rift."

"So, then it will be me and you?"Harold asked in high hopes.

"We may not survive this Harold. We are mortal."

The two continued with their task as they watched Zachariah and

Zanor open a wormhole. Great creatures emerged that were very massive and not affected by gravity. The creatures used their magnetism to push and pull the planets apart. Their moons followed. Rocks and debris between the planets either fell to the ground or fell into orbit. The movement of the planets sped up. After about two hours a bright light flashed between them, engulfing both in intense, blinding light. Seismic activity stopped, volcanism returned to a pre-Bloodbreaker state. Talaharian and Harold returned to the vessel, exhausted. They collapsed in front of Chorlanda who tried to shield them from the true sovereigns.

"Chorlanda, what is the meaning of the bright light in the atmosphere?" One of the onlookers asked.

"It is a shield as your electromagnetic field that usually envelopes your world is not present because of the events that just ended. It will fade as your normal shield reestablishes. I must warn all of you," she paused and went to the intercom. "All Earth beings, your world is safer now. The planet is no longer on fire, shaking, or under assault by the Bloodbreakers. However, I am unable to return you to your planet at this time. All of your chemical weapons, nuclear weapons and reactors, and industrial waste along with the gases and ash from the volcanoes have created a toxic land which is uninhabitable for the time being. I want you to know there were two people, one from Earth and one of Kluanaria, who have sacrificed themselves to save you. We owe much to the Rift Lords!"

The King Norway approached Harold, who was lying on the floor, motionless. "You did not have to prove anything to us Harold. We have always known you did not abandon us. We were not strong enough as a people to stop the invaders. But we coped and knew you would always be there. I know I speak for all of us when I say thank you for your sacrifices. Please wake up." He sat on the floor next to Harold. "Chorlanda, what will happen to us?"

"You will go with us to Kluanaria. We have more than enough room for all," she paused and looked at the many world leaders and sovereigns, "But we have specific laws. There is no person better than another. We work together and work as one if a major event occurs. The Morket, my race, and Fraeloch can traverse in these ships. The Kluanarians choose to remain in their current state."

"Why is that," a true sovereign asked.

"They were once like you and their world was almost destroyed several times by the Horsemen. The Kluanarians inability to work together caused most of the damage until an Interval, Dragon, Giant, Morket, Fraeloch, and a couple others made folks work together. You won't like to hear this, but they are you a few millennia in the future.

While under the care of Matelina's Shade in Bittern, Tatiana grew tired of waiting. She paced as she watched with her friends the attempt of the grown-ups to save to worlds. The massive amounts of rock and debris floated freely, she caught glimpse of her grandfather and a man dressed in animal hides both float to a large boulder and begin casting together. The kids squealed as a dark hole rimmed in red/orange electrical discharges. They froze in awe as gargantuan creatures, bigger than mountains, emerged. The creatures seemed to just walk across space.

"What are they, Shade?" Tommy asked in a concerned tone. "They seem to just walk like nothing was disturbing them."

The Shade answered, "I do not know. They come from a very distant land where gravity is much greater than these worlds. It is time children." The Shade opened a portal for them. "We must go now, while eyes are on the two worlds."

AFTERMATH

Agent Patriksen was onsite when the dragons pried the secret room open at the village at the crossroad of Mt. Salmo and Weelin. He paced as Eupepsians worked at ensuring the folk were transported safely to Zanor's small village on the edge of Weelin. Truance motioned Patriksen to follow them. As he walked alongside the Eupepsians, he reflected at the last conversations with LaCluae and Dunwoody. He looked over both of them as they were motionless. "Truance, is this normal? Why are they so lifeless?"

"Agent Patriksen, they will be fine. The room did its job. Spells did not injure them and the razing of our small outpost probably had some to do with everyone's state. Look around you; the Kluanarians are still as limp as your agents. They will be fine once we get them in the healing house."

Agent Patriksen continued observing his two team members and recalling the past week's conversations. He thought to himself, "If only I would have stayed. Maybe we would have all gotten out safely. What the hell is really going on? Will we be able to come together to defeat this new enemy and push everyone out of Earth who doesn't belong?"

Walther was waiting with a small group of Truncheon and Eupepsians. "Please bring them inside." He looked to the skies and noticed snow was beginning to fall along with ash that was still drifting in the atmosphere from the volcanic activity. "The ground here is fairly stable, but we will seal the building once everyone is inside." He directed the floating tarp-like gurneys into their positions as the Truncheon stood guard.

"Walther, do you know much about humans?" Truance asked as she started writing notes on Dunwoody.

"No, not much. What I learned from Myron's children when they were at the citadel is that all humans are very resilient. I am not sure about older humans.

"Those children are not human however." Truance responded as she used a seeing stone to observe the inner workings of Dunwoody. "Well then, their systems look very similar to ours, so I think this will go quite well."

Agent Patriksen stayed in a lounge type area that was very extravagant compared to what he was used to. The room was a brilliant white with pale grey stone floor. Brilliant spikes of herbs grew in planters that lined the walls and formed small staircase style planters to break up the room a bit. The ceiling was very high with cedar beams and skylights. A soft instrumental resounded through the halls and rooms which brought peace to all. The seating was airy, as the chairs had no legs and could recline to a full laying position. They adjusted to the persons biorhythms concerning sleep and wake modes. Tea and scones was served by Zephyrs. After Patriksen finished his snack, he fell asleep.

As Agent Patriksen dozed, Matelina's Shade transported the Newlings along with Rynn to Warroad. "You know what to look for. I placed you as close to the stream as possible. Edwina is going through the front gate with Wryn and Onachala. Tatiana, you, Tommy, and Irra need to stay close to me and we will begin our search in this room back here. I can only protect you if you do as I say. This will be very dangerous."

"I don't see how." Tatiana said as she surveyed the area. "Most of the Bloodbreakers are gone and I don't see anything else."

"Silly child, Dezire also has Trincotts and other dark creatures to protect her domain. There is great danger present, I can feel it," the Shade responded as they made their way to a door.

Irra paused. "There are demons here! They are in that room. We need a different way."

The Shade nodded and led them quickly past the door into a small recess. "Wryn, do you see anything ahead?"

"The hallway has darkened; I believe that Rynn and the others have drawn their gaze. How were you able to get her away from the battle so quickly anyway?"

"I explained that I would like you and her to accompany their cousins as you both have superior knowledge and experience that would make this successful," the Shade responded as Wryn motioned the group forward.

The five made their way down a narrow passage that was discovered inside a thin door. There was only silence. Wryn had cast a shadow over them to help protect them from unwanted attention. Several small rooms were checked out and recorded on a notepad by Tatiana as they made headway on the path. The sound of running water filled the air as they approached a large opening. Several demons were toward the far right side of the atrium.

Tatiana stood in awe as she gazed upon the room. She noticed a large seat toward the rear of the room with a water fall to its left. Stone columns supported the high ceiling and the walls were steel grey in color. Lighting came from large candles that floated freely in the room. It was a very desolate feeling to be in this room. Life seemed to drain from the group as they made their way behind the waterfall.

"I see it," Tommy said as they moved closer to the sharp rocks at the base of the fall. "I think I can reach it."

"I will reach it, Tommy." Wryn said as he climbed over the rocks to the center of the fall. He slowly lowered himself to the rocky ledge and instead of jumping across to the center stones, he walked.

Tatiana watched in horror. "How is he doing that? There is nothing there to stand on. What is going on?"

"There is an invisible ledge to the center. It is only visible by mages." Matelina's Shade responded as he surveyed the room. "Ah, he has it! Help him over this rock and we can get out of here."

Wryn nodded as he climbed over the last rock, assisted by the Newlings. "We will go out the front door this time."

"Why? Can't we just port from here? We have a Shade after all." Tommy said as he slowed his pace to almost a complete stop.

"No, we need Rynn and the other two. We can't risk losing this object now," the Shade responded as he cast a special spell over the group. "Not a word and follow my path exactly. One wrong move and the demons will know."

At the main entrance, Rynn and her group set up a diversion. She had communicated telepathically with her brother once he climbed off of the rocks. She had Edwina and Irra work together to darken the sky and disturb the Trincotts to the east so that the others could basically walk out the front door. She had not anticipated others. "Edwina, you and Irra need to take cover now."

"What is that?" I am not sure. I don't have a lot of knowledge about the darker entities."

Irra spoke up. "That is a demon. I believe that we are on the Earth side of the veil as none have been documented on Kluanaria. I think that somehow Dezire has found a way to summon them."

"Mithdrool?" Rynn asked as she observed the creature pass by.

"He is dead. He was placed in a prismatic prison and those actually do kill true Kluanarians," Irra replied. "Now, we need to move forward as it seems to be headed toward the diversion."

The group left there hiding places and proceeded along the path, through the grass. As they approached a large gate stood before them. It was about twenty feet high and 15 feet wide. There were only small slats in this immense wooded gate. Rynn examined it and found it to be three feet thick with metal bands sporadically placed on the gate as reinforcement.

"Time to knock." Rynn said with a large smile. She removed some form of explosives from her quiver and tied them to an arrow. She found her shot to be true and the arrow exploded at the exact center of the door. The sound was loud and echoed through the canyon that was part of Warroad on the Kluanarian side of the Veil. Loud screeches from Trincotts filled the air. Shades passed through the door looking for the cause, only to find the remnants of an arrow.

As the defenders of Warroad exited in search of the culprit, the three entered the courtyard where they met Wryn and the others. Matelina's Shade was unable to transport them. "I am sorry. I don't know what is wrong."

Irra raised her finger in the air and made a small tear in the Veil. "This should do it. If I calculated correctly, we should end up in Weelin. That is fairly close to Krosslaen."

"Krosslaen is on Kluanaria." Wryn interjected. "But I think once we are in Weelin we can get a Zephyr to relay our message to Ermenya." He stood watch as everyone went through the tear. Once through, they went straight to the healing house. Noticing the Truncheon standing guard, Wryn prepared the children. "Ok, I know you all have seen a lot of things. But this is a healing house and there may be people in here that are hurt really bad and some may not. So please be quiet and do not stare." He bowed to the Truncheon, "Please grant us access, we have returned from Warroad, sent by Kira, to retrieve an artifact." The Truncheon returned the bow and granted passage.

Truance greeted the group and showed them to a small room where they could clean up and get checked out. "What did you find, Wryn?"

"Something the dragons need. Is there a Zephyr who can tell Ermenya we are here with her requirement?"

"Yes, give me a moment." Truance exited and returned with a Zephyr. The message was relayed and the Zephyr left in a gush of strong wind.

"Is there any word on the Rift Lords?" Rynn inquired as she examined a slice on her left arm. "This is unusual." Truance approached Rynn and examined the slice.

"All of you, I would like to examine your left arms, please." Truance said as she studied Rynn's wound. "There is no sign of blood loss, did you brush against anything?"

"Not that I can remember. We had a thing from the Earth Realm pass by us, but I do not think it touched me. The only other things present were Trincotts, and they don't do slices. They rip and tear."

Truance left the room briefly as Ermenya had arrived. "Your group has returned successful. They also return with a strange slice on their left arms."

Ermenya nodded and took her humanoid form. "I wish to look at these slices. I believe I can fix them and take care of what caused them. Did either of the Dark Orders return with this slice?"

"I did not examine everyone as you arrived when I was starting."

"We will do this together then." Ermenya said as they entered the room. She examined each individual's left arm. "Ok, Irra and Onachala are good, the rest of you will need some help."

Wryn spoke up. "What is the cause and treatment?"

"I believe that since you entered Warroad and darkness is the main thing present, the darkness made the slice to track each of you. Now if you don't mind, I will heal each of you so you will no longer be tracked." Ermenya started with Wryn. She placed a claw on the slice and closed her eyes. Immense light filled the room. Intense heat radiated through Wryn's arm, and he did not scream in pain. Ermenya opened her eyes and re-examined the slice. "You are healed, please go and be at peace." This was repeated for the remaining six.

Wryn placed the artifact in Ermenya's claws. "Please take this and do what is necessary to reunite the dragons and hopefully stop this destruction."

Ermenya nodded and as she looked up, she had a sense. "The Rift Lords are here. They are injured severely."

Truance raced to the entrance and found Truncheon supporting Nebulos and the Rift Queen. "Quickly, we must help them now."

Nebulos looked up briefly, "We did what we could. Save her." He passed out. There were singes on his face and arms. His clothes tattered and burnt.

Truance closed her eyes and turned toward the Rift Queen. She saw that her injures were more severe, possibly because she channeled more energy. "Quickly, take them to the quiet zone and send for Walther and Lady Phallus. They will have the most experience."

Far above Earth, Chorlanda piloted her ship as the refugees watched in awe as great creatures hovered about. They saw two old men and dragons trying to do something extraordinary with the creatures. Ash from the volcanoes had spewed far into the atmosphere and there were massive mushroom clouds below as the ship orbited the seemingly abandoned planet. Tears filled their eyes as they saw first-hand, the devastation brought by the Bloodbreakers. The planet was engulfed in ice and fire. Falling ash and radioactive particles from nuclear reactors coated all continents.

The Kluanarians

"This is what we have to go back to, eventually. This frozen chaos. Our planet has been destroyed by a group of people totaling no more than 1000. If this is the case, how do we stop them? They are still down there and I believe we still have a chance. It is our home and we must reclaim it." General Thomas said as he stood staring at view screens that showed more detail than gazing out the windows. "We will defend our home."

"General, I do not think that wise. There is too much ash in the atmosphere right now, let alone the radiation."

"Chorlanda, you don't get it. If this was your home you would fight."

"I would, but our people have moved on from pent up anger and rage."

"And you think we are you in the past? I think you are delusional and I will fight."

A gasp filled the air as several refugees watched as the two Aantiri cast a spell and struck one of the creatures entering through the wormhole. The massive creature charged them and knocked them from the floating chunk of planet. Zachariah managed to recover quickly and grab hold of Zanor's wrist. They floated in space. He managed to get the creature's attention and it approached slowly, extending its hand to the Aantiri. Both stepped into its palm and they directed it toward the edge of the Veil, which seemed to flicker in an orange-pink color slightly above the Aurora Borealis.

The Aantiri's goal was to physically move Kluanaria back into its position on the other side of the Veil. With the Veil being so damaged, the likelihood of success was minute. The planets slowly orbited each other from the gravitational pull between the two. Even though they were stable, it was essential that Kluanaria return to the correct phase.

"Zanor, we need the dragons. These creatures have done much in stabilizing the planets, however the dragons are key."

"I know Zachariah. I know. We do not know if the Rift Lords were successful. That is a major factor for Earth to be stabilized. Its life needs a home and I know some of those people aboard the ships will retaliate."

"I realize that, but we also have order to restore on Kluanaria. We can deal with the Bloodbreakers there."

"Right now we don't have an option as they are still actively targeting lesser volcanoes and seeking more artifacts."

"Very well. We will have to wait this out."

Kren approached as they took a seat in the giant's hand. "The Rift

Lords are injured. The majority of the shaking has ceased and major volcanoes are quiet again. Talaharian and Harold are um, flooding the land to help cool it quicker."

"Did Talaharian open the land as he has done in the past?"

"I believe they were going to see if the heavy rains worked first. So far it is. I have traversed the planet three times now and have seen improvement."

"Well then, Kren, perhaps you can tell us if the Earth beings of all shapes, sizes, and species can be returned now." Zachariah said in a booming voice.

"You will need to address them directly." Kren said as he vanished.

"This is what you get when you want a solid answer." Zachariah said as he looked up at their host. "Please take us to Jaquesian."

The creature nodded and went through the wormhole with the Aantiri in hand. "What good will he be at this time?" A slow rumbling voice broke the silence. "I feel it is too late. The planets are slowly crumbling, emitting intense energy across the galaxy and into any open wormholes. This will attract things, savage warring things as my kind are. We will use these two planets energy to feed us for the next billion years, thanks to your so called Bloodbreakers." The creature stopped speaking as it neared Jaquesian. "Jaquesian, you have visitors."

In finishing their downpour across the globe, Talaharian and Harold took flight to study their accomplishment. Enormous amounts of steam rose from the ground. Ash and radioactive material slowly fell to Earth. They looked at each other in disbelief.

"Let's walk on the ground. It will tell us more than flying," Harold said as they observed lava cooling far below. "It is obvious we didn't do enough."

"We cannot walk there. The radioactivity will kill us. Not even protective spheres would save us from it."

"So we have to deal with a contaminated Earth. Then so be it. We can restore it to its glory."

"Harold, wake up. Plants, animals, everything below us are dead, dying or being mutated from this radiation. This is the exact reason Kluanaria is the way it is. We must let these creatures see their fate."

"So are we leaving them here? We surely can't put them on Kluanaria. It is just as unstable as it is here." Harold said as he paced.

"Well, if they cross the broken Veil, they will reestablish themselves. The plants and animals will do well, but the people will rise against us and from what I can tell, they will kill us all and destroy the planet like insects destroying a field."

"You really have nothing good to say do you?" William said as he joined the two.

"William, what do you recommend? Jaquesian may or may not help us in our plight. But he is the only one who has dealt with this deadly energy before in such a massive amount."

"I cannot say. But life will survive. It always does. We rode many times into battle against the horsemen. They have been contained. Have you ever considered using the horsemen together, as a team?"

Harold thought for a minute and laughed. "Are you crazy? I am one of them and once my brothers are released on to this world, hell will break loose on top of everything else going on. With the Veil broken, more frozen chaos will continue. Look below us. All that rain we created froze. Whatever the Bloodbreakers did, it is fairly permanent."

Talaharian rubbed is chin as he pondered the idea. "You know, it might just work. After all, all four are technically loose on Earth right now."

"Death will have no part of it, or Pestilence. Plague may, but I wouldn't count on it." Harold responded. "What happens when they discover I was able to be free this entire time? What then? I will be replaced."

"It is just a thought that we should keep in our minds as a possibility." William said as he looked to the ships orbiting. "We need all options on the table."

On Chorlanda's ship Agent Weisjord paced. He looked at maps, examined volumes of books, but nothing prepared him for the outcome before him. "Frozen... Everything is frozen solid. This is an event that should never have happened. Frozen chaos is not supposed to be the outcome."

"Time will give us answers, young one." Menosh spoke as he entered the room. "Time has always guided us. This unfortunate event is just one hurdle Earth must face with or without its inhabitants."

"What do you know of Earth? Have you seen this elsewhere, perhaps Kluanaria?"

"I will not reveal my knowledge to you. But I have seen this only once before."

"Ah, then it is Kluanaria. I knew it! How could it be anywhere else?"

"Young one, you are not hearing me. Perhaps your books and ancient history will point you to the right answers. And from what I see, you will have plenty of time and plenty of extra eyes to help you solve this."

"General Thomas, sir. I am Agent Weisjord, and I would like to bend your ear, if you have some time."

"Weisjord, eh. I guess I have some time. What is on your mind son?"

"Truth be told, we need to get to Earth. There is a zone that Dezire set up that is supposed to be for us to return to. I think she left information behind there."

"Can you be certain of it?"

"No, but my gut tells me we need to go to Elberton."

The General nodded. "We have to find a pilot amongst all of these folks, inconspicuously. And where the hell is Elberton?"

Agent Weisjord nodded and the two slipped off amongst some of the true sovereigns to solicit help for their plan.

Chorlanda was passing by as they were discussing various details of past events and how to solve the current crisis when she heard, "take the ship." She immediately returned to the helm and locked the hangars down. A message was sent to Lucien at Bittern via Kren.

Lucien roared in anger. "Those folks do not deserve our aid anymore. They are plotting against us and this event is just starting."

Matelina approached. She made a special announcement that all could hear on both sides of the Veil. "Grandson, I need you to trust in the Aantiri and dragons. They are our only hope. Our people who were on Earth during the Bloodbreakers' major siege along with Earth's own life that did not make it to the ship, are all dead or dying. Poisoned by radiation and choking on volcanic ash. This is not a legacy I want, but it is the one we were dealt. This is why Kluanarians rejected industrializing. Instead we developed our own skills, each of us, internally. This is why we have survived so long. Our minds are the only technology that is truly needed. You now see what happens when things turn sour in technology." She paused for a moment. "This is a warning to all. Stay away from Earth; it is now a radioactive, frozen wasteland. Too many have died trying to save it." As she walked off, her image faded from the rooms filled with people on the ships and from the minds of the Kluanarians. Tears filled her eyes thinking that her own daughter caused this chaos.

Sorrow filled the halls of the Fraust. Shades comforted the Newlings and their peers. Demitri was in Burwash with Thanias as the speech by the unchallenged ruler was made. All bowed in grief and reflection. Many entered the Great Hall and waited instruction from Demitri.

After an hour, Demitri stood. "We have suffered great losses both here and across the Veil. Most of the Bloodbreaker have rejoined the Fraust and are sharing their knowledge. Dezire is at Warroad with limited supporters there. Some form of creatures crossed the Veil on the Bloodbreakers' last return and are tracking anyone who approaches. Hundreds of our people sacrificed themselves to protect the Veil and our way of life. Those who have not passed yet on Earth, are suffering from radiation poisoning. The protective spheres do not protect them from this radiation. I am uncertain of the names as of yet, but once a full review is done and maps sent here, we can determine more accurately our losses."

"How do we stop the mergence? How do we defeat Dezire?"

Thanias stood beside his grandfather. "We are working with the dragons and with the Aantiri who have sought aid from Jaquesian. He is of another realm, and it could backfire. I am telling you this, as you need to know the plan and input any thoughts that may help us. Dezire is very powerful, and we are learning as much as we can from the returned Bloodbreakers to stop her without more senseless loss of life."

"It is so cold here! We only have so much material that we can use to arm our families. How can you help us?"

"Gather what you can and return here. Together, we will go to Bittern where the Fraust have their hall below ground." Demitri answered. "Please disperse and return within the hour. All Kluanarians have received this message."

Lunacerian ported himself to Burwash. He immediately went to the Great Hall in search of Lucien. "Dear friend, what news do you have?"

"Demitri is having all Kluanarians meet here and port to Bittern's Fraust Hall. I do not know how well this will work, but it will alleviate the dangers of freezing or worse. Chorlanda dispatched a message to me in which one of their generals' plans on taking over the smaller space craft to rise up against us. After all we have done trying to preserve all of their life forms and prevent all from perishing in the nuclear fallout and volcanic ash. Sure, the Rift Lords were fairly successful but it did not stop all of the tremors. Both planets are merging… And I… I can't protect Impresaria or anyone of the Paladins under me and their families. I…I am helpless, and those Earth creatures are going to rebel, at least they are all safe on ships."

Lunacerian took a moment to process what Lucien had said. "I believe that the General may have meant to use the craft to aid us in battle."

"He needs to sit still and be a refugee and let us…"

"No, Lucien. You need to calm down and breathe. I have spoken with this man briefly and he means no harm to us. Please, sit down." Lunacerian retrieved a mug of ale and gave it to his friend. "Drink, relax. It will all work out. I have this feeling."

Lucien chuckled. "The last time you had this 'feeling' is when we were young and decided to wander off in Treah, where we upset a group of Intervals who were training on moving rocks and boulders."

Lunacerian thought back and he too began to chuckle. "Now, give me a swig of that." The two sat patiently as Kluanarians began to arrive. "Do we have mages here or possibly a turning stone?"

"Yes. Thanias is in possession of it."

"How are you handling his return, so to speak?"

"It is hard. I mean, he died. He died by my niece but was completely healed by the dragons and a Star. I… I feel sort of relieved to know that if someone is worthy, they will more than likely be saved. Hope is not gone but challenged."

After the ale was gone, they joined Thanias and Demitri. Lucien somewhat paced around the group. He would glance at Thanias every so often, in wonderment.

"Why all the pacing, Lucien?" Thanias asked as he stepped in front of his brother.

Lucien hugged his brother, with tears streaming down his face."You died. They found you worthy. I am so happy and so scared for you. I feel torn by reality. We, we had your body here, lying in state, and then the next thing I see is this small lad and a crystal dragon revive you like you were just taking a nap. Bright light and flowers filled the air in the Great Hall. They chose you."

Thanias listened and absorbed what his brother said. "I did not ask to be redeemed or revived. I deserved what I got, and I… I should not be here because of what I had done."

"But you learned from it and you are still learning. They chose you." Lucien paused as many had gathered in the hall and could hear the conversation. "At any rate, we're glad you are home and have found your rightful place amongst us."

Thanias smiled. "Thank you, brother." He paused and hugged his brother and then turned to the group. "It is time we depart until we can stop this endless winter." He went to the center of the hall and a small stone rose from the floor. He inserted the turning stone and a brilliant flash of light momentarily filled the room. "Please step through."

The masses were calm and collected. Each took their time going through the gateway opened by Thanias. Several stopped to thank him as they passed by. At last everyone had been safely relocated and the four stepped through to Bittern.

At Krosslaen, Ermenya had returned to find her and Freiderich's brood fast asleep. Thallas had returned from the Earth Realm and was not doing well. "Lad, what troubles you?"

"It is my head. I feel like I got hit again, in the same spot. I am sorry, but I felt this is a safer place for me. My head might explode."

"Please lay here." Ermenya pointed to a very soft lounge chair that hovered above the floor. "It will not hurt you."

Thallas reclined in the chair as Ermenya removed a small stone from a shelf. He noticed it pulsate and change colors with the rate of the pulse. "What does it do?"

"I will place it on your forehead and then I will ask you to close your eyes. Once your eyes are closed, it will read your mind's pulse and record all anomalies and I can figure out how to fix them. Keep in mind you were hit very hard in the back of the head and Rynylla healed you very well. If I am correct, this will clear up soon. Now be still while you close your eyes. Now just relax with your eyes closed, sleep."

As Thallas dozed with the pulsating stone on his forehead, Ermenya found Fred. "We have the artifact. It is time to bring our kind home. Earth needs saving as does Kluanaria."

"It is going to be risky, trying to save both planets." Fred said as he peered in at Thallas. "How bad is he hurt?"

"I think significantly. The sword hilt to the back mended, but I am not sure if Rynylla was able to repair the electrical paths in his mind. This stone will answer that question. He probably is also very over-tired from the battle with the Bloodbreakers."

"I still cannot believe that Talaharian let him go to battle, with his latest injury especially." Fred paced a bit. "Perhaps we need to send him to the healing house?"

"The one at Weelin is locked down and is in transit to Bittern." Ermenya replied. "The Rift Lords are there, as are the Kluanarians who made their home by Mt. Salmo."

"Do we need to aid the Rift Lords? Were they successful? How serious are there injuries."

"For Mercurian's sake Freiderich, go there. Find out all you can and let them know we have the artifact. Also, take Thallas and the chair he is in with you. Truance can read the pulsating stone and do what is necessary." Ermenya paused briefly in thought. "Oh, and do return here so we can open the portal." She hugged Fred and watched as he dematerialized. "Good luck, you will need it." After a moment, Ermenya began setting up the great hall in Krosslaen for the portal. She found the Altar of Returns and placed it in the center of the room. She then left to check on her brood.

Dezire had watched from a tower as the Newlings entered Warroad. She ordered her Bloodbreakers who remained and the Trincotts to disperse and the Shades to keep watch from a distance. She paced in the tower, as the Newlings entered. Dezire asked her Shade to mark them for tracking and then went to a small pool of water in the room and watched as the

Newlings split into two groups and explored her domain. She leaned forward as Wryn's group followed the long hallway to the main hall where the waterfall poured into its basin and flowed out along the main corridor. She contained her anger as best she could when Wryn found the mage path to the blue-green artifact and removed it. Dezire's focus changed to the main entry where she watched Rynn use an explosive arrow to open the door and meet up with the others. Once they had gone, she screamed. Her voice carried through the tower and down its stairs. She immediately ported to Elberton where Arkronde was observing the outcome of their efforts.

"So far the plumes of ash have not covered the village. There is no radioactivity present either. I believe this will be successful, providing the worlds stabilize and the Veil remains down." Arkronde said as he bowed.

"That is good news. However, the mage, Wryn, has the artifact that controls the dragon realm and the ancient Aantiri is actually helping them stop my plans." Dezire paced back and forth as she went over everything in her mind. "I would like you to help me solve this slight dilemma. I did not anticipate the ancient one aiding Earth or two Rift Lords working side by side."

"Well, let's see here. First you knew that there was Nebulos who controls Riftan, and I am sure in our dealings with rift gates these past months, that you knew about Earth's version of Riftan."

"How would I know there is another place such as Riftan here, on this satellite?"

"Well, how else would a rift gate work? It has to be able to open or close from either side."

"That was all you, I thought, as a liaison for Nebulos."

"Well, a liaison usually has to communicate between to individuals."

"That was..." Dezire was very upset. "All this time... How do I know you are truly on my side?" She paced more; her steps were slower and louder. "I don't know if I can trust you now."

"I have been with you one hundred percent this whole time. I just had to do my job as the liaison between the Rift Lords to keep them pacified." Arkronde replied as he stepped in front of her.

"We'll see. Hopefully they are still unaware of this."

"Nebulos is aware, because of Tatiana. Which means...?"

Brenda M. Hokenson

"He removed you from Riftan, didn't he?"

"Yes. But I am still able to open gates; it is just a bit trickier."

Dezire breathed a sigh of relief and then thought again. "That means Nebulos has probably spoken to whoever is on the Earth-side of the rift gates." She kicked the air in front of her. "This is bad."

"Actually, what is bad is the fact that the Veil came down as planned and a mergence of the planets which has broken up both, partially. The good news is that they are now stabilized in orbit, for now."

"Well, well, well. Something is working. I just need to be let things unfold for now."

"I think you may consider sending some sort of spy to Burwash who can collect information for us." Arkronde said as he began pacing. "Perhaps we can persuade someone to do this."

"Hmm, perhaps, but I think we can use this seeing stone to do the same thing. It comes from Vale Kilowas, in the fortification built at its center. There are many other items that we have yet to exploit, I mean explore. Mithdrool left many things behind in his tragic death. Perhaps he still has deadmages that would be interested in our doings." Dezire smiled for the first time in months. "Yes, we need to go to Vale Kilowas and the Mithdroolean Forest next."

Arkronde smiled, "It is good to see you are feeling better. Come, I must show you the observation area that I set up. It is quite unique. Also, we have a wonderful antechamber where we may dine together."

Dezire nodded and followed him to the observation area. "You do realize that those making decisions are not in Burwash?"

Arkronde continued up the stairs as he thought about the ramifications of this next ploy. "Who do we trust to aid us in this shall we say, adventure?"

"The Newlings will help us." She smiled again, "trust me; they are right where we want them?"

DECISIONS

As the Orders arrived at Burwash, Talaharian asked that the true sovereigns and other national leaders, and one Agent Patriksen to join them in this serious discussion. "It is of the utmost importance that you attend. General Thomas, please join us as well. We will need your knowledge as well."

Portals were opened and the leaders went through as quickly as possible. The group looked around at the Great Hall which had a single throne to its rear. They stood in awe, admiring the detailed craftsmanship of each statue, column, the floor, ceiling, everything. The group was escorted to the front rows as they had never attended such a meeting and it would be the most logical placement. As the members of Orders spoke, their voices automatically translated into each visitor's native language in their minds and their questions were also translated similarly.

Demitri and Matelina stood near Thanias, the new Supreme Ruler, as he addressed the attendees. "Thank you for taking this long journey from your homes and shelters to assist us in determining how to proceed with our unique situation. First, and foremost, the worlds have stabilized thus far and the moons have adjusted accordingly as well. Many of you have witnessed Earth's fire, radiation, and let's not forget, frozen chaos. You have seen things that seem unworldly, but that does not make them any less real. Please, let us hear from Talaharian, as I know he was speaking with members who could not be present at this time."

Talaharian stood and bowed before the guests. "First, thank you for your hospitality on your planet. You let our people inhabit a very secluded area for such a long time, and I am grateful for that. I spoke with several Orders and one dragon to get a list of solutions that may or may not work. As you know Earth is very dead, except for microorganisms that can handle the radiation and ice cold. The tremors have ceased for the most part and the majority of the hostile air has been siphoned by our Rift Lords. Both are severely injured as is Thallas." He took a moment to pause for the people to process what he had said. "Harold would like to release the horsemen of Kluanaria on Earth in order to better assess the damage and remediate problems."

A roar from the crowd erupted. Walther stood, "Are you mad? Have you not heard of the last time the horsemen were loose here? Do you know the damage they caused?"

Harold stood in response. "I am one of them, I have not harmed…"

"No, you haven't, because you chose a path of non-destruction after finding a green-eyed little girl way back when." Walther spat.

"Yes, but I helped in capturing my brothers."

"It doesn't matter now. Are there any other ideas besides this horseman's?" Walther yelled.

Talaharian sighed, "Zanor and Zachariah are requesting court with Jaquesian. He has very powerful tools that could aid us."

"Jaquesian cannot be trusted," Lunacerian spoke as he stood to address the group. "Perhaps, Menosh can repair all of this. He is an Enygminite, just doesn't choose to use his powers"

"The dragons will help." Freiderich entered the room in a cloud of red smoke. "Right now, we have the key to unlock the door to our world. We need to know when you come to a decision so that we may evaluate it and calculate the Veil restoration into this plan."

Talaharian bowed to Freiderich. "What say you to these options?"

General Thomas looked around at the worlds' leaders who were openly discussing these ideas. "I for one want to seek this Dezire and Arkronde. They need to be dealt with before we can fix anything."

"Is there such a thing as a containment room where these 'horsemen' can be released and spoken to? I am sure that if we place Harold in there first, it might go over better. He is a good actor." Agent Patriksen spoke as the room filled with hundreds of conversations.

The Kluanarians

Thanias nodded, "Yes, we have such a room for this occasion. We just need the pouch of many pockets to release them."

"Where is it?"

"I have it. It is locked away." William said as he glanced at Freiderich, "The dragons have to agree to its use, and will have to be present for the discussion."

A true sovereign stood, followed by other true sovereigns who were in group. "We would like to know if all options can be exercised at one time. Can your Orders do that and what can we do to aid you?"

Thanias went to the group and stood with them. "It is the only way. I am uncertain if Jaquesian can be reliable, however."

Freiderich responded, very well. I will ask William to retrieve the pouch and meet me in the selected chambers. All of you will bear witness to this event. Harold, it is up to you to perform well."

"Put me in the pouch and have me come out last; that should suffice."

"Agreed."

The three exited the Great Hall and entered a medium sized room that was covered in many symbols that would help contain the evil within the pouch, once released. Harold handed over the hammer and was imprisoned in the pouch.

"First let us pray that this goes as planned." William glanced at the viewers who were fidgeting in excitement and fear.

William reopened the pouch, carefully releasing Famine first. "We need your aid."

"Who says I will assist you, William? I see you remembered the dragon."

"Yes, now if you don't mind, we are releasing you brothers."

Pestilence was next, followed by Death. The two turned and looked at Famine and nodded.

War was last to emerge from the pouch. "How long have we been imprisoned?"

"A long, long time, War."

"What do you want with us?" Death said as he paced the room, eyeing War and William. "Something does not seem right."

"Nothing is ever right when we have summoned you in hopes you will aid us." William spoke as he glanced at the four, each of which had taken a corner. "The terms of this aid are…"

"Enough!" Death picked William up by his neck. "If this is for the sake of your precious people, forget it. I won't help and War can't. His work is bound by blood and cannot interfere. Or is that why you summoned us?"

"Wha…" War started to say as Pestilence dropped him to his knees in agony.

"We are not so blind to see that War has been free in this realm, and somehow another realm." Death said as he tightened his grip on William. "Free to do whatever the hell you wanted, and no one could stop you, or wouldn't?"

"I…I don't know what you are talking about, you old fool. I have been imprisoned just as long as…" Harold was unable to finish his sentence. Death snapped his fingers and Harold fell to the ground, dead.

"As for you two, if there is any more mischief and deceit, we will not listen." Death said as he turned toward the dragon. "I can take your lives as well."

Talaharian stood aghast as Thanias looked on in the Great Hall. "This isn't going well."

"Now that we have your attention, William and Fred, perhaps you will listen to our terms." Famine spoke as he sat down at the table with Pestilence and Death. "Join us," he extended out his hand toward the two empty seats.

"First of all, how long have you known War was not with you?"

"Since the beginning. And the pouch has many secretive aspects that we will not delve into." Pestilence responded. "What kept you from placing his essence in the pouch?"

"His love for humanity that must have occurred sometime when he saw the carnage across the land, we crossed dragging him behind, bound to another."

"You bound him to a living soul?" Death seemed quite interested in this radical idea that worked. "So, why do you not bind those guilty to me, and I can alleviate some of your stressors? Famine and Pestilence can mop up Kluanaria."

"The problem, Death, is that the other realm is in dire need of your aid. The Veil has been removed and the planets have collided but stopped

The Kluanarians

short of merging completely. The Aantiri are speaking with Jaquesian and we are also looking to the dragons"

"The Rift Lords were of no use."

"How do you know this?"

"Let's just say this pouch has many aspects hidden within it. We have seen everything that has transpired, to include War having a family and extended family."

"And your point?"

"The horsemen are not permitted family as it, let's say, clouds their judgment. HE SHOULD HAVE RIPPED YOU ALL TO SHREDS! THAT INCLUDES EARTH!"

The people in the Great Hall were terrified beyond belief. Thanias and Talaharian looked at one another.

"Jaquesian will assist you, but we will not."

"How do you know this, Death?"

"Because he is in your Great Hall with the Aantiri. You do not deserve help. We must purge Kluanaria of War's family!"

Freiderich, who had remained calm throughout the process, stepped forth. He said through grinding teeth with smoke and small flames as he spoke, "Oh, believe me, you will cooperate or you will no longer have an essence item that restores you, mark my word!" He flicked death in the forehead with his massive claw and glanced at the other two, "Any questions?"

Jaquesian entered the room with Zachariah and Zanor. "Perhaps you should find Earth's legendary King Arthur and as him and Merlin to help you in this asinine dilemma. Greetings all, I am Jaquesian and I control those rather large creatures which have helped slow the convergence of the planets." He paused and showed off a rather large smile. "My realm is a very different place than this. Your two planets are very similar, if not identical in composition. You see, I spent some time with Gareth before I would let my creatures here to assist and found that in fact, these planets are one in the same. So in essence past is meeting present. Not sure which is which, but judging by the destruction, present blew itself to bits with the help of past technology and one angry Fraust."

"Dezire was never a Fraust!" Matelina said as she kicked in the door. "She is a dimwitted little girl who is to cowardly to accept her role in society."

"Not a Fraust? Tell me than, what is she."

"She was a Truncheon who thought she could become a Fraust. Fraust are not trained, the Order's spirit, for lack of a better description, selects one. Who is this King Arthur?"

"No one. He is a myth." Jaquesian said as he observed Matelina. "You are too old to deal with this. I should have Death take you."

"You are not capable of that, for the horsemen are of my realm. Now sit down and help us figure out the best solution."

As the group debated and the Great Hall observers looked on, the healing house glided safely alongside the large healing house in Burwash. Immediately extra Eupepsians entered the tattered building and started caring for the victims.

The Newlings were present as well. Truance had Malos assist with checking them out. "Do we let them go to the Hall?"

"No, it has too much potential to set off the little one, which would be bad for all."

"I heard that, Malos! I aint deaf ya know! What is at the Great Hall?"

Truance hated conflict, so she confessed. "A meeting is taking place for the two worlds' leaders, and another realm, plus the horsemen."

"Grandpa Harold is there! Everything will be fine without my presence." Tatiana said as she and her friends strolled out into the village square. They looked up and could see Earth and its moon near Kluanaria's two moons. They observed the large green creatures and a strange ship. "Where do you wanna go first?"

"Let's go to Ruan!" The group chimed.

Rynn and Wryn had a bad feeling, so they accompanied the children. They approached from the Palisade, which was destroyed. As they walked along the river they could only see a gaping hole where Ruan once stood.

The Kluanarians

"My, my home. My friends. What happened?" Tommy was devastated. "Tatiana, why did you destroy my home?" He became very angry which alerted the Shrike that accompanied the prismatic prison. "Fix it now, or I'll… I'll."

Wryn took his arm. "Tommy, it is okay."

"No it isn't. Look around. What is alright about this?" Tears filled Tommy's eyes. My family." He dropped to his knees and prayed, reflecting on everything they did as a family. "I HATE YOU! GET OUT OF HERE OR ELSE…OR ELSE I WILL IMPRISON YOU, JUST LIKE THE OTHER BAD GUYS!"

"I didn't do this. I swear on my horse, I didn't do this!" She ran toward Treah in tears. Clouds formed above her as she ran. Rain poured from the sky as the others looked on. "Stupid people anyway, I will show them! I will solve this."

When she reached Treah, Tatiana noticed that there was much damage from earthquakes. The small village was semi in-tact, so she entered. At first, she looked in the buildings and found that only a couple of folks were there. The lower mountains near Bittern had collapsed. She entered the main building where the few were gathered in a rite. She recognized the words; she had used those words to repair her sister, Edwina. At once she joined the group who welcomed her. Once the group finished their rite, Tatiana went outside, followed by the others, and took out her notebook. She drew what she saw and as she looked to the northeast a glimmer caught her eye. "Do you see that?" Tatiana said as she pointed to the glimmering object. "I think we need to look at it more closely."

She started to walk off but was grabbed by an Interval. "Tatiana, we must view it differently. Several of us have gone to look at it, and it destroyed them within moments of reaching it."

"Trust me. I know what I am doing." Tatiana whistled and her horse appeared. "My horse and I will check it out." With that, Tatiana mounted the horse, and both levitated to about 30 feet in the air. She guided it to the glimmering object, but just enough out of reach of spells. She took out a small telescope that Gareth had given her to help her investigate things. As she peered at the object, she could see waves of energy emitting from it. She adjusted the telescope and could see that it was a dagger made of obsidian looking material. The blade was extremely thick, and she could

411

Brenda M. Hokenson

make out some runes on it. She paused to draw this on her note pad and then looked at the waves of energy. "How interesting. I think we can deal with this, what about you?" She asked her horse, who seemed to dislike the idea and immediately returned her to the village.

"The horse told us you wish to take care of the object. Is this true?"

"Yes. But I would like to describe it to you as well as show you my drawing." Tatiana dismounted and removed the notepad from her pocket. "This is it. The handle was a grey metal, but the blade seemed to be obsidian or some other black stone. It shined and I could see energy waves coming out from it. Then I saw these runes, at least I think they are runes. The horse wouldn't let me any closer."

"Yes, those are runes, and they are usually not found on blades as this. You know what it says, you know what must be done."

"I know. But I don't think I am ready." Tatiana said as she paced. "Is Menosh coming?"

"He is waiting in there." The interval pointed toward a grove of trees that protected a raised pool of water.

"Well, then, let's go, together." Tatiana followed the villagers who led her to the grove and took their places in a circle with Menosh.

"Tatiana, I have given you all knowledge and your gifts as an Interval are extremely strong. The blade you saw is an artifact, which was placed by Dezire to disrupt the Veil. It also made the hills collapse in this area. It had extra consequences. This artifact triggered last which is why there is more destruction in this area, to include Ruan and the Palisade."

"I need to remove each artifact in sequence, don't I?"

"Yes. The first one is in Warroad, behind the waterfall that flows into the Great Hall there."

"Is that the one we removed with Wryn?"

"No, that one is needed to control the creatures the Aantiri brought through a void to help stop the worlds from colliding. Jaquesian will not help, even though he said he will. He wants these planets to perish, as his realm needs the minerals and energies of these to planets. He will lead the Orders astray."

"Grampa Harold is there. He will know better."

"No, Death and the other two horsemen were released by Fred and William. Harold was ended."

412

The Kluanarians

Tatiana took a deep breath and locked her tears back; there would be time for sadness later. "So, I need to get us to where they are meeting and stop the horsemen, Jaquesian, and Dezire?"

"You will have help." An Interval stepped forward. "I will get us there, as I lead the Intervals now. You will be my guest."

"Well, I know from Walther's story, we need to get the small devices into the pouch of many pockets in order for the horsemen to be returned to it."

"You learn well, Newling. Now let us begin this very difficult process. Menosh, can you grant us protection?

"No, not for what you are dealing with. However, Tatiana can, once inside. She knows everything."

"Well, then, umm…" Tatiana paused as she did not know the Interval's name. Watch after my horse, please.

"Let's go." The Interval said as a brilliant pink light filled the room. "Step through with me."

It seemed to take forever for the light to fade and reappear in Burwash. The retaining room barely accepted the portal as friendly. The two emerged in the middle of an argument. The argument halted as to two came into full form and stood in the center of the room.

Tatiana quickly glanced over everything and first snapped her fingers, which moved Harold to her. She placed her left foot on his chest and then looked to the Interval. The Interval nodded and placed a protective spell over Harold which began to heal him from the inside out. Breathe," commanded Tatiana. Once Harold stood, the Interval placed a hardened shield around him. In a matter of seconds, time froze, and the Interval retrieved the pouch of many pockets and Tatiana the horsemen's binding artifacts. They were placed back in the pouch and the interval placed it on his belt. Time began again. Those in the Great Hall witnessed the whole ordeal. They were frozen, speechless, as they watched this little girl take over an important meeting.

"Tatiana, what are you doing? They are almost our only chance." Thanias spoke as he moved away from Jaquesian.

"Uncle, Jaquesian will not help. He is using you to have better access to the minerals and energy his realm needs. By inviting him here, he knows

413

Brenda M. Hokenson

the resources of both worlds. If you accept his aid, you will lose everything on both planets."

"Who told you this nonsense?" Freiderich asked as he and William focused on Tatiana.

"I know all now. So, I hope you will pay attention this time."

Jaquesian had made his way around the room and grabbed Tatiana by her shoulders. He pulled out a special dagger from his overcoat. "If you so much as breathe wrong, I will stab you, you little hooligan. I will stab you with great pleasure."

"Enough!" Thanias roared. "Let the girl go. Let's everyone sit down quietly at the table and discuss our options."

The Interval blinked, causing Jaquesian to lose his balance and land in a seat, which bound him. Tatiana returned to her new leader's side and sat. The others followed suit.

"Freiderich and William. Why on Kluanaria would you even consider releasing the horsemen?" The Interval said as he looked at the dragon and the titan. "Harold told you not to, but you did it anyway. Is there a benefit to the dragons with having horsemen running loose here?"

"No. But we have no solutions. The Aantiri, God bless their souls, had no options but to ask for use of those creatures. There would be nothing left of either realm had they not done so. Jaquesian is needed to send the creatures back. The dragons are needed to rebuild the Veil." Thanias explained as best he could.

"Uncle, we can't fix the Veil. We can however stop it from worsening. I know where the artifacts are that caused the two worlds to collide and take out the Veil. I have to retrieve them in order, or it will get much worse. Laval will help me."

The Interval turned to Tatiana and nodded in agreement. "I believe the three Aantiri can use their combined knowledge to return the creatures to their realm. Jaquesian however can return on his own. The Rift Lords will be able to block his gates now that they have this knowledge."

"I need to know how bad the air is on Earth; because Warroad is the first point I have to go to. I know the artifact is on the Earth-side and then they alternate. The one by Bittern is the last one. I...I am sorry." Tatiana looked horrible.

Harold moved slightly within his casement. "I am glad I had not had

The Kluanarians

an opportunity to bind your powers then, young lass. Now, Talaharian can take you and Laval to assess what needs done. We will handle Jaquesian and talk to Zanor and Zachariah. Paul is very weak right now. I am assuming Menosh is somehow in the mix, or you wouldn't be here." His eyes began to close for the last time.

"Yes, Grampa, Menosh is in Treah and is hoping to get this patched up. Grandpa...Grandpa...Help"

Freiderich advanced toward the the dead horseman. "I will handle this." He absorbed Harold into his talon. "The Eupepsians may be able to restore him."

"I truly believe this Menosh could just snap his fingers, and this would end and be like it never happened," Agent Patriksen said as he observed. "I keep hoping this is just a terribly bad dream and I will wake up to find that my agents were investigating a perfectly safe and sane place where nothing went so wrong so fast."

"Thanias, we will need you and the Fraust to stymie the Bloodbreakers at Warroad so I can retrieve the artifact," Talaharian said as he dismissed the sadness in Tatiana's expression. "This is very hard Tatiana, but I need you to focus, for Kluanaria and Earth."

"No, for Grandpa."

"I will need a Keeper to assist me. I know Tommy has a prismatic prison."

"Tommy is very mad at me. You see we got to Burwash via the healing house. When were released we decided to walk to Ruan by the small stream? Well, the Palisade is destroyed and Ruan is a crater, Treah had some hills slide. Anyway, he said that I did it and should be in a prison with the other bad guys."

Talaharian stepped forward with one question. "Have we made our decision?" He looked to the wall where the image of those in the Great Hall was watching. "This includes your response as well, observers."

FROZEN CHAOS

GENERAL THOMAS SPOKE FOR THE United States, "If you can provide us some aerial vehicles, we can provide distraction for you to get to Warroad. Or we can try to thaw aircraft on the ground at the air bases nearby Warroad and use them as a distraction. Just because the nuclear stuff all went melt-down, doesn't mean that the jets are damaged."

The European sovereigns agreed to the plan as did the Americas' true sovereigns. "We must attempt to salvage our planet." The consensus of the Great Hall was yes, follow the Intervals.

In the retaining room Freiderich, William, Talaharian, Agent Patriksen, Laval, Tatiana, Jaquesian, and Thanias waited. Zachariah and Zanor were enroute as the ground below Burwash shook violently. The Intervals present protected the structure and ground below.

"We cannot wait much longer. Maybe dad will stop her." Tatiana thought aloud as she tried to ignore the shake and her mission for a few more minutes. Where is Thallas?"

William looked at the girl. "I am sorry, your father is gone. Dezire was using him as a window, to watch everything we did. Kira…Kira put him in a sleep and encapsulated him in a charm. Thallas is still being tended to with Paul in Krosslaen near Edziza."

The Aantiri both entered the room at the same time. Zachariah sat at one end of the table and Zanor the other. "I see Laval has come out of hiding along with Tatiana." Zachariah said as he looked them over. "I do believe that this will truly be frozen chaos once we start. We overheard that Jaquesian will dupe us, so we are asking him politely to leave now with his creatures."

Jaquesian stood, looking from one person to the next, trying to size up the power. "Well, I am outnumbered, but I do have great powers. I will bow out gracefully if you will not ever use my creatures for your benefit. I do believe you owe me something for their services as you both came to me for further aid, and I provided you with the resources and my assistance as well."

"You haven't done anything yet." Zanor said.

"Well then, you are truly blind. Your worlds are perfectly balanced. The debris between them is gone. The moons are in harmony. You are not capable of that."

"Well then what did you do with the rubble?" Zanor asked as he leaned forward, glaring at Jaquesian.

"It is in my realm, where we can use those minerals and such for a long time."

"Ah, so you paid yourself." Zachariah spoke. "Since that is the case, your services are no longer needed. You were paid in full plus some; so take your creatures and leave these two realms now, before I really get mad."

Jaquesian agreed and was allowed to return to his realm. The group watched as the creatures also left.

"Those are three less problems to deal with." Zachariah said as he returned to his seat.

"Now, we can safely move through the skies and get started with our own operation, I would like to call Frozen Chaos," General Thomas chimed in, trying to lighten the atmosphere.

Gareth entered with a large map that Tatiana marked locations of artifacts with sequential numbers. General Tomas marked bases that he knew of near sites, and Agent Weisjord marked other bases that could be used in Europe and a few others stepped forward to add their marks.

Walther sat down beside Tatiana, "This is where it gets interesting. Watch how all this plays out, ok?" Tatiana nodded and Walther started making a timeline. "We must start up here, so we will need to do a reconnaissance of the hangars to see if the craft are usable. Then the Fraust will move out under Thanias once we have a go from the Earth-side. This will be a long-fought battle, as Dezire will be prepared."

"Most Bloodbreakers have returned to the Fraust." Talaharian said.

"Oh, I am not worried about them. It is whatever else that has sided with her that bothers me. We need, I think a team needs to go to Vale Kilowas, in the stronghold. Ermenya and Edwina both know its contents. There are items worse than what we have seen locked in there." Walther paced.

Meanwhile, Dezire and Arkronde had begun sifting through Mithdrool's materiel. She found a large vault with many artifacts but wasn't sure of their uses. "We will need a warlock or mage of some sort who can decipher these. A priest might even work. Do you know of any?"

"Well, Mercurian used to be the hub of mage and priest activities. Perhaps I can stroll in and ask around. They have never seen me before, so I shouldn't stand out." Arkronde paced as he looked at the various objects.

"Very well then, I will take a handful of our allies to Vale Kilowas and began recovering artifacts. Will you be able to find me if something should happen?"

"Yes." Arkronde handed her a small turnkey. "Insert it in the ground and turn. The key will return you to my side from wherever you are located."

I will stay here for a bit more just in case I can find closer help and more support. Some of the Morket and Fraelochs are disgusted in the saving of the Earth's entirety. Those people…"

"I understand; let's just get started on this small undertaking." Arkronde disappeared and reappeared in Mercurian style attire for commoners. "I am ready."

"Very well, go. I will be here for two days and then to Vale Kilowas. Meet me there unless I tell you otherwise."

Arkronde nodded and ported to Mercurian. The area was a disaster. Many buildings were collapsed. Sanctuary was few and far between. The Chrinthold palace-like church was half collapsed. The mage towers were half as tall with makeshift roofs. The great hall of Beryth had been set up for shelter and healing. Tranquil Springs which was the great pilgrimage destination for Intervals and Chrinthold was unscathed for some reason. Arkronde took note and began looking for survivors who had not departed.

He reached the apothecary and found one person standing near the entrance. "Man, can you assist me?"

"I know why you are here. Leave now or I will have you taken to Blayne."

"I need your help, please."

"No. I don't think so. You are after the new shipment."

"I don't know about any shipment."

"LIES!" The man paused to clear his throat. "ALL LIES! YOU CAN'T HAVE THEM!"

Arkronde rolled his eyes. "Sorry I have to do this, but you leave me no choice." He raised his hand and slapped the man. "Now, I need your help in finding someone who can read inscribed objects. Do you know of such a person?"

The man, still reeling from the strong slap nodded. "Wryn, but he is not here right now. I am uncertain when he will return."

"Is there anyone else who may be of assistance? I think I found a way to stop the carnage of Kluanaria and Earth."

"Well, why didn't you say so? Ecklyn can read some inscriptions. She is an up and coming cross over. She found she has some powers from both Chrinthold and mages. She is a very prominent inscriptionist here."

"Where might I find her, please?"

"She should be near Tranquil Springs. She usually meditates there and does love puzzles and riddles."

"Thank you." Arkronde extended his hand to the man. In shaking his hand, the man felt a jolt. Unaware of what happened, he walked off leaving Arkronde to find Ecklyn. He smirked, thinking to himself. *That was an easy turn, now if Ecklyn will be as simple.*

The ground shook briefly as energies within were released as the land began to settle. Another two buildings collapsed as Arkronde made his way to the springs. He had been there a few times in his youth and had remembered the large trees and wildflowers. The thought was brief as he caught of glimpse of his quarry. He paused and studied her as she sat in meditation. As he approached, he decided it would be best to meditate in order to not alarm her.

"I see you for who you are gate keeper."

"I am no longer a gate keeper. The Rift Lord has passed."

"I see all and hear all. Why do you seek me?" Ecklyn spoke in a stern voice.

Arkronde opened his eyes only to see that she was standing before him with glowing gold eyes. "You… You are Ecklyn?"

"Do you know me in some way, gate keeper or do you have something you wish to ask?"

"I…I was not expecting…"

"Out with it man! Were you expecting some small slavering lunatic to translate an inscription?"

"Well…Uh…No." Arkronde was caught off guard by Ecklyn. He was scrambling in his memories of her race. "Where are you from? I only deal with Mercurians here."

"Lord Beryth would disagree with that statement, as you were a known participant in the use of artifacts throughout Kluanaria and Earth. What say you?"

Arkronde stood aghast, trying to size up her abilities. "I…I was seduced in to assisting Dezire in her successful ideations of the destruction of Earth in order to save the flora and fauna from utter destruction by human ignorance."

"Not likely. You see, I am very old and have been observing history unfold for millennia. I neither age nor ail. I am ubiquitous and see everything in detail."

"You lie! Only the ancient one can do that. And I happen…" Arkronde was cut off as Ecklyn closed her fingertips together causing him to be silent.

"You do not know me! Now, if you don't mind, we have a messy journey to undertake." She snapped her fingers and the two were translocated to Chorlanda's vessel, directly into an anti-magic zone. "Zachariah, I believe this person needs special care."

Zachariah nodded and summoned a special creature. "Do you know what this is, Arkronde? I will spare you the trouble of guessing." He watched and waited for a reply. "This Golden Eye is a baby. See the massive wings and piercing eyes. The talons are the worst. For once you are seated she will fly to you and perch on your shoulder. She will put her beak just inside your ear enough that you cannot move without her beak crushing into your brain. If you are still, she will read you and judge you. If you pass, you live, but in prison. If you fail, you will die most painfully, but instantly."

"Ecklyn was kind enough to bring me here, so why is she not speaking?"

"Are you that thick in the head? No one tells the ancient one what to do, ever. They answer to me and the Golden Eye."

"Since I will die either way, let me save you time." Arkronde used his mind and conjured a spell which ended his life.

The true sovereigns were witnesses to this and were taken aback at the finality. Rumblings amongst them erupted and discussions on how to proceed began. Zachariah paced in the room. He thought it was too easy to be over that quickly. "Truance, I would like his essence to be observed for awhile, to make sure his is not able to reanimate."

"Understood." She rifled through his bags and found a couple inscriptions in his possession. "I think these maybe of use."

Ecklyn wandered about the vessel, reading the individuals. Moments later, the Golden Eye perched on her shoulder and sang a brilliant song that brought levity to the vessel.

Talaharian sent a zephyr for Tommy in Burwash. Very defiantly he responded, "I am just a kid, and I don't want to go on another adventure. I had my fill. Tatiana broke this place and two worlds. I don't even know if my family is ok. You old people need to fix this mess." He slammed his hand on a table. "Please, don't ask again and it won't be fixed until the shaking stops."

The zephyr responded, "How do you know this?"

"No stability, which means the constant motion will slowly take the planet apart. I like Paul. He talks about science with me, and it is only logical. You need a focal point to stabilize. No pleas go back to Talaharian."

TRIAL AND TRIBUATION

IRRA AND ONACHALA WHISPERED AS they walked through the Fraust's halls of Bittern. Wonderment filled them as commotion concerning the ancient one echoed the long corridors. As they were both of darker Orders, they felt a sinking feeling about being judged by this being, but also excited about this rare opportunity.

"Do you think the ancient one will be ok with us?" Onachala asked as the two made their way to the great hall for supper.

"I think it will be fine. Maybe it only doesn't like the ones who destroyed things that are watched over by it."

"I think that you two will be just fine." Rithmas smiled as he answered their musing. "I have heard from Kren that she has taken Arkronde."

"Do you think she will visit here? How do you know the ancient one is a she?" Irra inquired, stopping in front of Rithmas.

"Ecklyn is a feminine name, so I am assuming."

"Well, do you think…?"

"I think you two need to eat something. Also, we have a bit of training to do. Guilles will join us later."

Onachala poked Irra in the side. "I wonder what we will be learning."

"Probably more absorption spells, so that we won't get hurt by the icy spells of the Bloodbreakers. Or maybe how to tame a…"

"Enough, Irra," Rithmas fumed. "YOU WILL BE TOLD WHEN IT IS TIME."

The two girls continued at a rapid pace to the dining area where they met up with more Newlings and Shades. They observed the hall being quite full for supper. There were many more Fraust than normal and a few folks had grim expressions. A gaggle of Earth folk passed them as they took their seats.

"This is interesting!" Irra exclaimed. "Something terrible has happened, I can feel it."

"I bet the ancient one did something bad!"

"Nah, I bet Tatiana did something bad." Irra laughed. "Her temper is bad you know.

A Shade approached, "War has passed. He was taken by Death before the three could be contained."

"Why were they out?" Irra inquired.

"The consensus was to get cooperation from the horsemen to find some kind of containment and halting of the destruction of Earth. But somehow, they knew War was not sealed in the pouch of many pockets as they were."

"And what of Arkronde?" Onachala chimed in. "What is his deal?"

"Ah, yes… Arkronde was captured by stupidity. The ancient one was requested by the Aantiri, who have no control over her, but she decided to help. As she sees everything everywhere across numerous realms, she caught a glimpse of Arkronde's intent and acted on it, posing as an inscriptionist."

"Brilliant! So we only have Dezire to contend with?" Irra added as she sat down for her meal.

"Well, yes and no. Shades have been returning with no powers and some have been frozen."

"How can a Shade freeze?"

"We look like a black in smear in the air when we freeze. Normally we are a light mist as you know. My theory is that Dezire has demons at her side that can destroy us. Once frozen, we never return."

"Oh, that is terrible. Is there a way…?" Onachala forgot what she was going to ask.

"Now, now, Onachala. Do not worry, for your training today is to save the Shades." Rithmas said as he joined the two at the table. I apologize for being harsh on the way here, but I have much on my mind and little time to sort out lesser things. Forgive me for the interruption, Shade."

The Shade nodded and continued his path. Tremors rocked Fraust Hold periodically as supper commenced. The brilliance in the ice carvings was waning, as if the structure was upset. Irra and Onachala watched as Sprites and Zephyrs frantically delivered messages. Something was not right.

The large crystalline orb came up from the center of the room. Images of the days' battle both victory and defeats were shown. Demitri followed with a stark message. "To all Kluanarians, we have tasted victory this day ending a very violent month. The majority of my Fraust have returned home, where they belong. Please honor them. Jaquesian has returned to his realm after helping solidify the gravity and removing the floating debris of the two planets. It is unclear if the dragons will be able to restore the Veil. A group is working on recovering the placed artifacts in hopes of helping end the process." Demitri paused and took a long breath before continuing. "A few hours ago, a horseman passed. Most know him as War, but his allies, family, friends knew him as Harold. His wife, Malificence, was badly injured. His children are fine as well as his grandchildren. We do not know what happens when a horseman dies, so everyone must be on alert for anything unusual. Arkronde was captured by the ancient one and is being dealt with, most painfully." Demitri paused again and as he drew a breath; he had the image turned off. The news was too much for him to bear and retreated to his home where Matelina was asleep.

As the orb lowered, many began interpreting the message. Could it be that the horseman, War, would rise as someone else? Is Arkronde gone for good? What about Dezire, will she be captured. Does anyone have a plan?

Chorlanda's fleet docked on Kluanaria's moon. It was a highly inhabitable satellite with many florae, fauna, and scenery as both Earth and Kluanaria possessed. All of the viewing windows were open for the refugees to look out. Empty, but recently built villages were visible. Zachariah spoke over the intercoms to all vessels. "Alas, we are not certain the fate of Earth at this time, let alone Kluanaria. I requested an expeditionary force to this satellite in order to prepare for refugees. I hope that everyone will accept this as a home, be it temporary or permanent. I have placed the Chrinthold in charge of the settlements, please follow their rule. They are both healers and fierce warriors, as some would call Paladins. They will rule justly, overseen by me. I have asked the true sovereigns to select their locales first as it is appropriate, followed by those who have no sovereign. Please pay attention to the directions given and please explore everything at your leisure."

Malos took over the intercom briefly. "Thank you for your attention. I won't bore you with a lengthy discussion but will cut to the chase. In a moment there will be a buzzing sound, after that a thought will enter your mind, which will tell you what to do. Do as the thought directs, as it takes you safely off the vessel and to your home. All species of flora and fauna have already been established here so some things will be recognizable. There is no mechanization of travel here, just foot or by a stock animal of some type. If you have questions, ask. Thank you for your time." As he finished, there was a loud hum that turned to a high-pitched buzz. Directions in each person's mind were translated to their language and the vessels began to empty.

Paul stepped off the vessel, looking for anyone he would recognize. His heart, heavy with the loss of Harold, his father and his mother were too much to handle. He wasn't sure how Tatiana and Edwina were coping. The past month was brutal, but this was a war, and he understood that. As he continued walking to a nice home, he could see images of his parents and grandfather. Tears flowed as he crossed through the iron gate and entered the structure.

"Paul! It is really you! I have been trying to find you!" Edwina ran up and hugged her brother. "We have lost a lot in a little bit of time. But remember that mom and dad…"

"We can't bring them back until Dezire is stopped. And Grandpa Harold…"

"I know…" Edwina began to cry as well. She sniffled and muttered, "Where is Tatiana?"

"She was to be with Wryn and Rynn, so I don't know. I think Krosslaen. Anyhow, I suppose we should eat and rest."

"Where is Grampa Zanor?"

"He was working with Zachariah on a plan to help the dragons restore the Veil last I saw. Hopefully he has a plan. I will be ready."

"No, Paul. You need a lot of rest. You did more than Grampa through most of the fighting."

As the two sat down at the table, food automatically appeared. It seemed to know what each needed to replenish. Edwina and Paul cautiously ate and glanced about the room. They noticed family pictures on a mantle and a nice fire burning.

"This is really nice, Paul. I hope everyone else has something like this."

Gareth made his way to the healing house which was translocated to Burwash. The tremors continued as Kluanaria was reestablishing itself in a new orbit with increased volcanism and a unstable rotation. He had seen the demise of Ruan, the Palisade and could see Treah in ruin. As he entered the building, he noticed new sections for healing. There were so many folk it was almost unbearable to continue. "Walther, are you documenting everything?"

"Aye lad. It is a terrible thing to behold. And the Eupepsians have set up a small room for us to do our recording. I am certain you have maps to do."

"Before we begin that task, we need to get a list of everyone in healing houses and their assessment. Think we will just start at the back and work forward, so we end up by our assigned cage, er room."

"Why aren't you on the ship with Chorlanda anyway?" Walther mused knowing the answer already.

"Here we are," Gareth said avoiding the question. "Oh, this is the room for the Rift Lords. Definitely not accessible but we…"

"You will not pass." Truance responded as she removed the lock pick from Gareth's hand. "They have severe radiation levels and massive burn areas or a large portion of their bodies, and we are trying our best not to lose them. We have acquired gear from the earth folk in order to even go near them. They have given us a few specialists who are doing their best to help us. We can't treat burns until radiation is no longer a factor" She sighed. "Next door to them is our fallen. This includes Harold. What happens now? Is he replaced, does he respawn, or absolutely nothing?"

Walther cleared his throat. "Time will tell. Who is in here?"

"That would be all of the agents who were in Weelin and their leader person. The two will be fine and he seems to be observing them. This room

The Kluanarians

over here has the bumps and bruises; the next one has minor breaks and lacerations." Truance paused as Walther and Gareth recorded the numbers. The room at the end of that hall has about 200 folk who are frostbitten, missing limbs. Yes, that number is low because we can't save them all. We are trying our best and we have so much help. We just don't have the supplies, especially the regrowth elixir that Paul discovered while studying the flora and their properties."

Walther stood as close to her as possible and looked her in the eye. "Amputate and use artificial limbs. We have done that for a very long time. It worked great at the Palisade. Their life isn't over because of that. Wake up Truance or I will see that you are reduced to a chamber maid."

Gareth walked ahead, "Ah, finally last room! Looks to be unconscious people."

"Yes. Is that everything?"

Walther nodded, and he and Gareth entered their assigned room to write reports and assess everything. A scrying pool was there to communicate. They gleaned more information from the other healing houses and the infirmaries set up on Kluanaria's moon. A sprite provided them with total casualty list and one for those who passed.

Gareth slammed his fist into the table. "We need to act fast before Dezire figures out Earth is abandoned and comes at us again. Darned nightmare! What a waste!"

Thanias entered their room. "What is your assessment, please?"

"Not good. Not good at all. We only have data on the folks, nothing gathered on what was lost in materiel, technology, communities…"

"That is all we need right now. Ecklyn is meeting with the dragons. We are still not sure about these spells that create all of the snow and of course how they manipulate the extreme cold."

"Why didn't I see it sooner!" Gareth exclaimed as he used a board on the wall to list the Bloodbreaker talent. "Only one knows how to do all this and he has disappeared again." Thanias and Walther stood in awe. "The Enygminite is the only one not accounted for. He is the one who pushed Tatiana. Heck, he probably is the leak to the horsemen and Dezire. Don't you see?"

"Get the Orders leaders here now!" Thanias commanded as several Zephyrs had been summoned to help.

"How will we stop him?" Walther wondered. "He isn't really in our lore anywhere. He just pops in and out of our lives, albeit very rarely."

"That is the answer! You are a genius! It has always been when there was small bit of turmoil that escalated after he had come and gone. Check your Edziza record and the first attack by Mithdrool." Gareth said to Walther as they opened up the travelling library. "Here, here!"

Thanias sat at the table and watched as his two scholars researched. Several Orders entered and took their place at the table and observed further breaking down of the battles and those directly involved.

Malos entered with a very special book. "This is the travel info for when Menosh arrives and departs every single outpost, village, town, campsite, etc. It automatically fills to track him. This goes back to our first encounter with him."

"How does it work?" Ecklyn said as she joined the group.

"It is something I believe Nebulos designed to track any non-Kluanarian who happens in. Each um, group has their own book, to include all the Earth travelers who would cross the veil to visit Ruan and Kluanarians who crossed the veil to Earth." Malos passed the book around.

"Does it give us the last location visited by said folk? And does Menosh have the ability to bend the weather like that?" Thanias asked as he puzzled over something. "Why would he pull the parallel planet into this?"

"Perhaps he is courting Jaquesian and his creatures." Gareth added. "Are we even able to destroy him if this is true?"

Ecklyn paced as she studied the Orders. "I will be out on a special project that will bring answers. Yes, I should know everything, but sometimes things are hidden that only I can search for. And Harold needs to be dealt with accordingly."

"Harold?" Gareth inquired. "He is dead."

"Yes, and he is also a Kluanarian horseman."

Dezire paced about the great hall of Warroad. Many of the remaining factions of Mithdrool arrived in her support along with a few Morket and Fraeloch. "My guests, I am humbled by your company and welcome you to Warroad. I have faith that we will accomplish great things within the next few days." She paused as an unidentified person entered the room. "Speak your name and your business."

"You know me, Dezire." A deep rumbling voice responded. "Did you think your plan would be a stroll through the gardens?"

"I don't know you."

"Did you think we would forget? Did you learn nothing from the past?" Bloodbreakers surrounded the person and forced him to approach the high seat. "How can you not remember? I am Zachariah. You have trodden down the wrong path for the last time." He snapped his fingers, and she was immediately standing next to him with special wrist cuffs. "Let's go now."

The Warroad guests stared in awe as Menosh appeared. Zachariah nodded in disbelief as they departed.

Thanias and the Orders adjourned to the high seat. His mother and father, along with key figures from Earth were seated as Zachariah appeared with Dezire. Zachariah forced her to kneel. "People of Kluanaria, Earth, and Phallas Minor I give to you Dezire. Thanias, provide a list of crimes the prisoner has planned and executed." Zachariah paused as Ermenya entered the chamber along with Thallas. He bowed to the dragon. "The floor is yours."

Ermenya read each charge aloud so as it would be heard by all. "Theft, coercion, war crimes, murder, destruction of two planets, disruption of a protective shield, creating a new order, violating the provenance of peace, possessing and utilizing weapons of grave destruction, illegal captivity, violating the sovereignty of a planet, violating a peace accord between two planets; do you have anything to say, Dezire?"

"You will never learn." Dezire smirked as if she knew something was about to happen. "I am truly surprised one of those bratty Newlings didn't nab me before this old man." Zachariah responded by forcing her completely to the ground.

"Very well then. Zachariah, Ermenya, please destroy her utterly so as to not have any remnant or shade or anything of her essence remains." Matelina said as she approached the high seat along with Demitri.

Brenda M. Hokenson

Ermenya approached as Zachariah adjusted himself. The dragon placed a talon on top of Dezire's head and closed her eyes. Zachariah used an incantation that stopped Dezire's bodily functions instantly and as the last movement left her body the dragon's talon glowed. The glowing intensified until the entire essence of Dezire was completely obliterated, leaving no trace and filling the room with silver and gold beams of light.

Thanias stood and bowed to Ermenya and Zachariah. I realize this is only the beginning of the end of the siege, but it is a grand start. Send word to all about this glorious hour!"

Ermenya spoke, "We must stand united as there is still great evil at Warroad. He is very much a threat and we must find a way to stop him. We dragons and Aantiri cannot restore the Veil until he is neutralized."

REST AND REGROUP

PAUL PACED IN THEIR HOME, hoping his parents would soon be returned. Staring out at the snow, scenarios of his parents were intertwined with many months of long events and all the hows and whys. Science, especially physics and astronomy were his greatest interest. After being on a spaceship, his mind was wide open to anything. He decided to get out his paper and pencils and start working on theory.

"What are you doing, Paul?" Edwina asked as she too was anxious to know of her parents.

"Trying to figure out how to get the planets separated better. Ya know, space time was altered horribly, so we need to see if we can get the wrinkle out of it."

"Why? Isn't this permanent?"

"I don't think it is. Do you think we can get to Vale Kilowas and search for a couple books?"

"Without getting caught, probably not. But we can ask Irra or Onachala... Why?"

"Edwina, the answer is in one of those books. I doubt anyone even bothers with books..."

"Would Gareth be interested in helping you?"

"I have no idea, Ed, but it was worth asking."

"However, we do it doesn't matter. But I am certain that there has to be a book or map on all of the contact points and one on the 'beings' in the universe, if Kluanaria is as old as I think it is."

Edwina ran down the hall and used a small scrying bowl to reach out to Gareth and a few of the Newlings. She explained Paul's plan and waited days for a response. The two were seated in the kitchen eating dinner when a Zephyr arrived with several parchments.

Paul read one aloud. *"Paul and Edwina, I am glad to find you both well. The Orders and several very important folks are working on both separating the planets and restoring the Veil. It is a very complex process and has never been done before. If you truly believe that this may aide us in saving two planets, so be it. However, even after successfully doing this grand task, Earth will remain uninhabitable for a very long time, due to the radiation that blankets the planet and continuing instability from the extreme volcanism caused by the artifacts used by the Bloodbreakers. Vale Kilowas is still treacherous and with Kira aiding those injured, entering without adequate 'cover' will prove most difficult. Signed Gareth*

Edwina read another. *"Rithmas and Guilles would like to assist us on this quest. Ona and Irra.*

"Well, that is a relief!" Paul exclaimed as he listened the short note. Also, Blayne got word and will support us once we get there."

"At least we will go in with some very experienced allies. We should learn a lot from them." Edwina added as she returned to eating. "We got answers pretty quick, and it is only midday. Now, when are we going to start on this?"

"Not sure, maybe in a couple days. Hoping not too late, plus we have to get to Kluanaria. It won't be a cake walk."

"Maybe the Zephyr can tell us how?"

"Too late. He is gone."

"Well, I am not." A voice never heard by the kids before said. A lady with golden eyes approached. "I am Ecklyn. I oversee pretty much everything everywhere, all the time. However, I have a dilemma, as an Enygminite has found a way to disguise his movements. I believe there is a way to restore things, but I need your help."

"Why do you need our help?" Paul asked as he stood up to greet their visitor.

"I am not to interfere in routine activities as it would disrupt the true historical path of everything. I can get you to Kluanaria and what you find most likely will help in a very massive undertaking. Also, I will meet your group very briefly. So please choose a time in which you would like to depart."

Edwina and Paul, uncertain of the newcomer, excused themselves briefly to entertain the thought.

"Paul, this is a good idea. And she is right here, right now." Edwina crossed her arms and stared at him, waiting for answer. Finally, she saw the nod that she had hoped for.

"Ecklyn, will our home here be safe if we go with you? Where is Tatiana if you don't mind? And thank you for doing this."

"Your home will be safe. Tatiana is now with Truance at the healing house. No, she isn't hurt, she is helping. And please let me know when you are ready to depart. Place this rock in your scrying pool whenever you are ready. I know it isn't today, and I will not rush this important decision." Ecklyn smiled and as she walked out their door a Golden Eye landed on her shoulder and they both vanished in a silvery mist.

Thallas returned with the dragons to Krosslaen. Freiderich assumed a human form to join Thallas at a table. "This, this isn't really happening, is it?"

"I am sorry, Thallas. I know you are very young, like your friend Tatiana, but I also know, you are very strong and very, very important. I hope you don't mind this room we setup for you. How is your head? I remember the injury from earlier plus the battles you were key in. How very extraordinary."

"I...I just want to go home. Momma will be crying."

"Your momma is here, and so are your father and sister." Freiderich responded as he pointed to the doorway. Thallas leapt out of the chair and ran straight to his family. "It is time for you to heal, little one. My clutch is preparing for some very big things to save the worlds. Now, let me show all of you your residence."

Brenda M. Hokenson

Irra and Onachala were elated to hear from Edwina. The Shade who had been training them became concerned. "Are you two plotting?"

"No." Irra responded. "What can you tell us about these Earth demons? Are they really from Earth or are the interdimensional?"

"They are interdimensional. I do not understand the Earth terminology so I am sure it is a term for things that they don't understand and can't see, since they are simply out of phase in a parallel plain like when you can cross realms at certain points, you become out of phase until completely through. Now, what is this about Vale Kilowas?"

"My you are nosy?" Onachala responded. "Anyway, Paul has an idea that requires us to return to Vale Kilowas, the old keep. You can go with us."

"The Fraust in charge of me, which would be Demitri. I don't think he is available right now, but this is a worthy cause. I will return." The shade vanished.

THE PAWNS' PLIGHT

MENOSH AND THE REMAINDER OF Dezire's forces began preparations for several key skirmishes across a vast area. The leaders gathered around a holographic image of Kluanaria, its moon and Earth. "My generals, it is time to strike them at the hearts of their homelands. The Rift Lords unwittingly helped us in our mission and now we must capitalize on this. The first zone of interest is here." Menosh enlarged an area of Earth's map and pointed out seven known super volcanoes and one extinct one. "The Bloodbreakers were instrumental in awakening a few of these already. While the Rift Lords were successful in removing the toxic airs at the time, they continue to erupt. I would like four teams to use these artifacts to disturb the remaining ones. I will take a fifth team to Scotland's Glen Coe and restore what has been quiet for far too long. Earth needs reset." He paused for a few minutes whilst the leaders assessed the objectives and measured up troops with the correct support capabilities. "Our second target is the moon of Kluanaria. If we disrupt "life" on the satellite, those from Earth will become hostile toward Kluanaria, with potential war breaking out amongst all of the factions. The final blow will come to Bittern and Fraust Hold. The Supreme Ruler will kneel before us and we will utterly destroy him. A diversion in Burwash will suffice to get them riled."

"Menosh, I do not believe we will have enough materiel and boots on the ground and in the air to handle these all at once."

Menosh addressed his highest general. "We will only need about 5 bodies in each of the squads going to Earth. I know for a fact that the

435

Orders declared Earth off limits to Kluanarians and Earth folk because of the merging, radiation, and the volcanoes. This trip will further destabilize it and hopefully the frozen chaos will continue to start a new ice age. I realize the dragons are going to try to reestablish the Veil between, but it will be too late. I plan on using the interdimensional allies to disrupt the moon. Our main force will be used against Fraust Hold. Two small tactical teams will provide a very strategic diversion in Burwash, one that will shake the Orders to their core."

Agent Patriksen woke up in a brilliant white room. He watched as a curtain in his hospital room was gently opened by a tall orderly. He looked at the artwork in the room and watched as the first heavy snowstorm of the season descended on the town. "How long was a I asleep?"

The orderly replied, "About 48 hours. You have had quite a long ordeal.

"Weelin! My team, General Thomas…"

A physician from Earth entered, "Well, now, I am glad you are among the living once again. I was concerned as you were so active and intensely studying your people and then were almost immediately asleep before you reached your bed. It was very difficult to tell to if you were in a state of unconsciousness. Do you remember any of the events that have transpired?"

"Oh. I…I don't remember much. My team? I need to see them, please." As the doctor nodded to the orderly, Agent Patriksen watched both depart. He had seen them somewhere before. *"Nah, they can't be from that. It was just a dream. No, no…More like a nightmare."* Agent Patriksen drifted off.

Will Agent Patriksen regain consciousness? Or was all of this just a really bad dream caused by a head injury?

CPSIA information can be obtained
at www.ICGtesting.com
Printed in the USA
LVHW110102090223
738979LV00010B/244/J